the JESUS boy

The One Who Would Change the World

by

Sean Elliot Russell

Copyright © 2016, 2018 by Sean Elliot Russell;
All rights reserved.

Print Edition

This story is a work of fiction. Names, characters and incidents are eithers products of the author's imagination or used fictitiously. Any resemblance to actual events, locales, or persons, living or dead, is entirely coincidental.

No part of his publication may be reproduced, stored in a retrieval system, or transmitted by any means, electronic or mechanical, recording, or otherwise without the express written permission of the author, Sean Elliot Russell.

***

Scripture taken from The Voice™. Copyright © 2008 by Ecclesia Bible Society. Used by permission. All rights reserved.

Any reference in this novel to "The Book" is speaking only of the Holy Bible.

***

Other books by the author—

(Fiction)
Shiloh's Rising: The Days *After* the Second Coming

**Should the Oaks Fall:
Short Stories to Enliven the Heart**

(Non-fiction/Devotional)
The Journey Home

***

This book and others by the author are featured as book trailers on YouTube.
Look for them by searching the book titles.

***

Please feel free to contact the Author:

Webpage:
http://shilohsrising.wix.com/sean-elliot-russell

Facebook:
https://facebook.com/authorseanelliotrussell/

Follow me at Twitter:
https://twitter.com/myshilohsrising

Search Amazon for the Author's Profile Page

Or feel free to write the author via E-Mail:
ShilohsRising@gmail.com

And find the author on Goodreads!

Dedication

I dedicate this novel to Von "Superr Von" Borilla, a man whose life and actions are like those of the Joshua Phillips character in THE JESUS BOY.

Owner and coach of UFK Martial Arts in Vancouver, Canada, Von often goes out onto the streets ministering the love of Jesus—giving food and blankets, praying for the sick (and seeing results!), and ministering His Good News to people who sometimes have little or no hope.

It's this kind of service and heart-position to the King that will draw down the Kingdom of God upon the earth into people's lives.

Contents

Part One: Seedlings ... 1

Prologue: The Weight of a Mountain ... 2

One: Back to Earth ... 5

Two: The Mystery of Lydia ... 13

Three: Unchartered Territory ... 17

Four: The Spreading Strange and Wonderful News ... 22

Five: Inner Warning ... 25

Six: Unfolding Plan ... 28

Seven: The Whispering of That Name ... 30

Part Two: Tender Shoots ... 35

Eight: Bless Your Enemies ... 36

Nine: Deserts ... 46

Ten: The Dream ... 52

Eleven: Wrestling with God ... 54

Twelve: Voices ... 62

Thirteen: The Four Boulders ... 75

Fourteen: The Mystery of Joshua ... 95

Fifteen: Keeping Watch ... 100

Sixteen: Lydia's Resolve ... 103

Seventeen: The Change in Cary ... 106

Eighteen: A Clean Slate ... 113

Nineteen: Burdens	*115*
Twenty: Broken Fred	*124*
Twenty-One: God's Gunslinger	*128*
Twenty-Two: Thirty Days	*134*
Twenty-Three: Lil' Samuel	*138*
Twenty-Four: Lydia's Confession	*143*
Twenty-Five: Tentacles	*151*
Twenty-Six: Interrogations	*155*
Twenty-Seven: A Mother's Plight	*166*
Twenty-Eight: Accusers	*172*
Twenty-Nine: Sorting Things Out	*180*
Thirty: Mr. Frank Gelb	*192*
Thirty-Two: The Turning of Events	*202*
Thirty-Three: November 15th	*211*
Thirty-Four: Something Amiss	*222*
Thirty-Five: Migrations	*231*
Thirty-Six: In the Face of Fear	*238*
Thirty-Seven: Taking Risks	*252*
Thirty-Eight: Revelations	*257*
Thirty-Nine: The Warning	*263*
Forty: One Called Tony	*269*
Part Three: Saplings	**275**
Forty-One: Double Life	*276*
Forty-Two: The Cry	*281*

Forty-Three: Room 103	*289*
Forty-Four: Into Your Hands	*297*
Forty-Five: Trials by Fire	*303*
Forty-Six: Trespassers and Advocates	*312*
Part Four: Immovable Trees	**322**
Forty-Seven: The Funeral	*323*
Forty-Eight: New Family	*329*
Forty-Nine: "The Incident"	*334*
Fifty: Salvation	*343*
Fifty-One: The Temperature of Love	*352*
Fifty-Two: The Mystery of Frank Gelb	*356*
Fifty-Three: Change	*370*
Part Five: Fruit from the Branches	**375**
Fifty-Four: The Outshining	*376*
Fifty-Five: Legacies	*390*
Epilogue: The Coming and Going of Seasons	**396**
Books Now Published from Sean Elliot Russell, author of *the Jesus boy*	
	400
Coming Soon from Inspirational Writer, Sean Elliot Russell	**403**

Part One: Seedlings

"a young plant, especially one raised from seed and not from a cutting"

Prologue: The Weight of a Mountain

It was in a small house on the edge of a small neighborhood where it all began.

One walking by that house on that night would never have known, never have imagined what it was that was about to take place within the walls of that home.

It was a night like so many.

It happened not in the father's bedroom or den. It wasn't a mother reclining in her favorite chair. It was a typical boy who extended his tongue to the offering of sweet honey. And as his tongue felt the gift upon it, it sat there, the sweetness enticing, dangerous, marvelous.

All at one moment, Joshua Phillips slammed the Book shut in both hands, the words he'd just read reverberating within him, probing inside his heart and mind, revealing for him in one moment his own insecurities, his failures, his joys, and his most ardent desires.

A struggle ensued. A war of decisions and fears and ultimate joy mired together, all began with but two words spoken by the Master: "Follow Me." Those words though spoken so many centuries before, whispered to him with a loudness that made his body tremble in anticipation of what they would mean for him, for his life, for those around him. He finally conceded, a triumph found only in surrender.

And then came wave after wave of liberty coursing through him, of life streaming through every atomic particle of his being. For a moment, the weight of a mountain came and rested upon the young man's shoulders and chest, pressing down upon him with an unspoken burden while lifting him to heights he'd never known before. The gentleness of the Unseen touched the vessel for just a moment and flooded his inner being.

But even as the boy rejoiced, there came also a sense of foreboding—something that seemed not to originate from himself. The days ahead would be treacherous and the path uneven and strewn with hazards. Joshua nodded to himself even as the joy washed over him once more like a wave of warm ocean water. He would do all that was necessary to fulfill the Will not his own—even if it meant his very life.

With that, he approached and closed his door quietly. Others in the house might've heard the door close not sensing its importance, not hearing the significance of the many boundaries that were about to be crossed beginning with a single step and a single moment of absolute surrender.

At that, the lad fell to his knees and began to pray.

Almost beyond human perception, there was, just outside that room, as if a darkened crow fluttering against the window, a lingering creature—its red eyes fixed on the goings-on in the room. It repeatedly rose and fell, shifting backwards and forwards like a dragonfly. More of its kind appeared, all drawn to the life within that they sought to feast off of. Then came the turning of the One toward them, His face like a giant, beaming searchlight—the light struck their bodies causing a great shrieking, sending them scampering away from the immediate vicinity to a safe distance—until they might attack at a more opportune time.

A cold draft passed through the seams of the window's brickmold causing Joshua to glance up at the darkened glass—as if seeing something there. For an ominous second, it was as if he sensed a terror there—its intent fixed on him. The boy was tempted to react; but he did not. He turned his face away from the window—his inner gaze returning to the insulation and warmth of the One Who surrounded him. Whatever would happen to him in the days and weeks and months ahead, he knew his source of security would always be hiding in Him. He rested his chin on his chest.

"Amen," he whispered.

One: Back to Earth

It was like wandering an unfamiliar and barren land covered with a thick haze, and then bursting through a misty wall into the brightness of wonders that had always been within reach, always there for the offering, always freely available—yet at incredible cost. Few knew of its existence. Still fewer knew of the consequences of what absolute and unrestrained obedience would bring.

On the morning of August 22nd, Joshua Phillips exited his bedroom, made his way downstairs to his living room before quietly stepping into the kitchen. Bailey, their rust-brown and white-furred border collie with white around its eyes, snout, and chest, one ear white, the other rust-brown, immediately but calmly rose from his bedding and stepped toward Joshua to greet him with an out-stretched nose.

His parents, too, believed in God, and drove to church each week. But even to them, to lock oneself away from everything—*everything*—had seemed a tad extreme—especially during the summer months. A fourteen-year-old could be known to be overzealous about things in his or her life. Perhaps the most troubling had been the skipped meals, and the disregarding of all external distractions including the television, the Internet, or going out to the cinema.

When during that three-week period he'd entered his room, they'd ask him if all was okay, if he was sure he was convinced of this course of action. Joshua would wipe away his strand of blond hair that sought to cover his eyes before looking up and smiling. He'd give a brief answer, but it remained filled with conviction and an unwavering certainty. To his parent's relief, there were no signs of disconnection from reality, nor a spirituality that seemed otherworldly. He merely sat there, reading that Book, speaking in a low voice to the Unseen. It wasn't always so calm, however. There were moments, sometimes in the wee hours of the night, when loud cries would escape the four walls of his room—not the meek and shallow kind of crying, but the sort that erupt from within one amidst an internal war.

Joshua had understood that people—including his own parents—might be shocked and perhaps worried about his actions. Perhaps he would be labeled a religious zealot, a freak of weakness desperate for God to live—or even insane. But whatever connection people placed upon him and his love for God, he'd decided at the beginning not to let his worries about what people thought concern him. There was only One to please.

What had happened to him during those twenty-one days he could never describe in words. His passion to touch the Untouchable had been fueled by more than emotion—but by words spoken by the Master millennia ago. "Follow me," He'd said to a tax collector long ago. And in those three syllables, one man's world had changed resulting in changes that no one could've fathomed because he had said yes.

It had all begun for Joshua when he'd been impressed to read the Scriptures in a disciplined fashion after a weeklong renewal service at his church, New Horizons Fellowship. When he'd read those words by the Master, he'd stopped reading. An echo began to stir up within him. He'd considered the ramifications—and for a moment declined to consider what the words really meant to him. But then, the words had churned within him not allowing rest for the next few days. And in that wrestling of divine and disciple, the Lord had taken hold of Joshua and refused to let go. That eventual struggle had birthed a sweetness, peace, and joy that Joshua had never thought possible. His family immediately noticed the effect on him.

    Mom, Joan Phillips, had thought the whole saga regarding Joshua strange, and something to be watched carefully. In her mid-thirties, she had slightly oval face with high, wide cheek bones and blue-gray eyes. As a habit, she wore minimal make-up upon her milky-white skin and yet still retained a youthful beauty and naturally pleasant disposition. Her hair, naturally light brown in color, was neatly tied to the rear indicating she was ready to roll up her sleeves and serve her family—something she loved and which took almost all her time and energy. Energy, however, was never in short supply with Joan. She retained an industrious and seemingly inexhaustible reserve to keep her household moving in the right direction. And included in her housekeeping was to remain diligent to shepherd her children in all areas of their lives. Chores were assigned and routines of the home life gently enforced. She'd always expected her children to eat at the table during meals even though few families did such anymore.

    That morning, she'd set the table for five not expecting to see the sixth member, not expecting to see her next to youngest son walk through the doorway. At the sight of him, her mouth had dropped an inch. She'd been in the middle of discussing with Dennis, Joshua's Dad, about the possibility of purchasing a used car for Kris, their eldest son, when she'd stopped mid-sentence and fixed her eyes over and beyond Dennis' right shoulder.

"What?" Dennis asked lowering his paper. He was a tall man with broad shoulders, thick, gold-blond hair, a finely trimmed beard, and a tanned complexion tinged with red. He wore his cleanly pressed, blue work uniform that scripted stark black letters on a white backdrop, *Sterling City Repair Shop*. Outwardly, Dennis appeared older than his actual thirty-eight years—such, perhaps, attributed to him being an automobile mechanic since a teenager. The characteristics of a quick smile and blue eyes, however, displaced any thought of Dennis being old. When he followed his wife's gaze over his shoulder, he saw Joshua standing there, looking confident and at peace.

"Hey, Joshua," he said visibly surprised with a subtle hint of relief.

He stood there, his hands in front of him, a content, happy grin upon his face. Stepping over to him, Bailey reared upward extending his white paws toward Joshua which he received happily. He bent over and gave his childhood dog a hug. "Morning, Bailey," he said joyously. After getting his morning routine rub down, the dog returned to his bedding and plopped down while keeping his eyes fastened on the activities at the table.

"Son, sit down," Dennis offered pulling out a chair beside him.

Joshua stepped to the chair and took his place quietly. The boy placed his hands in front of him on the table and gazed at both his parents.

"Well, I didn't expect you to have breakfast with us this morning," Joan said as she retrieved a plate from the cupboard. "How do you want your eggs?"

"Scrambled," Joshua said evenly as she set a bare plate in front of him. "Thanks, Mom."

"You're welcome," she said casting her son a sidelong glance. She stopped as if catching her breath and fixed her eyes on her boy. "Everything okay, Joshua?"

Joshua nodded with a grin as he sat ramrod straight. He pulled his hands to his lap.

She addressed him while placing two slices of bread in the toaster. "We know you've been on a journey of sorts, lately. Can you tell us what exactly you feel you've learned? What has it accomplished?" Joan asked as she emptied some egg mix into the frying pan.

"Obedience," he said quietly. "And that He is my sole comfort and reward."

"Oh," Joan replied in a plain voice as if it had been so obvious an answer. She continued to work the eggs that were sizzling in front of her.

"Obedience?" she finally asked.

"Obedience: I learned how to listen to Him."

"'Listen'? So, you...I mean, He speaks to you?" Dennis asked with a look of concern.

"Yeah."

"And He's your sole comfort and reward now?" Dennis followed up.

"Yes, when you're fasting meals and when you're not allowing things to distract you, you soon learn how to run to Him for comfort and strength—that He becomes your sole reward—not food, not entertainment, not other things."

"I see," Dennis said.

Joan set the scrambled eggs and two slices of buttered toast down in front of Joshua, stood over her son for a moment before turning without a word to continue her tasks. Joshua picked up his fork and began to eat.

"Joshua, what do you mean, 'He *speaks* to you'?" Dennis asked lowering his newspaper.

"I mean," he said swallowing his mouthful of food, "that I've learned to hear his heartbeat—to be led by Him."

"Hmmm," Dennis replied evenly with a thoughtful, almost puzzled expression on his face.

"Don't worry, Dad," Joshua said. "It's simple: instead of Him entering my heart, quite simply, I've entered His."

Dennis lifted an eyebrow slightly but only momentarily before returning his gaze to the paper in his hands.

Just then, Joshua's two older brothers descended the spiral metal staircase that sat at the opposite end of the kitchen. They were both tall, each of them mature and handsome. As they reached the ground floor, they immediately gave their younger brother glances. They, too, had observed their brother's peculiar behavior the past several weeks.

"You guys wanna play basketball a bit later?" Joshua asked. They sat at the table as they poured juice into glasses and awaited the new batch of scrambled eggs being cooked by their mother.

The two boys, aged sixteen and seventeen, both quick to smile, gave each other a sustained look. The younger, Bruce, looked at his younger brother with a grin. "So, you've returned to planet earth finally?"

Joshua laughed. "Yeah, I'm back."

Bruce chuckled lightly. "Yeah, well, don't expect the Lord to bail you out when we pulverize you."

All three boys laughed together.

"What about little Sammy?" Joshua asked looking toward his parents. "I could use his help. He isn't up yet?"

"He's not feeling well this morning," said Joan simply.

"Oh?" Joshua said.

"You boys work up an appetite," Joan added as she wiped down the counter. "Later this afternoon, we'll do a BBQ after your father comes back from a half-day at work."

It was nearly a week before the start of school—the scorching summer having seemed to stretch exceedingly long. There was only the immediacy of the present moment before each of them; all else did not seem to matter. There were no thoughts of school approaching, or girls, or even what they would do the next day.

Except, that is, for Joshua. Even as he played hoops, demonstrating his skills against aggressive and skilled brothers who tested his mettle in every way, there was a new look to the world around him. It was as if a new dimension had attached itself to everything he looked upon. There was more to it than the gleaning of the senses—this he was certain of. More importantly, he heard an echo from the One whose touch and majesty flowed everywhere in time and space. It was the echo of One calling for those who had been separated from Him. It was a heart, content in Itself, that would not relent, would not rest until every last one of the lost heard His Call. Joshua knew this—and that was what gave him the unique insight into a heart larger than the universe. At that moment more than any other, Joshua realized his purpose and mission for the day in front of him—and the days ahead. He would work to fulfill that purpose and mission by giving his will completely and wholeheartedly to the One.

Two: The Mystery of Lydia

Lydia Claremont rushed through the crowded hallway trying to squeeze between her co-students, her mind scrambling to remember the room number of her next class period. She knew she only had a couple more minutes to go before she'd be late. She'd forgotten her schedule at home which had forced her to try to recall where she was supposed to go. Finally, with a sigh of relief, she recognized classmates entering a room, which would be where she would spend the next eighty minutes.

   It was just before lunch, a time that made her glad that the day was nearly halfway over, but also gloomy because she still had to wait a whole period before she'd get something to eat and chat with friends. Not that she allowed class to stop her from socializing. She was always causing her teachers to border on disciplinary action simply because she liked to talk at her own convenience. It wasn't because she lacked self-control. Sometimes, she did the things she wanted because she wanted to even if it meant displeasing people around her—her teachers included. And while her adult instructors usually, eventually had their way with her when it came to her behavior, there remained something below the surface of who she was—an ever-present resistance to those in authority.

   She moved past the students gathered in front of the entrance before making her way to her desk which sat in row three, seat four—in the middle of the class. She carried with her a quiet confidence and an easy smile that seemed to make people around her feel at ease. She was usually the one to start a conversation, but equally true, also the one to end a conversation.

As she sat, she gave a subtle glance toward the seat two rows over and again noticed the boy within—a sandy blond-haired boy that had interested Lydia on day one and day two. Her first impression of him was that he wasn't that good-looking, but little by little during these three days, and seeing him in another of her classes, she'd noticed his keenly blue eyes and the friendly smile that frequented his lips whenever he was amid a conversation. Though a bit quiet for her tastes, she had noticed other traits about him—a strange purity about him, and a dreamy quality that surrounded his actions and the way in which he conducted himself. At times, it was as if he wore earphones listening to music…but there were no earphones or music. There was a strange disposition about him that seemed odd but not in a bad way.

"Hey Joshua," she said politely enough for him to hear. She'd not introduced herself to him though he'd definitely noticed her in their classes together.

Joshua turned his head toward her and gave her an amiable smile. "Hi Lydia. How's everything?" His voice was unrushed and calm.

Lydia heard the bell ring followed by the hurried march of the ultra-thin but tall science teacher, Mr. Opal, into the room. "Good morning, class," he said in a louder-than-needed voice. The class gave a superficial reply which the teacher challenged quickly. "I said, 'Good morning.'" The class echoed a forced, louder reply, "Good morning."

Lydia leaned over toward Joshua, the student in-between leaning back. "What do you like to do for fun?" Lydia asked plainly.

An unsure expression appeared on Joshua's face. It was obvious he was warring between speaking to her at that moment or waiting for a time when he wouldn't get in trouble with Mr. Opal. To her satisfactory grin, he leaned slightly toward her and dared to voice a reply. Just then, the teacher's voice boomed over their heads.

"Mr. Phillips."

Joshua looked up startled, and equally embarrassed. "Yes?"

"Save it for another time. We've a science class to conduct, yes?"

Joshua nodded his head while giving Lydia a glance of awkwardness at being caught.

Though brief, Lydia had enjoyed the scene. For a moment, it seemed as if the boy had snapped out of a light trance, as if the confusion and prospective of breaking Mr. Opal's rules had pierced his cozy bubble. It had seemed interestingly attractive to see Joshua in that state. She already sensed she liked him, though she couldn't decide why—or to what end such a friendship or relationship would be. It was true that he had thrown at her furtive glances in the past three school days, glances that Lydia had recognized as his interest in her. And every so often during class, she'd notice him look her way as if studying her, as if admiring her. Sometimes she'd act like she didn't notice, but other times, she'd turn and look at him—and grin at his attention. He, of course, would smile as his light skin turned a tinge of red with embarrassment.

    Despite the attraction, there seemed a vast gulf of difference between them—something Lydia had not identified until that very day. She'd asked a friend about Joshua, if she'd heard any tidbits of information about him. The words that came from her friend's lips had given her the information she needed: Joshua Phillips was a Christian. And that, she felt convinced, was all the reason to get to know Joshua. Perhaps with some leading, some convincing, and a little open-mindedness from Joshua, she would show him just what he was, and what he could be if only he'd turn from his naïve faith. Then, perhaps, the gulf of differences would disappear. And if not, she'd have her way with him, regardless.

Three: Unchartered Territory

Joshua had never known what he was getting himself into, or better, into Whom he was getting himself when he'd decided to obey the simplest of words ever spoken by the Master to a potential disciple: "Follow Me." He'd simply followed with the simplicity of a child, and with a determination to possess a faith that would be vigorous in all areas of his life. No area of his life had been left untouched.

But priorities for him had changed when his will had become secondary to His will. He no longer saw the things around him, or the people, in the same way. Life had become simpler, yet also more complex in that there were so many hurting around him. The question had not been if he would help such people, but how, and when.

The fourth day of school, Joshua had been late on his way to his next-to-last period class when he'd passed by a student whose form was twisted and unnaturally contorted within a wheelchair. Joshua did not know the student, but as he walked by, he felt an abrupt impression press down upon him.

Reach out and touch him.

The impression did not come in words alone, though the impulse was certainly direct and clearly understood. Joshua stopped. With more faith than it took to obey the notion, he turned and walked back toward the young man who wheeled along.

"Hello," Joshua said with a friendly smile. "Could I speak to you just for a moment?"

The student's downturned hand released the forward shifter, which brought the chair to a sudden halt.

His eyes glared through thick glasses as he gave a jerking motion of his head followed by several indistinguishable moanings, his speech abilities inhibited by his condition.

Nervously, Joshua continued even as he felt a haze surround him, making his clearness of mind vanish and his faith seem so distant from him. With his next words, he pushed out into unchartered territory, yet for every unsure step, he felt something pressing him to do this thing, to not be afraid, and to not doubt. "I know you do not know me since we've just met now, but I would like to…give you something I have."

The student managed a smile though he was certainly just being polite. Joshua did not know whether he had been given permission or not. Within the awkwardness, he leaned forward and laid his hands upon the boy's emaciated shoulders. For a moment, his mind drifted to the strange image that was now unfolding, how incredible this action undertaken by him really was, and how everyone must now be watching him with the utmost curiosity. He realized the pressure of the moment—but it was too late to retreat, too late to not pray for this boy. He leaned even closer about to whisper in his fellow student's ear.

Without warning, the late bell sounded filling the hallway, and, almost immediately, followed by a man's booming voice. "Hey, you two. You're late for sixth period."

"I only know that He told me to pray for you," Joshua said to his school colleague even as he heard the teacher's words. Joshua could not tell if the boy understood what he had just told him but he continued nonetheless. "So..."

"I'm not going to repeat myself," bellowed the stern adult voice. Joshua glanced toward the teacher and recognized Mr. Bell, an ex-Marine built like a heavyweight boxer nicknamed "Tyson" by the students for his resemblance—though his voice was significantly deeper. He knew he now had an excuse to not pray, if he wished, but something within him compelled him not to stop.

He leaned inward and said in a voice barely perceivable, "In the Name of Jesus..." He kept his hands upon the boy's shoulders, not knowing what he should do next, if anything.

The teacher began to walk toward them, his voice charged to tackle this challenge to his authority. The longest four seconds passed by even as Joshua heard the steps of the teacher draw closer. "What are you *doing*, young man?"

Joshua kept his heart on this incredible task despite the pressure of the encroaching teacher and those students who had stopped to watch the confrontation.

The teacher stood over them with a fixed gaze upon Joshua. "If you don't answer me, I'm going to escort you to the principal's office."

Ten seconds.

"Are you *listening* to me? I won't tolerate this behavior."

Students that had been passing through the hallway on their way to classes had now stopped and were watching the strange spectacle, all of them whispering and giving each other strange, fixed looks. All at once, Joshua released the student's shoulders and stood up, his body instantly relaxed.

He turned to face the teacher, a large black man whose face appeared especially flustered. Joshua gave an uncertain smile hoping to appease him. "Sorry, I just felt a need to…pray for him." The wheelchair-bound student moaned approvingly, a smile escaping his nodding head.

The teacher saw the wheelchair boy's gladness and his anger seemed to diminish quickly.

Knowing he was pushing things to the limit, Joshua bent to the boy's ear and whispered. "No matter what, just know *He loves you*."

Joshua walked off and turned to give a lighthearted wave at the boy. There was a reassurance within Joshua that he had done no wrong. But at the same time, there was a test of faith warring within him. He felt silly and the target of ridicule—not to mention how close he had come to being severely punished. Questions to God wrestled for answers. *Why had he just prayed for him? What had such accomplished?* Everyone stood watching, and it was the most difficult hallway walk he'd ever suffered.

Just as he was about to turn the corner, there came a large snapping sound that filled the hallway—like a tree limb snapping in two. Joshua stopped and slowly turned, almost afraid to look. His eyes doubled in size as he saw the boy had slowly risen from his chair, the teacher's face aghast at this scene taking place. The boy began to holler even as his arms straightened, even as his twisting head suddenly gained perfect movement and strength. Within seconds, the boy's frame had taken on a new form. Even as he yelled out, his voice began to change from grunts and jumbled syllables to clearly understood words of ecstasy.

"L-Look at me," he shouted as he walked and showed his hands and body to those gathered. Teachers had stepped out of their classrooms wondering what was going on, and students followed until they quickly overflowed into the hallway. The boy began to walk, his limbs strengthening with each movement. Everyone gasped in awe, the only sound heard being that of fierce whispers among students. No one said a word save for the boy. Mr. Bell looked from the boy to Joshua with muted amazement, his face reeling in shock at this which he was witnessing. Several began to mirror the boy and smile while others could only watch and ponder. There were some who had a look of fright upon their faces.

    Joshua, however, felt tears brim his eyes as he realized how he had just been used. He felt humbled even as he fell to his knees, at awe, afraid, and energized all in one moment.

    The same teacher who had shouted at them staggered as if he'd had one drink too many. It seemed he'd forgotten how to walk as he made his way through the crowd of students and teachers to Joshua who kneeled with his eyes closed. "H-How did you do that, son?"

    Joshua wiped away his tears before smiling and briefly laughing even as he stared at the boy who was now leaping and twirling about the hallway, his screams of joy filling the hallway. "I didn't do it," he finally said as he looked up intently at the teacher whose hands were visibly shaking. "It was *His* power, not my own," he added even as the tears continued to fall.

Four: The Spreading Strange and Wonderful News

The rest of that day at school for Joshua was anything but normal. News had spread throughout the school causing many to look at Joshua with mixed looks—some of surprise, some of suspicion, others of fear. Joshua, however, found himself not caring what people thought because at that moment, he felt at peace and the closest he'd ever felt to the One for Whom he served. It was one thing to believe without confirmation; it was wholly another to believe with sudden and unequivocal confirmation that the Most High's Spirit rested upon him—a simple teen who had taken literally the command of Jesus to follow Him—in every area of his life.

When the final relief of the last bell sounded, Joshua hurried to get to his bus. He looked forward to getting home and making himself the biggest cold-cut turkey and cheese sandwich he could put together.

It was just as he entered the heated brightness of the outside that a voice called out to him. Joshua looked to see who it was not recognizing the voice when he saw it was the boy he'd prayed for earlier. He stood short for his age, but the changes that had taken place were enormous. Accompanying him stood two adults—the resemblance indicating they were the boy's parents.

"My name's Brad," he said with a bright smile and extended his hand toward Joshua who took the hand firmly and smiled back. "It's amazing to me that I couldn't have done this earlier today."

"It amazes me, too!" Joshua added. "I almost didn't notice you without your glasses."

Brad chuckled lightly. "Yeah, they give me a headache to use them. I think I still need glasses—but not the coke-bottle glasses I've been wearing before."

Joshua nodded. "It's incredible what He's done in you! Your world's been totally rearranged!"

"Joshua," the tall man said stepping forward with a hand thrust in front of him. Joshua shook his hand with a friendly smile. "I'm Karl Young, Brad's father. And this is my wife, Stephanie. How can we ever thank you?"

Joshua felt the compliment's warmth momentarily wash over him; however, he decided to be cautious. "There's no need to thank me," he finally said. "It wasn't me who healed your boy; it was the power of Jesus."

"But *how*?" the mother asked with an uncertain grin. Joshua noticed the unhappy expression on Brad's father at the questioning of his wife. "We just don't know how this was possible. Look at my son. He's a brand-new boy!" she said, almost as if exasperated at the spectacle.

Joshua recognized this mother's lack of faith even in the face of such overwhelming evidence, but he excused her with a smile. "It *isn't* possible," he finally said. "Not without God. But give glory where it belongs. It's God who healed Brad. I should be getting on my bus before I miss it," he said with a wave and a smile. "Take care, guys."

"Wait," Brad said anxiously before beginning to walk alongside Joshua to his bus. "I was thinking. I'd like to serve this Jesus as you serve Him."

Joshua heard his words which caused a grin to appear on his face. "So, you want to know your Healer?" He stood at the entrance to his bus and saw his new friend give an emphatic nod. Several other classmates on the bus were watching closely and whispering feverishly to each other. Joshua suddenly felt tired. He wanted to go home, eat and rest—and most of all, contemplate what had happened today. But he knew he could not ignore this other hunger that was now resident within Brad. Finally, and happily after he'd done it, Joshua stepped away from his bus.

"Are you sure that you want to follow Him?"

The boy's face seemed to be calculating the cost in a single moment.

"I saw what He did for me. I want to know this Jesus…whatever the cost."

Joshua watched as the first of the long line of buses began to pull off. A part of him wanted to ask Brad to talk to him the next day—but this would not do. No one ever delayed a life-saving rescue because of hunger or tiredness. The unseen within Brad was crying out for answers from the Unseen above. Joshua finally conceded that his own comfort was secondary to the Will above. He would bring Brad to the Lord with gladness and with no regard for the cost. He would continue to pay the price and live in obedience despite his own desires.

Five: Inner Warning

Joshua got home just as the phone was ringing. After quickly rubbing the head of Bailey, he scrambled to get to it not knowing if he'd reach it in time. He picked up the handset and plopped down on the sofa.

"Hello?"

"Hi Joshua," a girl's voice said in a friendlier-than-usual tone. "Lydia here. What's up?" Just then, Joshua's Mom walked into the kitchen from the living room and gave her son an unspoken greeting and a quick wave.

"Lydia? Hey. How'd you get my phone number?"

"I have my connections," she said proudly. "What happened with you today? I've heard some crazy stuff. Is it really true?"

"Crazy?"

"It sounds crazy that a guy bound in a wheelchair all his school life suddenly becomes normal again—after you said a prayer for him or something."

"His name's Brad, and yeah, I prayed for him."

"How did you do it, though?"

"I didn't do it; I just obeyed God when I felt Him nudge me to pray for the boy."

There came only silence. And then, "Wow. I've never heard of that happening before."

"It's really no big deal when you think about it. God's life just poured into a broken vessel and mended it...in this case, Brad Young."

"I see. Well, it seems there are many broken people in the school who need that life. How come He doesn't fix everyone who's broken?"

"I'm not sure. That's why He's God and I'm His follower. I just do what He tells me."

"So...He speaks to you?"

"Well, not emphatically. It's more of a knowing that I'm to do something. Suddenly, He'll impress upon me to pray for someone or whatever. But hey, I never dreamed that He would heal a paraplegic...and right before everyone's eyes."

"Yeah, I heard some amazing things. Hey, are you busy this Friday night? I'd like to go out for some fun if you're not going to be at the monastery praying that evening," she said with a light chuckle.

Immediately, Joshua felt within himself a withdrawal—ever so slight. It was as if something within him had been pinched and pulled inward. "I'll let you know," Joshua said cautiously. He liked this girl but he wondered why he felt this inward warning.

"Ooookaaaaay," she replied, her voice unsure how to respond to his indecision.

"No, I just need to confirm it before I make a decision. I'll let you know tomorrow," he said.

"Well, pray about it," she said, her voice sounding serious. Then, however, her voice changed into a flirt. "This little vessel needs mending," she said with a laugh.

"Don't we all?" Joshua said giving a quick laugh, his sense of discomfort increasing by the second. He didn't like the

25 | the Jesus boy

way she'd said that. A moment later, he managed to say good night before hanging up.

Even as he considered these new plans for his upcoming Friday, he held his head in his hands as he mouthed a quick prayer. As he did this, he suddenly had a sense of something amiss in the room. Joshua turned toward a darkened corner in the living room as if something was there, still, silent, menacing. A shudder passed through him. Joshua immediately stood up from the sofa as if to challenge the internal threat he'd felt.

"The Lord is my High Tower," he mouthed as he turned and climbed the carpeted stairway to his bedroom. As he went inside, he closed the door and leaned his forehead against it while mouthing a prayer to the One. He slipped off his shoes and sat down at the end of his bed even as he struggled to understand what had happened to him earlier while talking to Lydia—the receding within that he'd sensed. And as he assessed it, he realized that that same feeling yet lingered.

"Lord," he whispered as he fell to his knees. "I don't want my closeness with You to change—or worse, to falter." He rubbed his eyes as he spoke. "I only want to please You," he said, his voice breaking. "What happened today—wow, Lord. It was all You. And I want to be used like that again and again," he said with conviction. "Thank You for healing Brad!"

Moments later, he entered a time of worship with all of his heart just as he had during his twenty-one days in August. A sense of comfort—the receding within Him no longer so apparent—coated his heart which calmed Joshua. As he finished his time in worship, he again prayed for wisdom regarding this girl named Lydia.

Six: Unfolding Plan

The television played softly even as Lydia hung up and laid back in the recliner. She felt tired while also feeling recharged having spoken briefly to Joshua. She contemplated Joshua's indecision—a rare event when it came to boys she showed interest in. While she liked the challenge, she felt an odd, slight feeling of resentment that she might not be considered—for whatever reason. Just as she arose to go upstairs to her bedroom to fall into her bed for the night, the telephone sounded its electronic chirp. Lydia turned and grabbed the handset.

"Hello?" she asked. Something within her had hoped that this was Joshua returning her call to say he would go with her...but she realized such was unlikely if not impossible. As it was, she'd had to make all the advances toward Joshua—him not making any visible advances toward her. The voice on the other end, however, wasn't Joshua.

She listened a few seconds before replying. "Yes, it's on track just like we talked about." "Don't worry." Lydia began to pace her living room running her long, slim hands through her long brunette hair. "I told you I would take care of things, and I *will*." She stopped in mid-stride visibly upset. "You know, you should trust me more! I know what I'm doing." And then, a few seconds later: "Bye!" she said angrily as she slammed the handset back into its resting place.

She wanted to run and never look back—but it was too late for that. Her temples suddenly ached as she felt the pressure pushing inward. She was where she was because she was proficient at what she did. So what if people weren't satisfied with her level of performance. She'd put in more hours than all of her predecessors combined—and with more to show for her work than any of them.

As she thought about her mounting stresses, her thinking turned to Joshua. Within a moment, her reflections went from dark to light and from misery to gladness as she realized the brightness and simple comfort seemingly inherent in Joshua. *What was it about him? How was it that one person could draw her so convincingly? What was it that he seemed to carry a dreamy peace about him and without appearing to be a dullard?* She became convinced that she would unearth what it was about him—this mystery of a boy. Besides, she loved this new challenge. And whatever challenges she tackled, she achieved and had her way. She smiled briefly even as her thoughts considered her newly unfolding plan.

Seven: The Whispering of That Name

Though still dark outside, Joshua awakened the next morning feeling refreshed and renewed. As he slipped out of his bed and smacked the hearty alarm of his clock, he sensed the Unseen surrounding him even as his mind tried to fully awaken.

"Good morning, Lord," he said aloud as he went to his knees and began to dialogue with Him. As he did, the Presence seemed to thicken and coat him bringing with it an assurance and vitality. Moments later, however, as he made mention of his school, there appeared before him a roadblock of dread. "What's going on, Lord?" Joshua asked. And as he thought about it, he realized there had come a warning within him. "Okay, Lord," he said. "Then thank You for Your added grace to face whatever's thrown at me."

Moments later as he stepped into the bathroom and turned the water faucet on full blast, Joshua considered the telephone call from Lydia the night before. He'd had girlfriends in the past, for sure. But Lydia seemed different—more mature and more rough-edged—as if she were used to a different crowd of people than her appearance let on. There was something else. More than any previous girl he'd courted, he felt especially attracted to her—to the point that he felt minutely intimidated by her. Then again, he considered, he wondered if there was anyone she couldn't intimidate.

Still, her entrance into his life had been unexpected. In some ways, it worried him what a relationship with a girl would mean for himself, and especially His relationship with the One. A part of him wanted to avoid the whole situation while another side yearned to explore what this all meant. She seemed pleasant enough though she didn't embrace his faith. Well, he'd work to change her heart so that she knew of His story and His desire and His truth. Perhaps the power's unexpected demonstration the previous day would be enough to begin turning her to Him. Regardless, Joshua decided he'd be cautious and take things slow.

Dressed, groomed, and cologned up, he felt a joy resting upon him as he departed his bedroom and went to the end of the hallway to descend the spiral staircase to the kitchen. As he came down, he was surprised to notice both his Mom and Dad sitting at the table talking in lower-than-normal voices.

"Hey," Josh said. Joshua scanned his parent's faces trying to figure out what was being talked about. He could tell, almost instinctively, that something was wrong.

"Morning, Joshua," Dennis said in a seemingly normal voice, his newspaper still folded, undisturbed on the table.

Joshua watched his mom, her back to him, lower her head and wipe a cheek before finally looking around to him and giving him a morning smile. "Hey, Joshua," she said trying too hard to be cheerful even as he noted the red puffiness beneath her eyes.

"What's wrong?" Joshua asked stopping, to a strange silence. He held a neutral expression but visibly concerned.

"Nothing," Joan answered with a brief, unsteady smile. "Just talking stuff."

"*What* stuff?" Joshua asked unsatisfied wiping away his straight blond hair strands away from his eyes.

Just then, Joshua heard the commotion of his older brothers behind him as they descended the spiral staircase.

"Hey," Joan yelled in a low voice toward Kris and Bruce. "Samuel's still sleeping!"

They immediately quieted with whispered apologies. The boys' tall frames moved past Joshua before taking their places at the table which brought Joan seemingly to life.

"Breakfast coming up, boys," she offered rising to the counter and oven. When Joan volunteered Dennis to drop them off at school on his way to work, the boys became animated with happiness at such unexpected news. Joshua, however, remained unsure what he would do. He stood there unable to ignore the concern and unseen tears on his mother's face. It was clear his parents had been hiding something from him though he had no idea what that something could be. For all he knew, it had nothing to do with him. Yet, he couldn't be sure of this, either, as he'd overheard his two brothers tell them the previous night about what people had supposedly witnessed regarding him and the wheelchair-bound student.

In a moment, Joshua felt sadness envelope his heart as he considered how important his parent's approval truly was. Could he bear the weight of knowing his parents did not approve of him, his actions, or his faith-actions on behalf of the One? He loved his parents. But could he love God even more if he were tested in such a manner?

"Thanks, I'm not that hungry," Josh said as he approached the kitchen door that led to the living room.

"Where're you going, Joshua?" his Dad asked over his shoulder. "I'll take all of you."

Bailey quickly scampered from his crate and ran up and stood beside Joshua wondering if he'd get to go where he was going.

"That's all right, Dad," Josh said even as he looked down at his dog who looked up at him with pleading eyes. "Sorry, boy. Not this time." Then he turned toward his family. "I'm gonna be late for the bus. See you guys later."

Joshua stepped into the living room and made his way to the front door even as he felt his stomach's emptiness churn within him. He felt disappointed in himself that he hadn't stayed and enjoyed his family's company, but he also felt he had no choice but to get out of the house so he could get fresh air—and to consider what all these things meant to him and his new walk with God.

As he walked out of the house and onward to the street that would bring him on a rendezvous with the #276 big yellow school bus, he whispered the Name which brought an immediate comfort and relief. Other feelings, however, stirred within him that equaled fear. He suddenly realized just how daring this new adventure of his was. If he wasn't careful, if he didn't prize his newfound relationship with the Most High above all, he might fall from grace only to find no one around supporting him, or worse, wanting to be associated with him. The raw realization terrified him.

"Please forgive me for my doubt," he whispered into the empty air in front of him as he glanced down at the road as he walked. The Unseen seemed to wrap around him even closer than previously which granted him a renewed hope that he would not perish regardless of circumstances, and that he would not ever be left abandoned or alone. He would pay the price—regardless of the results to him or his surrounding relationships.

***

The Presence was thick—yet even that Great Presence could not block out their concentrated shrieks and screams directed at the boy. This had begun from the moment he'd stepped down into the kitchen—the confusion being sown, the disconnection of the boy with his family, and the fear arising within him about losing all his relationships— including his closeness with the One. These all were quite satisfying. Yet the dark ones also hungered to get nearer to him—to latch onto him and his life's sustenance. Soon, they knew. They'd use his weaknesses to dethrone the One from his heart—and, in addition, use the shame and guilt to drive him far away from Him so that getting back would be unlikely if not impossible.

Part Two: Tender Shoots

*"a very young plant,
or a new part growing on a plant"*

Eight: Bless Your Enemies

As Joshua stepped off the bus, there stood Brad waiting for him with an expectant smile. He wasn't alone. Three other students, two boys, one girl, stood beside him in a line as if soldiers awaiting instructions.

"Hey Joshua," Brad said with a welcome grin. Joshua felt glad to see his new friend which seemed confirmation that he would always have a friend on this earth as long as Brad was upon it.

"Hi," Joshua said. "What's up?"

"I want you to meet Jennifer, Sergio, and Alistair."

Pleased though slightly unnerved, Joshua smiled as he gave them a sweeping wave. "Nice to meet you guys. Ah, you look like you were waiting for me to arrive—what's the occasion?" he asked Brad.

Jennifer spoke up. She was African-American with friendly, round eyes, and the smoothest olive skin Joshua had ever seen. She had a reed-slim frame topped by intricately braided hair that skirted her shoulders. "My friend Alicia told me what happened to Brad. And I think I speak for all of us when I say we want to know more about Him...and what his healing means."

"I see," Joshua said with an uncertain smile. He also felt a pang of embarrassment that he didn't know what exactly to do next. Just the night before, Joshua had felt the weight of an impression that the demonstration of power the previous day would be enough to begin a harvest with few words spoken. Yet there was also a realization that a darkness had settled into the school long before—the weeds and tares observed everywhere. It was as if the darkness had become settled into the landscape of the school and had had its way for so long that nothing could dislodge its effects. God's power, however, had begun to change the landscape, Joshua realized. He wondered what the repercussions would be, if any, on him and others that held to His Name.

Sergio, a tall, darkly tanned boy with short, straight black hair and brown eyes spoke up. "Yeah, we just want to know what's real. Me and Alistair here both saw what happened to Brad," he said putting one hand on his shoulder. "And if the truth be told, it freaked us both out."

Alistair, who was of Chinese-American lineage, nodded in agreement. He wore his black hair spiked atop his already tall, thin frame. He nodded to Sergio's words. "Yeah, it did!"

Joshua didn't know what to say. He just wasn't used to speaking to people. He opened his mouth to speak, unsure what would come—and he was more than a bit surprised when the words began to flow from his lips. "God's power is here because God is here. He wants to set all captives free—of whatever affliction or chains that may exist on people. Do you want to follow Him as I follow Him?"

All three nodded their heads, Brad watching giving an approving nod.

"Then...you guys can meet—"

"Well look what we got here!" an amused voice interrupted. Joshua turned to see three large boys walking toward them, the speaker of the bunch showing a smirk of a grin on his large, round face. His black eyes seemed closer to each other than they should've been but matched his straight, black hair. His round cheeks and face were plump and rested seemingly without a neck upon a large, rotund body. He stood easily over six-foot-tall—his considerable size impressive and ominous. His hands were like those of a gorilla—seemingly ready to clutch and dismember. Like his smaller buddies, he wore a blue jean jacket, oversized jeans, and immaculate-white sneakers. All three wore their red, straight-edged street caps turned slightly to their right side. Glancing at him, it was clear to Joshua that the guy was in a mood to play—that he would be, unless intervention took place, a cornered mouse. Josh was reminded of his prayer early that morning—the dread that had filled him.

Joshua prayed quickly internally for wisdom—and help.

The young man drew to within five feet but continued his tirade. "We got the preacher dude here right in front of our very eyes," he said to his compatriots who said nothing but nodded in agreement while maintaining their cynically cold eyes fixed on Joshua.

Joshua immediately stepped between Brad and his new friends and the approaching boys.

"What do you want?" he asked evenly, his heart pounding within his chest.

The large boy's grin changed to amazement, his eyebrows knit with subtle anger. "Hmm, maybe I want to smash you into the pavement just so your friends right here don't get the silly idea to talk to me like you just did."

Joshua hated confrontation. Even worse, he hated pain. "Look, I didn't mean any disrespect," he said with a soft steadiness. Just then came a word within him, like a rock lifting to the surface waters of his mind and heart: *Bless your enemies.*

Even as Joshua contemplated what he should do, if anything, the gorilla of a boy thankfully redirected the dialogue, though Joshua did not like any of this situation he found himself in. "So how did you do it? Magic? Mirrors?" he asked with mocking, sneering laughter.

"How did I do what?"

"How'd you make 'ol Brad there get up out of his chair?" he asked throwing a glance toward the timid teenager who immediately threw his gaze to the ground.

"I didn't. It was a power beyond anything you or I could imagine...from God."

"Is that so?"

Abruptly, without warning, Joshua felt himself being jerked upward by the oversized boy and then downward until his soft cheek slammed against the cool, jagged pavement. "What do you think now, *Jesus* Boy? Are you convinced of that? 'Coz I'm not!"

Bless your enemies filled his mind again even as he moaned as his cheekbone and temple were pressed against the rough hardness of concrete. *Bless my enemies?* Joshua repeated inwardly. At that moment, Joshua felt only the rage of being humiliated. His enemy deserved no blessing or kind words, words that he felt would be wholly useless. Within the reasoning of his anger, he wanted, instead, to do only one thing: to call fire down from the sky.

Brad and the others stood aghast at the situation, their eyes doubled in size at the scenario unfolding before them. They protested as much as possible not having any kind of advantage—though the hardened stares of the larger boys quickly made their outrage wilt to almost nothing.

"Hey!" bellowed a teacher's voice but from some distance away. Immediate relief did not come, however, before the brute spoke in a low voice into Joshua's ear.

"Tomorrow morning, I'm going to come here and ask you the same question—and the answer better be to my satisfaction, J-Boy."

"What...do you want the...answer...to be?" Joshua managed painfully through labored breaths.

"I don't care...but here's a clue: I *don't* believe in God."

Joshua felt the pressure being applied to his body and face immediately lift away. He sat up before tenderly touching his cheek and looking at his hand—blood coated his fingers. He felt the pins and needles flutter through his limbs. The teacher finally reached the gathered crowd though the bullies had already scampered off the school grounds.

"Make space," the teacher bellowed, the crowd opening up to allow him through. Reaching Joshua, he bent down to him. "Are you okay?"

"Yeah, I'll be fine," he said even as the phrase repeated once more in his mind, *"Bless your enemies."*

***

The shrieks of the darkened ones had sown confusion and embarrassment in the boy during his one-sided melee. And when the deafening sound of the Voice had filled the boy's insides, simple words with simple instructions, the boy had, to their delight and pleasure, resorted to his own wisdom above the One's. And now, they continued to concentrate on him—to make him doubt the One's faithfulness.

***

A heavy dread rested upon Joshua even though he tried to act unshaken and normal before Brad and the others. In honesty, he tried to get free of the weighted feeling—but no matter what he did, he still felt saddened—as well as traumatized. He felt a betrayal that he couldn't look past.

Brad, Jennifer, Sergio and Alistair followed Joshua into the school foyer. They each felt sad that they hadn't been able to do anything to help Joshua in his predicament. All four of them recognized their placement in the scheme of things when it came to structures of power within the school; they were but cowering freshmen that had just entered the dog-eat-dog world of high school. Joshua had forgiven their lack of action understanding their inability to do anything without themselves also being assaulted.

"You were brave," Jennifer offered as she followed behind.

"Brave?" Joshua gave a doubtful glance toward her as he reached and delicately touched his bloodied cheekbone. "How was I brave? I was disgraced back there."

After a momentary silence, she gave a quip of a reply. "You stood between them and us. I'd call that brave no matter what happened!"

The others each nodded and agreed wholeheartedly.

Joshua gave a light shrug although the comforting words had influenced him. In some ways, they'd given him back part of his dignity. Suddenly, he realized he'd just met some friends. He stopped and turned to them.

"Meet me at 2:30 p.m. today at the flagpole. If you're serious about serving Him, we'll talk about it then."

The four teens nodded before rushing off to their classes. Brad lingered behind.

"Are you okay?" he asked. "I'm sorry I didn't help you."

"It's okay, Brad," Joshua said with a light jab to his shoulder. "It was out of your hands and mine."

"Well, we should tell a teacher that they're coming back for you tomorrow morning, don't you think?"

Almost without thinking, Joshua shook his head. "No. I would rather let God handle this."

Without saying another word, Brad gave a shy grin and a polite wave as he headed off the opposite direction to get to his first class. It was as Joshua began to walk alone that he realized the look that had been cast his way from Brad: admiration, though Joshua couldn't say for sure if there was anything worth admiring about himself.

Joshua thought of himself as a naturally humble person, but not either meek, mild-mannered, or a wimp. He knew his own limitations and he generally used common sense when reacting to the people and situations surrounding him. He'd always thought he could talk his way out of a tough spot.

Minutes before, however, he'd found his circumstances run amok in the face of a bully who was intent on inflicting pain on him. For a moment, Joshua found himself hating the bully who had minced his cheekbone into the pavement. He wanted to fight back, to use whatever force was necessary to end the humiliation and harassment. What had he done to deserve such treatment? Did God really expect him to turn and offer the bully his other cheek?

As he entered homeroom class moments later, he delicately felt his mildly bruised cheek. He took his seat and considered the reflections churning within him. At that moment, he felt insignificant and he knew why... There he'd been, talking about God's power and suddenly, His power had *not* been. Joshua felt anger building...but more than that, a sense of disappointment, as if he'd been solely abandoned. He felt as though the jagged cement had become the reality—not his faith or his belief in God's power to handle any situation.

Yet, even as the teacher took roll, and as students talked in hushed tones around him, Joshua felt the enfolding Presence wrap around him as if to comfort him. Joshua noticed, however, that a slight barrier had arisen in the amount of time it had taken for him to be forced to the cement and humiliated until the time he'd reached the class and sat down. Despite the comfort given by the One, Joshua also noted a receding of the Unseen within him.

Joshua knew the problem remained in one place: his own heart. He knew deep down that he could never blame God for what had happened. He closed his eyes and whispered the Name apologetically to ask for forgiveness. Now, in the classroom came wave after wave of intimacy as the barrier slipped away and the Uncreated touched the created. His eyes closed, Joshua raised his brows in surprise when he heard a voice penetrate time and space and call his name.

"Joshua."

"Joshua!"

Joshua's eyes shot open. "Present," he replied to an impatient teacher and the titters of nearby students.

Embarrassed red, Joshua managed a half-smile to those around him so not to look too weird—hoping they'd thought him half-dozing.

***

"What happened to your face, Joshua?" Lydia asked. She'd sauntered into the science class and instead of walking down her own row, she'd walked down Joshua's before standing over him—a concerned look on her face.

"Just an accident," Joshua smirked.

"Playing rough with your brothers?" she asked, her voice probing to know but for more reasons than just his welfare, Joshua considered. The strange marks on his face were of interest to everyone, it seemed, and now Lydia.

Instead of lying, Joshua offered a friendly smile. "Naah," he said allowing his voice to downplay what had happened. He did not want to have to share what had happened—a moment that still jarred him and seemed unreal to him. "Just an accident this morning," he said.

She leaned her weight against the edge of another student's desk next to Josh's desk as if to get cozy. She'd given no concern whatsoever for the girl seated there who remained incredibly patient.

"So," Lydia said following a sigh. She looked down at him from her perched position.

"So," Joshua repeated with a quip of a grin trying not to display the momentary discomfort he felt.

Without warning, she leaned over toward Joshua's face. He had noticed her striking features before—but now they especially impressed him. She had rounded brows that complimented her dark eyes. Her perfectly shaped nose graced her oval face, a smile quick to appear in almost all circumstances. When she did smile with those thin, wide lips, she was able to light up an entire room. "Would you care to go with me to a youth group meeting this Friday night?"

"What kind of youth group is it?" Joshua asked as he slowly slunk downward into his seat so not to feel too uncomfortable.

"A witch coven," she said with a quick laugh, Joshua's expression remaining undisturbed. "Church, of course," she said simply and then turned and whisked off down the row before entering her own row until she took her seat. She looked over toward Joshua giving him a furtive smile as Mr. Opal entered the room with his characteristic greeting.

Joshua considered this new possibility. Perhaps Lydia was open to God working within her. To find out, he'd have to spend time with her, a realization that frightened him as well as thrilled him. She glanced over to him which gave him the chance to nod a smile to her. He would go with her on Friday night.

Nine: Deserts

The rest of the students had left on buses leaving the school grounds seemingly desolate except for occasional students going about their after-school business. The sun's brightened rays descended upon Joshua and the other students which would've been unbearable except for the shadows of nearby tall oaks which blocked the repressive heat. Every so often, Joshua would glance about him as he realized he wasn't too enthused with the idea of repeating what had happened to him earlier in the morning.

Brad, Jennifer, Sergio and Alistair sat there surrounding the flagpole, awaiting what they perceived to be a change in their life, but also an adventure of sorts. Joshua, however, wanted them to know that it wouldn't be easy—and that there would be a price to pay for each of them.

Sergio had been the first to ask a question. "Tell us how you came to know Him."

Joshua took a seat on one of the marble benches that was nearby. Then they gathered around. "It happened after a weeklong of renewal services. I'd really felt drawn to Him, unlike any other time. As I thought of His goodness and love, I realized that nothing else fulfilled me or gave me the peace that was within me at that moment. And it was then that I really felt the need to give Him everything I possessed—all of my life. So, a month ago, I went into my bedroom and remained there for almost all of three weeks."

"What did you do?" Alistair asked perplexed.

"I prayed. I read His Word. I listened. I worshiped. I went through a sort of desert experience."

"'Desert experience?'" Jennifer asked.

"Well, it's a bit difficult to explain but even God's Son had to learn obedience through time in a desert or wilderness...except He did it for forty days and nights." Joshua felt his heart lift in exhilaration as he began to explain. "Before Jesus faced temptation, the Spirit had rested *with* Jesus. When He came out of the wilderness having succeeded in His testings, however, the Spirit rested *upon* Jesus." Joshua waited to see if the idea registered with any of them.

Brad's eyebrows raised in excitement. "So something happened to Him only after He'd succeeded—after He'd passed His tests?"

"Yep," Joshua said. "In a sense, it was Jesus graduating with honors—except few if any people that have lived have reached that level of faith and dependence and devotedness to the Father. And it wasn't a diploma He walked out of the desert with: it was the Spirit of the God without limit." Joshua paused momentarily to let it sink in. "When I went into my bedroom, I stopped everything...to be with Him."

Sergio seemed genuinely amazed. "No television? No chatting? No PlayStation? No tunes?"

Joshua smiled understanding how radical it sounded. "Well, I listened to music that edified me, but everything else I eliminated. I also gave up two out of three of my daily meals, except for drinking juice and taking daily Communion before the Lord."

"How hard was it for you?" Jennifer asked.

Joshua didn't want to lie whatsoever. "There were a lot of times I wanted to quit, and to go do what I wanted. I fidgeted, and fought all the desires that I had to sleep, eat, and entertain myself."

Alistair and Sergio exchanged looks before turning back toward Joshua. Alistair asked, "So we have to do the same thing?"

Joshua stared down at the pavement, the memory of being shoved down into it that very morning an unkind reminder that the tests and growth and learning would never end. Regardless, Joshua knew what God expected— even if sometimes unexpected events happened.

Allistair shifted his weight as he pondered aloud his friend's question. "But it'd be worth it," he said looking around at those gathered, and especially Sergio. "To be touched by One so great, and then to somehow touch His heart... What price wouldn't be enough?"

Joshua nodded. "Exactly. You'll each have to look within yourself. You'll have to go through your own desert experience. The price, for some, is too great. But if you graduate with honors, I believe, the changes will never be the same for you or the people around you."

"What is the price?" Jennifer asked in a low voice as if she was afraid to ask.

"It costs...*everything*."

"Everything?"

"Everything," Joshua said emphatically, joy etched on his face.

"But why so many days? Why can't we just get jolted with His electricity and have His power if we decide to follow Him?" Sergio asked.

Joshua wiped away a strand of hair covering his eyes as he thought about the question. "I don't know. Perhaps He could jolt you, and perhaps He does that to some." Joshua suddenly glanced up at the trees surrounding them. "I mean, look at these oaks towering over us." They each looked upward at the far-reaching limbs covered in thick greenery. "Of course these giants," he continued, "started out as tiny seeds. I guess it's Him proving you…like a metal made pure and strong through intense heat and ice water. Perhaps more than anything else, it isn't so much Him moving into your heart…but you moving into His."

All four nodded, each of their faces displaying various levels of understanding.

"But it is a time of testing. You must be strong…or in actuality, weak, so that He might be strong within each of you. It's the building of character that He treasures most."

Brad stood up and faced each of them. "Well, I know that just yesterday morning, I couldn't stand here or talk in a manner that people could easily understand me. I lived, my body endlessly cramped into twisted knots. Every function of my body, every effort to exist was difficult and a struggle. Almost every day of my life, I wanted to know why I should even continue living…and what my purpose could ever be. I'd come to school and nod and smile…but inwardly, I was never convinced it was all worth it to keep going. I barely had a friend because of my condition. People were too embarrassed to try to know me or even to be seen with me. Sometimes I'd go an entire day without having a conversation with anyone—not even teachers talking to me. But when Joshua stopped me in the hallway to talk to me, God used him to change everything in my life. He touched me through Joshua's obedience. My life, and even the life of my parents, has dramatically changed forever." Brad paused to look down at his hands. His face seemed to be amid great computations. "I had nothing before He touched me. I have everything now...and I want to give back to Him all that I am."

Joshua's eyes met those of Brad. In an instant, he knew exactly what to do. With a determined look, Joshua rose to his feet and placed his hands upon Brad's shoulders. He began to pray for his friend, and within minutes, for each of them. Then, he sent them home and told them to do as their hearts—and the Spirit—led them in the hours and days ahead. If the world was going to be changed, it would first have to begin within each of them, and continue with equal fervor every day, something Joshua had warned them about with absolute conviction.

Almost an hour later, as Joshua stepped out of Brad's parent's car, however, he felt the measure of his own words that he had spoken to the others. Although he felt tired, and though he fought with the idea of eating a meal and going to sleep, he entered his room, closed the door, and went to his knees to pray—not only for himself but for his new friends and the path that was being laid for them in the coming days and weeks ahead.

Yet even as he went deep aiming to accomplish great things in the Holy Spirit, he was brought back to the image of himself being shoved into the hard, irregular pavement. And he was confronted with his feelings against the bouncer-of-a-bully who had threatened him—and would, within twelve hours or less, return to haunt him.

Just then, he looked up at his darkening window when he thought he heard several scrapings—as if the claw of some creature was trying to burrow its way inside.

Joshua turned back to the Lord. "How can I love someone like my attacker? Please, Lord. Show me how to forgive him—how to see him as You see him?" He felt already a relief having admitted these questions to the Lord—and he somehow knew He had heard his queries. He continued to pray for himself and the guys—his heart wide open to whatever the Lord wanted him to understand and know.

***

The ink-black creatures hissed and turned on each other like rabid dogs as they struck the barrier in their zeal to fill his room with their life-draining, dark plans—the glory of the One within the room too great to enter. They'd thought the boy was moving in their direction because of his bitterness, his hatred, and his unwillingness to do the most basic of things required of His followers—to give genuine love. And, they'd been overjoyed at his mounting pride—an amazing and effectual barrier to anything good from the One. But then the boy had gone to his knees and even fasted a meal—and now this: the turning back of the boy to the wisdom of his Master. They continued to watch—their hungry eyes fixed on the kneeling lightbearer. Soon, they knew. Soon they would have access to him and have their way with him.

Ten: The Dream

Joshua dreamt. He found himself roving rapidly through what appeared to be a golden wheat field that trembled in the wind. There in front of him scampered the frame of the behemoth bully, as if trying to get away from Joshua. Every now and then, he'd look back, a terrified look of desperation scrawled upon his face.

Just then, the boy stopped as a golden cloud surrounded him. He, however, seeing the light, grew increasingly hostile as he tried to beat back the hazy brightness. The gesticulating boy, seeing how helpless he was to cast off this strangeness, began to dash in another direction, and again Joshua saw himself following close behind.

The scene repeated several times, with the light each time surrounding the boy like a swarm of incessant bees. Soon enough, however, he began to grow tired until his fighting and running tapered to nothing. And there he stood, bathing in the glowing cloud.

A voice filled the air. *This one will do great exploits. My love will capture him.*

Joshua awakened and sat up quickly. The scene remained repeating vibrantly within him. Joshua blinked as his eyes slowly adjusted to his bedroom around him. And it was then Joshua turned and positioned himself on his knees even as the sobs came for this one who had never known love, not even for a single moment of his existence.

But how could God reach him?

Joshua began to weep deeply in a way he didn't—couldn't—understand.

"How?" Joshua whispered through his veneer of tears. "How can You do this?"

And then Joshua felt the words course through him as strongly as that first day when God had spoken to him to follow Him: *Bless your enemies.*

Eleven: Wrestling with God

He'd awakened from a catnap just as the school bus came to a halt, the first image in his mind being the threatening image of the burly face of the bully. As everyone stood to unload, Joshua became convinced he would again be humiliated in the next few minutes—before even his first class.

He'd somewhat laughed at the thought, but it had seemed a perfect way for God to teach him anything He deemed a necessity through the blows and disgrace of this overgrown boy.

Joshua stepped off the bus into the cool morning air. Already, he could feel the warmth of the rising sun encroaching as it hovered against the distant horizon. It would be another day of scorching temperatures. He inhaled a long breath, thankful for the delightful morning even though his very existence might be about to come to an end.

"Hey," shouted a voice from the side.

Momentarily jolted, Joshua turned briskly to find Sergio and Alistair, their faces seeming to be different from the previous day. It was as if a soft glow rested upon them.

"How are you, Joshua?" Sergio asked.

Joshua looked them over. They seemed content, thoroughly focused, and more aware of everything—their surroundings, other people, and themselves.

"We began to 'pay the price' last night," Alistair said with a smile, his dark eyes glimmering in a joy that Joshua had not noticed previously.

Joshua immediately forgot all about his own concerns and rejoiced with his two friends.

"Keep it up. Welcome to the School of the Holy Spirit," he beamed. "Have you seen Brad and Jennifer?" Joshua asked.

"We haven't seen them yet," Sergio replied.

Joshua scanned around him, wondering if today he would be fortunate. To his chagrin, there wasn't a teacher present. But part of him was glad, because now he'd have to depend solely on God.

"Oh, oh," came Sergio's low voice. Joshua heard the warning in his friend's voice and whirled around to find the three thugs stepping between the buses—their eyes immediately fixed on Joshua.

"Alistair? Sergio?" Josh said.

"Yeah?" they murmured at the same time.

"Could you guys pray with me for the next few minutes."

Sergio spoke under his breath. "We will do that, but we'll also be praying *for* you."

"Gee, thanks for that!" Joshua replied unable to keep from allowing a grin.

They gave their consents even as Joshua breathed his own quick prayer for wisdom and direction. As the larger boys stepped closer, Joshua gathered his courage and stood to await what would come.

"Hey, Jesus Boy," he seethed through lips that barely revealed teeth. "Been waiting for me?"

Joshua did nothing, said nothing. He continued to pray when he felt the impression rise from within him to the surface of his mind.

Bless your enemies.

This time, Joshua was convinced, he would do as he'd been told. He had nothing to lose.

"So, you have an answer for me? How did the wheelchair-boy," he said, "get up out of his chair the other day?"

Joshua steadied himself for what was about to unfold. "The power of God."

"*Not* a good answer, J-Boy," the boy said in a near croon.

Large hands seized around Joshua's collar and rapidly twisted him face down to the pavement. Several students had gathered to watch the confrontation and were now rewarded with this one-sided melee.

Bless your enemies.

Again, Joshua felt his cheek being minced into the pavement—the pain double what it'd been the previous day because of the existing abrasion. With his right hand that remained free, Joshua reached behind him to lay his hand upon his oppressor.

"What do you think you're doing?" the aggressor asked as he swatted his hand down.

But Joshua would not relent. He reached around quicker the second time. "The Lord...*bless* you," Joshua shouted with all his strength and through his pain.

Immediately, images flooded Joshua causing him to nearly forget his uncomfortable, pained position. *A young boy, possibly seven, running through an untidy house, hardly dressed in any clothes. Shrilled shouts. A confrontation. A lady being shoved to the floor by a large man dressed in a*

the Jesus boy

black leather jacket. The boy begins to cry at what he sees. He runs over to her as if he can help her—to do something to stop her pain. But the lady barely pays attention to the child in her nigh-drunk stupor, and it is almost as if he does not exist in her world. When she does finally see him, she screams at him to get to bed. But the boy isn't concerned with his sleep. How can he lay his own head down in peace when his own Mom cannot live without worries about what will happen to her each day?

Joshua had not known anything like this was going to happen…and even as this giant of a boy pressed him even harder against the pavement, Joshua spoke through his pain.

"He knows…what…you've gone through. He remembers…how lonely you felt when your mother wouldn't come home at night. It was Him who wanted to give you all the comfort in the world when you felt so scared for her, and for yourself, on so many nights." Joshua felt the sting of tears as he saw how empty and love-starved this boy truly had been and likely was even at that moment. "He loves you, Cary."

Without warning, the boy released Joshua and stepped back as if electricity had passed through him. He looked at Joshua in stunned amazement. "How'd you know my name, and all that stuff you just said?"

Joshua untwisted himself into a more comfortable position on the ground before giving the hint of a shrug. "I didn't. *God* did," he said. "And though you want to deny it, He is calling you to follow Him and know a love you've never experienced before."

The boy's mind seemed to become confused and overloaded in one moment. Angrily, he shook his head violently as if that would somehow push aside the realization that was intruding on his mind. The big boy's two pals watched in nigh-shock and confusion, as did the crowd of students that had gathered to watch.

Joshua stood up and dusted his knees of dust and debris. Looking sternly at Cary, he directed a palm of his hand toward the boy and spoke with authority. "I say again, the Lord *bless* you."

Cary collapsed to the ground as if all strength had left him—the two teens to his side looking down at him confused. The large boy tried to get up but it was almost as if he was fastened to the ground though nothing visibly held him. Joshua walked over to Cary and spoke down to him. "Your unrest will continue…until you surrender to Him. But when you do, you will rise new…and…you will know His love."

Joshua walked away rubbing his cheek, Sergio and Alistair following close by, their faces aghast at what had just happened.

"What just happened to him?" Alistair asked looking back at the downed, twisting boy.

Joshua turned and considered the boy's dark brown eyes even as he rubbed on his stinging cheek. "When I reached around intending to bless him by laying my hands upon him, suddenly, it was as if I was seeing glimpses of his growing up years in one moment of time."

"Wow!" Sergio's exclamation was a consensus shared by all three of them.

It was just then that Joshua, too, collapsed to his knees as he felt the surging emotions within him finally surface. Sergio and Alistair standing beside him reaching for him as if to steady him, Joshua tried to look away as more tears brimmed his eyes at the images that continued to replay in his mind. "He...has lived a hard life. You know, yesterday, I hated him. I wanted to call down fire upon him. Today, I only feel compassion for him."

"But he's on the ground," Sergio said looking back in disbelief at the giant boy, "as if he were wrestling with someone."

Joshua nodded emphatically. "Cary tried to pin me to the ground to get me to give up my love and trust in God. Now he's pinned to the ground to receive His love. When he surrenders and admits the truth, he will be able to get up."

"God would do that?" Sergio asked.

Josh shrugged his shoulders. "I'd say it's Cary facing the invasion of God's love—and that would pin a lot of people to the ground until they could finally accept—or surrender—to it."

"But when will he be able to get up?" Alistair asked astonished.

Joshua shrugged again. "*That* is between Cary and God."

***

Less than two hours later, Joshua found himself sitting in the Principal's office. The administrator's probing into the incident earlier that morning was not unexpected. The tone in Mr. Brown's voice, however, was unexpected.

"What did you *do* to that boy?" the balding man asked perplexed.

Joshua raised his brows at the question and leaned partially forward surprised at the question. "I did nothing to him. What could I have done to him?"

"Some of the students at the scene say they saw you strike him," the teacher answered on a sigh.

"I did not fight him," Joshua said plainly. "And the entire scene was one in which I was the least in control."

"Well," Mr. Brown said through thinly pressed lips, "the boy was unable to get up for over an hour, Mr. Phillips. And when he did finally get up, the boy was crying uncontrollably."

"Crying?"

"In a strange mixture of sorrow and something akin to…happiness. It really was very peculiar."

Joshua smiled at the workings that had taken place within Cary.

"What is so funny to you, Mr. Phillips?" Mr. Brown asked.

"I suspect that perhaps Another had His way with him."

"Another?"

"God."

"*God?*" he asked emphatically, but there was in his voice the traces of half-mockery.

Joshua slunk back against the back of his chair knowing his next words would be especially interesting in Mr. Brown's hearing. "I prayed for him."

"You *what*?"

"I prayed for Cary," Joshua said evenly and awaited Mr. Brown's reaction. Not a hint of any reaction, however, showed on his face. "I don't know if he'd ever felt a caring hand toward him in his life. But this morning, God's hand came upon him."

Mr. Brown leaned back in his high-back chair growing more annoyed. He swiveled on his chair and stared out the large office window—the day especially bright with golden light. "You mean to say he 'got' religion lying on the pavement?"

"No, *not* religion," Joshua said with a slight tinge of anger at such a suggestion. "He received...life."

"Joshua, I find this whole scenario highly unusual. In fact, I heard the news two days ago about Brad Young. Tell me please...*what* is going on?"

Joshua studied Mr. Brown's face realizing that these items would be strange and difficult for a teacher, and especially a critic, to accept. "Few people consider God in their daily equations of existence—except as a last resort. Perhaps that is why it seems unusual that God would touch people as He evidently has."

Before dismissing him, Mr. Brown mentioned that he would be investigating the matter further. Joshua nodded and gave a friendly smile as he walked out of his office.

Joshua wondered what else could happen, and if Mr. Brown or other teachers could try to punish him when all his actions had been beneficial and good. Perhaps they would try to give God detention, he thought with a snicker. Regardless, his goal would be to please God, regardless of what anyone thought. And at that, he returned to his class ready and willing to serve the Master's bidding—however and whatever that might require of him.

Twelve: Voices

Joshua detested the fact that he didn't yet drive a car. As it was, he remained at the inconvenient mercy of his older brothers or parents. Thankfully, however, his Mom had finally relented to give him and Lydia a ride to the church for the Friday youth meeting.

"So, school going okay?" his mother asked. "I've heard a few things from your brothers that seem hard to believe," she said as she turned and looked rearward before backing out of the driveway. The sun's red-orange light was draining behind the distant horizon, the cooling darkness fast claiming the neighborhood.

"Like what?" he asked with a faint sigh. He leaned his head back suddenly feeling more tired than usual.

"Things a little strange, things I wouldn't believe except I know your brothers can't keep a joke going more than a few minutes. Is any of it true?"

"Well," Joshua said as he lifted a head toward his mother. "It's really not difficult to understand when we realize God is real. And He likes to give His love away. He doesn't like seeing humanity shackled...by anything." Glancing over to his mom, he noticed her eyebrows knit in concern. "What's wrong?"

"Nothing...it's just a bit strange. You have to admit that much."

"Mom," he said with a moan. "It's called the supernatural, stress on the word *super*."

"Oh, okay…and that's supposed to help me and your father understand how it is that you can make a wheelchair-bound boy walk?"

"I didn't do anything except pray. God did the rest. And you don't have to understand it—just accept that God used me. And meanwhile, aim to be sensitive to God in your own life. He'll use anyone who's yielded to Him."

There came silence. Joshua wondered if he'd just overstepped an unmarked boundary, but his Mom said nothing.

Finally, Joan released a long breath. "Well, at least you're not a hermit or a monk anymore. I'm glad to see you're getting out. And I'm glad you're going on this date," she said with excitement in her voice. "Tell me what her name is?"

"Lydia and it's just a youth group meeting, Mom," he said with some amusement. "Before you know it, I'll be calling you to come pick us up."

"Hmm, too bad. Might do you some good to have some *normal* fun, stress on the word normal," she said with a sneer.

Joshua smiled knowing his Mom was just looking out for him and trying to protect him from becoming weird.

They arrived at Lydia's house at the appointed time. Finally, out stepped a slim, tall girl who began approaching the car. She wore tight jeans and a white top. Almost anything, Joshua surmised, looked good on her.

"Niiice going, Joshua," Joan said in a low voice. "She's a beaut."

"Mom!" he said with a grin, giving only a slight nod of his head trying not to exacerbate the situation. Quickly getting out of the car, and with a mixture of fright mixed with nervousness, he held the front door for her all the while trying to look calm, cool, and collected. Lydia beamed brightly and gave a meek "Thank you" before taking a seat beside his Mom.

"Mom," he said bending down so his Mom could see him. "This is my friend, Lydia. Lydia, my Mom."

Joan took Lydia's hand with a cozy, pleasant smile. "Nice to meet you, Lydia."

Joshua was glad to see the ladies getting to know each other. It felt strange but it almost seemed as if he were already dating this girl—though nothing formal had been established between them as yet.

Sitting in the rear seat, Joshua was glad for the opportunity to be able to occasionally study this new girl uninterrupted, perhaps for the first time since meeting her. He kept quiet as they made their way to the church, listening to his Mom and Lydia talk. Every now and then, Lydia would glance back at Joshua with a smile or include him in their chitchat.

As it was, though, Joshua felt a strange war taking place within him. For the first time since he'd come out of his room after twenty-one days, Joshua realized that his attention was being drawn in other, different directions, and that his diligence wasn't as strong as he'd thought it was. Suddenly, this cute, intelligent, laughable girl—with her eye on him—had entered his life; he wasn't so sure what that might mean for him and the Unseen within.

Joshua looked down at his phone and typed a quick message before sending the text to Brad, Sergio, and Allistair asking them to please pray for him—for the strength to escape any temptation, and to keep his heart and mind fixed on the One no matter what.

They pulled into the church parking lot creating in Joshua a strange mixture of gladness and uncertainty about what the immediate future would bring—a future that would be shaped by his present decisions. It was this reality that scared Joshua, even more than the onslaught and humiliation of the bully or a hundred bullies.

***

Lydia had been pleased that Joshua had given his consent to go to the church youth group. It was a place full of energy and people who were at least genuine about what they believed. Some might call them extreme or overly zealous, but hypocrites they were not.

Still, she'd appreciated the reception she'd received when she'd come here several months before. Both the leaders and the teens involved had been friendly. And there were moments when the peer pressure was astonishingly great for her to "give her life to the Lord." She, however, had only gone there for the coziness of atmosphere, and the quick friends she'd made. And, of course, for the other reason that few, if any, would ever learn about.

When she saw Joshua's Mom's car drive up her driveway, Lydia had felt her heart lift which was a momentarily relief from the subtle and unseen nervousness she felt. It seemed incredible to her because few if any previous boys had been able to stir her to such levels. Perhaps, with but a little bit of prying, she would be able to shatter the barriers that kept her from knowing him more fully. She wanted to understand Joshua.

Perhaps church would be the place for such understanding to start to be unpacked.

Joshua had held the car door open for her as she approached, which had impressed Lydia. She liked his easygoing style of dress, and the friendliness he radiated. Most of her previous boyfriends had never held a door open for her, nor treated her like someone special as Joshua had done. Perhaps old-fashioned, but he really was a gentleman.

She remained doubtful that he was fully interested in her...until she'd seen the way he glanced at her upon her approach to the car. He'd tried to hide his attraction to her by looking off in the distance, which had only made his face turn even more red. This had pleased her. Perhaps this invitation was the best idea she'd had in quite some time.

After the pleasant drive to the church, Lydia and Joshua both waved goodbye. Immediately, Lydia spoke up as they watched Joshua's Mom disappear down the road. "You have a really great Mom."

"Yeah, she's one-of-a-kind, I think," he agreed.

"Ready?" Lydia asked as they both glanced behind them at the church. It had a contemporary look to it—which was a must for Lydia. She didn't want to feel like she was either in a museum or a morgue though she'd been at rare times in churches that resembled, or felt, like such.

They walked up several steps and pulled on the glass double doors that opened up to a lobby with a shiny, marble-like floor and contemporary decor. Swinging open the heavy wooden doors that led into the inner sanctuary, Lydia was glad to hear music booming from mounted speakers in anticipation of the teen crowd that was about to show up. Across the front of the sanctuary was a handwritten sign in big, black, block letters that read, "No Compromise!"

"I like the whole set-up," Joshua said with a subtle nod. "How often do you come here?"

"I come on Fridays, but usually only when I'm bored out of my mind."

"Hmm, so you came to the last place on your list to be with me?" Joshua asked inquisitively with a hint of a smile.

"No, silly," she said entwining her arm in Joshua's, and glad for his hold. "I'm not bored out of my mind tonight."

"And why would that be?"

Lydia laughed at the question. "Because, I have you to myself finally," she said with a genial smile walking off to a refreshments area before casting a rearward glance at him.

So far, Lydia considered, everything was going exactly as she'd planned. Tonight, the walls would begin to fall...and if it took several of these "dates," she would continue until she understood Joshua and had won his heart and mind.

***

Two adults approached the two of them with smiles and said hi. Lydia introduced Joshua to the adult youth leaders, Paul and Tamara. The man was overly tall with a convivial smile. It was obvious that most teens would be impressed and appreciate this man's affirming attention. The woman who stood beside him was his wife, a rather petite, slim lady but whose presence immediately emanated an impression of brightness, warmth, and welcome.

"Hi Joshua," they both said warmly offering their hands to him. Joshua shook their hands with a kind smile. As he'd felt their welcome and their touch, he couldn't help but feel a witness within himself that there was something special about this couple.

"Hey," Joshua replied happily. "Thank you."

Seeing a small group of other teens entering, the two told them to feel at home and excused themselves to meet and greet the group.

"They're pretty cool," Joshua said impressed.

"Yeah," Lydia replied, though her tone gave the indication that she was more interested in moving on to other matters. "So, after the worship service, care to go for a walk on the grounds?"

Joshua felt a jolt within himself as he heard the question. He gave no immediate answer which left a bit of awkwardness lingering between them. "We'll see," he finally said plainly. In his heart, he tried to reassure himself that tonight would be all right, that he would maintain caution. Temptation was one thing, but temptation with such a comely girl concerned Joshua for his own welfare in every respect.

During the next hour and a half, over fifty teenagers enjoyed the contemporary style of various worship songs that filled the church building with energetic loudness. The group consisted of various types of teens, some of which remained within their cliques but who nonetheless participated in the worship—or, at the least, gave their respect to it. Some were more active than others with clapping or even dancing, while others sat silently and just watched. Some stayed in the back rows and seemed only marginally interested in what was happening.

Joshua felt himself recharged within the deepest parts of himself by the music, though his ability to worship freely, he realized, was somewhat held back by Lydia's presence—as she didn't seem to delight in the worship as he did. Still, Joshua felt something else—something akin to a warning within him that wouldn't disappear no matter what he did.

As Paul the youth pastor stood with the Bible held in both hands, Lydia looked at Joshua and gestured for him and her to walk out into the foyer. Joshua didn't like the idea of being rude and bent toward Lydia. "Let's wait till after his sharing," he whispered. He noticed by her sudden solemn face that she did not appreciate his suggestion.

Paul began to share his message, an exhortation to each of the kids to be sensitive to God's Spirit and voice, and not to give in to the rampant peer pressure as they interacted within their schools and other social arenas. He also brought up about being cautious who one was in relationship with—that being connected heart to heart could be a dangerous position to be in if the other person didn't walk with the Lord.

Several moments later, without warning Lydia shot up from her place and began to walk toward the rear exits. *Was she upset at him?* Trying not to look at anyone staring at him, Joshua rose and followed her. Stepping out into the lobby, he noticed Lydia staring out the tall rectangular window out into the parking lot, her arms folded.

"I thought you were going to go for a walk with me," she said evenly.

"Yeah, but I didn't want to be rude to your pastor—"

"He's *not* my pastor," she said turning to face him, her face flustered. "I just come here occasionally. You may or may not have noticed, but I'm not into this religion hitch like they are...or you."

Joshua felt a receding within him that made him feel a sensation of momentary emptiness. "Religious hitch? But it's not like that—"

She interrupted him again and stepped closer to him. "I like being a part of this place...the people are nice and I like the positive atmosphere, but I don't care for the preaching."

"Oh, I see," he said looking her in the eyes. He tried to hide his discomfort at standing in front of her.

"Do you?"

Joshua studied Lydia, unsure what to say. It felt as though he was now amid a minefield with every step increasingly treacherous.

"Listen, Joshua," she pleaded, her voice now turned more pleasant. "Can we go for a walk? I mean, can't we learn as much from God's world as we can from a dusty old book?"

Joshua thought to correct her perception but decided better of it. "Okay, let's go out—but just for a couple minutes?" he asked.

"Cool!" she said beaming a smile and suddenly excited.

"But *next* time, you have to promise to stay for the message. Agreed?" he asked.

"Next time?" Her face shown a puzzled expression. "Who said there will *be* a next time?" she laughed as she grabbed his hand and led him across the foyer to the front doors before pushing the doors and stepping out—the hot September air hitting them.

***

"I like Paul and Tam, but I don't care for their pushiness," Lydia said as she glanced about at the rich greenery of the trees and lush grass that surrounded the rear of the church.

There was also a volleyball court and an area of lounging at the bottom of the clearing. "I'm happy and content the way I am. I don't need what they have."

"Are you sure about that? What they have isn't just an irrational faith, Lydia. It's real and life-changing because they've encountered the Risen One."

"Don't get me wrong. I'm happy if it's real to them, or to you," she said brushing a wisp of her dark hair from her eyes. "But truth changes from one person to the next. I think it's just a matter of perception."

"Truth seems to lose it relativism when a person drives up to a red traffic light. Or puts on a parachute." Joshua replied calmly. "Perception is not an exact measure of truth."

Lydia laughed as she considered Joshua's words.

Josh continued. "If God is there, then that is reality, not just a matter of perception."

"Isn't that a big 'if'?" Lydia asked. "And even *if* He is there, why doesn't He do anything to stop the suffering that has engulfed our miserable world? Why didn't He do something to warn the Franklins?"

The community had borne the news of the death of an elderly couple when a midnight fire had engulfed their home several weeks before. Joshua had thought about the question of suffering and evil often. He replied softly after quickly and silently praying for wisdom and guidance.

"My faith says that God entered human history and became a man. That same faith says that He lived and died within this 'miserable world.' He never denied reality, or evil, or suffering. Instead He acknowledged the Unseen around Him, and made us aware of it, too, regardless of the circumstances."

"No, Joshua." Lydia shook her head emphatically. "If God is love, how can He do nothing when children starve to death or when terrorists have their way and kill innocent people? If He really loved, why wouldn't He intervene?"

Joshua waited several seconds trying to think through his own thoughts. "I don't know the answers though I could spout off theories all day long…but that would not change anything within you or within me. We live in a fallen world…but that does not remove us from our own choices or responsibilities—or needs—regarding the Creator."

"Joshua," she said stopping and turning toward him. She stood as tall as Joshua, and might even be a bit taller. She took his hands in hers and smiled. "I really hope we can become something more than friends. It's rare to meet someone like you; and I want you to know I respect what you believe…even if I can't be into your faith like you are."

Joshua had hardly blinked as she stood there holding his hands and facing him. His heartbeat quickened and he realized he must appear as red as a tomato. Her beauty mesmerized him even as he tried to concentrate on what she was saying to him.

Joshua finally spoke. And he suddenly granted himself the freedom to speak his heart's feelings. "I think you are stunning, Lydia."

He felt her hands release his as she stepped even closer to him, the fronts of their bodies almost touching each other, their faces nearly meeting. Her hands now held each of his biceps and gave a subtle squeeze every now and again.

If you love Me, you will obey My commandments.

The words seemed to rise within him even as he tried to bring action to the words—without success.

Her hands moved up to his shoulders. They just stood there even as he felt her warmth against him, smelled her alluring perfume, and stared into those gorgeous eyes that now shined into him with a brilliance that he'd never known from any other until that day and hour and minute and second.

"Hey, you guys!" came Tam's voice from afar off. "You need to come back into the church until the meeting's over."

Joshua glanced over and saw Tam's small frame facing them over near the side of the brick church, her arms folded. "I guess we should head back."

A look of disappointment crossed Lydia's face—but only for a moment. "Okay," she said evenly as they both turned and began to slowly climb the hill back toward the church. But even as they walked, Joshua had the strangest feeling of regret and a tinge of sadness that he'd for one long moment allowed the voice of another to distract him from the voice of the One within. And he shuddered at the precipice he now found himself. In his very near future, even on this night if he wasn't cautious, all could be lost. He prayed silently, seeking to make sure he was reconciled to the One, and, at the least, to be strengthened against any other torrents of temptation. His prayers, however, seemed to be weighted and go nowhere. He watched Lydia several steps in front of him walking up the hill toward the parking lot that led into the church. Joshua tried to discern who this girl was in his life and what her entrance into his life would mean to his future—and to his relationship with the One.

Joshua turned his head in the direction of the thick treeline—the branches swaying this way and that. The sun already gone past the horizon line, it was darkened. As his eyes fixed on this area, he felt a chill of cold pass through him that seemed to settle within the emptiness he felt inside him.

***

Because of their proximity to the girl who was hooked by cords to two large demonic brutes who almost always remained near to her and had great influence in stirring her emotions and decision-making, their subtle voices being quite convincing in their suggestions, gaining access to the boy had been relatively easy. Despite the worship and despite the preaching which had, incidentally, been planned from eternity in order to be injected into Joshua's life for his own good, his distracted heart at the presence of Lydia, however, had not adequately received the Word. Because of his subtle disobedience, the Presence had, for a time, become a dim light within the boy—dim enough so that the dark agents could harass and interfere with His link to the One. They managed to sever his communications with the Master—at least on the boy's end. And the disturbance that resulted—as well as the gaping emptiness—would allow for them to harass the boy for quite some time—to their satisfaction.

The boy was drawn by this alluring girl's physical looks—without concern for her inner looks. He was drawn to look on her with enticing passions and subtle but powerful lusts directing him. Though the world looked at it as harmless flirtation, to the One, it went beyond ancient boundaries set in place—both to protect the boy and to protect the girl who were of immeasurable value.

Thirteen: The Four Boulders

Joshua had returned just before midnight the previous evening wondering if anything good had come of his time with Lydia. Thankfully, Tam had been emphatic that Joshua and Lydia both wait inside the church until Joshua's mother arrived to retrieve them.

The young people's worship service had been grand, and although he'd enjoyed Lydia's company, he'd also felt a great deal of regret that he hadn't been more sensitive to the Spirit within him when the moment of testing had come. Although he hadn't outright sinned, he'd not been much better than Samson who had retrieved honey out of a carcass. Although he hadn't touched the dead animal per his vow to God, he'd still put himself in a dangerous position. Joshua had thought a lot about Samson's example. If anything, the man's behavior was simply wreckless and lacking wisdom—and eventually resulted in his own perishing.

Awakening early, Joshua had immediately positioned himself so he could reconnect with the One. But something troubling was evident in his inner life—a change had taken place since his interchange with Lydia.

"What's happening to me, Lord?" he asked. Yet despite his best efforts, his mind kept on returning to the moment when she'd stepped up to him. He shouldn't have been so easily engulfed in her wake. Yet that's exactly what had

74 | the Jesus boy

happened. He'd felt suddenly powerless—paralyzed by her hold upon him.

In fact, if it hadn't been for the watchful interference of Tamara, Joshua worried what the outcome could have been. Is it possible that he would've given in to such a test without hesitation? If another moment had been allowed to pass with himself standing in front of her, would he have been able to turn away, step back, or to sprint away from her—all to protect the special relationship he maintained with his Master?

He could envision her arresting smile. For a moment, it felt as though she were again standing in front of him, her face inches from his, their bodies touching. Others might've been happy at such thoughts, but for Joshua, it only made the internal struggle intensify as to where his allegiance truly was.

Having had no success in reconnecting to the Lord, Joshua hoped a change of setting would help grant him some serenity within his storm. He decided he'd get out of the house and go to a place treasured in his heart. He hoped there he'd be able to focus and reassert his connection with the One. As he came down the stairway and stepped into the living room to make his way out of the house, however, he noticed a body wrapped tightly in blankets on the sofa, Bailey asleep along the front of the sofa on the carpeted floor.

"Hey," Josh said inquisitively before noting the nigh-buried face of Samuel, his youngest brother. The body stirred until a tiny voice escaped the covers.

"Hi," he said in a barely perceptible voice. Bailey sat up and eyed Joshua's approach, his tail wagging briefly.

"What are you doing sleeping down here?"

"Mom said I could sleep here if I wanted. I'm not feeling good."

Joshua nodded. He stepped over to the back of the sofa and leaned down. "What's wrong, Sammy?"

"I don't know," he replied weakly. "Yucky is all I can say."

"I see," Joshua said feeling sorry for him. "Want me to pray for you?"

"Sure," Samuel replied.

Joshua stepped around and sat down on the edge of the third seat cushion where his little brother's feet rested. Bailey stepped closer to Samuel and placed his head on his torso. Joshua reached over and placed his hands on Samuel's forehead—almost too hot to the touch—and spoke a prayer against whatever it was attacking his brother's body. He prayed for nearly a full minute before finishing. He wondered if the answer would arrive as it had for Brad. Even as he walked out of the room, he somewhat expected something to happen. But nothing happened...at least not visibly.

He told his Mom he'd be back in a few hours, that he was going to his usual place. She nodded her consent but glanced at him with a puzzled, concerned look. Her look only made him feel more unsure of himself.

"Everything okay, Joshua?"

"Yeah," Joshua said quickly, though in truth, he knew something wrong but found it difficult if not impossible to pinpoint what it was. The balance in his life was, at that moment, out of whack. "I'm going out to clear my head. I'm leaving my phone here so I don't get distracted."

She nodded. "Take Bailey with you?"

"Sure," Joshua said, happy at the thought. "Come on, boy," he said pushing open the swing door that connected the living room with the kitchen. Bailey, his ears perked high, tail wagging, scrambled into the kitchen and bounded toward the back door, his excitement brimming with impatience to get out the door.

Stepping out from the comfort of the house's air conditioning onto his manicured back yard, Joshua immediately felt the wall of stifling heat. Although Josh didn't like the heat, he welcomed the sun's brightness which seemed to cheer him up and offer some relief from the internal struggle that he had yet to resolve. Within just a few steps, almost immediately, sweat formed on his brow and the back of his neck. For Bailey, however, there was not even a hint of hesitation as the border collie scrambled into the grass-cut backyard and began roaming, engaged in dog intrigue along the boundaries. Walking until he reached the tree line, Bailey following, Joshua slipped between two shoulder-high bushes onto a shaded path, the relief of shade from the canopy of tall trees immediately cooling him. Only some of the sun broke through the ceiling of trees, the golden rays slanting into the forest intermittently throughout the woods.

As he walked the wide path that might be used for small tractors or four-wheelers, numerous winged insects crossed in front of him seemingly in a hurry to get somewhere. Occasionally, he'd duck and weave past webbed architecture suspended between tree limbs (he didn't like to disturb them) unable to see its builders who were, themselves, hidden and tucked away from the heat. The wide dirt path moved north behind his and his neighbors' houses until they seemingly left human habitation and rose steeply to a summit before the land opened into a vast field of toughened, knee-high yellow-green grass, trees sparse.

About twenty minutes' walk later, the path narrowed significantly until it was only wide enough for one person to walk—medium-sized rocks, shrubbery, and mounts of earth on each side. A zigzag dirt path cut through the land until it rose to meet four large boulders almost at the summit of the hill, what his family had come to call the Four Boulders. As usual, Joshua couldn't help but notice the intermittent footprints of animals that crisscrossed the trail—deer, rabbits, dogs, and small critters—all delightful explorations for Bailey and the unceasing movements of his white muzzle. The deep impressions of motorbikes and dirt bikes were also evident on the path—none of them fresh, some of them appearing to be from weeks or months before.

When he'd finally arrived at Four Boulders, these boulders that had been seemingly placed in their resting places forever as silent guardians over the land, he walked another 500 feet to the edge of a cliff from which he could see the lower lands. Singular tiny houses and small, distant farms dotted the landscape. A wind crisscrossed the air giving added relief from the sun's heat.

He found the flat rock that he had adopted as his own since he'd started coming up here years before. It rested upon the slight incline of a hill fifty feet from the cliff edge, held up by a bed of grass, dirt, and tree roots from a lone, strong tree that rose behind the flat rock into the blue sky, its leaf-filled branches perched above casting a cooling shadow to the ground. Joshua sat down briskly expelling all the air from his lungs within him as if to also push out the anxiety he felt. He ran his right hand across his forehead pushing back his blond hair saturated with sweat, and removing the coating of sweat. He took in the entire view and felt altogether glad he'd come here. He was in the perfect position to realign himself—which, no matter what, offered him an advantage to his internal war.

This was his resting place with the One, the place he'd come to talk or listen, or both—whatever was needed. He pulled out from his backpack a jug of ice water and took a long drink. He bent over and poured water into a cup-shaped depression in the rock. Immediately, Bailey gulped the water down before looking up, taking a seat next to Joshua. Joshua ran his hand over the top of Bailey, his mouth open and breathing hard as he tried to cool down.

"What have I done?" he asked into the open air. He wondered if he'd lost the Lord's favor or His power that had poured through him before. Not feeling like he wanted to study the details of what he had and had not done, he simply gave what he hoped would be a blanket apology to satisfy the Unseen. "Okay, I'm sorry for anything I did or did not do..."

Just then, he felt an urgency to become specific or else all his effort of reaching out to the Lord, and this lengthy walk, would be in vain.

"Yes, Lord... I'm sorry for not listening to You last night...for feeding my own desires instead...and for allowing Lydia to replace You as my primary focus... But most of all, I realize that I did not acknowledge Your will above my own..." His words trailed off as he stared into the distance. This whole episode proved that even the minutest trespass could result in a splintering within him. "Lord, what am I without You? I can't do anything without You. I can't even breathe properly without You being close to me."

It hadn't taken as much effort as he had imagined before he sensed the Spirit's renewing presence draw near and embrace him. But nagging questions churned within him without the relief of answers: Was it okay to date Lydia? Could he date her if she didn't walk with the Lord as he did? Was it a desire for Lydia that was at its core unhealthy and ungodly? Or something else, something he hadn't realized about her, himself, about the Lord's will? He prayed for most of the morning, the Book open beside him. When the sun approached mid-sky, Joshua felt that any splintering that he had caused the night before had been dealt with. A new sense of confidence and joy settled upon him, which made him feel glad and relieved.

   It was as he felt this elation that he followed Bailey's suddenly fixed gaze toward the direction of the forest edge. Then he saw movement from the edge of the woods—someone coming up the hill toward him. Bailey let out several barks as he stepped forward and kept his eyes fixed on the approaching figure. Joshua couldn't see who it was but it appeared to be the frame of a young lady. Then he heard the person calling out his name and waving at him.

   "Joshua?" came the voice from the edge of the tree line.

   Lydia? Here? Now? Joshua quickly rose and stepped down to meet her, Bailey scrambling alongside him, as she drew nearer. Again, a cloud of confusion coated his heart as he saw her approach. He felt a pang of uncertainty in his heart. Yet he also felt a strange glimmer of gladness—even excitement—to see her figure moving toward him.

   "Lord, *please* help me," he prayed simply. "I need Your help to stay true to You!"

* * *

   "Hey there," Joshua said with enthusiasm as she came within arm's length of him. She looked great—her straight brown hair tied back behind her head, her attire of a yellow tank top and khaki shorts with running trainers what you'd expect of someone casually dressed on their Saturday. They hugged for a moment—a moment Joshua fought to keep brief. Bailey drew near which immediately pleased Lydia.

"Wow, what a beautiful border collie," she said kneeling and running both of her hands through the brown and white fur of Bailey's face, head, and ears. Her face was a tinge of red as she attempted to recapture her breath from her fast-paced trek. "It's Saturday afternoon so I thought I'd come by and see what you're up to," she said looking up at Josh.

"Come and sit under the shade," Joshua offered. "How did you find me?"

"Your Mom told me exactly where you'd be," she replied. "Are you hungry? She made grilled-cheese sandwiches for the both of us."

"Sure, grilled-cheese sandwiches sound great," he said happily. As they reached the shade of the tree and the flat rock, Joshua gestured for her to take a seat on the flattened rock. "Have a seat," he said with enthusiasm. It seemed to have been made by time and the elements for two people.

Gingerly, she sat, Bailey coming and taking up a position in front of her while looking out across the lands, fully expecting, and receiving, hearty rubs along his back and around to his whitened chest from Lydia. Joshua sat down beside her and scanned into the distance. Deep down, he continued to pray.

"Am I intruding on your privacy by coming here?" she asked with a sheepish expression.

"No," he said smiling broadly. "But you surprised me. It's a bit far for you to have walked."

"My friend dropped me off at your place. When I found out you were up here and not in your house, my ride was already long gone. Your Mom told me it'd be easy to find you if I followed the trail up to the clearing and headed toward the four large boulders."

"Yeah, she's been here with me a few times along with my family. Sometimes, we come here and have a cookout. Amazing view, isn't it?"

She nodded and glanced toward the horizon. "It is timeless here." But her focus wasn't overly keen to focus on nature or scattered houses or farms that sat across the land. "So, why did you come here alone?"

"Not alone; Bailey's been with me," he said with a laugh.

She reflected a smile to his humor, her alluring smile making Josh wonder for a split second what it'd be like to kiss.

"I like to come out here to pray," he finally said, his voice taking on a serious tone.

"Should I leave?" Lydia offered with a half-smile.

"No," Joshua said flatly. "I finished just before you came. I'm glad you came up here." He *was* glad, which is what concerned him.

"*Really?*" Lydia asked as she edged closer to Joshua with a flirtatious smile.

"Yeah," he replied, unable to keep from smiling back to her. He shot her a quick glance before turning away and looking to the safety of the distance. It would be better to not feed the desire that was already burning within him. In that moment, he determined he'd be careful not to be especially warm to her while alone with her, but he would also not be rude.

Lydia looked at him curiously. "To pray? For *real*?" She chuckled.

Joshua ignored the irritation he felt that she didn't yet regard what was important to him. Nodding briefly, he decided to be firm...but indirectly. "This is one place I can come to find strength."

"Okay, *'Arnold,'*" she said bringing her voice to a low pitch mimicking Arnold Schwarzenegger's accent. When she noticed his lack of amusement, she allowed her voice to become serious. "So," she said looking around, "this is where you come to find spiritual strength?"

"Yeah," Joshua giving her a fleeting glance. "But it's more than just spiritual. It encompasses all of me. My emotions, my intellect, my will...even my body."

"You find strength by praying?" she asked for clarification.

"Yeah, as strange as it may sound. But for me, it's actually more like two people sitting down and having a talk—like we're doing right now."

Lydia shrugged. "Hey, if it works for you. Where was God sitting...? Can you show me?" she asked with a grin.

"It's not quite like that," Joshua said seriously, hiding his irritation. He sensed the sooner they returned to the house, the better the outcome of this circumstance would be for him. "Lydia, let's head back," he said.

"But I just got here, remember?" Lydia said matter-of-factly. Then, she reached out even as he was attempting to stand up—keeping him in place. "Wait a minute," Lydia said with another of her striking smiles.

Joshua turned to face her just as her lips touched, and kissed, his. He resisted little, for the kiss had come and gone

83 | the Jesus boy

before he could do much about it. Then she nearly leaped up and stood admiring more closely the panoramic view.

"Maybe I want some spiritual strength out here too," she said as if nothing had just happened between them.

Joshua felt his heart sinking within him. He gave no reply but let out a slow breath even as he silently prayed not to be swayed any deeper into unwanted territory.

"Where does the trail go to?" she asked curiously and began walking until she was fifty meters above them, the thin grooves of the trail leading up over the hill and beyond.

"It ascends for quite a while before eventually dropping to the rock quarry on the other side."

She stopped abruptly. "Oh. Not very exciting."

Joshua sensed the discomfort lingering between the two of them. He truly didn't know how to remove the awkwardness without appearing too warm. At the same time, however, if he remained aloof from her, he might seem too cold, and forever lose her. A part of him wanted to take her hand and lead her. Another part wished for any other situation but this one.

She turned back toward Joshua and began to move back toward him.

"So, Lydia," he said in a friendly tone. He nearly smiled but kept himself as neutral as possible.

"So, Joshua," she aped.

Joshua grinned. "So, you have brothers, sisters?" he asked to make small-talk.

"I have a younger sister. My Dad...passed away when I was really young, just after Stacy was born."

"Oh, I'm sorry," he said with compassion on his face.

"The Big C took him before I could learn what having a Daddy feels like." She looked off into the distance for a second before resuming. "And you have three brothers, correct?"

"Yes," he said.

"I met Samuel. Sad to see him feeling so icky earlier."

"Yeah, I want to see him get better."

"Hey, I have a question for you," she said pulling out and handing him one of the grilled-cheese sandwiches from her backpack. "By the way, your Mom let me borrow this backpack."

Josh nodded. "What's your question?" he asked as he took the tin-foil-wrapped sandwich in his hand and began to unwrap it.

"You have two older brothers and yet you didn't ask for their help a couple days ago?"

"Help? What would I need their help for?" He took a bite of the sandwich before he slowed his chewing and tilted his ear toward her awaiting what she'd say.

"How 'bout protecting you from those bullies at the school yard?" she asked as she, too, unwrapped a toasted, gooey-cheese sandwich.

"You heard about that?" he asked.

"Yeah, I heard you knocked the boy down and he couldn't get up for nearly an hour."

"That was because of God, not me. I didn't do anything to him. I couldn't do anything to him."

"Did you know he was a part of the Jaded Heart gang?" she asked taking a small bite out of her toasted sandwich.

"Gang?"

"Yeah. I heard they weren't very happy with his sudden and strange change."

Joshua was surprised to be talking about this subject, about Cary who had tried to bully him until God got a hold of him. "What kind of change were they unhappy about?"

"I heard all of his aggressive traits had just vanished—like hot air out of a balloon."

"How did the 'Jaded Heart' gang take that?"

"I heard they gave him an initiation out of the gang."

"How'd you learn about all this?" Joshua asked.

She seemed to not hear his question, but asked her own. "If you didn't hit that boy, then what happened?"

"I merely did what God told me to do," he said as he took another bite of his sandwich.

"What did God tell you to do?"

"I said to him, 'The Lord bless you.'"

"That doesn't sound like a blessing to me. He was pinned to the ground for an hour, Joshua."

Joshua smiled at the awe of that moment even as he stood up and walked off near the edge before sitting down on a large log that appeared to have been there a long time. Bailey following him, Joshua waved Lydia to come join him. He felt a burning inside him as their discussion had turned to Cary and the news about him. In front of him was the charred circle of an old campfire. He sat down and patted the spot beside him inviting Lydia. Quietly, she sat down.

"It was a blessing because he found life, and God's love, and a sense of freedom during that time. God did that, not me. It was all *His* idea, not mine." Joshua couldn't help it but he laughed. "It's truly amazing what God can do in an hour what would take man years or even a lifetime to fix."

"You make it sound like God did some sort of operation on him."

"Maybe. I don't know. But I think all that guy ever wanted was to be loved…and in that time, though he fought it, I believe he wrestled with an all-encompassing love as if a moth caught by its wings. The more he struggled, the more helpless he became." Joshua became silent for a moment, his face serious.

"How do you know that's what happened, Joshua?" she asked, her voice serious.

"Because, what happened to him is exactly what happened to me."

"What do you mean?" she asked, sounding genuinely interested.

"When I spent twenty-one days locked away from the world, He touched me. And I can't explain it but I knew His love for me in a way that I'd only heard or read about. After those days in that room, however, I experienced His love as if He were there with me, wrapping His arms around me."

"That sounds a bit out there, don't you think?"

Joshua tried to be careful not to allow his irritation to seep through into his voice. "Lydia, it's said we were created in His image and that God is love. If that's true, then we would need love to survive—and just to operate properly. Without that love, we'd morph into something we weren't meant to be. Not just that overgrown bully…but every single one of us."

Lydia reached to her side and grabbed at a small tree's leaf yanking it free. "But if that's what we all need and if God is love, why don't we have it? Why did it have to take you weeks to discover it?"

"I could've found it that first hour…but I had to go through the removing of the excess clutter in my own life. Most people can't do that. They become Medusas looking in a mirror who literally become petrified by what they see of themselves—and then what they see of the Unseen God when they get to know Him. But it has to happen. And some are too weak or too fearful or too lazy to even try." Joshua noticed Lydia's face computing what his words might mean. He scanned the smooth rocks around him, their surfaces appearing wet in the sunlight's glimmer. "During that three-week period, I became an onion in which God peeled away at the excess layers until I began to see what was real about me—and about God—and what was not."

"So, *what* is real? Give me the fast-forward version."

Joshua hesitated to say. He didn't want to overload Lydia but her questions were thoughtful and could lead to a work of God in her life. And there was also a quality of holiness about these things. It wasn't something he wanted to speak lightly about.

"God's love. God's Son dying on a tree. Both of those things so personally committed...for me, to me, because of me... But during all that discovery, I also learned about...my own depravity."

Lydia gave no reply though her mind seemed to be racing to understand. "That's deep, Joshua," she finally said.

"It *is* deep, but it's *also* the greatest gift of understanding a man or woman could ever receive," he said, awe in his voice.

"So, God healed that guy the other day—but He did it in an hour," Lydia noted.

Joshua smiled and nodded. "There really is no formula. God can do whatever He wants as He sees fit and according to each vessel. All I know for certain is that until Cary surrendered, he was his own worst enemy—and everyone else's, too."

"So...what would happen if you blessed me...with another kiss?" she said with a smirk giving him a sidelong look.

With a shy grin, he allowed the question to linger. Since their discussion had turned to God, there had been a noticeable change within Joshua's heart, as if he suddenly felt the confidence of safety from temptation. Was this the strength he'd needed and prayed for? "Lydia, I really like you, too. But I want to move slow."

"Joshua," she said slightly flustered, but with a grin. "I was asking for a simple kiss on my cheek, not what *you* were thinking."

Joshua leaned back and studied her as she gave him a semi-icy look and turned her face away from him toward the distant horizon. "I," he finally conceded, "would be honored to kiss you."

Without any hesitation, he reached over and kissed her gently on the cheek. At first, he thought he'd kissed her too briefly...until a satisfied smile appeared on her face.

"Only the cheek?" she asked sheepishly.

Josh drew near again until he kissed her on her lips. "Happy?" he asked with a smile as he withdrew.

They sat there for the next hour talking about little things...but strangely not caring about what they talked about. Before they got up to return to the house, their hands held tightly. Suddenly, they looked at each other a bit differently than they had just two hours before.

Joshua felt relieved that Lydia had given him space and respect regarding his faith. Nothing of a compromising nature had taken place—to his gladness. He also felt happy that things had worked out as they had.

For now, however, he felt content and fulfilled. He didn't sense a change regarding his heart-connection to the One.

And although he still had questions that needed answers, he thought the best way would be to simply go slow—as he'd said to her—and do nothing that would cause him to compromise. The connection with her, to his surprise, had been made. Lydia and he were now more than friends. Still, there would be limits to their relationship as well as how she responded to the Lord on a personal level. That might change the trajectory for their relationship. He'd have to wait to see what would happen.

Arriving back at the house, they entered through the kitchen door to hear voices in the next room. Joshua and Lydia stepped toward the voices. Entering the living room, Joshua's Mom sat next to Samuel wiping his forehead with a cool, wet cloth—the boy's head propped up on her lap.

"Mom?" he asked, concern in his voice.

"He's gotten worse, Joshua." Bailey ran past until he sat in front of Samuel before licking his hand—the young boy's face flushed, his hands and arms the only part of him not inside the covers.

Just then, Joshua's father opened and entered the house through the front door. His father's eyes glanced over the room. Immediately, he greeted Lydia before noticing young Samuel on the sofa with his wife. "What's wrong, Joan?" Dennis asked.

"His temperature's 104. He seems to be getting worse."

"We'll take him to the hospital," Dennis said as he reached down and momentarily held Sammy's hand in his. "Joan, let's take him now."

Joan aided Samuel to his feet until he stood weakly, the blanket wrapped around the boy's torso.

"Is there anything I can do?" Joshua asked.

Joan shot Joshua a reassuring smile that quickly faded as she tried to help Samuel walk toward the front door. "Tell your brothers when they get back that we took Samuel to the hospital."

As they stepped out the door, Joshua's chest tightened. He felt angry with himself. Surely the power would've made Samuel well if he hadn't been sidetracked the night before because of his incident with Lydia. He'd fooled himself into believing he could be close to the Lord and be a regular teen. But the fact was hard to swallow: he *couldn't* be a regular teen with a regular life while in this season he'd dedicated himself to the One.

"Lydia, I have to go pray," he said as he felt the whir of the moment encompass him.

"O-*kaaay*," Lydia said looking down at the floor, dejection in her voice. "Do you want me to go?"

Joshua knew he must sound either insane or rude—if not both. "Look," he said with as much reassurance as he could muster. "This is serious. I need to spend time in prayer for Samuel."

"Fine," Lydia said coolly. "I'll call my Mom to come pick me up."

"I'll call you later, okay?" Joshua offered in an appeasing tone. "I'm going upstairs to my room. Of course, you can stay till your Mom gets here. I'm really sorry."

Lydia nodded with a look that was anything but happy.

It was clear to Joshua he'd upset Lydia, perhaps even hurt her feelings. Yet he also could not ignore the urgency he felt that had not been there moments before.

Lydia sallied toward the front door. As she reached the door, she glanced back at Joshua. "I can't compete with your god," she said flatly. "I'll wait on the porch for my

Mom." And with that, she stomped out of the house leaving Joshua feeling even more troubled and confused.

He decided he would do what he could to mend any grievances with Lydia as soon as possible. For now, however, he must not be distracted. His brother needed him. And Joshua knew the power of God could resolve any difficulty.

Climbing his stairs and entering his room, he flung himself to his knees as he sought to touch Heaven and be touched, as he sought to obey the Master's calling upon his life to follow Him with everything within him. He struggled to push away the regret he was feeling as he cast his eyes heavenward, of in one moment feeling so close to Lydia and in the next being momentarily torn from her. It made him consider if he could ever truly have a relationship with anyone outside of God and at the same time be a vessel for which God's power would pour through.

***

The dark forces had attempted to scream into his ears so to keep him confused and on an unsure footing with the One. Their attempts had only succeeded, however, until the boy reached a place that had become marked as a special meeting place between him and the Lord. Entering that place, the dark forces arrayed against him were themselves disoriented—even when the girl was brought—their tethers upon her temporarily cut. And, to their chagrin, she began, ever so faintly, to respond to the One—which brought on their angry reactions. The Presence had been strong—the boy's repentance, though having not dealt with all the issues, enough apparently that the Lord and boy were able to reconnect.

So, they returned to the youngest brother—to exacerbate his situation—the boy, they knew, being one of the keys to devastating the lightbearer's faith and trust in the One.

Fourteen: The Mystery of Joshua

Lydia sat in the car, her mother quizzing her with concerned glances as to why she remained so quiet.

"Everything's fine," she replied though her heart felt anything but fine. She'd not expected to be rushed out of his house...not like that. Not because of a prayer. She'd never had that happen to her—which might be comical if not for the simmering anger she felt churning inside her.

Strangely, however, there was another part of her—a small part—that appreciated the way Joshua had shown such concern for his little brother. He really believed God would and could do something for Samuel. Truth be told, she'd been amazed at the two stories that were already being whispered at school about Joshua's amazing abilities—the unexplained healing of the wheelchair boy and the transformation of the gang member-slash-bully in a single hour...

Could such be explained away? Lydia had queried inwardly. Perhaps Joshua had tapped into the unlimited potential and powers of the mind. Most people only used a tenth of their mental capabilities, she'd heard on YouTube. Perhaps God had nothing to do with it, only Joshua didn't know it. Of course, his belief system wouldn't allow for such as an explanation.

Still, she kept on remembering the statement Joshua had spoken to her about God's love, about how he'd always spoken of it or heard it but never experienced it until he'd spent that three-week period shut away. Though she'd not admitted it, she could agree that all human beings sought that one thing primarily: *to be loved*. She'd never considered God before and she wasn't about to. But she did feel an attraction, of wishing such a powerful love were true and actually available to her.

She, however, remained more practical. She wouldn't go off searching the cosmos for something or someone invisible when she could find it here on earth. And though she felt perturbed with Joshua, she suddenly made the decision that she would let him do his thing with God for the time being.

Despite the hiccups, she'd felt happy at the way Joshua had responded to her so far. Not wanting to spook him, she'd remained constrained both times she'd been with him. For the first time today, he'd opened his heart to her and revealed what it was that so-stirred him with the passion he carried about him.

The chirp of her cell phone rang. Lydia's heart sank a notch as she swore under her breath.

"I heard that," her Mom muttered not looking at her.

She'd forgotten to turn off her cell phone. She never liked to talk on her cell phone or talk any kind of business in front of her Mom.

"Hello?" she asked flatly. She listened but wanted to end the call as quickly as possible. "I'll call you back in a half hour." "No," she said in a slightly raised but controlled voice. "I will call you." "Bye," she said pushing a button and letting her arm drop.

Her Mom shot her a weary glance. "Who was on the phone that you couldn't talk in front of me?" she asked a bit offended. Her long, curly black hair waved as she turned

95 | the Jesus boy

away to watch for oncoming traffic at an intersection. "Hmmm?"

"Just a classmate calling about a test on Monday," she said lying. "Anyway, thanks for picking me up at Joshua's on short notice. I owe you one."

"You owe me a half dozen at last count," she said with a grin.

Lydia smiled. "Yeah, I do." She thought for a moment if there was a way to repay her Mom with an inexpensive gift—not something that would make her suspicious, though. Since arriving to Knott's End High School, she'd seen the power base spread satisfactorily. She'd completed her job faithfully—though much more always needed to be done.

Her mind, however, returned to the image of Joshua sitting there on the cliff edge, his blond hair being blown in the air. She could still almost feel his light kiss on her cheek...the way he'd bravely leaned toward her and kissed her, but with a bravery intermixed with such cute awkwardness.

For the second time, he'd been forced out of his shell and protective bubble because of her. She liked these wayward characteristics in Joshua and wondered if she could make such permanent in him without shattering his world. But another part of her wondered if she would even like him if such changes permanently took place. She'd thoroughly enjoyed her time with him. From the very beginning with him the previous night, she'd felt the freedom to remain herself around him. It was as if she could completely drop her guard in those rare moments when she was with him. There weren't any phony pretenses about him. He was who he was, authentic and even more important, completely accepting of her. She might not embrace his God but he'd not pushed her toward his God. But even as she considered her own happiness in being with Joshua...of dating him, she had to wonder if he would be able to handle knowing that there remained something especially different and unique about her, too. Not that she planned to tell him. That wasn't information she could freely divulge.

She excused such heavy thoughts. For now, she just wanted to go home and wait for his call. Who knows? He might call her at any moment to apologize. Or better, he might call to ask her to return later that day. He was, after all, into her. And that made her happy.

***

She rested on the end of her bed staring at her accursed mobile phone screen getting tired of playing Candy Crush, the sun's light draining from the room. Four hours had gone by—and still, no call had come.

Did he think of her at all? He couldn't *still* be praying, could he? Had he forgotten their time together that morning, the previous evening? So many questions passed through her mind. All in one second, she shrugged lightly, flipped onto her back, and decided she'd stop being angry and be less demanding. She allowed her eyes to close as she felt more tired than usual from her climb to the Four Boulders and back. He would, eventually, call. She was convinced of that. She'd just need to be patient. It was Saturday, early evening. Surely he wouldn't want to spend the entire day and that evening alone in prayer, she concluded.

***

Joshua had entered the wilderness of prayer by his own choosing and with a dedication to remain if necessary. He made his way through the haze, unsure where he was going and when, even if on this day, he would arrive.

Forgiveness was sought for focusing elsewhere when it was clear his purposes now were so much more important and vital—especially when Sammy was in need.

It took time but two wills slowly again merged as one as a reacquaintance of sorts took place between him and his Master.

Joshua smiled at the joy and peace radiating about him. He marveled at the love that so enfolded around him and in him and through him making him content and yet ever-hungry for more. There was no other place he'd rather be.

He was at home here.

Fifteen: Keeping Watch

Several raps came at the bedroom door. Joshua looked up at his wall clock and saw it was 9:30 p.m. He leaped up quickly hoping good news had come about Samuel. Opening the door, he found his father standing in the darkened hallway.

"Hey, Dad," Joshua said. "Is Samuel okay?"

The look on his father's face, however, wasn't one of pleasantries, nor of sadness. For some reason, he looked angry.

"What's wrong?" Joshua asked even as he realized the look was focused squarely at him. His father wasn't just angry. He was angry at him.

"You *didn't* tell your brothers where we went?"

Joshua remembered he'd been told to tell his brothers that they'd taken Samuel to the hospital. "I came straight up to my room after you guys left. I've been here the whole day praying for Samuel."

"Joshua, for the past five to six hours, they haven't known where we were. My phone bat didn't last an hour after we reached the hospital—and your mother forgot to bring hers."

"Sorry, Dad," Josh said.

"Your brothers didn't even know you were up here, son!"

His father was visibly upset—the first time in a long time he'd seen him like this. Of late, Joshua had noticed his father's irritation easily stirred. And tonight, he was the cause.   Joshua tried to show on his face the regret he felt. "I'm...really sorry."

Joshua's father stood there as if considering what to say next. Finally, words slipped from his mouth. "Maybe you'd be better off to remember that old adage about being 'so heavenly minded that you become no earthly good'?"

The words struck Joshua like a hammer. Immediately, there came a recoiling within him even as he tried to pull back from the caustic words. But there was no escape. Joshua looked away from his father and down at the floor even as the attack seemed to reverberate within him. He fought off his desire to allow his wound to surface on his face. It was clear that his own intentions, his desire for more of God and more of His power pouring through him was wholly misunderstood. How could they ever know what he'd discovered? How could they ever understand the brilliance that remained so nearby, but which continually cost so much to attain and maintain?

"Is Samuel okay?" Joshua finally asked in a low voice.

"Yeah," his father replied, his voice softer. "He's still got a fever, but the doctor's managed to bring it down some. He's asleep now in his room."

"What's happening with him?"

"Don't worry, he'll be all right. Just keep praying," he replied in a reassuring voice even as he quietly pulled the door shut.

Joshua felt the earlier words of his father lingering. Was it true? Was it possible that he was spending so much time keeping watch of himself and his spiritual health that his family was in danger of being neglected—even to the point of disrespect? He also considered his actions with Lydia earlier; had he treated her fairly, to ask her to excuse him and, oh by the way, to go home?

Opening his door, he stepped to Samuel's room which was next to his and looked in. There he rested, his chest rising and falling a bit too much, it seemed. He approached his brother's small frame and kneeled.

Closing his eyes, Joshua whispered the Name of Jesus. Comfort seemed to enclose around Joshua even as he gave grateful thanks for his brother's keeping. Joshua sat there listening to the rhythmic, slightly-troubled breathing of his sleeping brother. He laid his hands gently on his arm.

"Joshua?"

"Yeah, I'm here, buddy. How're you feeling?"

"I'm scared."

"We have to trust the Lord, even when things seem to be going out of control."

"Yeah," he replied weakly.

"Just rest, little brother. And don't worry. I'm here. I'll watch over you." At that, Joshua laid on the bed beside his brother and placed an arm around him and held him. "Love is all we need," Joshua said in a near whisper.

Joshua would do his part and trust God, no matter how difficult. He would keep his mind fixed on things above—for the sake of those around him, and for the sake of those who had not yet experienced His all-encompassing love and power. Silently, Joshua began to pray and rebuke the sickness even as his tiredness began to take hold of his mind and draw him into sleep.

Sixteen: Lydia's Resolve

She felt angry. Neglected. Disconnected. And all she wanted was to hear his voice, to know he at least cared.
You surely can't be praying...still! she considered. It had been twelve hours since they'd been together.
Then she realized this strange feeling churning within her. Strange indeed because of the jealousy she felt against this god of Joshua's... She chuckled at the thought all the while contemplating how she would bring Joshua back down to reality.

***

There came the muffled ring of the telephone, and then several seconds later a voice from downstairs for Joshua to pick up the phone.
Just then, almost with a jolt, Joshua remembered poor Lydia. She'd no doubt been waiting for his call. He looked at the clock. It showed 10:48 p.m. He hoped it was Brad, or Sergio, or anyone else so he could honor his promise and call Lydia right away.
"Hello?" he said evenly, hopefully.
"Hmm, you mean you have time for a two-minute call?"
Joshua winced. "Lydia, no—"
"It's okay. You go ahead and do your praying, and long walks, and whatever else you want to do."

"No. I've just been watching over Samuel the whole evening." An hour ago, his mom had come in and replaced him. She'd remain at Samuel's side overnight.

"Good," she said sounding genuinely glad. There came a pause. "Well, I hope you sleep well tonight, Joshua Phillips."

"Wait. Please, I didn't mean to hurt your feelings by not calling..."

"No need to explain, Joshua," she said, her voice cold. "I wouldn't want you to have to put priority on me when I'm clearly not." Before Joshua could reply, there came the long drone of the dial tone.

He pressed her telephone number and waited. It rang almost a dozen times but no one answered.

Joshua sighed. No matter what he did, he made a mess! He stepped over to the window and looked out at the darkness. In the sky gleamed the moon with its lighting coating the landscape with a soft, bluish hue. Intermittent clouds drifted lazily as if they had no care in the world, the moon at their backdrop, but always adamant about peeking through with its gift of silver light for the darkened world below. He wondered what she was doing. He looked down at his hands, fearful that he would never be able to make his will God's will. Still the questions echoed from within. *Was it God's will for him to be seeing Lydia? Could he bring her to know God? Or would the outcome be him being brought away from God?*

"Please," he prayed. "Give me guidance before I lose everything dear to me." And with that, he slowly undressed, pulled back his covers to his bed, and crawled beneath. "Don't let me fall away, Lord. Help me speak the truth to anyone and everyone who will listen, to all You place around me." He turned on his side pulling the covers up around his shoulders even as he tried to forget the worries and weights of the day. "In Jesus' name, amen."

Seventeen: The Change in Cary

Climbing off the bus, Joshua began to make his way toward the school entrance when he suddenly found himself nearly colliding into the wall of someone's broad chest. He stopped abruptly and looked up to find himself standing before the "bully" he'd met days before. His face bruised and swollen and his left eye blackened, he wasn't, strangely, unhappy. Still, Joshua wondered if he was about to face another challenge.

"Hi," the big boy mumbled in a low, gravelly voice.

Joshua noticed the incredible change that had taken place since their last encounter. Though beneath the discoloration around his left eye and several healing cuts, the boy's face appeared strangely at peace.

"Hi. I'm Joshua," he said before bravely extending his hand which was quickly swallowed by that of the larger boy's hand.

The boy seemed almost a bit shy, and perhaps a bit unaccustomed to these kinds of greetings or even regular conversations. "Well, God seems to have already told you my name?" he said with a grin. He looked down at his hands, a surprisingly timid expression on his face. "Do you mind if we talk for a minute?"

Joshua gave a slight nod, subtly astonished that this big guy was asking permission. "Sure. What's up?"

"I want to know more," he said rubbing his polar bearlike hands together.

"About?"

"Last week, I...gave my life to God. I don't know how to say it, but up until that day, I'd never experienced love before. And since then, I've had a hunger to know more...but I don't know what to do next."

Joshua gave a smile at Cary's interest.

"What's so funny?" the boy asked suddenly alarmed.

"No, no," Joshua answered quickly worried he'd just made a big mistake. "I'm not laughing at you. It's just that I understand what you're talking about. When you taste His goodness, nothing else compares."

"Exactly!" Cary said pounding his fist in excitement. "But how can I know more about Him?"

"Hey, leave him alone!" came a voice from the side.

Joshua turned to see Brad charging toward them. Behind him trailed Sergio, Alistair, and Jennifer. Joshua stepped in front of them raising his hands to stop Brad. "No, Brad...he's not here to hurt me. He's here because he wants to know more about the Lord."

Each of them shot each other quick, surprised glances. "Really?" Sergio asked. They all marveled at the incredible scene before them.

"Well," Jennifer said, "Let's pray for him. What's your name, anyway?"

"Cary."

They surrounded the behemoth of a boy and began to pray for him that God would begin to reveal Himself to Cary and to guide him in his new life. They prayed only briefly, but the boy seemed especially encouraged.

"Thank you," he said.

"After school," Brad added, "we meet in room 312 to read the Bible and discuss what it means to each of us. You're welcome to come."

Cary nodded with a big grin. "I'll be there. Thank you." Suddenly, he rose and stepped toward Brad before giving him a giant of a hug which caused a momentary expression of alarm on Brad's face at the unexpected display. Then, he turned and hugged each of the others. As he came to Joshua, he held him for an extra-long moment before whispering downward into his ear, "Thank you for the blessing you spoke to me the other day."

Joshua watched as the boy walked away and toward the entrance into school. A week ago, he'd have gone to wherever gang members go in the space of a day. Now he was attending school and seeking to understand and know more about God.

Joshua felt a tinge of emotion well up from within him. He could only breathe thanks to the One Who had brought Cary out of his troubled, unloved life into something robust and better. Joshua turned to the others finding it hard to erase the smile that was upon his lips. "How's the time alone with God going?"

Jennifer replied happily. "I'm doing well. It's been difficult to adjust my schedule, especially when I have three younger brothers who love to put their noses into anything and everything."

Joshua grinned. "I know about the brothers part. But you can do it. You can each do it. Our number one priority should always be to reach His heart and then remain there. After we reach that place, we aim to maintain a life that never grieves or troubles Him—or disturbs our connection to Him."

They each nodded. Sergio spoke up as the group began to move toward the school entrance. "I believe God wants us to do something special together on November 15th."

"What's that?" Joshua asked.

"I'm not sure, but I believe it's a day for all of us to do a work together for Him, but I don't know what."

Brad pulled on his book bag straps as he walked. "I told Sergio we should seek the Lord about it and ask Him to confirm it somehow."

"Good idea," Joshua replied. "If He's directing all of us, He will confirm to each of us."

Sergio nodded.

Alistair raised his hand to interject. "We're both confused about how to know if it's God or if it's ourselves. How do you separate His will from your own?"

The short clang of the warning bell sounded indicating they now had five minutes to reach their classrooms.

Smiling, Joshua shook his head as he considered a question in which the answer could fill volumes of books. "That's not something you can learn through words, I don't think. Like I said, it's about knowing His heart and then being responsive whenever and whatever He impresses or whispers to you. Get in the Bible and don't come out till you know His heart."

"But," Alistair asked pondering what to ask, "suppose I'm wrong. Suppose I do something and it wasn't God at all—but all me?"

Joshua nodded understanding the tension. "In that case, you lean on your faith in God. And if it's a good deed and it wasn't God, at least nothing bad can come out of a good deed, right? That's how I see it."

They all nodded.

"Just be obedient. And brave," Jennifer offered.

They each waved goodbye as they headed toward their individual homerooms. Joshua felt a special happiness at seeing Cary on a new path, and at hearing the news that the others were truly on their own journeys to a fruitful fellowship with God. It would not be easy; and there would never be a time when they could say they'd "arrived," but at least they would know Him intimately, and perhaps begin to give some of Him—or some of His life—to the lost and dying around them. That, Joshua realized just as he neared the corner that would bring him into his homeroom, made him especially glad and content. That was his feeling, until he heard her voice from behind.

"Joshua?"

He turned even as the bell rang, realizing he was now late.

"Hey Lydia," he said. She kept silent but stepped toward him. She seemed to be studying him somewhat.

"How are you?" Joshua asked as he glanced into his homeroom and noted the teacher thankfully not present yet.

"I'm fine," she said. "How's Samuel?"

"He's doing okay. I checked on him this morning and he was fast asleep with no temperature."

"That's good to hear," she said. "Look, I'm sorry about my call on Saturday night. I know you were worried about your brother. Lord knows I wish I had someone who'd watch over me like you did him."

Joshua gave a simple smile and nodded just a bit. He considered her beautiful eyes and suddenly forgot about his truancy. She stepped closer to him just as a cat-call came from inside the room.

"Joshy," an obnoxiously loud classmate yelled. "Don't forget to get her saved. She needs Jesus," a boy's voice mocked, causing half the class to burst out in laughter. Joshua looked and noticed it was Freddie, a tall, thin Puerto Rican boy who was known for getting a laugh or two at the expense of others. "Don't be a naughty saint," Freddie continued, which made the class laugh even more.

Joshua had nearly blushed. As he turned to look at Lydia, however, he noticed something he'd not expected. Lydia's face continued staring into the class, her eyes fixed on Freddie who was obviously fulfilling his destiny as class clown.

"Hey," Joshua said reaching out and touching her arm slowly drawing her back. Finally, she turned her attention fully back to him. "It's super early. He's just trying to make sure everyone's awake."

They stepped away from the entrance to have a bit more privacy. Lydia looked down at her hands. Without another word, one of her hands reached for and clasped tightly onto Joshua's hand. "I really think I feel something for you," she said with a smile.

He didn't want to appear insensitive. "I feel something incredible inside me for you, too," Joshua said, his eye locked onto her dark eyes which seemed to gleam with brightness at his words.

"That'll be enough, Mr. Phillips," Mr. Bryan's craggy voice came from down the hallway. Mr. Bryan was a hefty man who had a way of irritating indirectly...no matter what the situation was. "Romance 101 is for *after* school, not during."

Both Joshua and Lydia jolted apart at the teacher's approach and stepped between them into the classroom.

"I'll see you later," Lydia said softly even as that look he could not quite decipher remained. Even as she stepped off, her eyes probed into the class locking onto Freddie.

Joshua gave a quick wave to her as he entered the class. "See you later on, Lydia."

"And you're late, Mr. Phillips," came Mr. Bryan's voice as he approached his desk.

But Joshua did not mind being tardy. He was momentarily caught up in the moment that seemed to be now his to treasure. It seemed official to Joshua, but despite the last few days, he and Lydia were now in a relationship. He tried his best to cast aside any conflicts or confusion that he knew would inevitably enter his life because of this transition. And though he tried his best to hide it, he found himself grinning with satisfaction as he sat there causing several good-natured snickers from students sitting around him. His face turned an extra shade of red when he realized they'd been collectively watching him since he'd entered the class.

Eighteen: A Clean Slate

Lydia had thought the first half of the weekend something of a success in being able to connect with Joshua. She'd found him to be a gentleman, with a nice smile, fun to be with, and rather easy-going despite what she viewed as a restrictive faith. The second half of the weekend, however, had been less than what she'd expected.

It was clear that Joshua would not be the typical boyfriend. She'd thought several times about giving up any pursuit of him, yet there remained a keen interest and attraction. Perhaps that's why she felt so frustrated—because she found her heart newly captive to this new boy even though he looked heavenward a bit more than the average guy. But if she was honest, she didn't like the fact that she wasn't in command of her own emotions or able to steer her own course without wondering about Joshua or seeking to include him in her plans. Or perhaps this was what love was? She didn't know exactly what to think or what to do.

On this morning, however, she'd decided to start fresh. She'd wiped the slate clean. Instead of nagging and remaining upset, she'd decided to try to solidify her feelings and figure out where their relationship was headed—if anywhere worthwhile.

When she'd first seen Joshua and then held onto his hands just several moments before, she'd been filled with a bizarre warmth. The affirmation of their relationship gave her a sense of rootedness, as if she were now immovable. Her insides were steeled with a renewed confidence and excitement. Mystery, too. And so many other emotions. She'd been with guys before, but few if any had stirred her quite like Joshua.

 Only one part of her time with Joshua had been marred: That boy's mocking from Joshua's homeroom class. If he'd known who she was, he wouldn't have thought his bantering so amusing. If it was attention the boy was seeking, she knew exactly what to do. He wouldn't be laughing for too much longer after she was done with him.

Nineteen: Burdens

The after-school prayer meeting had been typical of the other meetings apart from Cary's entrance. Joshua had felt an excitement seeing the large boy enter the class—especially considering the dream he'd had about him. Truly, it seemed the Holy Spirit, the "Hound of Heaven," had gone on the hunt and brought home a lost soul.

   At first upon seeing Cary, however, Joshua didn't know quite what to think. The prayer group fidgeted uneasily from the coming of Cary who hadn't very much shed the outward appearance of being gang-affiliated. Cary, however, had brought with him two teens dressed like thugs, each with steel-like stares and carrying with them the flaunt of arrogance. But there was something else about these boys, Joshua realized. Though they did well to maintain a veneer of protective bravado, they also carried upon their faces an anticipation of something—as if they'd come expecting to receive something.

   "This is TJ and BL," Cary said simply.

   Joshua nodded to each and was surprised when both thrust open hands toward him. He shook their hands. They seemed as though they were just lingering, unsure if they should stay or not. And there was something else about the way TJ and BL looked at him—almost as if studying and trying to figure out what it was that had brought about such dramatic changes in Cary. And then Joshua realized these guys, despite everything, were displaying a respect toward him. Had Cary told them all of what had happened to him several days prior?

"How are you guys?"

They each nodded, and then Cary spoke up. "These two are my closest friends. Unlike the rest of the 'Jaded Hearts' gang, they made sure they were absent when they learned I was to be initiated out of the gang." As if punctuating his words, he pointed to his bruises and blackened left eye against the backdrop of Cary's blanched-white skin. There was a lengthy pause as no one quite knew what to add to that statement.

"And today," Cary continued, "they've come to find out if God is real. Plain and simple. They endured a whole day of classes just so they could make sure they were here now," Cary said.

"Really?" Joshua asked. "How could I or anyone prove God's reality? The biggest evidence is standing right before you," he said before gesturing toward Cary.

Both boys nodded slowly, though they seemed unconvinced.

Cary who had been leaning his bulk against the teacher's desk when he suddenly bolted by Joshua nearly shouting. "If you want evidence, all you have to do," he said stopping and pointing downward at Brad who looked just a bit timid at Cary's charge, "is take a look at this guy!"

"What's so special about *him*?" TJ asked flatly.

Brad raised himself up out of his chair conjoined with desk until he was standing up before speaking with a boldness Joshua had not remembered seeing in him. "Because, over a week ago, I couldn't even stand up, or talk to you like I am now. God did that for me in five minutes!"

At that, the boys stepped further into the room and took a seat without saying another word.

***

After the meeting, Joshua walked alongside Cary as they made their way out of the school toward the parking lot.

"When you came to know that you would follow Him with all your heart, what did He share with you?" Cary asked.

Joshua nodded. "Good question. I just knew that there was going to be a conflict before His power could go outward and rearrange people's lives."

"Conflict?"

"The Lord told me one thing during those twenty-one days. He said, basically, that through Him in me, there would come great change to the world."

Cary nodded. "Sounds good. After what happened with me, I'm in complete agreement that change is needed in so many people's lives."

Joshua nodded. "Your friends seemed to believe the message," Joshua said. "But why didn't they make a decision? I thought they were ready to...but then they seemed to back off." Joshua looked up for an answer and noticed a strange expression cross Cary's face. It was a visible look of concern and about what he should say next...if anything. Finally, with reluctance, he spoke.

"They're afraid of leaving the Jaded Hearts. If they leave, the gang might choose to make examples of them in the worst of ways."

"What, you mean they'd kill them?"

"There are some things worse than being killed, Joshua. They already unleashed their violence on me. Our boss,

Tony, will not like the changes that are happening right before his eyes…and especially if B.L. and T.J. also make the change. Three 'Hearts' leaving in a week will not be good news or good business. It could even cause personal problems for you."

"Who's this Tony?"

"I don't even know who he is. I just know his first name, and that he indirectly leads the Hearts and all they do."

"Indirectly?"

"Yes, because none of us in the gang have ever actually seen him. Occasionally, we receive directives."

"What did you have to do for him?" Joshua asked.

"Not a good idea," Cary said shaking his head. "I don't think it would be wise to tell you anything about that."

Joshua nodded slowly. "Is it something that effects our school?"

"All I can say is, it effects *everything* in this city."

"Everything, huh? And you can't tell me more?"

"Not now. I'll pray about it, and wait for His leading. But for now, I'd prefer not to say more. I don't want you to get hurt."

"Okay," Joshua answered with a bit of irritation. He stopped at the point they'd separate. "You pray about it. But realize that the more exposed the darkness is, the more opportunity God will have to pour out His light and life into that darkness. He's working in our lives not just for our own sakes, but for each one of the people at our school, and outside our school—even those in the Jaded Hearts and even, possibly, this Tony guy."

"I'll do what you guys do: pray," Cary replied. "And if somehow God leads me to share with you, I'll share. But," he said solemnly, "You may end up wishing you didn't know what I know."

It was then that Joshua remembered the warning about the darkness, and how it would not take kindly to the work of God. Despite all that, Joshua decided to trust God. There was nothing inside Joshua that would allow him to turn back now. Whatever was to come, good or bad, he'd face it with the determination and strength of Samson. In fulfilling the will of God, however great the burden, he hoped his end wouldn't be quite like Samson's.

***

"So, how are you and Lydia?" Joan asked as they neared their home.

"We're fine," Joshua said.

"Is it official yet?"

"I guess so."

His mom gave him a smile quietly impressed. "She is such a beautiful young lady. I hear your brothers are just a tad bit jealous."

"They are?" Joshua asked glancing over at her.

"You should try to find time to be with them a bit more. It won't be long before they're going off to college or into the military, especially Kris."

"Yeah, I'd like to spend more time with them." Joshua said considering his Mom's words. "They're really proud of me?"

"Yes," she said with a smile, her hands on the steering wheel.

Joshua chuckled lightly. "How was Sammy feeling this morning?"

"He was feeling better today so we let him go to school."
"Good," Joshua said. "Mom?"
"Yes?"
"Did you ever have a faith like mine...when you were younger?"

She seemed hesitant to answer. But finally, the words tumbled forth. "Ah, yes. I went to a Christian camp when I was fourteen. It really impacted me. That's why our family goes to church each week. I may not be a missionary or a door-to-door witness about Jesus, but I've tried to give each of you kids the opportunity to have the Lord in your lives if you so choose."

"What about Dad? How did he come to know the Lord?"

"Why don't you ask him yourself?" she asked giving him a sidelong glance.

Joshua didn't really want to ask his father. He could still remember his father's sharp words spoken on Saturday night. "He was upset at me on Saturday night for not telling Kris and Bruce about you guys being at the hospital with Samuel."

"Joshua, don't let that stop you from following your heart and your faith. Your father was tired and worried about Samuel. The truth is, he's happy as long as you're happy."

"Why didn't Dad go with us to church on Sunday morning? That's not normal for him not to go with us."

Just then, they turned to pull into the driveway.

"Mom?"

Joshua's Mom seemed to hesitate to give an answer. Turning off the engine, she prepared to get out of the car. She stopped for a second, however. "Just pray for him, Joshua. He's searching for God just like you are. He may not spend a lot of time praying, but he does believe...but sometimes, even the most stable of faiths can face testing."

Joshua nodded as he opened his door, but his mind was slightly puzzled at her words. *What's testing Dad?*

His Mom came around the car toward the front door. "When you get the opportunity, talk to him. You know he's fair. He'll tell you exactly what he thinks as well as answer any questions you may have the same way."

"Mom?" he said behind him as his mother followed him to the front door. "What's the test? I mean, for Dad?"

Without answering him, she stepped past her son and put the keys in the lock and turned before the door swung inward. Before entering, she gave her son another sidelong glance. "Talk to your father when you can, Joshua. And come back down for dinner in an hour," she said with a smile.

"Okay, Mom," he said, turning left and climbing the carpeted stairway up to his bedroom. As he entered his room, he closed the door behind him before setting his bookbag down on the bed that sat to his immediate right. He unzipped and removing his heavy textbooks. Stepping around to his desk, he arranged his textbooks according to the homework he had to do for the next day. Then he approached both of his windows and closed the curtains—one directly above his desk to the right of his bed, and the other directly opposite his bed. Before delving into the algebra problems that Mrs. Blackwell had assigned, however, he decided to lay down on his bed and rest a few moments. He stared up at his phone screen checking the statuses of his friends. As he did, he found himself thinking about what his Mom had said about his father being tested.

He heard the scratching. He sat up and stared at the window straight ahead. Then he heard on his left a massive squeak of a hinge—his closet door opening. He turned—a massive black head with eyes of red and thin, razor teeth stared back at him—its mouth forming a sneer mere inches from him. A gunshot exploded shaking him and the house.

Josh screamed as he sat up—the darkened room around him threatening and dangerous.

He'd fallen asleep.

He looked around suddenly afraid, feeling cornered by a darkened form—its hideous form still appearing in his mind's eye. Whatever it was, it wanted to crush him and to take his very life. He fully believed the darkness would reach out and take hold of him in his next few breaths. It still lingered and filled his insides with a sickly feeling. Quickly, he pulled his knees to himself in a protective measure. He whispered the Name. But then he felt ashamed he didn't have more courage. So he shouted it out disregarding his fear. "Jesus *is* Lord!"

Almost instantly, there came into the room a sweeping comfort and sweetness; it filled the room allowing for no empty or unused spaces. Then came to his mind a reminder of the Master's words he'd read the day before: "I will never leave you nor forsake you." The threat of the darkness made war with the comfort of the abiding Word—both indicating to him that his life was the pivotal point of a great conflict.

Joshua ignored the notion that something might be beneath his bed as he slipped to the carpet onto his knees and prayed intently as he sought the refuge of the Lord's abiding comfort, strength, and protection.

"My Lord," Joshua said nearly crying even as the presence strengthened and thickened about Him. But even as this took place removing the dread, there also came a sense of heaviness that came to rest upon Joshua's shoulders. "What is it, Lord?" Joshua began to pray mixing his supplications with both praise and worship—which seemed to immediately clear the air even more.

He prayed—deciding to simply trust the Lord. He knew this prayer must be vital because of the burden that now rested on him and within him. It was intense—like an ache that he couldn't remedy. He might never know what the burden was or for whom it might help until eternity unfolded. Could it be for himself—the concentration of darkness seemingly targeting him? He continued to speak to the Lord in utterances known and unknown—his eyes fixed on the Lord and on no other.

Twenty: Broken Fred

Arriving to his homeroom at the start of the day, Joshua saw the class whispering ferociously—even with the teacher standing at the front of the class. Even at Mr. Bryan's stern protest, there remained the cyclone of fevered rumination.

"What's going on?" Joshua whispered to Cheryl, a girl seated next to him.

"Did you hear about Freddie?"

"What about him?" he asked remembering the boy's jeering playfulness directed toward Lydia and him the previous morning.

"He was attacked this morning walking to school."

"Attacked? Is he okay?"

"He's in the hospital. I heard his arm was broken."

"Did they find out who attacked him?"

"They're still not sure, but they think the Jaded Hearts did it."

"Hmm," Joshua murmured turning away and suddenly troubled. Even as he felt sympathy for Freddie, his mind kept returning to Lydia's expression the day before, when Freddie had had his little bit of fun at their expense. Her facial expression had surprised him because it had appeared so thoroughly cold and seething with anger; it had been as if a storm had been silently brewing beneath the outward appearance of her face. Was there some sort of connection between this morning's event and her response to Freddie the previous day? He almost immediately dismissed such thoughts—but something within him wouldn't allow him to release the notion completely.

"Joshua Phillips."

"Present," Joshua answered Mr. Bryan's roll call. Despite such coincidences, Joshua shook off such a suspicion. Lydia was not like that and certainly wasn't able to cause such an attack on poor Freddie.

Later, still a whole class before the lunch period, a hungry Joshua made his way through the thick crowds of students toward his science class. He was about to enter the room when he heard his name called from behind. Turning in response to the familiar feminine voice, he saw Lydia's beaming smile. Joshua smiled back at her giving her a brief look-over before slowing down to wait for her to reach him. As usual, she looked amazingly graceful in the light blue top and dark blue jeans she wore and the way she handled herself with everyone around her.

"How's your day going?" he asked as he reached over and gave her a kiss on her cheek.

Pleased at his thoughtfulness, she grinned brushing back a dark strand of hair from her eyes. She cradled two books and a notebook. "Good here," she replied buoyantly. "And you?"

His lips formed a subtle smile. "Fine here."

"Why's that?" she asked over her shoulder as they continued to move through the crowds of huddled students.

"Coz I'm with you again," he said with a slightly flirtatious glance toward her.

She smiled before she replied. "Same way I feel."

"Hey, you remember that boy that was heckling us yesterday in my homeroom?" Joshua queried.

"Yeah, what about him?"

"It's sad; he was attacked and beaten while walking to school this morning? They think someone in the Jaded Hearts did it." They neared their class and stopped for a moment just outside the door to have some sort of privacy.

"Really?" she asked, her voice concerned. But then, almost instantly, her voice changed. "I suppose you think I should be sorry for him?" she asked, her lips pressed together.

"But his arm was broken," he stated and looked to see what her reaction would be.

"I repeat: 'You think I should be sorry for him?'" she said in an even voice.

"What does that mean?"

"It means, ugliness goes around and it certainly comes around."

"He was just joking with us yesterday. He didn't deserve to end up in the hospital." Joshua noted Mr. Opal's approach and shifted to let him get by.

"Good morning, class," he said after entering the class in his too-loud voice.

Joshua and Lydia took their cues to follow the teacher into the class even as Joshua considered her reply. Was he being super-sensitive about Lydia's insensitivity toward Freddie's plight? Regardless of how he tried to reason her answer, however, he found her viewpoint, no matter how much he tried to reason it, unacceptable.

The next eighty minutes seemed to stretch indefinitely. Joshua tried to act normal and give his normal attention to class and to Lydia. Yet there was something inside that made him feel as if the wind had been kicked out of him.

125 | t h e J e s u s b o y

Following class, Lydia stepped to Joshua's desk as he readied to leave for lunch. "I'm sorry. I hope Freddie's all right," she offered, her voice steady and sure. "It's just that I barely know him. My only perception of him is from yesterday—and no, I didn't appreciate being teased by him, especially in front of the class."

Joshua finished placing his books and folders into his backpack before looking up into her open face. "I don't think anyone deserves to be put in the hospital," he said.

Lydia nodded, though her black eyes seemed steel-like and lacking any signature of warmth. "Fine. I'll have some flowers delivered to him if it makes you feel better," she offered.

Joshua looked up at her and noted the hint of a smirk on her face. "No flowers are necessary," he said plainly and unamused. "Maybe some sympathy would be enough."

"Josh, *okay!*" she said in a seethed whisper. At that, she walked down the row of desks and out of the class.

Joshua wanted to call out to her, to stop her from leaving him, but something else within him would not let him do it. He let her go her way.

Twenty-One: God's Gunslinger

After school and the daily devotional meeting, Joshua awaited his mom's arrival to take him home. He'd forgotten to recharge his cellphone the night before which had left his phone with a dead battery halfway through the day. He waited nearly an hour before he realized she wasn't coming. Flustered, he tried to think of why she wouldn't have come. The school grounds were nearly empty when he decided he'd walk home. It would be a forty-minute walk, but he felt hungry and tired of waiting. Doing anything, even walking, would be better than doing nothing.

As he walked, he silently prayed. He whispered the Name and thanked Him for His love and daily provision. He even thanked the Lord for the ability and strength of walking. With a smirk, however, he lifted a supplication to the Lord in jest, "It'd be nice, though, if someone stopped to give me a ride home."

About halfway home, he decided to stop to get a drink at a small convenience store he'd traveled past perhaps thousands of times in a car without ever stopping once. Waiting to pay for his drink, Joshua noticed an older man standing in front of him talking with a slurred voice to an obviously disinterested clerk who seemed more interested in doing anything else rather than listen to the man's dissertation on life.

Joshua noticed the nearly empty bottle in the man's left hand and the worn, whiskered face, hued beet red from the past summer's scorch. His hair had receded half way to the rear—the remains of which were a bleached yellow. Likely in his mid- to upper-fifties, he looked to be a farmer of some kind dressed in worn blue-jean suspenders. The only thing he lacked to complete the impression, it seemed, was a brimmed straw hat.

As the man went his way and stepped outside, the clerk in his low twenties raised his eyes to the ceiling while shaking his head. "He comes in here every day," he commented to Joshua. "Always drunk or on his way to being drunk."

Joshua nodded slowly. "Does he cause you problems sometimes?"

"Yeah," the young man replied. "And he's always repeating the same stories."

"I see." Just then, the Voice whispered within. *Tell John what I am about to do in this man's life today.*

Huh? Joshua wondered inwardly. But rather than question or linger, Joshua gave in and spoke to the clerk named John. "You'll think this strange, but the Lord is going to do an amazing work in that man today. And you will witness it."

The clerk stood staring at Joshua as if he'd been suddenly paralyzed. "Oooo-*kaaay*," he managed in a half-mocked tone. Finally, he said, "It took the good Lord six days to create the earth; it'll take a whole lot more than six days for the Lord to change *that* man."

"I have to stress to you," Joshua added, "that you will see the work of God in his life with your own eyes...*today*."

Joshua watched John the clerk nod unconvinced, perhaps thinking the shop was truly on its way to becoming a magnet for all the town crazies.

"Bye," Joshua said trying his utmost not to seem strange. He stepped outside with his soda pop in hand. He turned to see the old man sitting in the shade beneath a tall oak tree at a complimentary table, bench combo. Walking over to him, Joshua gave the man a comforting smile before daring to lock eyes with him.

"W-What do you want, boy?" the man asked gruffly.

Joshua saw into those hard, hazel eyes, eyes that did not like being mocked or jeered—especially by a teenager. Joshua simply began to share. "The Lord hears your stories. But He hears more than that. He hears most of all your heart that's partially broken."

"W-Who are you?" the man asked visibly angry and troubled, his voice slurred and his face growing a deeper shade of red if that were possible. Yet despite the display, Joshua detected vulnerability in his voice.

"It doesn't matter who I am. But He will take your pain. He sees your heart in its barrenness and shattered state. He wants to help you."

The man nearly laughed. "Help me?! Did He help me six years ago when my wife died? What good is His help to me now when I'm a shell of what I once was?"

Only words would do no good. This situation required a demonstration. At the prompting of the Unseen One, and with a boldness Joshua had never known before, he stepped forward and placed his hand upon the man's shoulder. "The healing you require will come when you know that you're absolutely loved, and *never* alone."

What seemed to be a current of electricity passed into the man as he jolted backwards off the bench onto the ground—Joshua, too, shocked at what had just happened.

Joshua scrambled around to help him back to his feet. However, the man appeared to be conked out in a still, calm sleep! Tapping on his cheeks, Joshua finally drew the man out of his slumber. Finally, he looked up as if he'd just awakened from a quiet, afternoon nap—a peace and calm now etched on his face.

"What an amazin' dream," he said, his voice crisp and clear, his eyes vivid and vibrant with new light.

"Really?" Joshua asked standing up straight with a broad smile. "You had a dream?"

"Yes. I dreamt I was in my house by myself covered in darkness when a warmth of light came streaming into the room. And then just as that happened, arms enfolded around me before a Voice spoke. It said I'd be all right if I'd open my heart and accept His *tailormade* love for me."

Joshua nodded happily. "God is like that," he said simply.

"Who are you, by the way?" the man asked looking Joshua over as if he'd just now noticed him for the first time.

"Joshua Phillips," he answered with a smile. "My father's Dennis Phillips who owns the Old Sterling Repair Shop in the city center."

"I see." At that, the man stood up with Joshua's help before taking Joshua's hand in his and shaking it. He started to walk toward the store, at first appearing groggy until he'd taken several steps. He was thirsty again, he said over his shoulder toward Joshua. Moments later, he exited the store, four one-gallon cartons of chilled spring water in his hands. With a wave, he was off heading wherever it was he lived.

"What'cha going to do the rest of your day?" Joshua yelled after the old man.

The man stopped and turned back toward Joshua. He paused as he looked down at the ground and then up again at Joshua. Then he smiled. "I've a refrigerator and kitchen cabinet full of junk to get rid of—stuff I think I won't be needin' anymore."

Joshua smiled as the man turned with a friendly wave and walked down the road as if he had not a care in the world upon his shoulders. Joshua was about to start his walk home when a lone voice came from behind.

"What'd you *do* to him? He was completely sober." Joshua turned to see John the clerk standing there watching.

"I told you what the Lord told me to tell you. The Lord healed the man's broken heart. Remember what you've seen today." At that, Joshua turned to resume his walk home—and for a moment, he felt a little like a gunslinger having downed another enemy of God and now walking off into the sunset. He grinned at the silly image that filled his mind.

God always seemed to work His plans out, Joshua realized, especially through circumstances that made His people uncomfortable or inconvenienced. He now welcomed his walk home. Glancing back, he noticed the clerk, still standing there staring in his direction.

***

By the time the demons knew the lightbearer was near, it was too late. And as the Voice sounded within the boy, His Voice deafening to the dark ones, they shrieked with fear and outrage. This old one they'd infested for years was theirs—his life theirs, his warmth theirs, his dark moods theirs to feed on.

And then the boy's single touch had come—the life of God coming in like a flood, the enemy having no choice but to scream and rage as they departed into the oblivion freeze of the wandering lands.

***

As Joshua got home, he found the house unusually silent. On the kitchen table, however, was a handwritten note from Mom.

Had to take Samuel to the hospital again. I'll call you guys later.

Joshua sighed as he finished reading the note and nearly collapsed into the chair at the table. Samuel's condition had not improved—despite Joshua's best efforts to pray for healing for him.

"Lord," Joshua said aloud. "*What* is going on?" But there came only the still silence of an empty house. Going up to his room, Joshua dived onto his bed. Though uncertain and out of his control, it seemed, Joshua would not ruminate on the things he could not do, but on the things he *could*. Again, he went before the One. This time, he grabbed his guitar from the corner and began to play, his voice singing worship and praises to the One. Then, as his voice fell away, his hands strumming the guitar, occasionally plucking the strings in a way that relaxed and soothed him, he prayed for the next several hours—not just for Sammy but for the old man, for Freddie, for Lydia, for the Bible Club—and for the future that God was leading him into. He prayed he'd be kept faithful whatever came at him.

133 | the Jesus boy

Twenty-Two: Thirty Days

Lydia dialed a number on her cellphone and waited.

"Garrett," she said. "Yeah, good job. But did you have to go overboard and break his arm?" "Well, next time, don't be so zealous. Did you give him the message I told you to give?" "Good." "Are you sure there weren't any witnesses?" "No, I think he'll have learned his lesson." "Bye." She clicked the "end" button and then dialed Joshua's number. It rang half a dozen times with no one answering.

She considered what Joshua would do if he knew she'd been the cause of Freddie's present misery. Still, she bet the class clown wouldn't be in a mood to jeer and jest for a long time.

Just then, Lydia heard a car pull into the driveway. She expected it to be her Mom. Looking out the window, however, she noticed it wasn't her Mom's car.

"Oh *noooo*," she said. With a jolt, she flung the front door open and stepped out onto her cement front porch, the Fall's season nearly upon them, the cooler temperatures beginning to be more often than not. But the sight of the sleek black BMW was enough to add perspiration to her and raise her heartrate.

"What are you doing here?"

A tall musclebound man stepped out of the car. He wore dark-tinted Gucci sunglasses and a heavy, black leather jacket despite the September heat. Several gold necklaces sparkled in the sunlight around his neck. His face and neck were tanned, and even his hands—obviously gained elsewhere and not from the Iowa sun. Appearing to be in his upper thirties, he wore a dark goatee which looked as though it was expertly maintained.

"Just stopped by to visit...to make sure you're well," he said.

"This isn't a good time for a 'visit', Frank," she said looking at her small-face, gold watch. "My Mom will be home any time now."

"I won't be here for long, sweetie," he replied simply. "How's the recruiting going?"

"It's going okay, Frank. Now, can you get back in your car and leave?"

"Don't talk to me like that," he said evenly but with a slight threat in his voice. "We need more recruits. Can you make it happen?" he asked stepping toward Lydia before stopping just shy of the bottom porch step. Lydia stood just in the doorway with her arms crossed.

"Sure, with some time," she said, impatience growing in her voice. "But what's with this social visit? I've already made the operation three times what it was when I came into this mess."

"Just making sure you don't get religion. It seems to be spreading throughout the school like a bad case of the flu. Even a few of the Hearts have caught it."

"Frank," she replied. "Do I look like the kind of girl who'd try on old-time Gospel?"

"What's with this Bible Club that meets after school hours?" he asked flatly.

"It's a club for geeks, weaklings, misfits, Frank. No harm there."

"I want it shut down."

She looked at him curiously. "Why? All they're doing is reading their Bibles..."

"You heard me," he said turning and walking back toward his car. "I don't care for the competition. You have thirty days to make it happen."

"Thirty days?"

"Thirty days to get rid of this Bible group, and then another thirty days to double the recruiting."

"How can I do that?"

No answer came to her question. Opening his door, he stood and stared back at Lydia. "One of the main leaders—his name is Joshua Phillips. He needs a new hobby after school. Make sure he discovers it. Got it?"

"Frank!" she said, flustered. "I didn't agree to do anything for you except deal with recruiting for the operations and the passing of goods. That's it!"

The man gave a broad smile as if she'd just agreed to his demands.

"Frank!"

Climbing back into his BMW, he started the engine before reversing out of the driveway and speeding off down the street way too fast, Lydia thought to herself.

Staring after the car, she considered Frank's instructions. All at once, she felt as if she was in way over her head. And she suddenly realized just how lonely she felt. She'd been instructed to attack her boyfriend's most cherished activity—and to bring his group to a halt through whatever means necessary. That troubled her. But the loneliness she now felt seemed to acerbate her feelings. All at once, she just wanted to be with Joshua—to be held by him. She knew he loved her. But not more than he loved his god. She knew even now, he was probably praying somewhere—her being the furthest thing on his mind.

"Okay," she said aloud. "I'll do it...I'll bring down Joshua's little empire. And when it's all finished, he'll have no one left but me to cling to."

Twenty-Three: Lil' Samuel

Through the thin veil of his praying, Joshua heard the sound of someone entering the house; it was nearly eight o' clock. Sensing it was okay to stop praying, he decided he'd go downstairs to the kitchen hoping to find out news about Samuel. He came to the top of the spiral staircase when he stopped curious to listen to the conversation between his little brother and mom—and not wanting to spoil what he might glean.

"But what is it?" Samuel asked.

Joshua wondered, *What is 'what'?*

"It's what's making you sick, honey. But the doctor's going to try to help us make you well, okay? So why don't you sit down there and I'll heat up some chicken soup for you."

"Okay," Samuel said.

Finally, Joshua descended and stepped into the kitchen. "Hey," Joshua said.

"Oh, hi," his Mom said pleasantly surprised. "Want some chicken soup with crackers with your brother, Josh?"

"No thanks, Mom. How are you?" Joshua asked his brother who smiled broadly as he stepped over and gave his brother a hug from behind.

"He's going to be fine."

"But what's wrong with him?"

Joshua watched his Mom stop what she was doing and stand still, as if to compose herself. Finally, she turned, her eyes reddened. "I've been waiting for the moment to share with you and your brothers. Something's wrong with Samuel's blood, Joshua. It explains why he's been so weak of late."

"Samuel's blood, Mom?"

Bailey stepped over next to Joshua and looked up, as if searching the boy's face. When Joshua's question didn't receive an immediate answer, he decided to be patient and let his Mom answer when she was ready. She again turned back to preparing the soup. It was obvious that she was trying to hide her emotion in front of Samuel.

"So, it's serious?"

She nodded ever so slightly before giving a quick glance toward Joshua. "You sure you don't want some soup with your brother?" she asked, her voice wavering.

"Yeah, I think I will have some," he said in a low voice as he sat down beside Samuel.

"Mommy says I'll be all right. The doctor's going to make me better," Samuel said. Bailey nudged Samuel's elbow before he turned and pulled the dog close to him with a hearty hug.

Joshua tried to respond to Samuel's statement with a reassuring smile.

After Samuel had eaten and been ushered to bed, Joan returned and sat down in front of Joshua. She spoke softly but matter-of-factly. "According to Dr. Jackson, he has an aggressive form of leukemia."

"How long have you and Dad known about this?"

"We've known he was unwell the past few weeks, but the official diagnosis came to us a few days ago."

139 | the Jesus boy

Staring at his mother, Joshua immediately dismissed his anger at not being told. It was enough of a concern on his parent's minds that their youngest son's life was in this precarious state. Immediately, Joshua's mind scrambled to find a strategy on taking hold of this thing, this situation, and getting a grip on it to get rid of it. He'd seen the power of God—he knew it could bring even a such thing as a miracle, cliché as that word seemed to be in many circles of Christendom.

"Joshua, I want you to be praying for him. He's going to need all we can give him," Joan said, her voice amazingly firm.

Despite his internal strategizing, Joshua also felt an emptiness within him that would not go away but seemed only to enlarge with each passing second. It was amazing what one word with just two syllables, the "C" word, could do to a person's state of mind—how it could rearrange one's whole world in a matter of seconds. Even as he held onto Bailey and considered the march of time and the onslaught of cancer that would inevitably try to take him away, Joshua's mind raced to find some advantage, some word of reassurance. At that moment, Joshua was glad for the peace of the One's comfort; he had to wonder how people without His love could possibly fare when faced with such news.

Just before heading to bed himself, Joshua went to Samuel's small bedroom. "How are you feeling now?" Joshua asked.

Samuel, already tucked in bed, gave Josh a smile and a nod. "I feel pretty good."

Joshua returned the smile. "Want to go to a movie tomorrow night? Maybe Mom will take us," he asked. Joshua expected she'd give her approval.

***

After finishing his time with Samuel, Joshua walked outside toward the solitude of the woods, Bailey with him. As the gentle cool breeze and silence enfolded around him, he spoke toward the expanse of the sky that stretched seemingly endless. The sun's pale light was being pushed toward the horizon by the thick darkness gathering overhead. At that moment, Josh felt alone and so minute.

"Lord, I don't know what's going on. I barely have control of my own life, never mind my brother and Lydia and the rest of the world. I need to know You're there, and that You won't leave me alone to screw everything up."

Joshua walked along the trail for a short distance as his words seemingly lingered between heaven and earth. There was neither confirmation of message received in Heaven, nor a sense of His presence to reassure him. But Joshua knew He was there. He decided to be as honest as possible with himself and with his God as he prayed aloud.

"You know all things; you know my thoughts. I have prayed for Samuel repeatedly. Yet my prayers have seemed to do nothing; they've been worthless. Please, Lord. What am I doing wrong? I need to know what to do. He's my brother." Then the thought came to him, which he verbalized even as the tears began to well up: "I love him. I would gladly take his place if it meant he could live."

He fought to not break down in tears.

"Regardless, I pray not my will be done, but Yours." Even as that statement left his lips, however, Joshua worried if he would be able to accept that will, whatever it was to be. Did he truly trust the Lord? "Just help me to do my part. I don't want Samuel to die because of my failure recently to remain upright in You. Help me, Lord. And don't leave me alone. I need You so much. Sammy needs you."

There came nothing. No reassurance. No immediate sense of comfort even as his mind and heart churned with these new developments in his life. "Your will be done," he finally conceded. "I must trust You, regardless of what happens, regardless of my feelings. But help me in my weakness and human limitations," he prayed. "Help any areas of unbelief that remain in me that they'd be replaced by trust in You. Thank You, Lord. Amen."

***

They surrounded him—the boy's focus on the storm so intense that it made the dark ones' constant screams and shrieks in his spiritual ears all the more effective in helping to block out and prevent any words or sounds that might come from On High.

Twenty-Four: Lydia's Confession

The next morning, Joshua went to school as usual. Still, the aftertaste of knowing that his younger brother faced the indescribable struggle of a horrible and potentially deadly dis-ease—at such a young age—made a sober mark upon Joshua's heart. It had a way of changing the perception he had of the world as he made his way to school. Joshua momentarily wished the quiet, lighthearted chit-chat of his bus mates was his own. Instead, he felt a heaviness pressing down as if to squeeze the very breath from his lungs. It wasn't that he distrusted the Lord. It was that no matter what he did, no matter what he prayed, he could not budge the burden from his heart regarding Samuel.

Stepping off his bus when they reached the school grounds, Joshua met Sergio, Alistair, Brad, and Jennifer. A gentle, still haze clung to the green of the football fields that surrounded the high school.

"How's everything?" Joshua asked.

They each nodded that they were well.

"How's the praying? You guys finding the heart of God in your seeking?"

Sergio spoke up. "It hasn't been easy. But I'm still plugging away."

"Same here," Alistair agreed. "My parents are wondering what's happening with me, however."

"Yeah, that happened to me, too," Joshua replied. "Just tell them the truth: You're seeking God's heart."

"Easier said than done," Alistair said. "They're atheists. As far as they're concerned, I'm talking and praying to nobody."

"Then look for opportunities within your family and parents to counter that notion. *Show* them that He is real."

"How? If I do more chores, my parents just think that should be normal for their kids. If you lived in a Chinese household, you'd know this," Alistair laughed.

Joshua smiled and he nodded understanding. "Well, no matter, there will be opportunities if you ask for sensitivity from the Holy Spirit."

Alistair nodded. "Yeah, I think that's the only way."

Joshua turned to Jennifer. "Going good with you, too?"

Jennifer nodded with a smile.

"Well, would you guys please remember my brother, Samuel? I found out last night some news about him."

"What?" Brad asked concern in his voice.

"They found out why he's been sick of late. He has an aggressive form of blood cancer."

"Oh my," Brad said, sadness blanketing his face.

Each felt especially sad to hear such news. They each gave their consent that they'd pray fervently for Samuel every day until he was healed.

Having several minutes left before class, they lingered at the stone bench that sat at the side of the walkway that led to the main school entrance. Just then, Sergio pointed toward a crowd of students making their way into the school.

"Look, there's Freddie."

Joshua saw him, his right arm bent in a bulging, white cast.

"This city's getting dangerous to live in," Jennifer said. "Poor guy."

"At least it's only a broken arm," Alistair added. "Could've been much worse the way he was attacked."

Freddie saw them looking at him and suddenly changed direction and began walking toward them.

"Does he want us to pray for him?" Brad asked.

"I don't think so," said Joshua, preparing for the worst.

As he came nearer, he began to yell angrily in rapid Spanish.

Joshua stood up. Freddie was directing the verbiage directly at him. "What's wrong?" Joshua asked.

Finally, Freddie became silent as he stepped slowly, evenly until he was nose to nose with Joshua who stood several inches shorter.

"Is this how you spread your Message?" he asked angrily casting a glance downward toward his white, cocooned arm.

"What are you talking about?"

"The boy who did this to me gave me a message when he attacked me from behind."

"What message?"

"He told me *'I need Jesus!'*"

"*Who* said that to you?" Joshua asked.

"The boy who attacked me yesterday morning."

"You think I had someone attack you? I wouldn't do that to anyone," Joshua replied.

"Look at my arm. It's done. Are you happy now?"

"I don't know what you're talking about." Joshua said, visibly troubled.

145 | t h e   J e s u s   b o y

Throwing a disgusted look at Joshua and then at the entire group, Freddie stepped backwards before walking off, again sputtering in indescribable Spanish.

"What was that all about?" Jennifer asked.

"I'm not sure," Joshua said even as he tried to ponder the accusation. He excused himself from the group and headed toward homeroom. As he walked, he tried to figure out how in the world Freddie had thought him involved, and why the boy who had attacked him had mentioned Jesus. He was about to push the strangeness aside for the moment when he remembered the previous day when Freddie had been teasing both him and Lydia as they stood at the classroom entrance. What had it been that Freddie had said? "She needs Jesus"? Joshua could still picture Lydia's facial expression at that moment, how angry she had become at Freddie's play-acting. Was it true? Had Lydia been somehow involved in Freddie's beating?

***

In Mr. Opal's class, Joshua wrote a note and dared to have it passed to Lydia. He'd written: *Hey, Lydia. Listen, I need to talk after class.*

She wrote back immediately before having the note passed to him discretely: *Okay, talk to you in ten minutes. Hope Samuel's doing better.*

When class ended, Lydia joined Joshua as they made their way to lunch period. Joshua told her about Samuel. Lydia became especially sad at the news and offered to do anything possible to help.

"There's nothing anyone can do, except pray."

"Is it bad? The cancer, I mean?"

"They think they've found it in time, but it'll be really tough for Samuel. Even adults can't handle this sort of thing easily."

"I see," she said. She reached her hand and arm around Joshua and pulled him close to herself before reaching and giving him a hearty hug.

As they pulled apart, Joshua, glad for her comfort and support, allowed a few seconds of silence before he decided to ask Lydia again about Freddie. As they walked down the hallway, Joshua finally raised his voice. "What's going on, Lydia? I mean, did you get someone to beat up Freddie?" Joshua asked keeping his face neutral yet resolute.

Lydia stopped in mid-stride before turning toward Joshua. "*What* are you talking about?"

"He came to me this morning and told me the message he'd been told. Is it true?"

"What message?"

"That he *'needed Jesus'*? Just like what Freddie said to us?" Joshua watched to see how she'd react. If she lied to him now, that would be the end of their relationship. He'd always been honest with her. He expected the same from her.

She hesitated for the briefest of moments. "I asked a friend to talk to him, Joshua. It wasn't meant to get violent."

"Wasn't meant to get violent? Who was this friend of yours?"

"A friend, Joshua. That's all you need to know."

"All I need to know? *What's* going on, Lydia?"

Lydia looked down at her hands as she spoke. Finally, she looked up, her eyes locking onto his. "Okay, you want to know the truth? I'll tell you."

"Go on," he replied plainly, his face growing hot as he looked at her.

"I have friends in the Jaded Hearts."

Joshua blinked at the stunning words. "What kind of friends could they be? No one just has friends in that gang."

"They're friends, Joshua. Nothing more, nothing less."

Joshua felt confused and angry at the same time. "I can't believe you would do this. I'm a follower of Jesus, Lydia. And you made me look like I was involved in having him beat up."

"I'm sorry, Joshua."

"Me too!" Joshua shouted before walking off.

"Wait!" she said angrily. "Joshua, where are you going?"

Joshua stopped and turned toward Lydia. "I'll talk to you about this later."

"No, let's talk about it now," she replied matter-of-factly and walked after him.

Joshua took a deep breath while keeping his gaze fixed on the end of the hallway. "Look," he said finally turning back toward her. "I have to think about what you've just told me. Do I really know you, Lydia? And I have too many other things on my shoulders as it is to have to worry about more."

"Okay," Lydia managed. "Shall I call you tonight?"

"I guess," Joshua finally said, reluctance in his voice. "Goodbye, Lydia," he said before finally walking off.

***

Joshua was glad she had told the truth about her involvement in having Freddie talked to—what had turned into a violent assault. Though a complete surprise, and though he struggled with the knowledge that she had "friends" in the Hearts gang, Lydia's honesty did mean something to him. But even with her honesty, and even if he forgave her, nothing would help mend Freddie's shattered arm or his belief that Joshua together with Lydia had had him attacked.

Entering the cafeteria, Joshua approached Freddie. At the sight of him, Freddie became visibly disgusted, the others around him displaying the same looks. Regardless, Joshua stepped up to their table. "I'm sorry what happened to you. I had no idea anything like that was going to happen to you. I didn't have any involvement in what happened to you."

Freddie glanced up at Joshua. "And if I don't talk to you now, are you going to have my other arm broken, too?"

Some of the other classmates were now talking to each other in low voices as they watched and listened in on the conversation.

"No, no," Joshua said. "I had nothing to do with what happened. My girlfriend didn't like what you said to us yesterday. She only wanted someone to talk to you about what you said, nothing more, nothing less."

Freddie swore under his breath. "Man, there wasn't any talking involved! Just me being attacked from behind. Man, what did I say to you or to your girlfriend to deserve this?" Freddie asked lifting his cast toward him. "How could you do this to me? Would you forgive her if this had been done to you?"

Joshua considered his question. He would like to believe he would forgive someone for harming him on purpose—with God's help. He could understand the anger in Freddie.

"Or what if it had happened to your brother or sister?"

"Is there anything I can do for you?" Joshua asked simply.

149 | the Jesus boy

"Yeah, leave me alone," he said punctuating his sentence by lifting his lunch tray off the table some six inches and allowing it to slam down onto the table.

Joshua saw how futile talking to him was now. He conceded defeat before walking off.

"Oh," Freddie shouted after him. "I'm sure the police will want to talk to you later about what you've just shared with me."

Joshua turned around. "Do what you have to do." At that, he left the lunchroom. Still, he felt the nagging realization that he would likely be questioned by the police and that Lydia would be included in that questioning. "Lord help me," he whispered. His life was a mess from start to finish and it seemed only to be getting worse.

Twenty-Five: Tentacles

After school, Joshua met with the prayer and Bible club which had grown to fifteen members. As was usual now, Cary showed up. As their gathering came to an end and people began to leave, Cary approached Joshua.

"Hey," Joshua said.

"I did some praying," he said pushing back his long black hair that nearly covered his eyes. "And to be honest, praying isn't easy for me. But I believe it'd be wrong not to tell you what's going on. But remember one thing: what I tell you might change how you see this school and this city."

"Great, more weights to carry around," Joshua said taking in a deep breath and slowly releasing it.

"What's wrong?" Cary asked, concern in his voice. "Is it a bad time for me to talk to you about this?"

"No, it's not that. You know about my brother's cancer; that's just one thing. My grades are suffering. My girlfriend and I are having troubles." Waving goodbye to everyone, Joshua began walking down the nearly empty hallway with Cary's large mass walking alongside him.

"Oh," Cary said. "Sorry to hear about all that."

"Well, tell me what you know," Joshua said with a quick smile. "The Lord will sustain me."

Cary nodded. "The Jaded Hearts are affiliated with a drug network that operates throughout this school. Although they aren't involved in the drugs themselves for profit or distribution, they do occasionally help Mister Tony by being his muscle."

"Who is this Mister Tony guy?"

"He's the one who runs the drug network. He's in charge of making sure the demand for drugs remains high—everything from marijuana to ecstasy to crack. And the school is just one component of the overall strategy. They also have influence in the other area schools from middle school on up, in the local community college, and on the streets."

"Go on."

"Well, the way they run the network is to find teenagers and use them to distribute the drugs discretely. Usually, they're the most popular in the schools—those with pull with other students. They basically look for salespeople who whet people's appetites for the drugs. They're the ones you'd never suspect."

"I see."

"Have you ever met this Mister Tony?"

"No, I was just an oversized Heart, remember? But I've heard others talk about him. No one messes with Mister Tony or the guy above him, Frank."

"So, who actually runs the Hearts?"

"That's Pistol, the gang leader."

"His name is Pistol?" Joshua asked incredulously.

"Yep. He gets kickbacks from the drug-running whenever the Hearts do Frank's or Mister Tony's muscle bidding."

"So, how do we reach the other members of the Hearts with the life of God?"

"You've already reached me. And there are others considering changing their current affiliations in the gang, too. But it won't be easy. The consequences for leaving are dangerous and, for a lot of them, they'd be giving up the only real family they've ever known."

Joshua shook his head. He couldn't even comprehend what his life would've been like without his mother or father. "But you came to know Him. And you left the gang. Why?" Joshua smiled as he left the question lingering between them.

Cary stopped before turning and faced him. "I left because for the first time in my life, I experienced something I'd never known before." At that, tears began to brim his black eyes. He turned his head away before turning back managing a smile. "I suddenly realized I was loved. I experienced a love that completely accepted me."

"You've never told me...but what did you see that made you turn?"

"I would love to tell you, but I can't...not yet," he said as he turned and began walking again. "It's just too personal. Maybe...when the time is right."

Joshua seemed surprised that he wouldn't tell him. Already, the intricate levels of Cary's intelligence and charisma mesmerized Joshua.

"How's your seeking going?" Joshua followed up.

"I'm doing it. What else is there for me to do? My wild days are over, at least in the natural."

Joshua smiled. "Yeah, just remember, you have something I don't."

"What's that?"

"You know what it's like for people who haven't experienced His love. I don't—at least not like you've experienced. That alone should be the greatest motivation for you to reach God's heart—and eventually bring that same love to others."

"Agreed," Cary said with a grin of satisfaction on his face.

Just then, Joshua's mother drove up. As she did, the window came down. "Joshua, does your friend need a ride?"

"No thanks," Cary said appreciably. "I'm staying at a friend's house just down the street." Then, turning to Joshua, he waved. "See you tomorrow."

Joshua got into the car and immediately asked about Samuel.

"He's doing fine," his mom said in an upbeat tone.

Joshua considered the new information he'd just learned about this Tony character and the Hearts' "enterprises." God had laid the impression upon him previously that there would come a great harvest—but not without first the need to disperse the darkness that had unknowingly attached to the very fabric of the school and community. Joshua prayed silently for the coming days and weeks that God would have His way in the hearts of his classmates and those within the Jaded Hearts—regardless of what happened to himself. Equally, he hoped that Lydia would soon find Him as he had. That would indeed fill Joshua's heart with joy and contentment.

"Arrest Lydia like you arrested Cary," Joshua said to himself. "Like You did me. In Jesus' Name, amen."

Twenty-Six: Interrogations

Several loud knocks at the front door of their house interrupted Joshua's nap followed by several barks from Bailey. Dashing to the window, Joshua peeked out to see who was there. He noticed a police car sitting in the driveway. Joshua tried to speak to the One, lifting a rapid prayer for help and His peace whatever was about to happen.

"I trust You," he said despite the panic of the moment threatening to overwhelm him.

Going to the bottom of the stairway, he thought he'd try to hear what was being said. That is, until both his brothers, Bruce and Kris, came down behind him. Joshua raised a hand toward them and seemingly by the force of his will, kept them back and silent.

"What's going on?" Kris whispered.

"Shush!" Joshua said. A low, booming voice laced with authority asked for Joshua Phillips.

"Joshua?" asked his father to the officer.

"Yes, are you his father?" the officer asked.

"Yes," Dennis said, his voice sounding both ominous and curious. "Joshua?" he yelled toward the ceiling of the house. "Come down here, please!"

"Right here, Dad," he said descending the steps to the living room. Before he did reached the bottom, he turned

155 | the jesus boy

his head around to see both his brothers standing there, puzzled, in-awe expressions on their faces.

"What have you done?" Bruce whispered, an expression of amazement on his face.

Too nervous to reply, Joshua stepped down into the living room wherein the county deputy stood having removed his dark blue brimmed hat.

"Evening, Joshua. I'm Officer Thomas," he said. Shorter than Joshua had imagined based on the sound of his voice, the officer wore a rotund frame with an especially ruddy face. "I need to ask you a few questions about an incident that took place yesterday morning."

"Okay," Joshua replied, all the while trying to remain calm and keeping a fleeting eye on his father's face.

"A boy, Fred Gonzales, who shares a class with you was attacked on his way to school yesterday morning," he said with very little emotion. "Do you know anything about that incident?"

Joshua felt like a butterfly caught and about to have its wings pinned. He'd not even done anything wrong yet he felt as though he'd been an accomplice to Freddie's woes. He eyed his father, who now held his arms in front of him crossed. His face seemed to be a bit too dark for Joshua's tastes. But why should he be worried. He'd done no wrong. And, Joshua could not and would not lie. That would only make things worse and entangle him even more in this situation. But, he worried that he was about to become the cause of Lydia's worst troubles.

"Joshua," the officer said amiably at Joshua's hesitation. "You need to help us out. That boy's arm was shattered. All I need to know are all the facts you know."

Joshua managed despite his nervousness to let out a breath slowly. Glancing at his father, he noted the face that had grown especially dark. Would his father be able to detect if he were to now withhold information to save Lydia from trouble? What would happen with his relationship with the One if he didn't tell the truth about what he knew?

"Lydia's my girlfriend. Freddie caused the whole class to laugh at Lydia and me two days ago. She didn't like it."

"What did she do after this?"

"Nothing, as far as I could tell. But then the next day, yesterday morning, I heard Freddie had been attacked. I didn't connect that incident to Lydia—not until Freddie told me what the attacker had said to him."

"I see," the police officer said scribbling into a small notepad. "Do you know the boy who attacked Fred Gonzales?"

"No."

"What did Fred tell you?"

"That he remembered what the attacker had said to him as he attacked him."

"What was it he said?" the officer asked.

"That Freddie 'needed Jesus'."

"Why does that stick out to him or to you?"

"Because Freddie had said those exact words to Lydia and me. He'd joked that she 'needed Jesus'."

"Go on," the officer said calmly.

"When he came to my school this morning, he came up to me accusing me of having him attacked. When he told me what the attacker had told him, it was later that I remembered what Freddie had teased while we stood outside the class."

"Has she told you that she had Fred attacked?"

157 | t h e J e s u s b o y

Joshua's next words would be syllables that would affect Lydia for the immediate near future—perhaps even the rest of her life. But he would not, could not, lie. "No. But according to her, she only wanted Freddie to be 'talked to'...*not* physically attacked."

The officer said nothing further for a few seconds. "What is your girlfriend's address?"

Joshua gave him the information he needed.

"Okay, Joshua. Thank you for your time. That'll be all, for now."

Joshua's Dad escorted Officer Thomas out the front door. Upon closing the door, he turned to his son with a serious expression on his face. Joshua had sat down and prepared for the worst. His two brothers came into the living room just as Dennis stopped them. "I need a few minutes with your brother," he said with no hint of discussion about the matter.

"Everything all right?" Kris asked toward Josh.

"Your brother's not in handcuffs, which says a lot," their Dad said. "Why don't you two go upstairs to your rooms so I can talk to Joshua?" which sent the two reluctantly up the stairs. Somehow, Joshua suspected they'd be listening to everything said from the top of the stairs.

"I'm very proud of you, son," his father said plainly as he ran his long fingers down across his beard. "It took guts to admit the truth despite what it might mean for Lydia. It's not for you to decide if and how Lydia should be punished. You were responsible only to tell the truth—what you knew."

Joshua nodded. "Yeah, but I've just got Lydia into a heap of trouble."

"You did nothing wrong. You did the right thing, son. Whatever she's done, it needs to be scrutinized and punished if she's ordered this boy to be attacked."

"*If* she ordered him to be attacked, yes. But if it was just to talk to him, no." Joshua pulled out his cellphone. "I have to at least warn her."

His father let out a slow sigh. "No, Josh. Just let things be. She'll learn soon enough."

Joshua slowly let his phone fall to his lap, unsure if his father was correct. He sat back against the back of the sofa shaking his head slowly. He couldn't shake the guilt and sense of regret that now coursed through him. Just at that moment, Bailey stepped near and laid his head on Joshua's lap and let out a single whine. Instinctively, Joshua rubbed his dog's head and ears that were pricked tall and turned toward him. Josh patted his lap which brought the dog to climb up and turn slightly before plopping down on his lap. Joshua wrapped his arms around Bailey and leaned forward before laying his head atop his soft, long-fur coat.

"So much crazy stuff going on these days," Joshua said unsure if he should say such a thing. It'd only lead to countless questions. But at this moment, he felt nearly overwhelmed.

"Anything you'd like to talk about, son?" his Dad asked as he collapsed his big frame into the love chair adjacent to the sofa.

"Dad, what's up with Sammy? Is it really looking that bad for him?"

Joshua noticed the same hue of darkness from earlier suddenly descend upon his father's face. "The doctor's not sure," he said soberly but firmly. Rubbing his hands downward over his temples and cheeks stopping above his beard, his father appeared especially tired. "But I know one thing," he said suddenly animated, "if I could do anything for him—*anything*—I would."

"So would I," Joshua said. Watching his father, he noticed a sudden spark ignite on his father's face, weak but sustained.

"I know you would, Joshua. For now, we just need to be there for him, and make sure we don't give up on him. He still has a lot of strength in him. And he has us. We can't let him think he's alone in all this."

Signaling to get up, Bailey immediately climbed down to the carpeted floor and moved off toward the kitchen. "Going upstairs, Dad." Joshua stopped when his father extended a hand toward him to wait.

"Yeah, Dad?"

"Tell me why it is that God used you to heal that boy at your school...but when you've prayed for Samuel so many times, nothing seems to happen for him?"

Joshua shrugged. "I'm not sure, Dad. I know for certain we shouldn't give up on the Lord, too. But what I suspect is that there's something bigger going on than just Samuel."

"Like what?"

"I'm not sure. I just know that for some reason, God hasn't touched Sammy like he has others that I pray for. I don't know if it's a failure in me," he said with disappointment in his voice, "or something else. But my friends and I are really focusing our prayers on Sammy."

Saying goodnight, Joshua returned upstairs to his room. Yet despite his thoughts for Lydia and Fred, he couldn't shake the question his father had asked. It was an enigma as to why God hadn't allowed His power to touch Samuel while touching others. Still, Joshua would not give up. He'd continue to do his part—and only that gave him comfort and reassurance. He would be his brother's keeper and never stop doing what he could to fight this enemy of God that was seeking to slowly take Samuel's life.

Just then, his cellphone rang. Joshua saw it was Lydia.

"Hi Lydia," Joshua said. "You okay?" he asked, though he wondered how she would be in another hour or less.

"I'm good," Lydia said with a sigh. "How 'bout you?"

"Lydia, the police came by my house in the last half hour. I think they may be on their way to talk to you."

"Talk to me?!"

"Yeah, they're trying to find out what happened to Fred."

"You mentioned my name to the *police*?"

"They already had your name through Fred, Lydia," he said, wishing he could slow down the runaway train he felt he was on. "If I lied, it'd be worse for both of us. I had to tell them what I knew."

"And what exactly *do* you know, Joshua?"

"I didn't lie to them. I told them what you told me, that you had someone 'talk' to him. But I also told them that you didn't intend for Fred to be hurt."

Although unspoken, Joshua felt angry at Lydia. He didn't feel much like talking to her at that moment. "Lydia, I have to go."

"Joshua! *You* must go? *You* do this to me and 'you have to go'? I can't believe you'd let them haul me off to juvenile without even a second thought."

He shook his head. "Why, Lydia? Why'd you have to create this mess in the first place?" And Joshua finally allowed the anger to have its way. "Good night!" Joshua said and without another word ended the conversation.

Moments later, there came several quiet knocks on his bedroom door. "Come in," Joshua said.

The door opened to reveal his father's large, lingering frame leaning on the doorframe. "Everything okay?"

Joshua shook his head. "No. Lydia thinks I betrayed her. I don't know what to do. She's so angry at me. But I'm angry at her, too!"

"You told her?"

"She called; I had to tell her, Dad." Joshua looked down at his hands. "I don't know what to do now! Everything's a mess!"

"Pray. For your own heart? And for her heart?"

Although there was no mockery in his father's voice, Joshua waited for an indication of whether his father was being serious. Joshua nodded slowly even as he made eye contact with his father. "I will pray. Right now."

His father gave a nod. "I'm downstairs if you need me, son."

"Thanks, Dad," Joshua said. As his bedroom door gently closed, Joshua turned and closed his eyes, even as he lifted the eyes of his heart toward the One to lift the concerns of his heart, of Lydia's situation as well as that of his family and poor Samuel.

***

Lydia saw the police officers climb out of their car and make their way toward the front house entrance. She sat silently but knew the shock that was about to be visited upon her mother. The doorbell rang.

"Hello, officers?" her mother said as she opened the front door.

"Good evening, ma'am. I'm Officer Thomas. This is Officer Smith. Are you the mother of Lydia Claremont?"

"Yes," she said, the sound of her voice sounding weaker by the second.

"We need to speak to her. Is she home?" Thomas asked.

"Yes, she's upstairs in her bedroom. Why?"

"I just need to ask her a few questions about an incident that took place yesterday morning to a young man who was attacked and had to be taken to the hospital due to the injuries he suffered."

"What would my Lydia have to do—?"

"May we please come in?"

"Yes, by all means."

Lydia heard the front door close and then the shout of her mother's voice. "Lydia?"

"Yes, Mom?" she replied hating this whole scenario that had been thrust upon her.

"Come down here, please. Officers Thomas and Smith want to speak to you about an incident that took place?"

Lydia came downstairs to find both officers standing with their eyes' fixed upon her. Both were young-looking in appearance though the subordinate had the dark moustache and glasses that reminded her of the Todd Flanders character from the Simpsons.

"Have a seat, Lydia," Officer Thomas requested. Not very tall but stocky, he wore a mild complexion and neatly combed, gel-set red hair.

Lydia took a seat. She avoided looking at her mother whom she could feel was glaring at her. Her younger sister, too, naturally inquisitive, sat quietly on the carpeted steps while holding onto the railing.

"We've received information that you ordered another person—someone from the Jaded Hearts gang—to 'speak' to one of your classmates, a Mr. Fred Gonzales? Is this true?"

"What? Where did you get—"

"Ms. Lydia. We have statement from your boyfriend that you—"

"Yes, I had a friend speak to Fred."

"According to the victim, he was attacked from behind as he was walking to school, and then words were said to him that may link you to the attack."

"I don't know how or why he was attacked," Lydia said with a look of defiance.

"I need the name of the boy that you directed to confront Mr. Gonzales."

"I don't know his name."

"You don't know the name of your friend?"

"Well we're not actually friends—just acquaintances," Lydia said feeling upset at herself for not being more careful with her choice of words.

"I need a name, please," the officer said as he loomed over Lydia.

"Lydia," her mother said in an appeasing tone. "You should tell the officer all—"

"Butt out, mother!" Lydia retorted caustically through clenched teeth without looking at her.

"Lydia?" Officer Thomas said in a serious tone. "If you won't tell me his name, I'll have to take you into custody. You cannot impede the investigation of a violent attack that happened on one of your classmates."

"I don't have a name," Lydia said, her arms crossed, her eyes fixed on her hands in front of her.

"Then I'm sorry but we'll have to take you in. I need you to stand for me, please?"

"Why?" Lydia said defiantly.

"Please, Lydia," her mother pleaded. "Tell the officer if you know anything."

"I don't," Lydia said as she stood up. It was only as her hands were placed in plastic zip ties behind her back that she began to realize just how silly she'd been to start this whole debacle in the first place. But it was too late. And most of all, her boyfriend had been the one to betray her. *How could you do this to me?* she seethed in her mind as she was led out of the comfort of her own home to the squad car. *How?!* Her anger seemed to build with every second. And all she could now feel for Joshua was a new emotion toward him she'd not felt up until now: *Hatred*.

Twenty-Seven: A Mother's Plight

Arriving at the front of Joshua's house, Dottie Claremont turned the car off and allowed herself a moment to listen to the calm of the warm night air. She listened for a moment as her car's engine cooled, subtle pangs and taps escaping from some mysterious place deep within her old car's engine. Choirs of crickets chirped from all around her car, the darkened world seemingly happy and content. The very air around her felt heavy with warmth from the heat of the day, yet the cool touch of a gentle night-breeze made the air feel carefree and refreshing. Everything around her felt at ease. It was the internal part of her that was anything but at ease. She felt frayed and worn. She regretted that she had few friends in the neighborhood that she could turn to, and that she had allowed herself to even consider coming here to Lydia's boyfriend's house. Still, she had to know if the accusations just might be true of her daughter.

   Dottie had thought her daughter to be a typical teenager, with good looks, inborn wit, and a sharp mind. She'd witnessed her daughter's vivacious social life without a second glance. Despite her suspicions that there might be more going on with her oldest daughter, she'd been thoroughly shocked when Officer Thomas had showed up, complete with the probing questions about a boy at school being beaten senseless. Dottie had stood by in disbelief, listening to question after question, helpless to help her daughter. It was instinct to want to shield her daughter, to stand in the way of any harm or unpleasant confrontation. But she could do nothing but feel a foreboding alarm begin to sound within her as the deputy seemed to unearth answers from Lydia—answers that said not all might be well with her daughter. After all, what kind of person would know gang members, and, have someone "talked to" or attacked to such a vicious degree by gang members?

Officer Thomas had been especially polite and professional, even when he had taken Lydia into custody. She'd been charged with impeding their investigation into the assault of Fred Gonzales—and being complicit in the assault and battery of her fellow student. Dottie had stepped back into her living room shocked at the sudden silence, unable to quite believe what had just happened. Her youngest daughter just sat there on the carpeted stairs—even she, normally the biggest talker of the family, stunned into silence by the events they'd just witnessed.

Finally climbing out of her car and approaching the front door, Dottie wanted only one thing this night: To see Joshua's face—to know if such a violent act could have been the result of her daughter's malice. Or was this all a big misunderstanding? Was her daughter telling the truth, that she had only asked a friend, oh, an acquaintance, who happened to be a gang member, to just "talk" to the class clown who had verbally teased her the day before?

The door opened to a towering, bearded man. Dottie's first impression was that he was a good-looking man. She also noticed the tired expression on his face as well as the textured imprint of the sofa lightly imbedded onto the skin of his cheek. He'd obviously just awakened from a deep nap.

"Can I help you?" he asked politely, but with just a hint of irritation.

"I'm sorry it's a bit late. I'm Lydia's mother, Dottie Claremont. I need to speak to Joshua—just for a few minutes?"

The man nodded slowly. "I'm Dennis, Joshua's Dad," he said offering his hand to her.

"Nice to meet you," she said as she shook Dennis's hand.

"Please come inside."

"Thank you," Dottie said stepping into a cozy, spacious living room. The quietness gave the impression that the house had settled down for the evening.

"I'll get Joshua for you," Dennis said. "Please, have a seat."

"No, that's fine. I won't be staying long."

Dennis stepped to the bottom of the stairway before shouting up toward the landing.

"Joshua? You have company. Again." There came the screech of a door opening at the top of the stairs.

"Who is it this time, Dad?" Joshua asked, a slight tremor in his voice.

Dottie stood by with her hands held in front of her.

"Lydia's Mom is here."

"Lydia's Mom?"

"Who is it, Dennis?" asked a woman's voice from another room upstairs.

"Lydia's Mom," Dennis repeated on a sigh before stepping to one of the living room chairs and taking a seat.

"Thank you," Dottie said meekly with a smile. "So sorry for the disturbance to your household," she added.

"It's entirely all right," Dennis replied. "Please, rest yourself," he added pointing to the chair opposite. She finally stepped to the chair and sat down.

Several seconds later, a lady wearing a body lounger followed by Joshua came downstairs and stepped into the living room.

"Hello, Mrs. Claremont," Joan gave a pleasant smile as she stepped to Dottie and gave her a warm hand shake. "I'm Joan, and welcome to our home."

"Hi," said Dottie, an embarrassed expression on her face. "I'm truly sorry for coming by so late. Please call me Dottie."

"Would you like some coffee or tea?" Joan asked.

Dottie accepted the offer gratefully. "Yes, thank you. I just had to talk to Joshua tonight about a matter to do with my daughter."

Joshua stepped forward visibly concerned. "Is Lydia all right?"

"No," she answered, suddenly struggling not to cry. "She's been arrested and taken to the Juvenile Facility."

Joshua said nothing at the revelation but stared down at his hands. An awkward silence lingered.

Finally, however, she continued. "Joshua, do you know if Lydia had that boy attacked?" Her words seemed on the verge of begging that such wasn't true.

Joshua shot her a quick glance, both sympathy and sorrow in his eyes. "I told the officer what Lydia had said, that she had had a friend talk to the boy who was attacked. I don't think Lydia wanted him hurt. When the officer asked me, I couldn't lie about that. I had to tell him what I knew."

Dottie nodded. "I know. I know you're a decent boy. Do you know who the boy was that attacked this Fred?"

"I don't know who, but I know he's a member of the Jaded Hearts gang."

"The Hearts gang?" she asked incredulously. "How would Lydia know anyone in a gang?"

"I'm honestly not sure," Joshua said.

Just then Joan came in from the kitchen offering Dottie a steaming mug of coffee. "Be careful, it's piping hot."

"Thank you." She cautiously lifted the mug to her lips and took a sip before placing it on a coaster on the side table.

"Mrs. Claremont?" asked Josh.

"Yes, Joshua?" she replied.

"Could I come with you to see her…when you go to visit her?"

Dottie's eyes widened at the question. It was almost as if she thought all this some sort of incredulous dream. Finally, she seemed to assert herself and answered. "I'm not sure about that for now. I would be happy to take you with me, but I'm not sure how Lydia would react. But I will tell her you want to see her. Why don't you give her some time?"

"Okay. Thanks," Joshua answered, sadness in his voice.

Several moments later, Dottie stepped outside of the house, Joshua accompanying her. She turned back to Joshua. "Please; keep praying for her."

"I have been. But perhaps more would happen if you were to join with me in praying for her, too. Good night, Ms. Claremont," Josh said as he eased the door shut.

The words of Josh churned within her. They had, initially, revealed a momentary hint of confusion on her face that lasted until she'd turned away and stepped toward her car. Once inside, she sat there again in the cushion of her seats, the harsh silence collapsing around her just as it had at home. But despite her momentary worry and concern, she found herself speaking to the Unseen, even as the tears slipped down her cheeks, asking for His help and direction, both in her own life, and in the life of her daughter.

   It'd been the first prayer she'd whispered in years.

Twenty-Eight: Accusers

Joshua had awakened the next morning feeling both tired and emotionally drained. There also was something else—an impression that did not dissolve with his usual time spent in early morning prayer. There seemed to be a heaviness clinging to his spirit, but something that Joshua realized to be a warning to remain vigilant, that he must not waver nor allow himself to become unfocused. He accepted the warning, and asked for the strength he would need to maintain his stance.

Still, he wondered if perhaps the ominous feeling had been the result of Lydia's plight...brought on, at least in part, by himself.

Arriving at his homeroom class where Joshua and Lydia normally chatted before the start of class, he felt especially strange. Most notable was the nonappearance of Lydia, something Joshua might have to get accustomed to. As he took his seat, he realized how much he looked forward to seeing her. The whole idea of her being taken away and housed in a juvenile facility had seemed unreal—until now.

Fred, however, *was* there.

Stepping close, he bent low to speak into Joshua's ear. He had short curls of black hair that matched his dark eyes. "Where's your girlfriend?" he asked, his arm wrapped in a bubble-like white cast.

"She's in custody," Joshua answered evenly.

"That's comforting," he replied. "But it won't help me when baseball season comes around, will it?"

Joshua looked up at Freddie. "I'm really sorry what happened to you but I had nothing to do with what happened."

"Yeah, whatever. If your God was real, maybe He'd fix my arm and all this would go away," he said as he stepped toward his desk on the back row.

Joshua heard the words and considered them for a moment, but he did not react. He had learned that the best way to be used of God was for the vessel to be used by the Master, not the Master to be used by the vessel.

After school, Joshua spoke to the group and gave them the same warning he'd felt earlier that morning. They said they'd be cautious all the while they continued to seek entering the heart of God.

Upon reaching home, Joshua noticed Lydia's Mom's car parked along the front of the house. As he came inside, his Mom shouted toward the front door.

"Joshua? Is that you?"

"It's me, Mom."

"Ms. Claremont is going to visit Lydia shortly."

Entering the kitchen, Joshua saw his Mom and Dottie seated at the kitchen table. He gave both a smile.

Smiling back, Ms. Claremont waved. She seemed much happier than the previous night.

"You're going to see Lydia now?"

"Visiting hours are from five till eight o' clock. I had the chance to call Lydia before noon. She wants you to come visit her with me."

Joshua felt a sudden rush of gladness that she wanted him to come see her. "She asked for me to come?"

"Yes," Ms. Claremont answered.

***

Arriving at the single-story, brick-faced juvenile facility, Ms. Claremont and Joshua were escorted into a waiting area that had a cozy feel to it. The chairs that lined the room were set in various bright colored leathers; the walls had various framed pictures with a nature motif; a television sat perched from the corner looking down on all, its blackened screen asleep. Only several minutes passed before Lydia stepped into the room, dressed in the drab of a gray, long sleeve sweater and sweatpants, her hair dangling loose. Despite everything, she appeared well, though admittedly quite flat in her demeanor. Joshua was glad for that; he feared a reprisal of anger that would make the atomic attack of Hiroshima appear small. Joshua watched as Ms. Claremont extended her arms and moved toward her daughter. Their hug, however, seemed cold. As the two separated, Joshua cautiously stepped forward, despite her defiant stare, and gave her a quick hug. Although he had shown the effort to greet her with the hug, there had been no effort on her part to return the greeting—her arms had remained at her sides.

"Hi Lydia," Joshua said, neutral in tone, as he stepped back before taking a seat.

Lydia kept her eyes fastened on Joshua's eyes, even while she sidestepped to a sofa and plopped down.

"How are things here?" Ms. Claremont asked, her voice even and trying to be upbeat.

Lydia shrugged her shoulders, but her eyes remained fixed on Joshua. Joshua felt uncomfortable and quite confidant Lydia had not forgiven him, yet.

"How's the food here?" asked her mother.

"Fine," Lydia said coolly.

"That's good. Mr. Derby said you can receive one care package per week, but it has to be mailed to you and the contents shared with the rest of the young people."

Joshua was glad for Ms. Claremont asking Lydia questions, which gave him an excuse to look away from Lydia and not be drawn into a staring contest.

"I wouldn't be here, if someone had showed they really cared for me," Lydia said. She maintained her fixed stare.

"Lydia, that isn't fair—" Ms. Claremont said appealing to her daughter.

"He betrayed me, Mom!" she said, her face growing red.

Joshua sat leaning forward, remaining silent while looking between Lydia, Ms. Claremont, and the shiny off-white ceramic floor.

"Did you want him to have to come here for lying to the police?" her Mom asked. "You put him in this predicament, not him."

Lydia took her eyes off Joshua for the first time before turning and glaring at her Mom. She seemed to hold her breath as the anger gathered in her chest and torso—her face growing redder with each second. Standing to her feet, she stepped to within half a foot of Joshua. Joshua tried to remain calm as he sat up positioning his back against the sofa even as she stared callously into his eyes. A tall black guard opened the door and stuck his head in the room.

"Everything okay in here?" he asked, but it was obvious he was directing his question specifically toward Lydia. "Hello?"

Finally, Lydia backed off. She turned to look at her Mom for a moment before stepping toward the open door. "Take me to my room," she demanded as she turned and marched out of the room, the guard closing the door behind her.

Silence. Joshua stared at the doorway that she had just passed through. He couldn't believe what had just happened. Besides his friendly greeting, Joshua hadn't had a chance to say a word, but his mind was racing. He didn't blame her for telling the truth about how she felt toward him, but he hadn't expected to see the glaring face of someone who now seemed to absolutely hate him.

***

Joshua pleasantly thanked Ms. Claremont and said goodbye before climbing out of her car. He looked up as he walked toward his front porch and noticed the sun on its descending path—a coolness now coating everything as the shadows replaced all the sun's light. Joshua noticed the beginnings of reds and oranges appearing on some tree branches. Walking into his house, Joshua immediately went to the sofa and collapsed.

"Joshua? Is that you, honey?"

"Yes, Mom."

She came to the window opening that connected the kitchen to the living room. "Did you get to see Lydia? How's she doing?"

"I felt like a dart board...except she was using her eyes as darts."

"She's that angry with you?"

"Anger is not the word, Mom."

"Okay," she said leaning on the windowsill. "Be patient. Give her time to think about what's happened."

"That's just it…she doesn't see what she did at all. It's all my fault, according to her."

"Juvenile Hall will help her realize who it is who's the real cause of her problems."

Joshua sat up and repositioned the pillows before plopping back against the softness. "Yeah, I guess."

"Keep praying for her," she said as she stepped away to tend items in the kitchen.

Joshua forced himself to his feet and climbed to his room. When he entered inside, he closed the door, turned on some worship music, and began to pray. Even if Lydia never spoke to him again, even if she cursed him from now on, Joshua was ready to pray for her, to bless her, and do everything he could to usher her into the graceful, loving hands of the Risen One.

***

"Ms. Lydia Claremont, we are trying to make this easy on you. But your non-cooperation is grounds for the harshest legal punishment the law will allow. We want to know the name of the boy who attacked Fred Gonzales." The judge sat still awaiting a response, her head propped up on her hand. Despite being no-nonsense in her demeanor, there was a sense of fairness, of wanting to mediate this situation. "Are you going to say nothing?"

The room was tiny, rectangular-shaped, and its light seemed to be suffocated by the wood panel walls and the proximity of the walls to each other. This room was created, Lydia was convinced, so a person would want to get out of it as soon as possible; the claustrophobia was a key ingredient in getting scared young people to confess or tell the authorities what they wanted to hear.

A large guard stood at the door behind Lydia, the door closed. Ms. Claremont sat next to her daughter. "Lydia? Judge Peterson is trying to help you avoid harsher consequences. Are you going to ignore her kind offer?" The hope between all parties was that little or no court would be necessary, that the punishment could be meted out through cooperation and contrition on Lydia's part.

Lydia lifted her shoulders as she pulled her arms in closer to her body. She kept her eyes fastened on a swirling wood grain on the heavy, mahogany table.

"Your scheme cost a young man a shattered arm," Judge Peterson said. "From what I hear, he'll be fortunate if he can play baseball for his team next Spring. Doesn't that mean anything to you?"

Again, there was only silence, as if no one else was in the room with her.

"Well, Ms. Claremont...I cannot regard your daughter's behavior as cooperative. Her record is spotless. If she wishes to live in a juvenile facility for the next twelve months or more, so be it." She pushed the chair back on the ceramic floor and then stopped herself momentarily.

"Lydia," her mother said forcefully. "Please! You need to tell the judge what she needs to know!"

As if jolted awake, Lydia blinked twice before lifting her face toward the judge. "Garrett Collins."

"I need his address, phone number—anything you can give me," the judge said and pushed a stencil notebook with a pen on top toward her.

Lydia wrote for thirty seconds, her head cocked to one side. She pushed the pad back across the table and resumed her blank stare at the table's surface.

Taking the pad into her hands, the judge stood and hovered over the table. "Ms. Claremont, the court will be in touch with you."

"Thank you for being willing to work with my daughter."

The judge gave a single nod before allowing the corners of her lips to upturn just enough to indicate a smile before the door was opened and she walked out.

Twenty-Nine: Sorting Things Out

Coming home from school, Joshua dialed Lydia's home number. He hoped to learn good news about Lydia from Ms. Claremont.

"Hello?" Joshua recognized the voice as Lydia's Mom.

"Hi, Joshua here. Just wondering if there's any news about Lydia?"

"She's cooperating with Judge Peterson. And I just finished reading today's newspaper. They picked up the boy that attacked that boy early last night."

Joshua expected the news of the attacker's arrest to make Ms. Claremont happy, at least hopeful. Instead, however, she sounded upset and troubled. "That's great...but what's wrong?"

"It says," she said looking for a place to read, "'Supposed Jaded Hearts gang member, who cannot be named for legal reasons, said to be seventeen years old, was taken into custody last night by city police for allegedly attacking a boy several years younger that resulted in the victim suffering a broken arm. According to officials, however, the gang member's actions were allegedly instigated by another student from Knott's End High School, a student who also cannot be named for legal reasons.'"

"Oh no," Joshua said almost in a whisper. "But at least she hasn't been named by the newspaper. No matter what, though, I suspect she'll never stop hating me for putting her in this mess."

"Well, Joshua, I would never expect you to have lied to the police. This whole matter was never in your hands to begin with. Lydia made choices...and although I do not understand why, and how she even had connections with this Garrett-character who's older than her and a gang member, she will need to learn the consequences of her choices." She paused just briefly. "Joshua?"

"Yes?" he replied bringing the lower part of the handset in front of his mouth.

"Has Lydia been involved in anything suspicious...at school or after school that has troubled you? Have you heard anything at all about her?"

"Not that I know of. She's just like any other girl that I know—except for being the most beautiful and sharpest of them all."

Ms. Claremont laughed briefly. "You have a great head on your shoulders, Joshua. I appreciate that you're sticking by Lydia's side through all this."

"The real question is...if she'll stick by me after what I did."

"She'd be making another foolish choice if she gave you up for something that she caused."

"I guess." Joshua thought for a second. "Did Lydia lock up her bedroom before she left?"

"They came and arrested her before she could go up to her room."

"If you're worried about anything, why don't you check her room? I don't think you'll find anything that will trouble you, but at least it would ease your mind some."

"I don't know. I don't want to betray her trust. Our relationship is already on thin ice as it is, I'm afraid." The line became silent.

"Yeah, I can respect your thinking about that."

"Call me anytime, Joshua. Hopefully I'll learn more soon about what's going to happen to her."

"I'll call or you can call my house anytime, too. Do you think it would be okay if I were to send Lydia a letter or card?"

"Why not? It can't hurt. Do you want the address?"

"Please."

There was shuffling as if Ms. Claremont were reaching and momentarily straining. "Okay, got a pen?"

Joshua took down the address of the facility. He hoped to immediately write her and try to resolve the issues between them. Perhaps she'd never date him again, nor walk with him or talk with him in school...but he wanted to at least be at peace with each other.

He could still remember the day they'd gone to church and walked out on the church grounds together. Although they had broken the rules of the youth group, Joshua had felt the electricity of the moment when he'd stood next to Lydia, hands held, their sense of connection strengthening with each heated second. Joshua was glad but also disappointed that the youth director, Tamera, had broken up their romantic flight. He still wondered what would've happened if she hadn't interrupted them. Would he have fallen? Could he have remained upright before the Lord had that temptation been fully unleashed on him? It worried him, even now, that he had to ask the question.

Joshua knew that God had ordained sex to be an awesome thing, and a rewarding thing, but that the Creator had set up permanent boundaries designed to prevent woundings or scars in people—both physical and emotional. Joshua didn't want to move outside those boundaries, not now, not ever. Still, it was one thing to believe something, but wholly another thing to still believe something when your emotions and body seemed to be pulling so wholeheartedly in one direction versus what your intellect and spirit wanted.

Pulling a notebook to himself, Joshua settled back on the sofa and began to write: *Hey Lydia, how are you? Listen, I just want to tell you I'm sorry. I don't know if my being sorry will mean anything to you, but I do feel that way. Although I know I did what I had to do (not lying to the police), I regret that what I shared with them ended up becoming a hardship on you. I didn't mean to get you in trouble...*

Joshua continued to write more but attempted to move off the whole affair and just write about normal, everyday stuff—what was going on at school, at the Club (kept brief, however), how Samuel seemed to be getting better, and how Joshua had barely but satisfactorily beat both his older brothers in basketball the day before. He kept the letter short, as it didn't make sense to write a ten-page letter when she might discard the letter completely. As he finished writing, he signed the letter, placed it in an envelope, found a wallet picture of himself to send her, and clasped the envelope between both of his hands: "Lord, I pray that you would minister to Lydia where she is right now, that she would come to know Your love, and the love I also feel for her. Please help her get through this time and find You in the process."

***

The Club met after school. The whole affair between Lydia and Joshua had become fodder for the masses, but Joshua wanted to make sure the Bible Club knew exactly what was happening. When all had gathered, twenty-one in number, Joshua called on the group. Sergio, Alistair, Jennifer, Brad all stood with the rest. The club had grown because of the events over the past several weeks. There was a sense of expectation in the air, but all of it was tapered by the news regarding Joshua and Lydia.

"I realize that there may be gossip flying about because of what has happened to my girlfriend, Lydia. She was placed in the city juvenile facility for being involved in ordering Freddie Gonzales to be attacked and beaten. I was surprised to learn this as I'm sure all of you were. Lydia is not a believer, yet, but I am confident that I can bring her to the Lord with time and patience."

"Missionary dating?" Jennifer asked with a grin.

Joshua heard the question from Jennifer. "I know it may seem that way. I have had to keep on my toes to keep from doing anything that I would regret later. But this whole relationship came about so quickly that—"

"That you forgot to ask the Lord about it?" Sergio asked.

"No, well, I didn't feel a prohibition from the Lord in being with her," he said, which was truthful although he could remember the receding of the Holy Spirit at several points during discussions with Lydia.

"Scripture says not to be unequally yoked with a nonbeliever," Sergio said. "It would be the same as if I and Alistair were hanging out with friends for long intervals of time, or at parties on the weekend...except that what you are doing could have a worse result."

184 | the Jesus boy

Joshua recognized that this had become an unspoken issue within the group without his knowledge. "I see. Do all of you think this?"

No one spoke up, but most faces looked grim.

Brad stood up from sitting on a desk. His voice was friendly and reconciliary. "Joshua, what Sergio is saying is that light has no part with darkness. You didn't have anything to do with the attack on Freddie, but some think you did just because of your link to Lydia."

"I regret that anyone would think that. Perhaps I did move too quickly in dating her but I want to pursue this to its natural end."

"Perhaps?" Sergio said standing up. His caramel skin became red as he approached being angry.

"I don't think," Joshua continued, "that all things are necessarily black and white. There are some things which defy labels and dogma. It's kind of like saying that God can't reach young people through rock music or other forms of music like rap or even thrash. We know that such forms of music, with the right message attached, can reach and influence young people."

"God used you mightily, Joshua," Sergio said. "But when we confront you about being linked to her, you tell us that not all things can be labeled black and white. We don't have anything against Lydia as a person."

"I am not being haughty. I just recognize that sometimes, God crayons outside the lines. His way of doing things doesn't always fit into our boxes nice and neatly."

"Joshua, I love you as a brother," Sergio said. "But has it occurred to you that Lydia came into your life just after you had made up your heart and mind to serve the Lord?"

Joshua nodded. "That is true."

"I do not believe it is God's will for you to date Lydia," Sergio said. "To be her friend, perhaps. But not to be joining yourself to her when she rejects Christ."

"I see you feel very strongly about this, Sergio. What about the rest of you? Brad? Jennifer? Alistair? Anyone else?"

Brad spoke up. "I agree that you should be very, very cautious. It is your decision and only you know what the Lord is speaking to your heart." Jennifer and Alistair nodded in agreement, as did others in the group.

"Or," Sergio interjected, "perhaps the Lord has already tried to speak to you but you did not listen. You were blinded by her comeliness or something else. You should consider that the Lord is using us to speak to you now."

"I am, but I feel I have kept myself pure and upright before the Lord. My first heart's desire is to bring her to the Lord. But I will not dump her because of ideology."

"Joshua! She had a guy beat up—" Sergio said, flustered.

"She told me she wanted Freddie talked to, not attacked. The boy that talked to him attacked him of his own volition."

"C'mon, Joshua! That's silly," Sergio laughed almost mockingly. "The boy was supposedly part of the Hearts gang. Do you really think the boy wanted to sit down and have a cup of tea with Freddie?"

"What are you saying?"

"I'm saying that she had him attacked, and that her connection to the Hearts makes the whole situation even more strange."

Joshua shook his head. "I know Lydia. She isn't like—"

"You don't know that, Joshua. You've been with her for what, two, maybe three weeks?"

"Yeah."

For the first time, there came silence in the room.

Joshua finally broke the silence. "Listen, I'm trying to sort this out, and I'm asking for patience with everyone." What troubled Joshua was the truth that he didn't truly know Lydia, that he had only been with her a short time. Was Sergio right? "How are you guys doing in your seeking?"

Everyone nodded. Brad spoke up. "It's been difficult, but I've been spending the time with Him. It's been a major thing to ignore the television, computer, and my phone."

Joshua nodded. "It takes diligence. And we need to guard against being complacent or letting our guard down. But as you seek Him, just remember that the first hour, just like the first day of a fast, is always the hardest. But if you press in, go with the intention of staying. If your heart is divided about being there, the Lord's presence and communion will be scanty at best and you'll only waste your time." Joshua flipped open his Bible and turned to a passage that he'd read long before that suddenly stuck out in his mind. He began to read from Isaiah 58.

Everyone listened. Joshua expounded on the passage. "The Scripture is saying that with the fasting will come a bridging of the generations, that the breach of unbelief, of ungodliness, that it will all be bridged because of dedicated fasting and sanctified living before Him."

"Amen," the students said in agreement.

Sergio folded his arms. "It is good to pray to the Lord," he said. Everyone turned their heads to listen to what Sergio. "But I have concluded that spending hours praying when we could be out there in the world helping to bring change, to usher people into the Kingdom, is a waste of time. I do not believe we need to be praying as Joshua says. If we pray an hour a day, God will still honor us as we do His work."

Joshua shook his head in stark disagreement. "When you spend time before the Lord, you learn what His heart is for the lost. You learn about your own heart and its lack of compassion for the lost and hurting in the world. It's as much about seeing the truth about yourself as it is seeing the truth about others."

"I can discover that through reading the Word."

"Then why did Paul go into Arabia for three years, Sergio? Why did our Lord Jesus go into the wilderness for forty days and nights?"

Sergio tried to think of an answer but became more flustered as he stood there. "I am going to be starting a separate group. Everyone here is welcome to be a part."

Joshua's eyes doubled in size. "You're going to divide the group?"

"Not divide. Find people like me who will work for change without spending hour after endless hour in prayer. God wants practical people, Joshua, not mystics who live in a monastery."

"But this seeking is only for a season, it won't last forever. It's a major key to having the power of God work through us." Joshua looked around, wondering if there would be anyone in the room with him after Sergio left. "Brad? Jennifer? Alistair? Do you agree with him?"

Brad shook his head. "I have experienced the power of God. I will stay the course here."

Jennifer agreed with Brad, as did Alistair.

"Can we pray for you before you go, Sergio?" Alistair asked.

"You're not going with me?" he asked his buddy.

"I don't feel right in my spirit about leaving. God isn't about division," he answered.

Sergio threw up his hands in disgust. "No need to pray for me! Enough with praying; time for some action!" With that, he walked out.

Everyone stared at each other in disbelief.

"Alistair, how long has he been feeling this way?" Jennifer asked.

"For the past week," Alistair said. "He was feeling frustrated that he couldn't settle down enough to spend time with the Lord. Then the stuff about Lydia and Freddie really set him off. And he also wasn't sure why it was presumed that Joshua should be heading the club."

"What about you, Alistair?" Joshua asked. "How has your seeking been? And are you okay with me leading here?"

"I have no problem with you, whatsoever. I echo Brad: Be careful with Lydia. As far as my seeking has been going, it's been a challenge just as Brad said. But I am seeking the Lord," he said with a wide, satisfied grin. "It's been actually amazing. Since seeing the miracle in Brad, I'm convinced totally."

"But," Joshua added sadly, "Sergio also witnessed the miracle."

Everyone nodded. Joshua spontaneously took the hands of those around him, and they all formed a circle. "Let's pray for Sergio. He's angry about a lot of things, and only the Lord can break through and help him."

***

That night, Joshua felt the irritation of seeing the club divided. It made Joshua feel sad, and he also felt genuine concern for Sergio's spiritual well-being. But also playing through his mind was the realization that Sergio was right, at least partly. He'd not stopped and sought the will and direction of the Lord regarding his dating Lydia. He had violated the Scriptures, which warned not to be unequally yoked. Still, he had hoped he could be a catalyst for change in Lydia. He had never planned to do anything unwise or impure. Had he been persuaded because of Lydia's outward beauty alone?

As Joshua sat in the presence of the Lord, he hoped the Lord would give him a renewed sense of direction. But nothing came. After fifty minutes of still silence, Joshua came off his knees and sat at the end of his bed.

He asked in a low voice, "Do I already know the answer?"

No hint of an answer came.

"Do I already know the answer to my question?" Joshua remembered the story of a Carolina preacher in the late-1800s who had come upon a poor family whose wagon-pulling horse had died in the middle of the path. Sheffy had been about to go off and pray when the Lord stopped him. There was no need to pray, because the answer was already provided: he'd give the family the horse he'd traveled upon for many years.

Was this the case for him? Had He answered but he'd ignored His words? Was only obedience needed? He noticed his gleaming white telescope sitting on its tripod over near the window, its lengthy lens stretched toward the blackness of the distant stars and planets. He wished he could peek through the telescope and be able to see a placard with the answers to his questions. Joshua hated these moments when he had to be cautious to find the right path. This was either a test of the heart or the answer had already been provided which meant he'd be risking his closeness with the One if he didn't recognize the answer and obey it.

"Do I really need to ask You these things? Is it true that I have overstepped, that it was never Your will for me to date Lydia?" Joshua could still remember the sense of withdrawal he had experienced when talking to Lydia, as if the Holy Spirit were telling him, "This is not a good idea."

"I ask Your forgiveness, Lord. I have grieved You." He fell back to his knees and leaned on the side of his bed. "Just give me time, Lord. It would be wrong for me to just abandon her. Wouldn't it?"

Joshua felt suddenly frustrated, both at the silence and the circular thinking he found himself in. Because of his not being sensitive to the Spirit, he'd left himself vulnerable, and not only had he been influenced, but so had the Bible Club and Sergio. The worst thing was, soon, it might result in Lydia being especially hurt as well.

Thirty: Mr. Frank Gelb

Upon Garrett Collin's entrance into the juvenile facility the same day that she had submitted his name to the judge, Lydia had considered the look of the young man: A large athletic boy shaped like an upside-down pear—the mass of the boy beginning with a large head planted atop a massive torso that tapered to long legs. The curly black-haired boy already had several pronounced tattoos on his tree-trunk arms. Collins had been brought in after the evening meal, so the boy had been given a sack lunch with a small plastic cup of juice. With the television blaring some ten feet in front of them—the other kids in various activities about the room, some playing table tennis, others pool, some huddled at the various sofas—Lydia sat at the middle of the same table as Garrett.
   "Hey," Lydia said.
   Garrett lowered the sandwich to the table and he turned to look at her. It was almost as if he'd turned to glare out a window instead of turning to greet someone. The look said, *Why are you speaking to me?* Clearly irritated but remaining silent, he turned back to his half-eaten, soggy sandwich ignoring her greeting.
   "Tony has a message for you."
   This time he turned and focused his eyes directly at Lydia, his expression suddenly softened and became more

approachable. "Is that right? What message would that be?"

"He knows you've already done a great job of putting that Gonzales boy in his place. But in doing what you did to him, I am now sitting here."

He turned his face and mouth back to the sandwich. "Who are you?" he said before taking a hefty bite, which left only a small portion of the sandwich left.

"It doesn't matter who I am."

"And?"

"And, you went too far in what you did to Gonzales."

"I did what I was told. Someone needed that boy to learn a lesson on manners. And nothing works quite as well as pain."

"Pain is one thing. Disability another!" She said biting her lip not to say any more. She stared at her hands in front of her. "Did you tell the police that you were told to attack that boy?"

"No," he said as he lobbed the last part of the sandwich into his mouth. Chewing and swallowing, he added: "I kept my mouth shut and told them I wanted to see a lawyer."

"Forget the lawyer. Tony wants you to admit that my instructions to you were only to talk to the boy, not hurt him. Do you understand?"

"Oh, so how do you know Tony?"

"That does not matter."

Without hesitation, Garrett picked up the small green apple took a huge bite—thereby eliminating half—and turned and smiled with a mouthful of apple. "You want me to be the fall guy for you?"

"This is Tony's instruction. Not mine."

"And did you give up my name to the cops?"

"I did not," she said lying. "Either someone saw you and turned you in, or the Gonzales boy was able to pick your photo out of the police album they have. From what I hear, you've been in trouble before on many occasions."

The boy chuckled. "Nothing new in that department. Coming to juvee is like homecoming for me; three meals a day, a bed to sleep in, basketball almost every day... Hell, I even get to learn a trade if I want to."

"What about your family?"

"I don't have a family, per se. I guess the only family I've known is the Jaded Hearts. They're the closest thing to a family I've ever known." He took another monstrous bite leaving essentially only an apple core.

"But you're just seventeen."

The boy swallowed. "Yeah, and I've seen enough in my seventeen years to fill a man twice my age."

"Will you do this for Tony?"

"Yeah, I'll do this for him. If they send me upstate, that's cool. I have friends up there anyway." He paused to rip open the bag of Lay's potato chips. "So how do you communicate with this Tony character?"

Lydia smiled. "I have my ways. Thankfully, not all the adults who work here have much of a salary."

***

Ms. Claremont had been tidying the house, going about her business as usual. She went upstairs to enter her bedroom when she found herself abruptly stopping in front of Lydia's room. She then felt a moment of surprise that her hand had lifted to the door handle and turned it so that the door seemed to float open as if inviting her inside her daughter's room. It was darkened and a bit stuffy, her bed made, almost everything in her room in its place. Walking to the window, Dottie pushed the curtains to the side and adjusted the blinds until light flooded the room. As she stepped away, though uncertain she was if she would leave or not, she heard something fall to the carpet floor. Bending down, Dottie noticed Lydia's cell phone. She presumed the phone had been sitting behind the blinds on the windowsill until she'd caused it to fall. She picked it up and sat on the edge of the bed. She pressed the menu button which brought up different options. Scrolling down to the "address book," she clicked on that which brought up a lengthy list of people and their addresses. She read through the list until her eye caught the name of Garrett Collins. She noted the date of its addition to the directory, September 12th, the day before Freddie Gonzales was attacked. She clicked on the caller ID function and began going backwards in time, hoping to see just whom she had talked to on September 12th. Only one name came up: Frank Gelb. Entering the number in the cellphone, Dottie heard the dialing.

A low male voice answered. "Hello? Shut up, I have a call!" the voice said to someone in the background, loud music playing. "*Tony?* You get out of jail already?"

"This is not Tony. Who are you? Why does my daughter have your number on her phone?"

It took less than two seconds before the phone went dead.

Nervously, and not quite sure what to think, Dottie turned off and replaced the cell phone where she'd found it. Going downstairs, however, she wrote down the phone number she'd memorized. Perhaps the police officer who had picked up her daughter would check the number out and find out who this Frank Gelb-character might be.

***

"Ms. Claremont? Where did you get this number? Frank Gelb is a dangerous man," the man's voice asked through the phone.

"He is?" Dottie scooted herself backwards on the bed, as if to steady herself from falling off it. "Why would he be involved with my daughter?"

"I'm not sure about that myself, Ma'am. Gelb is wanted on several arrest warrants out of Sioux City, but no one's been able to catch up to him as yet."

"What has he done?"

"He's thought to be behind most of the drug activities in Iowa. From what I've heard, he's known to travel to Chicago often, as well as Milwaukee and Detroit. But his home base seems to be Sterling City."

"So, he's from here?"

"Yes, ma'am. He's been around these parts going on twenty years."

"Okay, thank you, officer." She said. She'd hoped calling Officer Thomas would help her feel better, but alas, she now felt completely depleted and even more troubled.

"We're going to be using the number you gave us to try to locate this man. If you get any more information about Mr. Gelb, please let us know, Ms. Claremont."

"I will," Dottie said as she let the phone fall to her lap.

***

Dottie sat down on the bolted-to-the-floor steel bench awaiting her daughter to be brought to the visitor room. Finally, the door opened and in stepped Lydia. She wore a dark blue sweat suit with large white letters that showed Radford Juvenile Facility.

"Hi," Lydia said, seemingly at calm and a lot happier than on the previous visit.

Dottie sat ramrod straight and looked at her daughter without a blink.

"What's wrong?"

"Frank Gelb?"

Irritation appeared on Lydia's face for a split second, and if it hadn't been for the fact that Dottie knew her daughter intimately, she'd surely have missed the traces of alarm that she had seen flash across her face. "Who are you talking about?"

Looking down at her lap with a feigned smile, Dottie interlocked her hands and brought them to her lap forming a V with her arms. "I can remember," she said looking away and then up to the corner of the room, "the very first day that you told me a fib. Do you remember that day? You were just about to turn six."

"No," Lydia said plainly but pleasantly.

"You don't remember? You had asked me if you could make some blueberry Kool-Aid, and I had told you no, that we still had half a gallon of fruit punch in the fridge. Well, a few minutes later I heard this shattering of glass in the kitchen," Dottie laughed. "I thought the worst. As I ran into the kitchen, I remember you turning to me, you with the pig tails, covered in blue dust, your eyes scared and as big as golf balls. Do you remember what you said?"

"What, Mom?" she asked allowing a slight grin.

"You said, 'Momma, I didn't do it.'"

Lydia looked down at her hands on the table, and for all of two seconds allowed a smile. "I remember that now," Lydia said. "My problem was the fact that there wasn't anyone else around to blame."

Dottie smiled but then her mouth became a thin line. "I don't care about the past. I don't care about what you've done or not done. But I want the truth, because I love you. Who is this Gelb character? If you've gone down the wrong path—"

"I don't actually know him. My friends at school asked me to find some pot, and his name came up. I was told he'd be able to help us get what we wanted."

Dottie nodded as she brushed aside a long strand of her black hair. Although she did not show it, she was impressed that Lydia had admitted this, even if it was disheartening to think that her daughter was experimenting with drugs at such an early age.

Lydia continued. "We didn't actually get any drugs from him. I guess we were scared to go through with it."

"I see," Dottie said.

"Then I met Joshua, and it was as if I didn't want to try drugs anymore."

"That Gelb character is said to oversee the illegal drug traffic business for all of Iowa."

"How did you find that out?" Lydia asked.

"I called Officer Thomas and he warned me as soon as I mentioned his name." Dottie said. "Do you remember him, the one who came here and took you away in handcuffs?"

"They were plastic ties, Mom," Lydia rebuffed.

"The one who arrested you, Lydia," said Dottie calmly.

Lydia nodded reluctantly but said nothing. A few seconds passed with uncomfortable silence lingering between the two. "How's Joshua doing?"

"I think he was a bit disappointed about the visit the last time around. He really does care about you."

Lydia shook her head. "I don't know, Mom. I'm trying to forgive him. The fact is, he may care for me, but I'm not so certain it's the 'me' he wants, or whether it's just my soul he wants."

"I don't know that you can separate the two, and I understand if you don't want religion crammed down your throat—even by Joshua—but he is a good boy."

"You heard about the crippled boy at our school that was supposedly instantly healed?"

"Yes."

"Does that prove that God is real?"

Dottie gave a subtle shrug. "I happen to believe in Him," she said unashamedly. "The part I have difficulty with is the belief that He personally cares for any of us—or for me."

There came a light knock on the door, which meant to wrap up the visit.

"Well, thanks for coming by," Lydia said flatly as she stood to her feet and began to turn and move toward the exit.

Dottie quickly rose from being seated and walked briskly around the table toward her daughter. Without a word or warning, and before she could stop or protest it, her mom had already wrapped her arms around Lydia from behind. She held her gently yet firmly for several breaths.

***

Lydia walked in front of the female guard till they came to room thirty-five. Lydia felt intruded upon and embarrassed, almost as much as she found herself glad, and, somehow completed by her Mom's hug. She couldn't remember the last time, if ever, that they had hugged. The gesture had only lasted a few seconds, but the effect stayed with her; it was strangely warm and reassuring.

The guard unlocked the door and Lydia immediately spread her feet and arms apart so she could be patted down. Once inside, the door was closed behind her and abruptly locked. Her roommate, a chunky girl with deep red hair, lay on her bed quietly writing in a notebook. Lydia ignored her and plopped on her own bed. Thankfully the girl, named Stephanie, had kept mostly to herself since her arrival.

Although no one might've noticed it on Lydia's facial exterior, perhaps because of her Mom's last minute, unexpected, touch, she felt the annoyance of fear nibbling at her. Did Frank know what her Mom knew about him? If so, was he angry? Would her Mom be safe? As Lydia laid her head down on the hard, lumpy plastic that the juvenile facility called a pillow, she tried to think of how she could somehow appease Frank without something bad being done to her Mom.

Lydia also felt the irritation at lying to her mother. Normally she'd not have been concerned about the lie, since her concern was purely business-related, not personal. But the concern in her mother's face, and the sudden hug, had awakened Lydia enough to rouse her conscience.

But she was quick to remind herself of the stories she'd heard about Frank, about how dangerous he could be. And then, of course, there was the matter of Joshua. Was she to forget the boy—a naïve boy who had no idea about the real world? If she decided to forgive him, could she look past his blatant betrayal? Was it even sensible that she try to date, or even befriend, a boy who so obviously represented everything opposite of herself? Or was it okay to use Joshua if it helped preserve her image for the greater tasks she was responsible for? Was she truly willing to gain full-reign and leverage in the schools in the area but in the process, lose people she cared for—Joshua, her Mom, or even herself?

***

The next day, Lydia was surprised to hear her name being called at mail call. She retrieved the long envelope and saw Joshua's name written on the upper left-hand corner. She ripped the end of the envelope so she could pull out its contents, which was a single, folded page and a wallet-sized picture. She read the handwritten letter, which was warm and friendly. He mentioned Sam feeling better, the after-school Bible Club going well, his own sadness at not being able to see Lydia at the school, and most of all, his hope that she was doing okay. Despite still feeling the anger of Joshua's betrayal, she couldn't help but feel glad he had written her. And there was another realization about her...that she had been responsible for her own woes. Still, there was another part of her that nagged at her. How could Joshua have done the thing he had done with hardly any hesitation? Did she mean that little to him? But even as she resented Joshua's actions and questioned his betrayal, she also approved of the fact that he had come to visit her, that he had sent this thoughtful letter. She held up the picture, glad to have something that would remind her of the few times they had been together. But was there a future for the two of them together? She wondered.

Thirty-Two: The Turning of Events

It was within three weeks of Joshua's first letter (there came many cards and letters from him during her stay at the juvenile facility), Judge Peterson presided over the case in the juvenile court. It was there that Garrett told the judge that he had not been instructed by Lydia or anyone else to break the Gonzales boy's arm, but that Lydia had not been amused at his teasing and asked for the boy to simply be "talked to." Since the judge had been told the same testimony by Lydia at the beginning, she saw no reason not to accept her testimony, and especially since there wasn't any other evidence to the contrary.

    Almost one month later, Peterson would convict the Garrett boy, due partly to the heinous nature of the attack and in part due to the boy's lengthy juvenile record, of aggravated assault and sentence the boy to a little over three years in the Iowa State Juvenile Facility in Sioux City where he'd remain until he turned twenty-one years of age. The boy had not seemed unpleased nor angry at the verdict—there was simply no reaction from him at all.

    To Lydia, the judge spoke. "Your actions seem to me to have been minimal. Because of your reluctant but eventual cooperation, your containment for six weeks within Radford Juvenile Facility, and the belief by this court that you did not order the physical attack of Fred Gonzales, you are free to go."

"Thank you, your honor," Lydia managed to say to the relief of her mother.

"Very good. I hope you'll be careful who you interact with in the future. You have a bright future. It's truly up to you how your life turns out."

For the first time in a little over six weeks, Lydia walked past the court guards and joined her mother to go home.

"What a long stay," Lydia said relieved to be finally be free.

"Yes. But it could've been a lot worse," Dottie said as they walked side-by-side to exit the court room and head toward the elevator.

Descending to the ground level, they walked through the foyer to the outside of the courthouse. As they stepped outside, the sun beaming brightly, Lydia scanned the roads and parking lot as per usual before noticing the BMW parked opposite the courthouse. It was unmistakable. She tried to act as normal as possible and without alarm so not to arouse her mother's suspicion.

Lydia and her Mom found their car in the parking lot.

"I am so glad you'll be home. Your sister and I have really missed you."

Lydia nodded, appreciative that she seemed to be so happy that she was finally coming home.

Her mother put the car in reverse before stopping it abruptly. "What the—"

"What?" Lydia asked. Turning to look, Lydia saw the car—Frank's car—sitting in the way blocking them.

"That's strange. I didn't see that car there a moment ago," Dottie said matter-of-factly.

Lydia, looking in the side mirror, watched as the tinted window slowly descended to reveal the face of a man all-too-familiar. He wore dark sunglasses. And sure enough, the face turned toward Lydia for several seconds. It was menacing and unhappy.

"Is he going to move or what?" Dottie asked frustrated.

Finally, the car began to move forward out of the way. And it was just as it did that the man brought upward a clenched fist before lowering it again.

Lydia tried to maintain her control. "He's moved, Mom. It's okay. You can go ahead."

After getting out onto the main road to go back home, her mother tried to talk about this and that, and although Lydia listened and tried to be a good sport in making small-talk conversation, she found her mind fixed on the realization that Frank was especially angry with her.

"Did you hear me, Lydia?"

"What, Mom?"

"I said I'm going to be leaving the house this weekend for a work conference in Chicago. Can you watch after your sister for me?"

"Yes, no problem."

Nearly an hour later, Lydia had settled in her home again, glad for being home, finally. She dropped her plastic bag of various items she'd collected over the last six-plus weeks. Beginning to put the various items either in the garbage—she wasn't about to keep the generic shampoo, soap, toothpaste, and stubby toothbrush—or in their respective places in her bathroom, Lydia pulled out the small stack of letters and cards that Joshua had mailed to her. She wondered when she would see Joshua again—and what she'd do and what she'd ultimately feel toward Joshua at that moment they were reunited. For whatever reason, she'd not replied to any of his letters. Her feeling had been one of numbness, of being indifferent to take any action that would determine a path for the two of them. She'd just see what happened. Tomorrow in school, she considered however, she would see Joshua. And perhaps then she'd know what she wanted of Joshua, if anything.

Thankfully, Lydia's guidance counselor had coordinated with the juvenile facility, so she had been able to keep herself caught up in her school subjects. Lydia lay on her bed, and was glad for the quiet. There wasn't a single sound unlike what she was used to at the juvenile facility where there always seemed to be noise—people shouting, voices echoing down the hallway, metal doors slamming shut, chairs scraping across the ceiling above. She was home. She felt strangely warm and content for the first time in a long time.

***

She felt something scamper across her cheek. She looked up with a start. Joshua backed off with a jolt and a smile, a piece of string that he'd used to run across her cheek held in his hands.

"Hey," she said. She sat up to look for the clock and noticed her Mom standing in the doorway.

"Joshua wanted to come over and welcome you home," she said as she pulled the door three-quarters closed.

She sat up and looked at Joshua. "Hey." She ran her long fingers through her disheveled hair. "What time is it now?"

"It's just after eight."

"Wow, I must've been tired. I was out for almost five hours."

"Welcome home, Lydia," Joshua said, his voice hopeful.

Lydia stood up. This was their first time together since the first week of her time at the juvenile facility. She gave Joshua a neutral expression and walked to her mirror that sat atop her dresser. "I'm glad you came by tonight. I wanted to talk to you."

"I thought so. I didn't get a letter back from you. I still don't know how you feel toward me."

She kept her back to Joshua as she sat on the padded stool and stared at her reflection in the mirror. "When I first went to Radford," she said looking at him in the glass, "I believed I knew what my heart said, that what we had, ever so briefly, was over…that what you had done to me was inexcusable…that you had betrayed me, that I could not forgive you for that."

Joshua slowly lowered himself onto the end of Lydia's bed.

"Your letters were sweet. Your cards helped me think beyond where I was. I was able to think a lot in there—probably too much…about myself, my family, and you."

"And?" Joshua asked. "Was that a good thing?"

Lydia allowed silence to fill the room between them. "Yes," Lydia finally said plainly. "I needed that 'time-out' to think about what is important, and what I want to do with myself."

"So…what is important to you? What did you decide?"

She swiveled on the stool and faced Joshua. "That I am responsible for my own actions and choices."

"Go on," Joshua said, clearly impressed with Lydia's words thus far.

"I recognized that I needed to own up to the reasons I was in the juvee facility in the first place: it was my choices that led me there. And if I was to be true, to myself, to you, to everyone around me, I also could not date you again." Her expression remained neutral and matter-of-fact. She swiveled back to face the mirror.

Joshua leaned forward toward her. "You don't want me to be in your life?"

"It's not that you can't be in my life. It's that I don't think I can be in your life, Joshua. On the second week of my time at Radford, I realized that you are a quality person, a rarity among guys…that there is something bright and innocent about you. But in the end, I realized, you have shown me what priority I have in your life."

"But I had to obey—"

"And," she interrupted with a pause, "I expect you to obey. But that is exactly why I cannot be your girlfriend. I have never been second fiddle for anyone, and that includes you, Joshua. That includes even your God."

Joshua looked down. He stared into his hands. Without thought, he picked at a flake of excess skin on his hand. His voice shook, "But Lydia… Don't you know by now…that…I really love you?"

Was he almost crying, Lydia wondered? "You don't love me, Joshua. You love your God. It's Him you should be dating, not me. As you can see already, I'm not quite a Mother Teresa."

"I don't want a Mother Teresa. I want you."

Lydia stood up, approached Joshua, and reached down and pulled him to his feet. She looked into his eyes, and for the first time since knowing him, she saw the tears welling up.

"I've missed you so much," Joshua said. "I didn't want to hurt—"

Lydia moved closer until her lips finally touched his. Then, as suddenly as she had engaged her lips with his, she pulled back. "Good night, Joshua."

Joshua hesitated, but eventually turned and walked out. Waiting until she heard the front door close behind him, Lydia approached the stack of letters and cards that were bundled tightly within a rubber band. She picked them up, stared for a moment, and then dropped them into her wastebasket. It was time for her to get back to her work. She had things to do, and being in a love affair was the lowest of her priorities now.

***

Joshua had asked his Mom to drop him off at Lydia's house. He had not expected what had just happened to happen. And since he didn't feel like calling his mom to come back and pick him up again, he decided to walk the distance; although it might be a thirty-minute walk or longer, he didn't mind.

He'd been walking for ten minutes when a familiar car pulled up alongside Joshua.

"Joshua, let me take you home," Dottie said through her lowered window.

With some hesitation, Joshua finally nodded and crossed the street. He wanted to refuse, but he couldn't find it within himself to be rude, not to Lydia's Mom. Besides, perhaps she would have insight into what was going on. He climbed in and said hello.

"She ended it, eh? I'd asked Lydia where you were, and when she didn't answer me, I knew the answer."

"I deserved it. I shouldn't expect her to forgive me."

"Just give her time, Joshua. At the least, she'll always have a good friend in you. And the truth be told, I know she still cares for you... But right now, she's looking out for herself, first."

Joshua nodded. He didn't quite know exactly what to say. On the one hand, he felt a churning within himself that left Joshua feeling almost sickly. On the other, he realized that he was free now to pursue the Lord, that his attention would no longer be divided. But still...he'd wanted to be with Lydia. He'd not expected the brushing off he'd just experienced. But being brushed off wasn't quite the feeling he felt; it was more like being crushed by a mountain's weight.

Getting home, Joshua walked inside his house and headed toward his room.

"Mom, I'm home," Joshua yelled. His prayer several weeks before had been answered. Proceeding into his room, and happy no one had intercepted his entrance, he closed the door behind him. He had a little white stool that he would sit down on to pray. The answer to his prayer several weeks before about Lydia had been answered. Sitting down, he closed his eyes, lifted his hands, and approached the throne of his Father.

In the next hour, he communed with the Lord, feeling the fullness of His upholding power course through him. As Joshua stooped low with a humble heart, there came a lifting up, as if the hand of God Himself had lifted him, so that the joy filled him, and strength anew came in mighty waves. There was the temptation to be content with that and depart, but Joshua remained. He knew the secret. He knew that what was offered at the outset of entering communion with the Lord was just the edge of what a person on earth could experience. He pressed in, keeping his heart and mind focused on the Father, lifting Him up in heart and spirit, with voice, and with uplifted hands. In those moments of reunion with the Most High, and with considerable effort of his own, everything in his life was forced to fall away, like the rockets falling away from a space shuttle climbing to reach its orbit. There wasn't the heartbreak and disappointment of leaving Lydia's house; there were no homework or tests to worry about; he forgot about his brother being sick, or Sergio leaving the club angry. It was just him and the Lord. But one thing did remain on his mind: The onset of the 15th of November. It was two days away, and the others had prepared. They still did not know where they would go, or what the results would be, but they were prepared, ready, and willing.

Thirty-Three: November 15th

"Where should we go, Lord?" Joshua asked as the group prayed and listened for His guidance. "Show us where we should go. We want to be led by You."

It was Saturday early afternoon. Despite a chill in the air, Joshua, Alistair, Jennifer and Brad had gathered in the city square of Sterling City. Two sat on the cold steel of the park benches; Alistair sat Indian-style on a patch of grass while Joshua calmly paced a 3- by 5-foot area. They had been praying for a little over forty-five minutes, asking the Lord what they were to do today.

Alistair stood up. "I want to impact Sterling City!" he said. "I want them to know His power!"

Joshua grinned. "Alistair, people want to know His love. And that must be our motive."

Alistair nodded. "Amen!"

"Anyone sense a leading from the Holy Spirit?" Joshua asked. No one gave an answer for several moments.

Jennifer spoke up. "Joshua, where could we go that the impact would be both immediate and even verifiable?"

"What do you mean verifiable?" Joshua asked.

"If God does a powerful work through us, it would be good if it were in a place where questions to its authenticity wouldn't arise."

"How 'bout the hospital?" asked Brad. "Anywhere else, the Lord's power could be questioned. But surely not a hospital."

"Sounds like a good place to me," Joshua said. "Anyone sense something different from the Spirit?" When no one answered, Joshua continued. "But how can we get in there? There are so many rules nowadays about protecting people's privacy and the like."

"Leave that up to me," Jennifer said with a grin. With that, the four began heading toward the hospital which was located several blocks over from the city square.

When they walked through the hospital doors, a dark-haired receptionist with a kind smile greeted them. "Hello, can I help you?"

Jennifer took the lead. "Yes, is the chaplain in today?"

"I believe so," the woman said. As she picked up the telephone receiver, she asked, "Can I ask the reason for your visit today?"

"Well, we're from Knott's End High School. As part of the Bible Club, we were hoping to glean anything we could from the chaplain, to learn how he ministers to people—especially in distressing circumstances."

"Oh," the woman said, surprise in her voice. She seemed quite impressed. "Have a seat and I'll try to get a hold of Chaplain Davis. That's nice that you young people want to help people."

The teens nodded and listened as the receptionist picked up the telephone and dialed. "Yes, Chaplain Davis? There are some young people here from the high school's Bible Club wanting to meet you." "Yes." "There's four of them visiting today." "Okay." When she hung up the phone, she smiled and said, "Chaplain Davis will be with you in just a few moments."

The hospital had been recently been modernized, so everything within the facility had a new, modern look to it.

A few moments later, a tall, silver-haired man came walking down the hallway. "Hi," he said cheerily, a smile on his face. He wore red button-up shirt and dress slacks. He would've looked like a visitor to the hospital were it not for his official-looking identification hanging loosely from his neck.

As Joshua stood to shake his hand, he noticed the significant silver moustache that failed to hide his warm smile. Joshua noticed the chaplain had the etchings of crow's feet around his eyes, but they seemed to convey warmth and an unspoken wisdom about life. Everyone joined Joshua to greet him, introduced themselves before shaking his hand.

"I'm Chaplain Davis." He appeared stout with a slightly bulging stomach, but fit otherwise. "How can I help you today?"

"We're from the Bible Club," Jennifer began, "out of Knott's End High School. We wanted to learn firsthand how you minister to people."

"Oh, very good," he said pleased. "Follow me." They walked down the same shiny hallway the chaplain had come until he stopped, opened a door, and directed the teens into his office with a pleased smile. "Please, come in and have a seat."

The chaplain sat down behind his dark mahogany desk. "I must say, it's a rarity to have young people sitting in my office. What a pleasant change!"

"We were wondering," Jennifer asked, "if we might accompany you when you visit with the hospitalized today."

"That's a difficult hurdle to grant. The people here...well, some of them are very private about their faith—if they even have a faith. We don't want anyone feeling uncomfortable or any kind of pressure."

"Chaplain Davis," Joshua said. "We came today because we felt the Lord leading us to come."

"Leading you? How do you know He was leading you?" the chaplain asked respectfully.

"We just know," Brad said as he pushed his glasses against his face with a hint of professionalism and something akin to pride.

Chaplain Davis's eyebrows arched. "Is that right?" he asked with an uncertain smile.

Brad continued. "The Lord wants to show Himself strong in the lives of His people; He wants to work through us—and anyone who is humble of heart."

Again, Chaplain Davis smiled. "That's wonderful that you want to mirror His heart to help people. But I'm afraid I can't give you permission to visit those who are with us here." He paused. "But if I can answer any questions you may have about ministering to the sick or their loved ones, I am glad to listen and share any experiences that might help you learn something helpful."

"What if we accompanied you only," Alistair asked with his characteristic smile, his face aglow, "and if people ask for prayer, or you know people who are open to prayer, then we could have the chance to exercise our spiritual muscles?"

"Spiritual muscles, eh?" Chaplain Davis asked warmly. "And what if a Hindu asks you for prayer. Are you willing to pray to the god or gods that that person believes in?"

For a moment, Alistair closed his eyes at the question, as if searching for an answer. He ran his fingers through his raven hair. "That would be hard for me to do," Alistair admitted.

It was clear that Mr. Davis was being more than courteous, Joshua thought. "Mr. Davis...might we pray for just one person?" At that question, all four leaned toward Mr. Davis awaiting his answer.

"Well," the chaplain said, teetering on the edge of giving in once for all.

Alistair interjected, his eyes taking on a determined look. "We promise to be courteous. We just want to be an encouragement to people in need."

The chaplain shrugged his shoulders. "How can I refuse? Okay," the chaplain said which caused the teens to leap to their feet and congratulate each other. "I must say," he added in response to their enthusiasm, "I've never seen such zeal to pray for people—especially young people!" He watched them quickly sit back down, their excitement brought to a controlled, if suppressed, level. He continued. "Here's the deal. We have a patient who's in intensive care. He's been in a coma for about three days now."

"What happened to him?" Jennifer asked.

"A car crash," Chaplain Davis said soberly. "It was pretty bad. The point is, he's unconscious. I don't think he would mind if you said a prayer for him. However, his wife is there. I'll need to get her permission." At that, the chaplain stood. "Follow me," he said with resignation in his voice.

Together they took an elevator to the 3rd floor, which was where the more serious medical situations were kept under close observation. The chaplain asked the teens to stay in a specific area till he had made sure the man could be prayed for at that time. Within several minutes, the chaplain returned. "The man's wife says you can pray for him. She's happy for your concern for her husband."

Joshua's eyes enlarged in pleasant surprise, glad how things were turning out. "Can we see him now?"

"Let's go," Chaplain Davis said before leading them almost to the end of the hallway. The offense of urine, excrement, and detergent assaulted the nose, but Joshua ignored it. This was a place of weakness and of recovery. And, he hoped, of miraculous recovery if the four of them had their way. Entering the hospital room, they found a man with his eyes shut tight, laying in the bed, many tubes of various diameters thrust into his mouth and down his throat as well as attached to his arms. A heart monitor beeped incessantly. The wife rose from her sitting position to greet them. Her eyes were red and puffy. "If you can help my husband, please… We have three children. My husband's name is Tom Snyder."

Joshua lowered his head. "We can do nothing," Joshua said truthfully and evenly. "But we will be obedient and ask the One Who can."

"Thank you." She stood off to the corner. The chaplain joined her side.

The four moved toward the man. Jennifer piped up, "Can we lay our hands on him?" The chaplain looked at the wife who nodded.

Immediately, they laid their hands on the man, two on each side. They lowered to kneeling positions and began to pray quietly, mumbling their intercessions. Five minutes passed, and then ten. When fifteen minutes came and went, Mr. Davis moved to end the praying.

"Young people," he began until Joshua had raised his hand to suddenly quiet him.

"In the Name of Jesus," Joshua began and raised his voice for the first time during their time praying. "Awaken. We command the broken in this body to be mended. We come against the spirit of darkness that wants to rob, steal, or kill Tom. In Jesus' Name, we give thanks for the complete restoration!" A full minute passed. Several more minutes. But nothing seemed to change for the man. Finally, Joshua stood up with his head fixed on the floor, along with the others.

To the wife, Joshua finally looked at her before saying, his voice level, "We will continue to pray for him, even after we leave here."

"Thank you," she said with a smile bordering on crying. She reached out and took Joshua's hand. "Thank you for caring enough to come here." She was about to let him go when she instinctively gave Joshua a hug, and then the others.

Walking down the hallway, Joshua felt puzzled, even depleted. He felt ashamed that he felt this way. He didn't want the others to know his uncertainty of why the man had not been immediately restored.

"What happened?" Brad finally asked from behind as he followed the others. "Did we do anything wrong?"

"It's all in God's timing," Jennifer said, though she seemed to be trying to convince herself as much as the others.

As they got to the elevator and pushed the button to descend, Joshua felt the sting of tears at his eyes. He desperately wanted to be alone.

Jennifer must've noticed. She placed a hand on his shoulder. "Don't be disappointed, Joshua. We did all we can."

"I just wanted the best for that man...for Tom," he said, his voice shaking. "I can just imagine if that was my Dad in there—and it was me and my brothers facing the prospect of losing him."

As the elevator doors opened, there came a shout from down the hall to hold the doors open. They turned to see the chaplain scuttling toward them. They stepped inside the elevator holding the doors open before the chaplain joined them.

"Great job, young people!" he said facing the teens.

They each nodded, though their demeanor was both pensive and crestfallen.

"What's wrong?"

Jennifer answered. "We were hoping to see God do a miracle in that man. And *nothing* happened."

"I see." The chaplain nodded. "But you are wrong," he said beaming.

"How?" Alistair, wearing a distressed look, asked, all four attentive to Mr. Davis even as the elevator reached the ground level.

"Didn't you see how special that prayer—that show of support—meant to that lady? For a moment...my God...you helped her carry a burden so heavy. You gave her hope and you helped her to believe herself. You let her know that others care."

Joshua looked away, fighting to keep from crying. Finally, he felt himself collapse to his knees even as the elevator doors opened. There was nothing else that he could do. He hid his face from the others even as his shoulders shook.

The other three kneeled down beside him and laid their hands on him, trying to comfort him and hold him. Even the chaplain placed his hands on the boy's head. "The Lord comfort you," he prayed, "and make His face to shine upon you. May you know the richness of your service today, that it was *not* in vain."

A moment later, Joshua raised himself and wiped away the trail of tears that had coursed down his cheeks. The chaplain gave the kids his business card and asked them to return soon. He would be waiting for them.

Stepping outside, the blustery wind met them and reminded them that winter was coming. They walked for some time, still silent.

Suddenly and as if no one else were there beside him, Joshua lifted his hands heavenward. "I praise you, Lord God. I give You praise and thank You for the joy of walking in fellowship with You. We are obedient...we want to be obedient even if not one is healed. But we cry out for those who need Your healing grace. Extend Your hand, O Lord, and show forth Your power, that Your Name might be glorified and many people come into Your Kingdom."

With that, the others sensed the spoken prayer at an end, and they all said in unison, "Amen."

* * *

Joshua had expected a great move of God, and yet all that had happened was that his own faith was moved in a direction he'd not expected, if only briefly, but enough to shake him. Had their work and preparation of almost two months been for the wrong motivation? He didn't think so. They had been careful to ascribe all glory to the Lord. They had sought to do this work for the purpose of testifying to people of the Resurrection of Jesus, just as the early Church had done.

Still, the whole situation brought Joshua to a point of self-examination. It was conceivable that something in his life had caused the lack of power to flow. Or was this all a test of their hearts? Some people would lose heart and give up. Others would scoff and make fun of the whole idea that God wants to work miracles through a human vessel. This idea Joshua ignored entirely. He had witnessed with his own eyes the power of the Lord, for it had worked in Brad, and in Cary, and the drunk who was made sober after a catnap. The fact remained that those truly called, or chosen, would not—could not—give up. They would continue regardless of the difficulties of the journey. And, they would never turn back.

Joshua arrived home and as was custom, he ascended to his room and quieted himself before the Lord. He prayed for a heart that would reflect His character and the likeness of Christ, that he would trust regardless of outward appearances. And it was there that the air of dread seemed to drop into his spirit like a lead weight in a fish tank. It was almost as if a dark cloud had drifted into his room. There seemed to be a physicality to it. Like before, Joshua sensed that the group, specifically the four, were about to enter a time of grave testing, and that before things broke loose in the natural, the hearts of each of them would come to the denominator of who they truly were in Christ. Joshua began to intercede and ask the Lord to help and strengthen them for what lied ahead.

***

The darkness had watched with the equivalent of a bated breath—their forces arrayed and pressing in on every side to keep the man named Tom Snyder from recovering. Even with reinforcements brought forth from the rear, the strong ones, there was little that could stop the Spirit's power from entering the man as the foursome prayed and petitioned and commanded that the broken body be restored and change direction—to move toward life, and not toward death.

Thirty-Four: Something Amiss

The onslaught came quickly, without warning. The darkness moved in concentrated patterns—their strategies in place as they began to attack those who bore the Risen One's light.

***

On the Monday morning after their visit to the hospital, all gathered under the flutter of Old Glory, the cling-clang of the rope and metal against the pole sounding as if to beckoning everyone to come near. The usual people, Jennifer, Alistair, Joshua met beneath its shadow. All, that is, except for Brad.

"Where is he?" Jennifer asked. Today she'd worn her hair pulled back into a braided pony tail that reached down the middle of her back. "He never misses school."

"I hope he's okay," Alistair said crouching down and laying down his book bag on the cement all in one motion.

Joshua felt something amiss in his spirit. Jennifer was right. It wasn't usual for Brad to miss school. Even when he had been wheelchair prone, he still was vigorous about being in school every day.

"Is everyone doing okay?" Alistair questioned. He looked up briefly but cast his dark eyes toward the horizon, the sun now hovering over the tree tops, its warmth streaming toward the group casting off the brisk chill of the morning.

Everyone nodded, but there wasn't a great deal of enthusiasm. Joshua saw how everyone felt. "Listen, why don't we gather together after school and we can seriously pray?"

Again, everyone nodded. "Sounds like a good idea," Alistair said. "I don't know about the rest of you, but I could use it."

"If you can," Joshua asked Alistair, "try to invite Sergio. Give him the message that we're missing him. And I'm sorry if I offended him."

"I'll see him in a few of my classes. I'll let him know."

"Cool, thanks."

The warning bell suddenly pierced the still morning air. Just as Joshua and the others began to walk toward the entrance, Lydia walked past them at a steady pace. Seeing Lydia jarred Joshua, for he realized how much it hurt that she hadn't said anything to him nor acknowledged his presence as she walked by him. He tried to walk with the others and act unaffected, but perhaps he tried too much, for both Jennifer and Alistair placed their reassuring hands on his shoulder. He felt better with their touch, but then as Lydia pulled open the door, she turned and briefly looked Joshua in the eye. Joshua wasn't expecting this. The look was stony and flat—no emotion exhibited, neither anger, regret, nor gladness to see him. It lasted only a split second, but it was long enough to remind Joshua that he was no longer with Lydia and that he was the furthest, it seemed, that a person could be from her. It would've been one thing to experience the break-up and still be friends; in their case, however, there was the complete shattering of all ties.

Joshua didn't quite understand Lydia, or her actions against him. He did understand her anger, and her resentment toward both him and the Lord…but not the decision that the entire relationship be cut off.

Being so blatantly reminded of his loss, however, he prayed to the Lord asking for His comfort and strength. He neared his locker and prayed quietly—just beneath his breath—as he opened it up and grabbed the necessary books he'd need for his first three classes. "Lord," he whispered as he slowed down long enough to release his prayer. "You know my heart. I feel the pain of knowing I am no longer together with Lydia. But I'm also glad You helped me to remain true to You—that I didn't lie. Just please help me, and help her." He finished his prayer and slammed his locker door.

When he walked into science class several hours later, he'd already prepared himself for the realization that he would be in the same class, two aisles removed, from Lydia—yet it'd be as if they were on opposite sides of the planet from each other. He took his seat at his desk and kept his eyes directed toward his textbook and notebook. He didn't know why he was trying to avoid looking at her though he realized it was likely that he didn't want to feel any worse than he already felt.

"Hi Joshua," she said in a low tone. Joshua turned toward the voice and tried to hide his surprise. She had spoken to him.

"Hey Lydia," he said turning to her briefly—maintaining a calm and neutral expression. He turned and faced the chalkboard feeling slightly awkward. He turned back toward her trying his best to hide his discomfort. "How are you?"

"Okay," she said giving a slight smile. "And you?"

"Been better, to be honest," Joshua answered even as Mr. Opal entered the class and gave his customary greeting.

Joshua sat staring forward, but clearly felt astonished. What did these things mean? Had she forgiven him? Was she wanting to be friends? More than friends? Or was this some sinister scheme to get his hopes up? It occurred to Joshua that she might want to play with him for a bit. Was she really that spiteful? Was it possible that she had ordered the beating of Freddie? And regardless of what she had had done to Freddie, how did she have such intimate connections with the Jaded Hearts?

When the bell rang fifty minutes later, everyone exited to head to lunch. Joshua, however, deliberately loaded his book bag slower than usual to see what might happen.

"I saw Brad earlier," Lydia said as she rose and prepared to leave.

"You did? I thought he was absent today."

Lydia slowed and there appeared a somewhat smug expression on her face. "He was in a wheelchair again."

"He was?" Joshua couldn't believe the look on her face. Was she glad to have seen such?

"You sound surprised."

"I am," Joshua admitted. "I saw the Lord heal him."

"Are you sure it was God?"

"Who else would it be?"

"The mind is powerful. Perhaps the healing was always inside Brad and you helped him unlock it."

Joshua didn't like that answer whatsoever. "No. You can have your theories about how it happened if you want, but I know that I know what happened to Brad was the hand of God."

Lydia nodded but it was the "I-know-better-than-you look." "Okay, let's say it was. Then why is this miracle suddenly not so miraculous? Doesn't this validate that God doesn't really care?"

Joshua did not give an answer. In his mind, it was worthy of an answer but he knew Lydia wouldn't hear it. She began moving toward the doorway before she slowed and in a neutral tone, said, "Bye Joshua," and then walked out.

Joshua waited a few seconds before also leaving the class and then began a search throughout the hallway to find Brad. *What's happening?* He felt troubled, and he didn't know what to say. He felt the churning within him, and a hint of something strange within him: anger. Was what Lydia said true? He knew God was good, and that He cared for people. But despite this, there was a part of Joshua within him that had receded. But as he thought about it, he realized that he felt more than anger, but something even more dangerous. It was betrayal. And as much as he tried to reject the onslaught of feeling betrayed in his heart, it kept rearing its ugly head like angry ocean waves pounding a desolate beach.

Several moments later, Joshua saw the wheelchair moving down the hallway and the one he was looking for inside it. He raced to catch up to it. "Brad?"

Brad swiveled the wheelchair toward Joshua who bent low toward him. He did not say anything but merely looked at him.

"What's happened?" he said in disbelief. He saw the twisted look of the boy's wrists and hands. His face was ashen, appearing thinner than he'd noticed of him the previous week.

"I don't know," he said. "Yesterday before going to church, I felt fine. But during the afternoon, I began to have extreme pain in my various joints and muscles. When I woke up this morning, the pain had subsided but I found I could barely rise out of bed." Brad lowered his head. "I had to have my parents help me get out of bed and get dressed. I was helpless...again. My Mom took me first thing back to my doctor this morning. He said whatever reverse happened before isn't holding."

Joshua heard the bad report but was equally concerned about his level of trust in the Lord. "Are you okay spiritually, Brad?"

"No, I'm not." He looked around him before continuing. Seeing no one there, he added, "I'm scared, Joshua." He took in a deep breath. He asked softly, "Do you think I did something wrong?"

"No, Brad," Joshua answered. "Absolutely not! Any healing from Him is according to His grace and love—not based on things we have done or not done. Do you feel you've done something wrong?"

"No."

Joshua thought aloud. "Lydia said she saw you in the wheelchair. I truly can't believe this is happening to you!"

"Don't worry. I don't understand what's happening, but I'll just trust Him no matter what."

Joshua reached out and placed his hand on Brad's shoulder. "Yes, I know you will. And I'll be with you no matter what happens."

"What's going on?" Brad asked, and for a moment, he appeared on the brink of crying. "How can I ask or expect God to do miracles if He won't even do them—or sustain them—*in me*? I'm afraid I won't be much of a faith-builder when they see me bound in this chair."

"No matter what, you've got to trust in the Lord," Joshua said. "No matter what! You must trust in Him despite the circumstances."

Brad nodded. "It's so embarrassing. I feel like I'm a reproach to the Lord," he said as he began to roll toward the cafeteria. "Everyone's been looking at me, and without words they shout, 'Where's your God now?' and 'What about your testimony of healing?'"

"Your testimony remains the same," he said walking along with Brad. "You were healed. You did come to trust in Jesus. Nothing about your testimony is a reproach to the Lord. And you can't control what happens to your body. But you can control your mind and aim to position your heart so it doesn't get bitter—that it remains open to Him and His love."

Brad began to move off without saying anything.

"Do you want me to pray for you again...now?" he said as he followed along.

"I don't know if I can go through being well again and then fall backwards to sickliness again. That's too much for any heart to go through."

Joshua felt frustration at this whole scenario. He knew full well that although he himself believed in healing, even though he wanted it especially for Brad, it was ultimately the move and power of God's Spirit that brought forth healing. "Let me pray." Joshua laid his hands on Brad's shoulders and began to pray. After nearly a minute, Joshua ended his prayer. No immediate change, however, in Brad took place.

Brad looked up. "What happened specifically last time...I mean, did you initiate the conversation with me, or was it the Lord specifically leading you?"

229 | t h e j e s u s b o y

"I remember the way the thought dropped into me as I walked by you. The voice spoke softly, yet so strong. And I was so petrified to obey."

Brad nodded and grinned. "I was surprised because few if any other kids would ever talk to me. So when you began to, it was refreshing and so welcome. I knew it must be important, especially when the teacher began to grow irate and come at you."

Joshua chuckled. "Yes, I was scared. Mr. Bell is the biggest teacher in this school! And when nothing happened, I was even more scared. But you know I had to trust the Lord. And there I was heading down the hallway, late for class, when I heard from behind the loudest crack. But then I realized that it was bones popping into their proper position and alignment."

"I will always be thankful to the Lord for that gift of goodness," Brad said. "No matter what happens to me now or in the future."

"Amen," Joshua said. "Come on, let's get lunch.

***

Later, after school, the Bible Club gathered. Altogether, there were thirteen students. When they saw Brad enter the classroom in the wheelchair, everyone gathered around him and effortlessly showed their concern and support. They prayed, hugged, and talked to him, giving him encouragement both in seeking the Lord about the situation at hand and in trusting the Lord, regardless of what had happened. Joshua quieted the club.

"Listen, we must not lose our focus or our hope. It is God Who has called us out of darkness, and it is He Who will keep us from it. We must not allow the distractions—any distractions—to cause us to be sidetracked. Do we agree?"

"Amen," everyone shouted in unison.

"We will face tests, trials, and tribulations," he said. "As we are seeking the Lord, we must not forget that the enemy is going about like a lion, seeking whom he may devour. But we will not be victims to his attacks. We will fight back, but not alone. The Lord will go before us, and He will be our rear guard."

They began to pray, beginning with spoken praises to the Lord. As they began to move into worship, a sense of joy and unity began to fill the room. Soon, without anyone directing, they reached for each other's hands and just prayed. Although the sheep could not see the Shepherd, the more they prayed, mixing their prayers with upward flowing praise and worship, the more the sheep recognized an immovable peace begin to arise within them. The Shepherd had not forsaken them. There was the sense that He was watching and with them.

Even Brad noticed a change in his own heart toward his own predicament; he would trust in the Lord, and wait on Him patiently. He would not allow the torment of fear to fill his mind; instead, he would steady himself and keep his eyes on the One Who could save him, or give him the power to pass through the test at hand—even if it meant to live in a wheelchair the rest of his life.

Thirty-Five: Migrations

Arriving home, Joshua went into the kitchen to find something to eat. His Mom was there working a crossword puzzle at the kitchen table, her dictionary right beside her.

"Hey Mom," he said as he opened the refrigerator and scanned it for anything quick and easy to replenish himself.

"How are you, son?" she said without looking up.

"Fine," he said, which was partly true. The Monday had been difficult until the afternoon club had had their time of rigorous prayer. From then forward, however, the day had taken a turn for the better. Even the air around him felt different as if he could breathe easier.

"What's been going on with you and Lydia?"

Joshua felt a momentary encroachment with his mother's question. He preferred not to revisit that part again—at least not now. But then he reconsidered: Perhaps it would help to talk about what he'd been feeling. "We broke up several days ago. She couldn't handle me giving her name to the police."

"I see. It didn't seem like her to be that way, did it? She seemed so nice when I met her."

"That's true," he said as he pulled out lunchmeat, cheese, a tomato, ketchup, and Miracle Whip. Setting the things on the other end of the table from her mother, he continued. "Her whole personality changed after it became known that she was tied to Freddie being beat up. It's like she was a different person."

"So, are you both still friends?"

"Nope. She doesn't want anything to do with me. And then Brad seems to have had a relapse in his healing. He's had to revert to using his wheelchair again though his present condition is still better than before," he said avoiding his mother's eyes. "Believe it or not, but Lydia seemed to relish that he's been forced back into his wheelchair again."

"Really?" she asked, disbelief in her voice.

Joshua nodded. "Yep." Pulling out four slices of bread, he began to build his sandwiches. "She wanted me to admit that God had abandoned Brad, that if He is there, He doesn't care."

"She sounds jealous of your relationship with God."

"That's exactly what it is," he said as he spread globs of Miracle Whip across the bread. "But no one will change my relationship with Him. I'm sold out to Him—no matter what happens to others—or me."

Joan took in a deep breath and let it out slowly. "Stay strong, son. You've seen Him move in others, and in your own life. He is the one thing in all of our lives that is a tower of strength."

Sam nodded. "So true."

Joan continued. "Sam's on a relapse, I'm afraid. He was very sick this morning. He could use some prayer."

"Okay, I'll go sit with him after a bit."

Just a short time later, Joshua was sitting beside Sam. "Hi," he said reaching down and rubbing the top of his head. The intensity of heat emanating from his forehead surprised Joshua.

"Hi, Joshua," he said weakly.

"You're feeling bad today?"

"Icky," he answered.

"I'm sorry about that. Be right back," he said as he walked out into the hallway into the bathroom, retrieved a hand cloth, placed it under cool running water, and returned to the bedroom. He folded the cloth and then placed it delicately on his forehead. "There you go, Sammy."

"That feels nice," Sam said.

"I'm going to pray for you. Do you believe God can heal you, you know, make you well?"

"Yes," the child said meekly.

Joshua began to pray again for the boy. He prayed silently by laying his hands on his brother's sandy-blond head for nearly an hour. As Joshua stood up to leave, Sam sat up. "Hey, I feel better."

"You do?" Joshua asked surprised but smiling. "Come on downstairs then. We can sit on the sofa and watch the cartoon channel."

Sam smiled. Dressed in pajamas, he followed his older brother out of the room and downstairs. "Hey Mom," Sam said excited. "Joshua prayed for me and I feel better."

"Very good," she said as she reached out and drew him into her arms.

"C'mon," Joshua said. "I think the Stooges are on in a few minutes. I think we could all use a good laugh!"

***

Lydia received the call at 7:11 p.m. that evening. In her room, she answered the phone. "Hello?"

"What have you done to disrupt the Bible Club?"

"Frank, nothing, yet," she said. "If you recall, I've only been out of Radford a few days now."

"That was pretty careless of you regarding that Gonzales boy."

"I admit I could've handled that situation much better."

"I don't like it that you would risk blowing our entire operation on something as trivial as that."

"I'm sorry. It won't happen again."

"I know it won't," the husky voice said. "You've a job to do, and it needs *all* your attention."

"Well please tell me how I'm supposed to disrupt the Bible Club when it's clear they have the right to assemble? If we have them attacked, they'll get a martyr's complex. If we threaten, they'll just gather and pray all the more."

"Hey, you were hired to take care of the details. Use your imagination."

"Frank, it's a group of less than twenty. They're not going to be a threat to the network."

"How can you be sure?"

"There haven't been any major migrations out of the Jaded Hearts, not since that first week or so after school started. The fact is, this club has settled down. Even the boy who was majorly healed is back in his wheelchair. They're not worth our time or effort, Frank."

"Fine. If it stays as is, leave it as is. But I want you to keep an eye on it. If there are any significant changes there, I'll need it shut down!"

"Fine."

"And what about increasing the network, especially within Knott's End?"

"I've been doing that as I can. But I don't want to increase our numbers too much or else those already involved will start to feel stepped on."

"Either you make the network increase or the sale of goods increase. You make sure one of those two happen in the next thirty days," he said, his voice deep and without emotion.

There came momentary silence.

"Got it?" he asked.

"One more thing, Frank."

"What?"

"I want you to find a replacement for me. I want out before the start of Spring."

"You want out? Why?" he said, his voice conveying reserved frustration.

"I don't know. My heart isn't into the whole thing like at the beginning."

"Don't tell me you've caught some of this religion."

"No, but I'm sure I don't want to continue doing this all of my high school career."

"You will not give up your post. Don't you dare even think about it."

Lydia didn't answer. She felt the fury of realizing that she had very little power, that her will did not matter where she was. "Still. I want you to be on the lookout for someone else to take my position. This is my notice."

There came only the click of the call ending abruptly.

Lydia wondered if she had just made the biggest mistake of her life. Still, she had been true to herself, and she felt glad for it. She knew Frank and the gang might try to bully her, but she would stay true to herself. Thinking back, she thought about what she'd said earlier that day to Joshua about Brad. She regretted her nastiness, even though there was some sort of satisfaction at having said what she'd said to him. She could honestly care less if Brad was in a wheelchair or happily healed. Her questions had been directed at Joshua because she knew it would make him squirm and hurt him. She still resented the way he'd completely disregarded her when the police came knocking.

"Hey Lydia," came her Mom's voice from down the hallway. "How's everything?"

"Not much," Lydia shouted back and turned to see her Mom standing in the doorway. "Just a reminder I'm going out of town this weekend," she said, seemingly hesitant to put any part of herself into the room than needed. "You can keep an eye on Stacy, right?"

"Sure."

"I wish you would reconsider about Joshua," she said as she stepped away. And then she added as if shouting back over her shoulder, "He was such a charming young man. And this house was lighter when he was in it."

Lydia stared at herself in the heavy mirror that leaned against the wall parallel to her bed. There were a lot of things she was reconsidering. But it would take time, and something on the par with divinity to bring it all to pass. She didn't know exactly what was happening, but she could feel the charge in the air, of positive change, even of new directions. But such could not happen without dedication and being steadfast. She wanted to live a good life, a normal life, but what did that mean? Could she ever find contentment outside her life as she knew it now? Was there anything worthwhile to cling to, to hang her identity upon? She couldn't match herself to religion which always left a bad aftertaste in her mouth when she was exposed to it.

"Please help me, whoever You are. I'm lost and I can't find my way through this maze called life." At that, she laid her head on her pillow. "I pray tomorrow will be a better day than today."

Thirty-Six: In the Face of Fear

Despite the momentary, visible improvement upon Sam at the moment of Joshua's prayer previously, just two days later upon returning from school, Joshua learned that Sam had suffered a seizure. The news lodged in him like a splinter compelling questions in his mind as to what was happening, what he should do, what he could do. Joshua's oldest brother, Kris, drove Bruce and him to the hospital where Sam had been rushed earlier that afternoon. From the perspective of those outside the car looking in, there might not have been anything amiss or of weighty significance about the car's three occupants. Yet within the moving car, within the brothers, there was the silent, crushing burden within each—eclipsing the bright, heated sunshine and carefree blue skies. Though no one said so, there was within each a vast chasm that had formed, growing with each onslaught of bad news about Sam.

    Joshua felt unsure what, if anything, should be said. There was a part of Joshua that wanted to be an encouragement, to tell his brothers to seek the Lord on Sam's behalf, but he didn't want to be insensitive or sound like some sort of Pharisee. The shout of reality was what each of them was registering as fact, that for all of Joshua's desires and praying, there had been no long-lasting change in his little brother. But despite appearances and hardship, Joshua recognized these events as tests, and he would not give up on the Lord to heal Sam, and, to help and strengthen his family through this entire ordeal. But he wondered how he'd be able to encourage his family—if he really could. And he thought for a moment how he himself would find strength when the time came. But then the Voice sounded within him—an echo of the verse he'd read earlier that morning from the Psalms: "I will be your strong tower."

Just then, another voice spoke breaking Joshua's contemplation: "Joshua," Bruce asked from the back. "Why did God hear your prayer for that wheelchair kid but not for Sam, your own flesh and blood?"

"His name is Brad," Joshua said unflinchingly. "And I don't know why. I'm not God, am I?" he replied with irritation.

"That just doesn't make sense," Kris added as they turned a corner.

"A lot of things are a mystery to us. It rains on both those who are close to God, and those who pay Him no mind. We all live in a fallen world," Joshua said, unsure if he liked the direction of the discussion. "Maybe you should consider," he said with a pause, "the idea that God wants our family, all the family, to be in right relationship with Him. Maybe He's waiting for one of you guys, or Mom and Dad, to pray for Sam. Maybe there is a specific mission for each of us—for all of us—to what appears sometimes to be a world of madness."

"You got it right, Josh. It *is* madness!" Bruce said angrily.

No one else said another word as they made their way to the hospital, but Joshua could tell they were ruminating what he had said. Perhaps Joshua had stumbled onto a hidden truth.

They arrived at the intensive care section of the hospital. They had moved Sam upstairs and would keep him overnight for observation. All three brothers stepped into the room that Sam was being kept. Joshua stepped up to his little brother. Sam's face appeared as white as chalk, with smudges of dark circles under his eyes. But despite everything, he still managed to smile at his brothers' approach.

"Hey little guy," Joshua said.

Sam nodded toward Joshua with a labored smile. Joshua touched his arm which was fevered. Intravenous tubes were taped to his arm where the tube had been inserted.

"Hi Kris. Hi Bruce," Sam said weakly past Joshua which immediately animated the two brothers to step over. Joshua moved out of the way, glad for their brotherly comfort. Smiling, they ruffled Sam's hair and gently squeezed his little arm.

"Joshua?" Sam asked. "I guess God didn't listen to you, or to me."

"We have to trust Him, regardless of what happens." Joshua looked around. "We're all here for you," Joshua said which brought a smile to Sam's little face. "And I know He loves you just like we love you."

***

The night had started out well for Lydia. Ten-year-old Stacy had been unusually cooperative, being content to lie on the sofa and watch a movie, a small popcorn bowl in front of her.

"Stacy, can you turn the television down? It's blaring!"

"It's not that loud," Stacy protested.

Lydia enjoyed having the house to herself, but not babysitting. Still, it was a nice change to be king of the hill for a short time and without anyone looking over her shoulder. She wasn't one to throw parties, though she did have one two years before when she'd held a summer party after completing the seventh grade. The plan had been perfect: Mom gone and Stacy away at a friend of hers all weekend. But when Stacy had come home unexpectedly because she wasn't feeling well, she'd walked into the middle of a world unbeknownst to her. Most of Lydia's classmates plus many from the high school had descended on her humble home and turned their normally docile home into the place-to-be on the weekend. Music roared, young people huddled in groups throughout the house, and lots of food and lots of alcohol was that world. To Stacy's credit, she'd been better than Lydia expected; she'd not told their Mom about the party for a whole two days. Lydia had experienced one night of freedom but which had cost her the next four weeks of freedom sitting at home grounded.

Despite everything, however, there had come some good out of that party. It had been at that party event that Lydia, under the coaching of older high school friends, had met Frank, an adult in his early-30s but who still had an older teenager's face. He was good-looking and appealing to look at, but, on reflection, had cold, untrusting eyes that never seemed to stop shifting this way or that. Before the end of the party, he'd approached Lydia. After a thirty-minute talk and some upfront cash from him, Lydia's involvement, effectively a partnership, had begun with the initial six months set forth as a trial run. She'd had the summer to prepare and then the beginning of the school year to launch. In truth, Lydia couldn't exactly pinpoint the reasons for her acceptance, whether it was the power she would wield, or the money, or the sheer boredom of her life. Perhaps it had just been her administrative drive that had compelled her— or simply the challenge. At first the coordinating and moving of items through the Knott's End Middle and High schools had been exciting. So many vetted students were under her command. But with her success had come increased responsibility. Soon the distribution was also being moved through several other schools in the region as well as the college campuses—all with her as the administrator.

    Lydia had completed all her assigned tasks with fevered attention and without complaining. The yield of items being distributed had increased, with growing numbers of vetted young people part of the network. The higher-ups were especially pleased, including Frank. And therein was birthed Mister Tony. Lydia would represent one who would be forever whispered but never seen.

    Lydia came down the stairs, peeked into the living room and saw Stacy nearly asleep on the sofa. Walking through their dining area to the back of the house, Lydia opened the sliding door and stepped out onto the wood decking that hugged the entire rear of the house. She looked up and her eyes met the face of the moon, its yellow-white gaze seemingly fixed upon her, casting black shadows around and behind her. Leaning on the railing, she took in a deep breath. She couldn't help but stare upward into the darkness, the stars so bright and brilliant. The air was brisk and immediately clung to her body's warmth causing the hairs on her arms and neck to stand up. But Lydia liked the cold's assault on her: it made her feel freshened and alive.

    The night sky in its vastness often triggered her to think about her life, and what purpose her life had, if any. Most people her age didn't ask the who, what, and why questions about life. They were content to be herded into the future with little or no restraint. And yet she wondered why they were in such a hurry to go forward.

Lydia, however, felt more cautious about the future—despite the outward appearances and her actions that seemed to indicate otherwise. She didn't like going into any situation without knowing escape routes and alternatives to what had to be. She wished she was like some of her other friends who were carefree and free caring about life. But Lydia had always asked questions and thought up answers, if only inwardly. Despite her contemplations, however, she'd not fixed herself to any of those answers.

Life: Was it just a big cosmic accident? Or a big gift wrapped up and cruelly dangled in front of people to be kept out of reach for all time? Why did she exist? Why did she have the consciousness of life, and memories, and the perception of a very real future? Why was it that at that exact moment in time and space, she was alive to ask the questions? Why did she have a conscious awareness of herself? It made her feel grateful and scared—because it seemed to validate the truth of the Creator's imprint on life. Was Joshua right? Was there a responsibility upon all people to come to know God and live according to His ways? If people rejected Him, what would be their result? These were the things that filled her mind, especially when she'd do things like stare into the upper expanse of the night sky; it made her all-too reflective. It was as if the external universe mirrored her internal universe.

Eventually, she plopped down onto the wooden steps and leaned against the railing looking up. It was after several minutes while in that inactive position that the scream came. It came as a shrieking and filled the kitchen. Absolutely horrified, Lydia thought only of Stacy before jumping up and running back into the house, her eyes alert and all her adrenaline pumping. She immediately closed the door and locked it, all in one swoop. She saw the kettle on the stove, its water boiling, the hot steam rising, the scream still bellowing—all despite Lydia having not turned it on. It was just then that she noticed the mug with leftover dark grains sitting atop the counter. She had washed dishes earlier, and she knew Stacy wasn't a coffee drinker—*This cup shouldn't be here.*

Warily, she extended her hand toward the stove and turned counter-clockwise the knob which silenced the kettle. This served only to make the room silent—which seemed as terrifying as the shrieking. Lydia looked around, suddenly aware of everything. She needed to be, for she realized what was happening right in her own home. Frank had been in the kitchen. She remembered some of the stories whispered about the man before—stories that made the hairs on the back of her neck stand up. Instantly, she felt the realization of what might be happening to her—and she found herself not ready to meet God. Pulling on a drawer, she retrieved a large butcher knife and held it defensively as she slowly approached the living room, keeping the right-hand wall of the room to her rear.

Still, the television was playing and Stacy lay on the sofa sound asleep. But could this be some sort of prank by Stacy? Lydia noticed the front door was unlocked. Had they left it unlocked?

"Stacy?" Lydia called in a hushed voice.

But Stacy did not move.

"Stacy?!" she called in a low but emphatic voice.

There came a sigh-like groan. And then, "What? It's still early. I don't want to go to bed yet."

"Stacy...come over to me," Lydia whispered, and she suddenly realized how much she loved her sister.

This caused Stacy to sit straight up, as if a rag doll being sat up by an unseen hand. Stacy's eyes were suddenly large and staring at Lydia, as if she had awakened from a nightmare.

"What's wrong?" Stacy said quietly, a scared expression on her face, suddenly looking about her seemingly paralyzed. "And why are you holding a butcher knife?"

"Stacy, look at me."

She finally fixed her eyes on her, fear in her eyes.

In a low voice: "Please. Come over to me now."

Finally, she unstuck herself from the sofa and came quickly before standing behind her big sister.

"Upstairs, quick!"

"Why?" Stacy moaned fearfully. She appeared on the verge of crying. She now scanned around her, more with her eyes than her head, as if even moving her head might attract unwanted attention.

"I think someone's in the house with us."

Stacy looked around as if the very shadows of the room might dash out at her and grab her. With apprehension, they both scanned the long drapes that spread across the large front that faced the front of the house. This time, she really did begin to cry. "W-Who?"

"I don't know," Lydia said.

Pointing the blade of the knife away from her and flicking the hallway light on, Lydia began the slow, cautious ascent on the thick-carpeted stairway.

"Shouldn't we call the police?" Stacy whispered.

But Lydia had had enough of the police in the past few weeks. She would find out what, if anything, was happening on her own. "Just stay close to me."

They reached the top of the stairway, the hallway turning an immediate left. Along this hallway were three rooms, all located on the right-hand side of the hallway. The first room was Lydia's mother's room, the second Lydia's, and the last Stacy's. All three doors were open which could be either comforting or terrifying, depending on how you saw it. For Lydia, it terrified her, because at any moment and without warning, there might come rushing at her one who wanted only to do her and her sister harm.

Stepping into the first room, Lydia scanned the room and saw no sign of anyone's presence. Stacy followed quietly closing the door behind her before locking it. She whispered to her, "I want you to watch under the doorway. If you see or hear something move in front of the door, tell me." Stacy continued looking frightened but she nodded in agreement to her assignment.

Checking the bedroom, Lydia noted the closet which sat on the left and was easily large enough for a person to hide. Pulling on a knob quickly brought the doors folding outward and sliding open. Lydia stepped back quickly yet clutching the knife all the while surveying the closet. Only several boxes and her mother's numerous shoes sat along the carpeted floor. Pulling the other side open, she found only hanging women's jackets, suits, and dresses. She pulled open the second set closet doors—this section used for odds and ends. Dropping quickly to the carpet floor, her knife held in front of her, she lifted the edge of the blanket up quickly before scanning. From the darkness, two shiny orbs glared at her. Lydia held her composure, however, realizing it was Stacy's tattered, burgundy teddy bear staring at her.

Satisfied that the first room was secure, Lydia turned to Stacy. "I want you to stay in here. The telephone's over there if you need it—"

"You can't leave me," Stacy whispered with a look teetering on the edge of crying again.

"There's a lock on the door. I'll be back for you. Now lock it!" Lydia said with no room for discussion. She walked past Stacy and pulled the door shut quietly. She heard the door being immediately locked.

Cautiously, she turned right and walked into her own room before pushing the door so it was more closed than open. All remained quiet within the house. She slowly slid open her mirrored closet doors that had been built alongside the left-hand side of the room. She checked that no one was hiding inside—the hanging clothes appearing like ominous creatures from her nightmares. Nothing amiss, knife in hand, she then checked under her bed—no boogeyman present. Quietly, she proceeded to step out into the hallway before closing her door and approaching the last room.

As she stepped into her sister's bedroom, she noted the eyes focused on her—those of the celebrity teen boys from various bands and television—the posters of Stacy's idols spread out across the bedroom. The room had an especially feminine touch to it which Lydia inwardly despised, with pink bed covers and a large dresser and attached wooden mirror that shone a deep pink. On the bed were dozens of stuffed animals, all of them eyeing Lydia as if she were trespassing. Cautiously, she slid open her sister's mirrored closet doors and searched under the bed but still, thankfully, no one was discovered.

She suddenly felt at ease. But, seeing plenty of horror movies had taught her not to let her guard down—not completely. She walked back down the hallway and knocked on her Mom's door.

"Everything looks okay," Lydia said in a normal voice. The door unlocked and swung open. Stacy peered out, still uneasy, her cheeks wet from her quiet crying.

"Were you playing with me?" Stacy challenged unsure whether to believe what had just happened to them.

"No," Lydia said. "I wouldn't play like that—especially tonight."

"What made you think someone was here?"

"Because, I've heard stories about this guy I know," Lydia said, but not elaborating on the fact that it was Frank. "He was known to go into people's homes—people he didn't like—and he would do something as simple as making coffee. It was his way of saying, 'I'm the boss and I can go wherever I want, whenever I want. I can do whatever I want.'"

Stacy looked around again suddenly troubled. "You're scaring me."

"I'm scaring myself," Lydia admitted. "Let's go check the rest of the house," she whispered.

"Can I stay here?"

"Sure," Lydia said. "Be back shortly."

Within twenty minutes, Lydia had checked the house, made sure all the windows and doors were locked, and returned upstairs. She felt better, but the earlier sudden scream of the kettle still made her tremble. Stacy went to her room, closed and locked her room, and Lydia did the same. She lowered the knife so it was resting within arm's reach on the carpet floor.

The house was quiet, completely still. She wished the next day would come, so she could take comfort that the night was over, that she had merely scared her sister and herself and nothing else. But her mind kept replaying the kettle's screeching whistle and the scene of the cooling coffee mug set out—which defied all explanations.

Lydia fell asleep.

The abrupt shudder of something thudding against the bedroom door startled Lydia awake. Her eyes opened large and stared into the darkness. She fully expected a hand to reach out from somewhere and clutch her throat to snatch the life from her.

The house had seemed to shake. The feeling of terror—of near paralysis—seemed to extend to all her limbs. Had her door been struck with a sledgehammer?

She saw the clock's red numerals glaring at her—3:33 a.m. She had been asleep for two hours, if that. She felt for the knife but no matter how much she patted the floor, she couldn't find it. She sat up cautiously and then lowered herself so she had her back against the bed. She felt some more for the knife. It had to be there. Still, she couldn't find it.

She reached for her lamp to turn on the light. Upon turning it on, she rested her back to her bed and visually searched for the knife—but still there was nothing. She turned to look at her door.

"What is going on?" she said quietly. She felt regret and anger at herself that she hadn't had Stacy sleep in her room with her.

The door lock was unlocked. *But I locked it!* She thought. Opening the door inward, she saw the blade of the knife she'd had stuck almost two inches into the wood of the door's center. She heard something from her right and looked quickly. Stacy peeked out her door.

"Are you trying to scare me again?" she asked. "'Coz I won't ever make you mad again; I promise!"

"Close your door and lock it," Lydia said seriously. Her sister did not question as she quickly slammed the door shut and engaged the lock.

Stepping out into the hallway, she grabbed and worked the knife out of the door. She suddenly felt the adrenaline of anger coursing through her. She hated feeling powerless and at the whim of another. She had had enough! With only some caution, she walked briskly down the stairs finding the front door wide open.

Before going upstairs to bed previously, Lydia had turned on every light in the house she could find. Yet...here she stood—every light off.

"Okay, Frank," she said. "I know you're here." She said this with an air of confidence, but inside, she was terrified. As she drew closer to the kitchen, she noticed several items on the island counter. Several knives with their blades facing her sat on the shiny counter's center, deliberately placed. At this, she could handle no more of this. She pulled her phone upward and quickly dialed the police.

"Nine-one-one emergency services. How can we assist you?" a woman's voice asked.

Just then outside, there came the sudden squeal of tires from a car as it roared to life before racing down the street. Lydia ran toward the window to see what kind of car had sped off but it was too late.

"How can we assist you?" the 911 operator asked.

"N-No," Lydia finally said. "Everything's okay. False alarm." She pressed the "Off" button and replaced the phone.

She walked into the kitchen and turned on the light. She noticed a second coffee mug placed neatly in the sink. With grave reluctance, she reached and touched it which revealed a warmth still present on the cup's exterior.

Thirty-Seven: Taking Risks

Late, or rather early, the next morning, Joshua and his brothers returned home. Sam with his weary face and weakened body rested in his hospital bed, his too-small body in the oversized bed seeming odd to Joshua. His brother's condition had certainly not improved. Joshua had remained by him, his hands laid upon his brother's arm, quietly praying till it was time for him to go. After a whole evening and part of the night, Joshua's parents finally told the sleepy brothers to return home, that they would call them if anything changed.

His own phone having died several hours before, Joshua walked into the house and noticed the answering machine blinking a red "1". He pressed the playback button expecting to hear something from the hospital. When he heard Lydia's voice, however, he was momentarily surprised. He listened to her garbled message. He heard something he'd not heard before in her voice: fear. And then something else he'd never heard from her: a request, bracketed by urgency, for him to...*pray*?

Picking up the phone, Joshua dialed Lydia's house. After half a dozen rings, and about to hang up, her familiar voice spoke on the other end. "Hello?"

"Lydia? Are you okay?"

"Can you come over now?"

"Why? What's wrong?"

"I can't explain on the phone."

"My parents would kill me if—"

"I need you. Right *now*."

"I don't kno—"

"Please, I have *a lot* to tell you."

"Like?"

"Oh, forget it! Silly of me to think you'd be around for me when I really needed you."

Joshua was altogether shocked by the statement. He thought to reply before the blurting drone of the dial tone filled Joshua's ear.

Joshua replaced the phone in its cradle. He thought to dismiss her and wait till the next morning. But the very fact that she had called him must mean something was wrong. Joshua walked over to the stairway and stared up the steps as he weighed his next action. Joshua listened for the sounds of his brothers but there was only quiet. They'd be already settled—and waking them to take him to Lydia's would be futile, if not a health risk. He turned halfway and noticed on the kitchen table…the car keys. He knew it would be a risk, but he had to do something.

***

It took several seconds of knocking, but finally, a porch light came on before the door was opened with the chain still attached.

"Joshua?" Lydia said, astonishment in her voice.

"Hey, are you okay?" She didn't reply but closed the door quickly as he heard the scrap of the metal chain before the door was yanked open.

"Come in, quickly," she said, visibly jarred.

"What's going on?"
"He was here."
"Who is 'he'?"
"Frank."
"Who's Frank?"

Lydia turned and walked into the living room. She walked to the large front windows and visibly checked the curtains to make sure they were adequately closed.

"Who is Frank, Lydia?"

Lydia finally stepped to her sofa and eased herself down onto the seat cushion. Her face looked older and drawn downward with lines of worry and something else, something Joshua had never seen before in Lydia: fear. She stared down at her hands which held a slight tremor. "There's a lot you don't know about me."

"What do you mean?"

"When I was about to complete my seventh-grade year, I was approached by a high school student, a brother of a friend of mine, who asked me if I wanted to make money every now and then. I suspected what he was talking about—that it might not be something your average Girl Scout would be interested in. But when I thought about the alternative of working in a grease trap like Burger Castle, I really began to consider it."

"Okay. What kind of job are we talking about?"

"Let me tell you the story, please," she asked brushing back her long hair, looking in Joshua's eyes as little as possible as she talked. "Not long after, I met with this man named Frank, and he seemed to be impressed with me based on the recommendations of people that knew me. At first, I thought I'd just be doing odd jobs, but then he expressed interest in me actually being a leader for the goings-on at the middle school."

"A leader of what?" Joshua asked.

She gave Joshua an impatient look. "Are you going to let me tell you or not?"

Feeling tired, Joshua ignored his own irritation. "Go on."

"Because of our age, we were perfect candidates for the job, which was moving desired substances through the school, both to those who were users and to those who were simply gateways to the city's adult population."

"And your age was perfect because…"

"There were risks, but that's why we were paid so well. If arrested for anything, we would be punished only for a short time, and our records would be expunged before we became adults. Before long, I had made such a great impression that there were other schools—including local colleges—in need of my leadership acumen. So, I was asked to administer them too."

"Are you serious?" Joshua stood up. He had had no idea. But perhaps that was why the One inside him had been withholding him from fully embracing Lydia since the beginning.

"I know this must be a shock to you," Lydia said, sadness in her voice.

"What kind of drugs are we talking about?"

"Anything people want," she said plainly.

"You mean to tell me you've been involved in the Jaded Hearts after all?"

"Yes," she said, this time with some regret in her voice. "But indirectly only."

Joshua sat back down again and placed his face in his hands. He rubbed his temples even as he tried to process all

Lydia was sharing. Finally, he looked up. "And who's the Mister Tony guy?"

"*'Tony'*? How'd you hear about him?"

"One of the ex-gang members talked to me. The name came up."

"*I* am Tony."

Joshua stared at her wide-eyed unable to say another word. He stopped all movement and seemed paralyzed. It felt as if he'd been knocked off his feet by a rogue ocean wave.

Thirty-Eight: Revelations

Joshua was sitting in the living room of a drug dealer for schools and college campuses—and beyond—in the county. He still couldn't believe Lydia's confessions. But now it was necessary for him to find out if she really wanted to change or not.

Lydia looked contrite. "I'm sorry to share all this with you, Josh," she said, her hands in front of her. The truth is, I want to change direction in my life. But it's so complicated—I don't know what to do. And because…"

"Because?" Josh asked.

"—because Frank came to see me tonight."

"And…"

"Somehow, he got into the house."

"How?"

"I don't know. He has his ways."

"How old is he?"

"He's in his late-thirties, I think."

"What can I do?" Joshua asked lifting his arms and shoulders in bewilderment.

"You're not mad at me?" she asked.

"I don't know what I feel right now. For whatever reason, I guess I'm not mad," Joshua said. He ran his fingers through his hair, trying to figure out what to say next. "I can't believe what you've just told me, to be honest." Even as he said this, however, he realized how his heart felt toward Lydia.

He felt an inclination to hold back, but he disregarded the thought and instead surrendered to his feelings. "No matter what, I do care about you. I don't want anything bad to happen to you."

"Thanks," she said with a quick smile. Standing up, she stepped over to Joshua and stood in front of him. She ran her long fingers upward over Joshua's cheeks as she fixed her gaze downward into Joshua's eyes. "I care for you too, Joshua," she said. "A lot."

What's happening right now? Joshua wondered. He felt the surge of emotion and the sense of touch was nearly overwhelming any sense of restraint in him. Silently, Joshua said a short prayer, asking for God's help, yet there was another part of him whispering to him that he had done nothing wrong to stop what was happening, that there wasn't even a need to pray, that no lines had been crossed. He shouldn't be a prune when nothing wrong had happened, a voice seemed to suggest. The room's ceiling light shone atop her head creating a bit of a halo effect, the light shading her features. She looked wonderful to him.

Without thinking, almost instinctually, Joshua lifted and placed his hands over hers before lifting them away from his cheeks. He held them even as he stood up hoping to escape his feelings of helplessness. Face to face, he stared at her, examining her smooth face and neutral expression that several moments before had been apprehensive, but now seemed entirely at ease.

"Would kissing me be a sin, Joshua?" she asked.

"I don't kno—"

She leaned forward and kissed him without warning. And he moved to pull away, but she followed and held tightly, the kisses becoming deeper. Finally, he resigned, even as his insides struggled to understand what was happening, and what he should do.

"Lydia?" said a small voice from atop the stairway. "Are you there?"

Lydia stopped but kept her position. She was obviously keen on restarting what had just begun. "Everything's okay, Stacy. Go *back* to bed!"

"Lydia, I had a night terror," she said.

"I'm gonna be a night terror to you if you don't go—"

Joshua leaned forward and kissed Lydia on the cheek before side-stepping her and moving apart from her. Immediately, he began to pray in the Spirit inwardly. He felt it was important that he leave as soon as possible, but he also wanted to make sure Lydia was safe and okay.

"Go to bed, Stacy," Lydia yelled, louder. No reply came from her sister, which seemed to satisfy Lydia.

"Let's pray for your situation," Joshua finally said and he noted the visible change in Lydia's face. Praying was obviously the last thing on her mind. Finally, though, she reluctantly agreed, and they sat down together—hand in hand on the sofa.

"Father in heaven, we come to you in Jesus' Name. I just ask—

"Oh, what's the use of us praying, Joshua? This is pointless," she said with disgust in her voice.

Joshua stopped out of respect, but he clearly felt unhappy with her rationale.

"Lydia," Joshua said. "If you don't believe in prayer, or the One that hears, then that's fine. I'm not going to force you to do anything. But I believe. And I know He hears—even if sometimes I have to be patient and wait—or when I have to learn to truly trust Him."

Lydia nodded subtly. "I guess."

"Can we continue, Lydia?" Joshua asked lightly.

She nodded finally.

"Lord, we pray right now for Your comfort in this uncertain time in Lydia's life. I pray that You will continue to reveal Yourself to Lydia, that she would see You as her refuge, and that You would help her as she seeks direction on removing herself from these illegal activities within the schools. And I ask for Your protection over her tonight and in the days ahead. In Jesus' Name."

Joshua immediately gave her a tight hug before pulling away and walking toward the front door. "I'll be praying for you, Lydia. I need to head home now."

"Wait. Please don't leave yet," she said. Then she added in an even but vulnerable tone, "I'm still spooked. And I don't want to be here by myself."

Joshua nodded understanding. "I'm sorry," he said looking at his watch. "It's nearly five o' clock in the morning. Me staying here is not a good idea. If my brother wakes up and finds his car not in the driveway by six, or if my parents come home for any reason, you won't see me for the next six months," he said managing to smile and waiting for Lydia to respond.

Lydia finally nodded allowing a momentary smile in return as she conceded Joshua's decision. She looked unhappy, disappointment plainly shown on her face, but only for a moment.

"Look at you," she said smiling again. "Stealing your brother's car. Getting spoken to by the police. And dating a very naughty girl," she said as she stepped close to Joshua again. She reached for him and wrapped her arms around his waist. "Can't we have some 'us' time—when there's no one around, when we can just be ourselves?"

Joshua embraced her back. "I want that, too. But I don't trust myself. And I don't want to do anything that we might regret later."

"Like?"

"Doing something He," he said pointing upward, "won't approve of."

She sighed before letting him go. "Fine," she said gently, giving up.

Opening the front door, Joshua stepped outside making sure to look about first. A chill greeted him. Joshua turned to Lydia, holding his arms so to ward off the cold. "I won't be at school tomorrow, but I'll call you tomorrow afternoon—if you want to talk."

"Why won't you be there?"

"Sammy took a turn for the worse. That's why you got an answering machine when you called my house. We were at the hospital watching and praying over him."

"Sammy's not getting any better?" she asked sadly.

Joshua shook his head. "But we're still hopeful for his recovery. I believe God has everything in control despite how everything looks!"

"Please let Sam know I'm thinking of him."

"I will," Joshua said before leaning forward, taking her face in his hands and giving Lydia a kiss on her forehead.

Once in the car and driving home on some back roads that would get him home without risking a run-in with the police, Joshua began thanking the Lord for interrupting him through Stacy... But the real question pressing upon his heart was what he'd now do with the information he'd just learned about from Lydia. How would it affect his relationship with her? What could he possibly do to help her? And it was then he began to do the most powerful thing he could think of for her: he began to pray for Lydia with all his heart.

Thirty-Nine: The Warning

While on his way to the afterschool prayer gathering, Joshua still thinking about the events surrounding Lydia, and still voicing prayers to the Lord on her behalf, suddenly he felt himself being jostled into a darkened corner of the hallway. Someone tall and big dressed in a blue denim jacket had picked him up by his collar and shoved him into this corner out of sight. No teachers were about since it was after school.

"You're going to stop this Bible Club as of today—or else!" Joshua noticed the denim jacket was what was normally worn by the Jaded Hearts. He saw the face of the older teen. He had an oblong face, extra pounds giving his face a genial, friendly look. But there was nothing friendly coming from his face at that moment. Joshua felt the pressure around his collar, his button up shirt tightened around his neck until he could barely breathe, his lanky frame lifted off the floor some three inches pressed against the lockers. Still, Joshua managed to reply, though with some difficulty. "It's...not my decision...if we meet or not."

"You're the leader, aren't you?!"

"I just do...what the Lord...says. He led me to start it. He's the Leader. Take it up with Him."

"If you don't do as I say, if you so much as show up at that meeting today, I'm going to inflict enough pain on you to make you wish you'd never heard of God. Am I clear?"

Joshua couldn't agree. "Do what you want to me. Our group is bigger than just me."

"I'm warning you. You better make the best decision you've ever made and go straight home. If I find out your face was in that classroom, it's going to be a sad day for you."

Joshua listened for an inkling of leading from the Holy Spirit. But nothing seemed to surface in his mind. Except one thing he'd read that morning: "Offer him your other cheek."

"It's already a sad day for me!"

"What'd you say to me?" he said tightening the noosehold around his throat.

"It's sad that you...don't know Him. That you don't know how much He loves you."

The boy laughed before turning to his teenage accomplices who stood to the left and right of him. "The boy's trying to preach to me about Jesus. Do I need Jesus?"

The two teens nodded, one of them laughing. "Yeah, you do!"

Without warning, the boy jolted Joshua's head sideways with an open hand strike across his cheek—a loud slap filled the hallway.

Joshua yelled out, shocked at the abrupt quickness and force of the strike.

"That's a foretaste. Don't go near that Bible Club today, or ever again." The boy released Joshua's shirt which caused Joshua to drop to the floor abruptly. He began to move off while giving Joshua a darkened look as if to rein-force all he'd just said.

"Wait!" Joshua cried.

The boy looked back incredulously before stopping. "What do you want?" he said through gritted teeth.

"I can't do what you ask. So here I am. Do whatever you want with me here and now."

The boy turned around and moved toward Joshua just as an adult's voice filled the hallway from quite some distance away. "Hey you three! What are you doing?"

The boy saw the teacher hastily moving toward them from the opposite end of the hallway.

The boy said almost in a whisper. "You heard what I've said. Don't make me come find you."

The teacher finally reached Joshua's location, the three boys having escaped through the corridor that would lead them out of the school.

"Are you all right, young man?"

Joshua nodded, rubbing his cheek. "I'll be all right."

"What was that all about?"

Joshua wanted to tell him, but he realized that this was a matter that only the Lord, and prayer, would be able to truly rectify.

***

Entering the classroom where their meeting was normally held, Joshua found the group already started. The room reverberated with prayer from the students' lips. They were praying more animated than usual, the room thick with a sense of presence greater than their own. Joshua joined them, immediately feeling himself at ease and at peace. It was almost like coming home.

They prayed that they'd be able to have His heart for those who didn't know Him, that they'd also have a heart even for those who were their enemies—who wanted to persecute and harm them. They asked the Lord to turn every device, every plan, every maneuver of the enemy to His glory, and His gain. As the room prayed, some in the room began to cry to the point of seeming brokenhearted. Yet others felt an intensity of joy fall upon them—so much so that they began to laugh and smile. Others became still and unable to talk. Still others voiced their devotion in small utterances of song, sometimes in languages that seemed unknown and unlearned. Nearly an hour later, the group began to wind down their prayers until all issues seemed settled, all burdens lifted. It was a strange goodness that pervaded upon each person's face.

Joshua stood up and addressed the students. "We face an enemy who is not flesh and blood as we might suppose. Our enemy is unseen. And our Lord goes before us fighting the battles that are too great for us. But we must do our part—to remain faithful to pray, to remain faithful to stand no matter who opposes us. Let's remain in prayer, and not be shaken by any trial or tribulation that comes our direction. He's worthy of our lives. He's worthy everything we have and everything we are," he said which were responded to by the nodding of heads.

When all was said and done, the group hugged each other. No one was without a smile of joy upon their faces. In fact, as the group spilled out into the hallway to go home, the cheerleaders who were working on their banners saw them and looked on in bewilderment. They couldn't help but notice the expression of something that they all admitted was strange but also oddly attractive from these Bible Club members. What they saw was all very natural, but there was something unique about each person that came out of that classroom. It defied description.

One of the cheerleaders caught Joshua's eye as he walked by. He slowed down as she ran over to him. "Would you please pray for my Mom & Dad? They've been having a lot of problems lately."

Joshua stopped and turned to her. "Let's both pray for them right now. What's your name?" And he prayed at that moment, his action catching the cheerleader off guard. "Lord, take control of this situation in Jenna's family. The greatest prayer that I can pray for this family is that they'd know You, too, as I and so many others have come to know You." He said amen before turning to the girl.

"Jenna, would you like to know Him personally? Would you like Him to come into your life so you're not alone and trying to do life alone?"

She heard the question but seemed to dismiss it. "I don't think I can follow Him like you do," she said looking suddenly dispirited.

"He wouldn't want you to follow Him like I do. That'd be boring," he said which caused her to smile.

"Can you please tell me more about Him?"

Joshua began to share with her. And suddenly, it wasn't just Jenna but the whole cheerleading squad surrounding him to listen.

***

Joshua was relieved to see no one waiting outside to end his life. His time with the cheerleaders had lasted almost an additional hour—perhaps that was why no one was outside waiting for him. They'd grown too impatient to wait.

Joshua had to admit his amazement that the outsiders to the Gospel should be drawn to the Lord not through just words, but through the evidence of His presence upon His people after time spent with Him. The joy upon Joshua seemed to be without limit. It felt very close to the moments months before when he'd first felt the Spirit of God fall upon him in his room. But the joy was there because he had sought after God despite the outside pressures, despite the distractions and worries. He'd felt the Lord impressing upon him that he must not forget that his source of joy, of strength, of love was always centered on fixing his eyes on the One above first and foremost—through prayer, through worship. If he did that, he'd be able to continue the path designated by the Lord.

In that moment as Joshua set off to walk home, he felt invincible with an assurance of God's presence and reality with him. And in that moment, he prayed with every step for his family, for Sammy, for Lydia, for the cheerleaders who had surrendered their lives to God earlier, for his enemies who wanted to harm him—and even for this man, Frank Gelb.

And he wondered if the sense upon him of God's goodness at that moment was because of the trials of the past few days and weeks, or if it was all in anticipation of what was about to happen in his life—perhaps something unseen but which would require the fullness of the Holy Spirit's power and presence. Would he be able to stand firm, to remain faithful through all the tests and trials about to come his way? He didn't know about tomorrow. But he knew today would be fine no matter what happened, for God was with him.

Forty: One Called Tony

It hadn't taken long for Lydia to get the call from Frank demanding a face to face meeting. She was to come promptly the next day at 5:45 p.m. to the local park. Although she didn't like the idea, she thought it best to just meet up with him and try to get the situation ironed out before something was done that would cause regret. Entering the park which had shed its green and turned a dowdy brown from the encroaching winter, she noticed the shadows of the distant tree line stretching, the sun and all its light plummeting toward the horizon. A chill had already begun to reclaim the ground from any semblance of residue warmth from the day.

    When she saw him sitting on the park bench at the open-space corner of the field, she looked about to see if there should be anything to be concerned about. Nothing appeared, however, out of the ordinary, either menacing or dangerous. As she came to within a stone's throw of Frank, he finally looked up at her and fastened his eyes on her. He wore his black hair shortened on the sides and back, rising perfectly into one-inch-high spikes. He wore a neutral expression on his face. Today, he looked like anyone you might see in a park. He wore basketball attire and6 held a black Spalding basketball in his hands.

    "Hello Tony," he said when she was a stone's throw from him.

"Why did you come to my house and scare me and my sister?"

Frank snickered irreverently to her question while keeping his look fixed on the park's perimeter where massive oak trees lined the park. "I go wherever I want. Whenever I want. You should know that by now," he said.

"My sister was there. You had no right—"

"'Whenever I want,' I said. And I don't like it when things—or people—start to change around me. It makes me feel a bit funny inside. It makes it where I can't sleep at night. And I love my sleep."

"Oh, so you're just going to harass me and scare me nonstop till I do what you tell me?"

"Fear is just an emotion. There's something much worse that comes after fear, Tony."

"Just call me Lydia," she said with a hint of impatience in her voice.

He raised his eyebrows at her statement. "*See?* That's what I'm talking about. You've always been 'Tony' since we met—the name I gave you. Why must I start to call you by a name I've never known before?"

"I told you. I want out! I've grown your business to efficient levels. I don't feel I'm an asset to continue its growth."

The man looked down at the ground just as a canary-yellow butterfly landed between the two of them on a patch of brown. It fanned its large wings slowly up and down as if regathering strength. Without warning, Frank brought down one of his pristine white hi-tops on the insect with brute force startling Lydia and making her body momentarily jump.

"Why did you do that?" Lydia asked seething with rage, her face reddening. She stared at the crushed insect feeling sorry for it.

His face contorted with repressed anger as his eyes fastened on her. "This butterfly didn't have a choice about its future. But you do, Tony," he said matter-of-factly, his face regaining its normal appearance. "So, you better think a bit more before you finalize this decision of yours." He looked down at the dead, crushed insect. "Such a waste of beauty." Then his eyes rose to meet hers once more. "Give me your phone."

"Why, Frank?" she asked, protest in her voice.

"Don't make me ask again," he said simply.

Reluctantly, she handed him her phone. "What about all my pictures and vids on there?"

Without a reply, he handed her a folded sheet of paper before he leisurely began to walk off.

Lydia sat there stunned, unsure what to do. Her eyes followed Frank's movements to the edge of the park before he'd gone out of view, and then they fell again to the shattered insect. She felt sad for the poor creature.

Opening the paper, there was a message with irregularly cut-out words from newspapers, magazines and brochures. The message said:

> *So many broken hearts to see you leave,*
> *But Tony's still mine, do you believe?*
> *Mine to control, mine to command,*
> *Give your consent to avoid deadly backhand.*

Lydia rolled her eyes and scoffed a laugh. *Didn't finish eighth grade with that level of poetry, did you?* she thought to herself. But then her eyes shot to the edge of the park. And sure enough, standing at regular intervals around the park's perimeter stood guys and girls wearing the blue denim jackets of the Jaded Hearts gang. The reference to "broken hearts" was obviously regarding the gang. Some leaned on tree trunks while others were simply standing with their hands held in front of them—all facing in her direction. She looked behind her to see the same; wherever she looked, they were there standing, watching, waiting at the edge of the park. They looked relatively young—teens given this task of teaching her a lesson?

She didn't know what to do. And then she saw them beginning to slowly move in her direction. She began to move toward the exit of the park which only caused the gang to adjust their heading toward her. When she saw there was no way to get out of this situation, she thought she'd just face them—see if she could talk her way out of the situation.

When the gang had got to within 200 feet of her, surrounding her, five of the group drew closer toward her. She waited for the leader to address her—or perhaps this wasn't meant to be a discussion at all.

"Who's the leader here?" she asked evenly even as she attempted to remain in control.

A young man with reddish hair and heavy freckles stepped forward as the other five maintained their place. But he said nothing. His face showed no emotion, no hint of what they were going to do with her.

"So, this is what Frank wants?" she said to him, her voice without a hint of weakness.

"There's two ways out of here," he finally said. "Walk out of here as you came in—if you're a friend and partner of

273 | t h e J e s u s b o y

Frank's. Or get carried out—if you're not! You just need to make the decision in the next thirty seconds." He stood with his arms on his hips. "So...make your decision."

Lydia nodded understanding, her face resolute despite the threats. "I've already made my decision," she said pausing. She found herself in a situation where she thought there no way out. But she couldn't let this go on or else she'd never be free again. "Tell Frank I said, 'I'm out!' And I meant it!"

It was then that all five of the Hearts pounced on her—fists and feet being used all at once to pummel her.

Almost immediately, she slipped to the ground and curled into a ball covering her head in a desperate attempt to protect herself. Strangely, she pictured Joshua's face even as the pain began to be felt in every part of her body. For a moment, she realized not just how much comfort she received from having him in her life, but she also realized another emotion resident within her. It was no longer rationally controlled or withheld: she loved him.

Even as she sought to protect herself futilely against the raining blows, even as she tried not to cry out from the so-strong pride she felt within, she also found herself thinking of Joshua's God. She wondered if He would help her even now despite all she'd done—to her Mom, to her community, to people she cared about like Josh. Even as the continued kicks and punches struck her, desperation reigned in her. She screamed out to Him—to the God of Joshua—to save her. The thought came to her how empty her life truly was even as all around her suddenly was swallowed up by darkness.

***

Like puppets on strings, the young ones were brought to attack this one—their desire for violence amplified, their anger and hatred brought to an overflow as they attacked her. The demons were all-too-glad to unleash their evil designs upon the girl—to snuff out her life. Initially there had been just the empty space of an unlit vacuum—nothing to resist their onslaught.

But then appeared His face over her—pure light that deflected the demons' attack. He was, despite all her sin and rebellion, standing over her, protecting her, loving her—fighting for her against the tide of darkness.

Part Three: Saplings

"a young tree, especially one with a slender trunk."

Forty-One: Double Life

When she awakened, she saw only the hazy outline of Joshua's face above her. Then she began to realize that her surroundings were no longer the park but a hospital room. In the same moment, however, she suddenly felt pain wash over her body; nowhere did she not feel pain. She struggled to intake a breath, the pain filling all her chest cavity causing her to wince.

"Hey Lydia," he said with a subtle smile. "You're going to be all right."

"What…happened?" And even as she asked the question, she started to remember her last conscious moment before she'd been attacked.

"A plains clothes police officer saw what was happening and intervened. The gang all ran when he came to your aid."

"Oh," she said lifting her left arm with great effort—patches of black and blue bruises and red cuts along its surface. "I guess I'm lucky," she said through gritted teeth.

"Or maybe the Lord saved you."

"Oh, my face…it hurts," was all she could reply. "It's bad?"

"Swollen. They said you suffered a facial hairline fracture on your cheek bone and some badly bruised ribs."

"How did you find out?"

"Your mother called me when she learned you'd been brought to the ER. She let me come with her to see you. She's gone out to get a coffee."

Lydia began to cry—but even that action caused a wave of pain to pass through her. "I don't know why. I...prayed. In the park. Your God."

Joshua gave a subtle nod. "He doesn't have to be just my God. He can be yours, too."

"I don't think my life...is one He'd want, Joshua."

"I heard this saying and it's true: 'He isn't looking for golden vessels or silver vessels. He's just looking for yielded vessels.'"

"But what if I'm just asking for His help," she said letting out a moan as she tried to sit up, "for selfish reasons."

"He knows us in all of our contradictions. He knows you in all your ways. Yet that doesn't change the fact that He still loves you...just like He's loved me."

"Joshua, how'd you come to know Him?" she asked.

Joshua grinned happily. "Lydia, you're talking about Him like you believe Him to be real now."

"I guess I am," she managed a smile to Joshua. "I'm still just trying to understand. I'm not sure what to believe to be honest."

"I gave my life to Him when I was in a camp. But it wasn't until a few weeks later that I decided I'd do more than just coast through life with Him. I'd fight to go through life *with* Him and be used *by* Him to help and reach others. So, I began to fast and pray for twenty-one days. And I felt a change in me after that time."

"A change?"

Just then, Lydia's Mom came back into the room. "Lydia? You're awake," she said with a concerned smile.

"Hi Mom."

"Tell me how this happened to you?" She asked in disbelief. "What were you doing in that park by yourself?"

"I've been living a double life, Mom. I'm so sorry." With that, she began to cry softly, her crying making all of her tremble and cry out from the pain that racked her body.

Dottie kept a steady eye on her daughter. "Lydia, look at me."

Lydia turned her eyes toward her Mom, her cheeks wet from the tears.

"No matter what you've done, that's all in the past. The main thing is that you rest, get well, and whatever the future holds, we will handle it *together*."

"I'm sorry, Mom," was all she could reply softly, almost inaudibly, as the tears continued to fall. Dottie leaned over toward her and lightly kissed her forehead and placed her hand on her very delicately.

Just then a nurse stepped in. "That'll be all the visiting for today. Lydia needs to get some rest. You can both come back in the morning, or, if you want, Ms. Claremont, I'm sure you can come back later and use the empty bed overnight," she said pointing to the bed.

"I'd like to stay. I'll run Joshua home first and come back a bit later."

As he departed the room, Joshua waved even as Lydia gave him a subtle wave back even as she grimaced to move even her hand.

***

On the way home, the two of them sat in silence for several blocks before Dottie turned and addressed Joshua.

"Should I prepare myself for what she's done or been doing?"

Joshua decided to focus not on what would be a shock to Lydia's mother regarding her daughter being "Mister Tony," as well as her overseeing the illegal running of drugs through the area's schools. Instead, he decided to focus on what seemed most important about tonight's events. "The main thing is, she wants a change in the direction of her life. It doesn't mean it'll be easy to manage that change, and there may be consequences she has to face. But at least she's asking for help from others. I think she really wants to open up to you."

"But who can I go to for help?" she asked almost to the air, worry etched on her face. "I don't know how I can handle this by myself."

"Do you want prayer? We can pray together."

She looked at Joshua for a moment unsure if she should take his question seriously or not. But then she finally nodded, tears brimming her eyes. Pulling the car to the shoulder of the road, she shut off the car's engine and turned to Joshua. "What is it about you that's so different?"

Joshua was taken aback by the question for a moment. "Different?"

"There's just something different about you, how you do life."

"I'm just like the next person. I just know He's there for us, and He'll help us even in this situation with Lydia."

"I-I don't know what to pray. Or how..."

"I'll agree with you. Just pray...or better yet, just talk to Him from your heart. Tell Him exactly what you need."

She hesitated before reaching for Joshua's hand. "Lord, I'm new to this business. But I need Your help. I can't go on another moment without Your help. Please… Help my daughter. Help me to know what to do. Give us both strength—and Joshua as well…"

As her prayer trailed off, Joshua continued. "We need Your help, Lord. This situation is bigger than any of us. But I know You'll help us in our situation. You'll help Lydia get through this."

As Joshua finished, Dottie glanced over toward him. "Already, I feel something different."

Joshua smiled. "He will move on our behalf. He'll help us—including Lydia—whatever all of us must face."

"How do you know," she asked as she turned to see if the road was clear, "that He'll help us?" She pulled the car onto the road to continue toward Joshua's home.

"Because the way I understand Him, He is moved more by our faith than by our need alone." Joshua stared out the window at the passing trees, their leaves increasingly gold, orange, and red—many of them fallen to the ground. The chill of the air passing through the partially lowered window fluttered across Joshua's face.

After being dropped off and approaching his front door, Joshua noticed a car parked on the side of the road opposite him that he'd never seen before. The windows were darkly tinted, and there seemed to be the outline of someone in the driver's seat. And then he noticed the burning light of what Joshua thought must be a cigarette. Joshua prayed a quick prayer as he stepped inside his house, wondering who the person might be. "And I hope You'll also be moved by our needs, Lord. I for one need You in a big way."

Forty-Two: The Cry

Several days later, Lydia eased herself from her bed onto the wheelchair, a nurse guiding her, her mother nearby ready to assist. Her stay at the hospital was about to come to an end. She winced in pain from the throbbing that surrounded the region of her ribs, and the other parts of her body that remained bruised and aggrieved. Immediately upon settling into the chair, Lydia's face showed immediate relief. Just as they were about to depart the room, the three of them sensed someone else present at the doorway. There stood a police officer with his brimmed hat in his hands in front of him.

"Hello," he said simply before walking in as if he were visiting someone he was on a first name basis with.

Lydia looked up but the face of the police officer didn't register.

"This is the police officer who intervened during your attack," Dottie said politely as the nurse excused herself.

Lydia nodded and locked eyes with the man who stood before her wearing a somber look. He appeared to be in his mid-twenties with thinning brown hair, and a reddish complexion from too much time in the sun. She noted the officer's nameplate: *Browder*.

"Thank you, Officer Browder," she said hesitantly. There was something about the man's demeanor that didn't bode well, Lydia sensed.

"I don't know what to say." The police officer met her eyes but quickly looked down at the hat in his hands. "I wish it was for other business, but I've come to arrest you, Miss Lydia Claremont."

"Arrest her?" her mother asked taking a step toward the police officer as if to stand between the two.

"We've received details of your daughter's involvement in the distribution of drugs throughout her school. There's evidence from several witnesses that you've been involved in such for over one year complicit with several members of the Jaded Hearts gang. In the last twenty-four hours, two from the gang have come forward to confess because they don't want to be involved in this activity any longer. They named Lydia as the sole implementer."

"Is that right?" Lydia asked, even as she considered this shift against her by Frank. She recognized his handiwork in all this. They'd shattered her body, and now they'd shatter her reputation and, if possible, her very way of life. She knew, if she were to give Frank a single call and accept his "advice," that all this might somehow go away. Lydia's face changed to a look of acceptance, however. Wincing, she tried to adjust herself so she was more comfortable in the wheelchair. "Mom," she finally said softly. "It's all right. I've been living a lie for the past year and longer. I'm ready for a change—and for whatever happens to me."

"But she's not well," Dottie pleaded to the police officer nearly ignoring her daughter's words. "Look at her! You can't just—"

Officer Browder tried to appease Ms. Claremont with two raised hands toward her. He spoke calmly and softly. "We'll take her to the station, book her, and talk to the judge about placing her under temporary house arrest since she's not yet fit to be held in a juvenile facility. She should be home by tonight, Ms. Claremont."

As they exited the hospital into the special van that would take Lydia to the police station, Lydia noticed the car of Frank sitting in the parking lot, and sure enough, there propped against the front of his BMW car stood a sturdy Frank puffing on a cigarette as usual. He wore a business casual grey jacket with a white turn down collar shirt beneath, his black hair set slickly in place, as well as his shades. She locked eyes with him before looking away, a big smirk of amusement on his tanned face. She dared to look once more at him and instantly regretted it when he saw him now laughing at her—a defiant expression on his face.

After being loaded onto the van, Lydia took a deep breath as much as she could before the pain stopped her. She could only think of the first day when she'd awakened to Joshua's face. She'd found herself wanting to believe in his God, to share in the comfort that she'd witnessed in his life—despite the hardships he'd been having regarding Samuel and the cancer. But there was also another thought that replayed incessantly in her mind—that it was too late for her to invite Him in her life after all she'd done. In truth, she tended to agree with that thought almost wholeheartedly. This was her reality, not the alien worldview that was Joshua's. Yes, there was a brightness in him—even something attractive about it all. But that wasn't something, she was convinced, that she could honestly take hold of in her own life. She was too far gone, she gathered. And, she felt some sort of peace at the realization.

***

It was after 9 p.m. when Joshua heard Bailey let off several barks from the living room. A moment later, his Dad called him from downstairs. He flew down the stairway to the living room to see Lydia's Mom, Dottie, standing there holding her hands in front of her. Her eyes red and puffy, she tried to look composed. "Would you please pray for Lydia? For me? I just don't know what else to do."

Joshua invited her to sit down on the living room sofa. His Dad sat in the chair opposite him appearing especially tired from the long day. Yet he also held a compassionate disposition toward their unexpected guest.

"You believe in God," Joshua began. "And the passion you feel for your daughter will touch His heart. So why don't you pray, and we'll agree with you just like we did the other day?"

"But I'm not a follower like you are..."

Joshua smiled briefly. "There's always now. He'll come into your life if you surrender to Him, if you ask Him to come in."

She began to shake her head noncommittally at first, until something changed in her demeanor and she suddenly began to slowly nod in agreement. "You're right. I need Him so much in my life."

"Just ask Him to lead you, and your family. Ask Him to come into your life—into you."

She began to pray to the Lord from a heart bursting with emotion and need. "I have watched Joshua these last days and weeks. I think there's a reality to His beliefs, and You seem to move in his life. Would You come into my life as You have his?"

Joshua prayed with her, and his Dad sat quietly and respectfully. Joshua remained in awe of this moment,

285 | the jesus boy

amazed at the turn of events. Here they were in his living room, Lydia's Mom accepting Christ into her life, asking for His help, and about to be rearranged and changed forever!

Dottie began to cry, but it wasn't out of pain, but something else.

"What's *happening* to you?" Joshua asked in wonder.

"I feel different," she said wiping away a tear. "Something good's really happened to me."

"He is real. He will help you because He cares about you. Maybe you can now sense His immediate love for you?"

Joshua left Dottie with his Dad for a moment before flying upstairs before returning with a book in his hands. "Here," he said handing her a small black Bible. "This will help you understand more about God and His heart for you. It's His love letter to you."

She held the Bible in her hands and flipped through it.

"May I pray for you now?" Joshua asked.

"Sure," she said with a half-smile—looking a bit overwhelmed by all that was happening around her.

Joshua placed his hand upon her shoulder and took a deep breath. "Lord, I pray that You would now fill her with the Holy Spirit, that she'd sense Your Presence right now to an even greater level. May Your personal love and joy reside and flow from inside of her to all whom she interacts with."

She began to momentarily tremble. "Your hands have become so hot, Joshua," she said, her eyes closed.

"Just receive all that He has for you," Joshua admonished with a joyous smile on his face. He looked at his father who looked on, something of an amazement in his face.

"What's happening to me?" she whispered.

"Just focus on the Lord Jesus. Ask Him to give you all He wants to give you."

"Really? Is there more?"

"Yes, there is always more from Him."

She began to thank Him. And then she followed Joshua's instructions. "Please, I need You. I need everything You've got to give to me. And I want to give You all of me, too."

And for the next few moments, she sat in that exact position, her eyes closed, her hands raised, and a peace upon her face and within her heart that she'd never known before.

"He's immersing you in the Holy Spirit as He promised to do to all who come to Him seeking more, otherwise known as hungry," Joshua said with a jovial smile.

Joshua's Dad continued to sit watching all of this. He'd closed his eyes as well during the prayer of Lydia's Mom and during Joshua's blessing. As a few minutes turned to nearly half an hour, Dennis tapped on Joshua's shoulder.

"Yeah Dad?"

"Would you please...pray for me, too, son? You know how I've been so worried, so consumed with Sammy's situation. I-I just need more faith right now," he said, his voice trembling.

And so, Joshua led his father to pray from his heart, too. And then out of his father without being coached came the words, "I re-surrender myself to You, Lord. I've been a fool to try to live apart from You—and to carry these incredible burdens all by myself. Please forgive me. I can't go another minute—another second—without You," he said as tears streamed down his face. Something wonderful was happening in the living room. And Joshua was beside himself in wonder at witnessing it all.

***

The darkness had been gathered—in glee at the fracturing world of the lightbearer—piece by piece, it was being torn asunder. Here came the girl's mother—herself chained, her eyes seeing yet not seeing, as much a part of the dark kingdom as they.

But when He came—like the explosion of a cruise missile from beyond—it had struck with such force and such abandon that all the darkness was knocked back. And though they tried, there was no getting past what was taking place within the lightbearer's home. They screamed and clawed—but their efforts were futile.

The ground had become holy.

The light and Spirit entering another—no longer a slave, no longer dead—suddenly blazing with Resurrection life from the Risen One.

So, they turned their attention elsewhere.

***

Later, as the evening ended, there was an uncanny joy upon each one—but in double portions upon Joshua. Unplanned, spontaneous moments like this, like with the cheerleaders, like when Brad had been healed and Cary received His love, were incredibly powerful and sobering moments for Joshua. He realized just how vital these moments were to his spiritual fortitude, and how much he wanted them to be much more commonplace in and through his life.

Just as Dottie went home—one could truly say a new person—there came a call to his Dad's cellphone. It was late—probably his Mom giving an update. Answering the phone, Joshua could immediately hear his Mom's crying voice coming through his father's cellphone.

"My Sammy," she cried over and over, Joshua able to hear her voice. A chill passed through Joshua. Her voice continued, "He's slipping away. My Sammy, my Sammy…"

"We're coming," Dennis replied. "We'll be there as soon as we can!"

Forty-Three: Room 103

As they arrived at hospital room 103 where Sammy was being kept, Joan met the family outside the door. She instinctively buried her face in her husband's chest while wrapping her arms around him with all her strength. She began to sob quietly.

"Joan, what has the doctor said?" Dennis asked downward in a calming voice to his wife.

Joan finally pulled away and looked up at her husband looking all too fragile from what he was used to seeing of his wife. "It's not looking good, not at all. I don't know what to do… How can I save our son?"

Dennis held her tight wishing he could do something, anything, yet feeling the numbness of just how powerless he truly was settle within him—a dead weight of dread.

"All we can do is be here for Sam. And believe that no matter what, there's hope in Christ." He said these words hoping to comfort Joan, to help her not to give up. But he realized even as he uttered the words how good it was for himself to hear those words.

***

Joshua stood back watching his parents as they embraced—both having been tossed to and fro by the throes of their youngest son's grave illness for too long now.

His two towering brothers stood in front of him, their shoulders rounded and the frames of their bodies sunken and seemingly without strength. Joshua let his chin fall to his chest. He felt a growing pressure within him—of frustration and irritation that this was even happening! *Where are you, God?* Joshua wondered.

"I'll be back, Dad," Joshua said.

"Where are you going, Son?" his Dad asked turning halfway toward him.

"To the chapel."

"Come back when you can, okay?"

Joshua nodded before turning and heading down the hallway. As they'd entered the hospital, they'd passed by a delightful little room set off from the main hall. Red carpeted and set with modern upholstered chairs, there was at the front a place for people to kneel. Flowers and unlit candles sat along the perimeter. Thankfully the room was empty. Closing the door behind him, he ran to the front and fell to his knees and then forward onto his elbows, the front strands of his blond hair brushing over the red carpet.

"Lord! Tell me! What must I do? Please, Lord. Sammy is so small, so vulnerable. He's on the verge of disappearing from our lives forever. I need You right now! I need You to bring Him back to us, Lord!"

Joshua looked down at his hands. He realized how they could be open, to lift the Lord in worship or praise or, alternatively, to be clenched into a fist of bitterness and anger against the Lord. This thought frightened Joshua. Suddenly, the silence seemed no longer a comfort but a jab deep into his heart. He began to quietly sob as he pounded the carpet with his fist. He felt so alone, depleted, and no comfort as he poured out his heart. As the tears fell, he managed to see in the corner a large family Bible. Slowly climbing to his feet, almost distraught with his emotions, he reached for the Book before picking it up and holding it close to his chest.

"My Lord, Your Word is a lamp for my feet, and a light for my path," he said as he slipped back to the floor. He opened it randomly and then his eyes fell upon a Scripture.

He read aloud the verse that seemed to be highlighted. "'Now the God of hope fill you with all joy and peace in believing, that ye may abound in hope, through the power of the Holy Ghost.'"

Joshua nodded. "I want Your joy and peace. You know I believe. I need your abounding hope. And I know it's by the power of the Holy Spirit. So, help me, Lord. Help me not to look at this storm in front of me—in front of my family and poor Sammy. Help me to fix my eyes on You because You are my ever-present help in a time of need. You surround me with Your love and Your grace." At this point, Joshua began to pray in the Spirit. And soon the tears were no more, but a fury of faith arising from within him. Comfort was again his, and hope, and peace. Yet despite it all, he did not feel a freedom—or a release—to go pray for Samuel.

"But why, Lord?" Joshua said pondering the whys in such an uncertain time. "Why can't I just pray for him and see him restored? I must fight for Sammy!"

Joshua became still. He closed the large Book before arising to set it back in its place. And it was then just as he set the Book down that it dropped in his spirit filling his insides.

This battle is the Lord's, not yours.

And then, just as succinctly as that first thought had come, there followed another.

Give Me Sammy.

Joshua crumbled again to the floor as he realized this whole time, he'd been cradling Samuel in his heart so much that he'd never truly put him in the Lord's capable hands. "Lord, I'm...so sorry," as tears stung his eyes.

And then that familiar and comforting Spirit leaned upon him once again, the weight pressing down upon him and lifting him to new heights all in the same instant.

Do you forgive Me?

"What?" Joshua said aloud to the still, small voice that echoed within him. "Forgive You? What would I possibly need to forgive You for, Lord?"

"It's because He is a living Person, Joshua," came a booming voice from behind him. Turning, Joshua noted Chaplain Davis he'd met previously during his hospital visit with the Bible Club. He stood half in the doorway, half in the hallway as if uncommitted to entering. The man had opened the door to the chapel without Joshua realizing it.

"What do you mean, Chaplain Davis?"

"Even though He has done no evil, in your heart, you have seen Him as aloof and indifferent. He's not been in sync with your timing—and that's because He is Lord, and you are not. I have a hunch that's because you feel a hidden bitterness and possibly even anger to Him."

"But why would He ask me to forgive Him?"

"Because He loves you. And He knows you are hurting inside. He wants all the debris—any of it—to be removed from between you and Him."

Joshua nodded slowly. "I understand that," he said before closing his eyes and beginning to pray aloud with a lowered face. "I do, Lord. I...forgive You. You are good."

And he sat there for a few moments as he felt the joy slowly rising within his heart and mind. Almost immediately the peace filled him with such force that it brought with it a strengthening hope.

"But I don't know," Joshua said looking upward toward the chaplain, "if I fully trust Him. I can't stand the thought of losing Samuel. I just can't."

The chaplain nodded. "But you're powerless as it is. You might as well put the whoooole situation in His capable hands and then trust Him with it all."

"How did you know I was here, Chaplain Davis?"

"I was visiting Samuel and got to meet your parents. From what I can see, you've got quite an amazing family, young man!" he said, his kind smile appearing beneath his silvery moustache. "They told me you were here which didn't in the least bit surprise me."

"Why?" Joshua asked.

The chaplain smiled. "Because, you're a watcher for your family. I knew you'd be here praying and interceding for your brother and family. And, I trust, you've never stopped praying and watching over them, have you?"

"No, I haven't stopped. I love them too much—sometimes maybe more than I love God, if I'm honest."

"Joshua, if there's one thing that I've discovered," the chaplain began before pausing and finally taking a few steps into the room, allowing the door behind him to softly close. "It's that if you love God with all your heart, mind, and strength, you'll be able to love everyone—your family, your enemies—with such incredible passion. In fact, you'll love more perfectly everyone in your life if you love Him first, and if you know His personal love for you."

"Hmm, I hadn't thought about it in that way," Joshua said. "Thank you, sir."

At just that moment, the chaplain's phone began to vibrate. Holding the phone to his ear, Joshua could just barely hear the person's voice—a lady—on the other end. "Really?" the chaplain asked. "I'll come to you right now," he said before ending the call. Then, turning to Joshua, he opened the door and said simply in an upbeat tone, "Follow me, would you?"

They walked down the long corridor to the front reception desk where a mass of people now stood— probably a dozen or so people. Drawing closer, Joshua recognized the faces—the people from his church, *New Horizons Fellowship*. The chaplain greeted them and allowed Joshua a few seconds to wave, hug, and shake several of the people's hands.

"I gather you've come here to show your support for a certain family?" the chaplain asked with a pleased grin.

An older man stepped forward whom Joshua recognized as the church pastor. "I'm Pastor Hemmings. We've come not just to show support, but to also pray for Samuel's recovery."

The chaplain explained they'd have to keep their noise levels down and pray in the waiting room, though if Samuel's parents were open to it, they'd be allowed to go in pairs to Samuel's bedside to pray for the boy. The group enthusiastically accepted the chaplain's instructions.

***

Joshua began to lead pairs of the church to stand beside Samuel and offer their prayers on his behalf. About an hour later, there appeared familiar faces—Sergio, Alistair, Jennifer, and even Brad in his wheelchair. They, too, went next to Samuel's bedside to pray for his recovery. Then, to the surprise of Joshua, there came Lydia's mother together with Stacy to offer their prayers and support. The news about Samuel's grave prognosis had quickly spread throughout much of that part of the city.

Chaplain Davis came frequently to check on the comatose boy offering any practical helps to the family.

Meanwhile, the church crowds began to leave to go home followed by Alistair, Sergio, Brad, and Jennifer. Now it was just the immediate family present at Samuel's bedside doing all they could to believe this nightmare would soon pass, that little Sammy, perhaps in the morning, would soon sit up and ask what all the fuss was about. The hours passed, however, with no significant change. Eventually, nearing midnight, Kris brought Bruce and Joshua back to the house to get a proper night's rest for school the next day.

As Joshua sat in the back car, he thought of the entire day—so full of ups and downs—the good, the bad, and the ugly. During it all, he'd sensed the presence of God when Lydia's mother and his own father had opened their hearts to the One. It had been then, despite all happening, that he felt the most alive. Deep down, Joshua wondered what was going to happen—to Samuel, to Lydia, to Brad, and all his family. He wanted God to show up in these situations. He knew, just as earlier during the afternoon, that He would show up. And when He did, His power would be evidenced and result in changed lives even in the face of the greatest impossibilities.

***

The darkness struggled to get a foothold, however as they found a place to hide until an opportune time allowed them to press forward, there came the high-pitched whirl of incoming light that struck their positions—scattering their forces, causing those advancing to retreat. They came repeatedly, nonstop, and shattered their schemes. The demons continued, however, as the one called Samuel was key to their strategy. How else to dim the light in the bearer of light who continued to replicate himself in others?

Still, they continued to move forward and hold their ground until the light strikes faded. Then they began to move toward their target with all speed.

Forty-Four: Into Your Hands

The next morning came too quickly, Joshua surmised, as he pulled back his covers and eased out of his warm bed. A chill in the bedroom air immediately met him. Stepping to his window, he used his fingers to turn the wooden blinds enough to see what kind of day it was going to be. To his chagrin, he could see it was dark and dreary with rain—not the kind of day you want to step out into. Joshua thought for a moment to have a day off from school. After all, he'd been through a great deal the last few days. No one at his school would question him staying at home today.

Yet there remained in Joshua a sense that he must be in school today. It felt like he was being streamlined to go—no matter how he felt. "Okay, Lord. It must be for a reason. Let me get ready," he said as he went into overdrive to prepare himself.

After showering and dressing, Joshua received a message from his father. Every message that came now influenced Joshua—filling him with feelings of both apprehension and hope—about what the content of the message or phone call would be. His father had written to say that Samuel's condition remained unchanged.

Joshua dialed Lydia's house.

"Hello?" came Dottie's voice.

"Hi Ms. Claremont. Is Lydia there?"

"Yes, Joshua. I'll get her. And," she said, "it's been amazing to awaken to such incredible peace—and the sense that He's really here with me."

"Wow, that's amazing to hear."

"Let me get Lydia for you."

A few moments later, the phone was picked up. "Joshua, I'm sorry to say this to you. She's asked me to convey to you that she's sorry but she won't be talking to you again."

"What?" Joshua asked, alarmed.

"I don't know how to explain but she's just feeling really low this morning. She's been banned from coming to the school pending the investigation against her. And because she's going to cooperate with the authorities, she's thinking she'll soon be sent to the juvenile facility in the capital for quite a long time."

"Sioux City? Please, can I stop by there tonight after school? Don't tell her I'm coming."

"Okay, Joshua. But just be prepared for whatever mood she might be in when you get here."

"I understand. Have a good day, Ms. Claremont," he said as he ended the call. "Please work in this situation, Lord. Amen," he said calmly despite the churning within his heart.

***

Cary met Joshua at the bus stop as he stepped off his bus. "Hi Cary," Joshua said. "Have you heard anything through the grapevine about what's happening to Lydia?"

"I'm not quite in the loop like before, but according to BL, the guy you met before, Frank's got it in his mind to make some examples."

"Examples?"

"Yeah, he can't let it be seen that he's weak. He, after all, has to answer to someone too."

"But why bring attention to a drug distribution network within the school? That doesn't seem to be strategic thinking, does it?"

Cary laughed as they neared the primary entrance into the school. "A network like the one that's been operating in the school for years can cease for a time and start up again weeks later. Demand and supply will always be present. Hey, I hear the gang might be infiltrating our club, too."

"Really?"

"They're unhappy about the club's influence. They don't want it to spread. So, we can expect something might happen shortly."

"Interesting. Thank the Lord it's not my club, but His. I'll leave that to the Lord to take care of. If He has me to do anything to protect His work, then I'll act."

Cary smiled. "Yeah, if He goes after those guys like He did me, they'll soon be one of us, too."

Joshua nodded. "May the Lord extend His hands to all who need Him. May they, too, taste His goodness—even, and especially, His enemies."

"Amen!" Cary said with a thunderous clap that filled the hallway.

***

The after school gathering took place, and sure enough, there appeared two new faces. They introduced themselves as Hugh and Thomas—both appearing as normal teenagers, both sophomores. When Joshua nudged Cary if they looked familiar to him—perhaps members of the Hearts—Cary had shaken his big head. "I've not seen these guys before."

Joshua decided to give these two guys an overdose of spiritual medicine; besides, he really felt like he needed the reconnection again. If they were, indeed, facing a war of sorts from the darkness, better they be fully aflame with His Spirit than to be cooling embers. If these two guys were sincere and present on their own volition, they'd be open and glad. But if they were there for ulterior motives, they'd soon find it a bit difficult to remain there. Joshua directed the group to go deeper than usual in their time of worship—Alistair having brought his guitar. As they lifted their voices in unison, Joshua sensed the Spirit falling upon all gathered.

Joshua glanced over the classroom thankful to the One for His help in working in each of the guys' lives that filled the room. Jennifer stood with her hands uplifted, a glow upon her face. Brad sat in his wheelchair with his face upturned, his eyes closed. Despite the strange reoccurrence of his previous condition, he still looked better now than he'd ever looked prior to his amazing healing. Still, Joshua felt an ongoing puzzlement at the return of the boy's previous condition. "I put him into Your hands, Lord," Joshua prayed quietly. "May You be glorified in his life and situation. May Brad be brought closer to You despite what's happened to him."

Joshua watched as Alistair played with all his heart while seated on one of the desks. And Joshua felt the joy of seeing Sergio having returned to worship with them though he didn't know if this was permanent or temporary. His presence with the group especially blessed him. Then Joshua looked upon the new faces—over a dozen or so young people, some of the cheerleaders included, all now dedicated to knowing and walking with the Lord.

Joshua felt the joy of the Lord sweep over him. "And You are the most important One here, Lord—even if no one else was here, *You* are enough! Welcome, Lord," Joshua said softly with a smile as he opened up his heart to the Lord afresh inviting Him to come and to fill all of him—and everyone in that place. "Come and take full control of me and this group, Lord. If we have You, no darkness or deception can remain here for long," Joshua said grinning ear to ear, glad for the joy and peace that permeated this place and now his heart. No matter what was happening in his life—whether great or small—if he turned and kept his eyes on the One, no matter the situation, he'd experience a joy overtaking him and resetting him. Lifting his hands in worship, the others joining in, Joshua noted the two guys remained in their places, respectful though reserved—their manner calm but uncommitted to what was happening around them.

When the time of worship ended, the two were still present and seemed to have adjusted well. Joshua greeted them as they were about to leave but nothing seemed amiss about them. They'd simply come because they'd heard some of the stories—strange and wondrous stories—of God doing crazy things in the school. They had come seeking to know more about the Lord. When Cary had heard this, he'd become especially animated. Like it or not, the giant young man herded the two of them to sit down in the rear of the class so he could share with them what had happened to him not too long before. Joshua could only chuckle at the spectacle of seeing this ex-gang leader, once a bully to do works of the flesh, now being a bully-for-the-Lord herding people to hear his story—whether they liked it or not. It truly had been a miracle what had happened to the big guy.

On his way home, Kris having picked him up, they stopped at the hospital and visited Sam until about nine o' clock. His condition remained unchanged. To alleviate his symptoms, the doctors had begun to treat Samuel with various transfusions which would help the boy to have respite from his fatigue. Heading home, Joshua staring out the window as his brother drove them home, Joshua could only pray as he again put Samuel into the Lord's hands. "He's all Yours, Lord. And Lydia. And my family. And the Bible Club. All of it, I place in Your hands. Amen!"

Forty-Five: Trials by Fire

"Kris, is there any way you can you stop by Lydia's place?" Joshua asked with pleading in his voice.

"What? It's getting late, Joshua."

"I know. But I've got to talk to her," he said giving his brother a concentrated look. "It's been on my mind all day. Everything else is going wrong. I want a chance to make things right with her."

Kris gave him a sidelong, knowing look. He smiled briefly. "Girls," he said with a grin. "They'll drive you crazy—when you're around them and when you're not."

Joshua nodded. "I know, tell me about it."

"Okay, I'll drop you off. If you want, I can come back and get you in an hour."

"Thanks, Kris," Joshua said as he felt hope again. "You can be all right sometimes," he laughed.

Kris mimicked a laugh before forming his right hand into a fist and delivering a light jab to Joshua's side.

They pulled up to Lydia's home before Joshua got out and waved his brother away. Feeling a bit shy about showing up at nearly ten o' clock, Joshua rang the doorbell. A few seconds later, Stacy opened the door.

"Hi Joshua," she said and opened the door enough for Joshua to step through into the house. Just then, Dottie came from the kitchen. Seeing it was Joshua, she smiled warmly.

"Sorry about stopping by so late. I just got back from the hospital."

"That's all right, Joshua. Are you hungry?"

Joshua could smell the aroma of something good lingering from the kitchen. "Something smells good, Ms. Claremont. Sure!"

"How's lil' Sammy?" she asked in a reserved tone.

"He's stable but unchanged from the past day or so."

Dottie nodded. "Sorry to hear that. Just hang in there. He's got an amazing family waiting for him to get through this time."

Joshua nodded before stepping into the living room and taking a seat on one of two sofas that faced each other. He felt rather sheepish. Stacy, who reminded him of Pippi Longstocking, complete with the blond pig tails took a seat opposite Joshua and seemed to be studying Joshua without much restraint.

"Is it true you made a lame boy walk?" she asked flatly.

"Stacy!" bellowed Ms. Claremont's voice from behind which was set to the rear and to the right of the dining room.

"I just wanted to know," she said with the hint of petulance in her voice.

Joshua spoke up despite feeling timid and a tad embarrassed. "Brad is his name; yeah, he was touched by God."

"Really?"

"I just did what God told me to do," Joshua said patiently.

"What does He say about me?" she asked, this time her voice soft and inquisitive.

Joshua smiled briefly. "Do you want to find out?"

Stacy nodded.

305 | t h e   J e s u s   b o y

"Let's ask Him, then," Joshua said. He rose to his feet and stepped into the dining room for a second. "Ms. Claremont?"

"Yes?" she said standing over a saucepan that was being heated.

"May I pray for Stacy?"

"Sure, of course," she answered with a pleased smile.

Joshua stepped to Stacy who remained seated on the sofa. She looked up with an uncommitted and unsure look.

"Don't worry," Joshua said with a grin. "This will be painless. Just going to pray over you."

He began to pray for a few moments inviting the Holy Spirit to fill the room. Then his eyes sprung open even as he sensed the holy presence filling the room. Joshua laid his hands on the girl's shoulders just as Ms. Claremont came into the living room and joined in praying for her. "We just lift up Stacy to You, Lord. I just pray now to have a glimpse into Your heart for Stacy."

They stood for a few seconds quietly and receptively. Finally, Joshua began to share. "I just see a father figure picking you up and throwing you into the air and catching you again. I believe Daddy-God is saying you're His special daughter, that He delights over you and desires that you'd come to know His special love for you. He also knows your heart's concerns. He's been waiting for you to turn toward Him with an open heart so He could show you how much He loves you. He's never let you go even though at times you've felt as though you were alone."

Stacy smiled at that, even while keeping her eyes shut. "I'd like to be closer to Him," she said.

Ms. Claremont leaned over slightly and hugged her daughter from behind.

Over the next few moments, Joshua led Stacy in prayer—a conversation really—between her and the Lord. And when, finally, she said "Amen" echoing Joshua, there was something visibly different about the twelve-year-old girl's disposition. "I feel different—in a good way."

Ms. Claremont reached down and wrapped her arms around her again. "Yes, Stacy, my baby girl. When you invite Him in, everything changes."

Joshua smiled, glad, even overjoyed, to see this unexpected, unplanned result in Stacy. A few minutes later, Joshua seated on a stool at the dining room's table, Ms. Claremont served Joshua some steaming chili con carne on white rice.

"I'll go up and talk to Lydia—let her know you're here," Ms. Claremont said with a grin.

A few minutes later, Ms. Claremont returned. "I think she's already asleep, I'm afraid. She didn't answer her door. Sorry, Joshua."

"Oh," Joshua replied, trying very hard to hide the disappointment he suddenly felt. "Thanks for trying," Joshua managed with a grin.

About twenty minutes later, his large bowl now empty, Joshua started to say his goodbyes as he headed toward the front door. He thought he'd start walking home and wave Kris down when he approached; he honestly didn't feel like ringing Kris. Even if he had to walk the full distance, he welcomed it by the way he was feeling. It was as he drew near to the front door, Ms. Claremont and Stacy standing with him at the front door, that he heard his name being called from upstairs. Joshua looked toward the sound of his name, then to Ms. Claremont who gave him an approving grin.

"Good luck, Joshua," she said as he smiled back hopefully before climbing the stairway.

***

He turned left at the top of the steps and stood in front of the first door before giving a light knock.

"Come in," she said in a neutral tone.

"Hiya, Lydia," Joshua said, peeking inside. She sat on the edge of her bed. She patted the edge of the bed beside her for him to take a seat. As he did so, she reached around him embracing him in a tight hug. Then, she laid her head on his shoulder.

"I've missed you, Joshua," she said simply. He returned the embrace while being absolutely surprised at her sudden, unexpected displays of affection. He tried to find a way to separate himself from her to have a safe buffer; yet she clung to him too tightly to allow this.

"I've missed you, too," Joshua admitted to her looking at her.

"Under house arrest is better than the juvenile facility," she said with a laugh. Again, he tried to release her to get a safe distance from her. But she continued to hold onto him firmly.

"I think I heard you praying for my sister?" she said, finally releasing him.

"Yeah, I could really feel the Lord's compassion and love for her."

"I see," she said flatly, with a hint of disinterest. "What if I were to tell you what I feel—or rather show what I feel toward you?"

Joshua nodded, and although subtle alarm bells were going off telling him to excuse himself or rather, to insist on them visiting each other in another part of the house, he calmly resisted doing that. It was possible, after all, and desired in his heart, that Lydia and him be finally reunited with each other after so much uncertainty. They needed privacy for that to happen. Despite all the inner warnings, he felt glad to be invited up to her room—even giddy (though he was very careful not to allow this to be on display to her). And if the truth be told, with all that had been happening the past few days, he suddenly felt relieved to be in a place where he could just be with his special someone—nothing expected of him except to receive and give love. He wanted to feel something good for a change—to be comforted by being with this girl who had so filled his heart and mind the past months. The thought of her, even at the worst of times, had, in the brief time he'd known her, granted him a sense of strength and well-being—even identity. He could still remember the looks on his brothers' faces when they'd heard he was dating Lydia—a tall girl with a fine body and even finer face. Sitting here now, moreover, he realized just how worn out he felt from seemingly always having to wear burdens uncommon for adults, never mind one his young age. He wanted to rest—to let down his guard. For a moment, just five minutes, he told himself. He wanted to be normal—to have the chance to experience what was burning within his heart for Lydia at that moment. He wouldn't allow himself to go too far, he repeated to himself.

But even as these preventive, putting-the-brakes-on thoughts filled him, her hands lifted to his face and pulled him closer until their lips touched; he felt the battle raging within—and the Voice present but increasingly being diminished. Like flood waters appearing out of nowhere, he felt himself suddenly being carried along. He stopped resisting as he wrapped his arms around her pulling her closer to him, her alluring perfume, the flutter of her breath across his cheek. Never in his life had he felt what he was feeling at that moment. Was this love? Or something else? His body was already fully endorsing his every movement and their every touch of each other. Joshua recognized in his intellect what was happening—but each argument was side-swiped away as he surrendered to the driving passion within. There was no stopping what was happening to them. Within moments they were lying alongside each other as they kissed and caressed each other.

There came the honk of a car horn outside. *Kris!*

"Joshua?" came the muffled voice from downstairs. "I think your brother's just drove up outside."

Joshua felt the panic of the moment. He did not want to leave, not now. For once he was where he wanted to be—with his girl. Quickly stepping to the door and opening, he poked his head out into the hallway toward the staircase. "Okay, Ms. Claremont!" he said trying to sound like nothing was out of sorts.

Joshua returned to the bed and sat down with a hearty sigh. Lydia raised to a sitting position before bringing her hand to rest on his shoulder. Even as he pulled out his phone and rung Kris, she was, even at that moment, kissing him on his right cheek.

"Kris?" he managed, trying his best to sound as normal as possible.

"Why aren't you coming out? Mom and Dad told me to come fetch you. It's getting late and you've got school tomorrow."

"Kris, please. I'll get Ms. Claremont to—"

"If that's what you want to do," Kris interrupted. "Call Mom or Dad now and get their permission, or get your butt out here *now*!"

"This isn't a good time for me to leave, Kris."

"I don't care. You've got all of five minutes or I'll call Dad."

Joshua ended the call and threw his phone down on the carpet beside them. He reached over and pulled her close. Then, just as he was about to kiss her goodbye, he had an idea. He had to do it as he wanted—needed, really—this time with Lydia. Releasing her and quickly retrieving his phone, he rung Kris back. When he answered, Joshua spoke up. "I just spoke to Dad. It's cool. Lydia's Mom will bring me home in thirty minutes." Even as he said these words, for all his justifying reasons why, he felt his insides sinking within him. He felt an emptiness that caused his heart to race at the actions he was allowing to happen.

"Okay, fine." And then the call to Kris ended.

"Whoa!" Lydia said with admiration in her voice. She laid back against the stack of pillows against her back while pulling on his shoulders which drew him backwards to her. "I like this new Joshua," she said before leaning over him and giving another kiss from above. She ran her long fingers through his blond hair, a smile appearing on his face.

"By the time Kris finds out, probably when he gets home, it'll take him another twenty minutes to come back—if he comes back—which is enough time to spend with you."

"Only forty minutes, kind sir?" she asked acting a disappointed look.

"It's the best I could do. But don't get used to it," he said.

"Why do you say that?" she asked.

"'Coz I'll probably be grounded for the next month or longer when my family finds out what I just told Kris."

"Hmmm, yeah. So, I suppose we should take advantage of the time we have?"

"So, are we back together now?"

"Do you really have to ask that?" she asked.

"Well, I—"

She shushed Joshua. "Let's stop with the words. I'm tired of words. I want to feel something together. Don't you?"

Joshua gave a subtle nod and kissed her. Already in his mind, he'd crossed several lines that he shouldn't have crossed. And now, this latest do-not-cross line of telling a lie, had astounded him. A fleeting glimpse of himself praying for Stacy made him even more astonished—to go from such heights to such depths in so short a time! Yet for all the wrongs of his actions, he somehow felt at least partly justified. He needed this time with Lydia. For the sake of his relationship with Lydia, this was important. This had been the make-or-break moment in their relationship.

"Hey," he began. "We should slow dow—"

"Hey," she answered in a corrective, almost-whispering tone. "I said, no more words."

He thought to resist her but that thought was only fleeting as he allowed himself to finally surrender to her.

Forty-Six: Trespassers and Advocates

The vacuum had been the ideal spot—the place where the trap was set. The lightbearer succumbed—the Voice replaced with the voice of another, and replaced with his own wisdom.

   Immediately, they clung to the boy—their fangs drawing from him the life and light that they so craved—like leeches. Their victory was sure, now. And soon, the victories would spread to the other boy when he breathed his last.

   And when that took place, they'd have permanently suffocated the life and light of Joshua Phillips.

***

   It was in a house not unlike any other on the street. Anyone walking by wouldn't have considered the boundaries being crossed—boundaries set in place by the Eternal One for a purpose—so that all would be protected and valued. It was a desecration of something meant to be sacred and contained within a holy and enduring covenant, something intended to be handled with care—for the sake of human hearts which could be so fragile and so easily dashed to pieces.

   As the door had closed and the lock had been engaged, and no more words were uttered within, it had taken only the inborn instinct of a mother downstairs to realize what might be happening. She'd given a shout of warning—her goal not to embarrass the teens—as she climbed the stairway and stood in front of Lydia's door.

"Lydia? Joshua?" she queried.

There came a flurry of movement within and muffled mumblings.

"It's getting late. Joshua? Want me to drop you off?"

"Yes, Ms. Claremont," came the boy's voice in an all-too-friendly voice.

"Five minutes, Joshua," she said through the door. "I'll be waiting downstairs for you."

***

Lydia sat against the back of her bed. She felt a tinge of anger at her mother for interrupting their time together. Yet for any anger she felt, there was also something else within her, feelings she'd not encountered very often before. They had lodged in her mind—regret, and, she surmised, something else akin to shame. Her motives, not too long ago, had been to bring Joshua back to earth—to ground him by seeing his wings melted by the scorch of the sun's heat. She had wanted him—all of him, not just a part. She hadn't wanted to share him with his God.

Now, however, something had changed. She didn't want to hurt him—she simply wanted to be with Joshua. A haunting look upon Joshua's face had appeared as he'd got up to leave. It was as if the light, always present before, had been dimmed to almost nothing. Lydia sensed he'd been silently crushed by their actions.

She lowered her head for a moment. She felt self-conscious, even foolish, yet there was something—a drive—to say something.

But to whom?

Then like something inborn within her, she prayed very quietly, her eyes closed.

"God, I'm sorry for wanting to hurt Joshua to get what I want. Please, help me to be a better person. I hate myself for what I allowed to happen with Joshua. And I ask You to help Joshua so he'd get back some of the joy and life he had before he came here tonight. I'm sorry."

As she ceased to pray, she continued to keep her eyes closed even as she found herself finding strength in the stillness—and something akin to a presence? And though hard to notice, there was on her cheek a tear that trickled down her cheek, which she quickly dabbed away.

***

Joshua sat in the car as the car moved in the direction of his home. He felt so many emotions as he sat there—but most of all, he really wanted only to be alone. Any traces of the One seemed to have receded in his heart until there seemed to be nothing but vague traces of His once vibrant, infilling presence.

"Sorry if I interrupted you two," Ms. Claremont said. Joshua heard her and for a moment was surprised that she was the one to be sorry. There was only one in the car needing forgiveness, Joshua considered.

"No," Joshua confessed. "I'm grateful you called me when you did."

Ms. Claremont nodded her head. "Yes, I was getting concerned when it became a bit too quiet up there."

Joshua lifted his hands and covered his face and lowered his head to his chest. "I-I betrayed Him," Joshua admitted even as his voice struggled to remain strong and even.

Ms. Claremont kept her eyes focused on the road in front of them which Joshua was thankful for. "I was a teenager once," she added with a laugh. "Might be hard to believe, but it's true."

Joshua wished he were alone even more so. He just wanted to crawl up into a little ball and cry for the way he had moved so quickly and without hesitation toward feeding his flesh—of going against the so-clear Voice of the Holy Spirit.

"Joshua, lately you've been through more than most," she said. "I could understand why you'd suddenly feel weak and overwhelmed—"

"I love her," Joshua said simply. "I love your daughter—probably too much for my own good. How can I be in a relationship with her and God at the same time?"

"Because of you, Joshua, I've experienced a change within me. I see the world differently. The same for Stacy. And I suppose, when the world gets a little too much inside of us, we will experience a different kind of change—not the change we want, or that He wants."

For the first time, Joshua turned and glanced at Ms. Claremont, an astonished smile appearing on his face. "Hey, that's pretty insightful."

"You may've disappointed yourself, and the Lord. But somehow, I suspect that it won't take much for you and Him to be reconciled," she said with a knowing grin.

"But how can I ever trust myself again? I failed Him. It was so clear what He was speaking to me—yet I ignored and pushed Him away. I just wanted to be with Lydia—to forget about every problem, to just be happy with her."

"Joshua, you'll just have to set up boundaries that will keep you from being in that situation," Ms. Claremont said as they entered the street that Joshua lived on. "And if it'll help you, I'll make sure you're not allowed to go up to her room again," as they pulled up alongside Joshua's home. "Living room only, please!" she said feigning a totalitarian voice.

Joshua chuckled at that.

Ms. Claremont put the car in park and then turned for a moment. "Mind if I do the praying this time?"

"Thank you, Ms. Claremont," Joshua said with a smile before lowering his head. She reached over and placed one hand upon the handsome lad's shoulder.

"God, I really want to lift up Joshua. He's had a hard week. So please put your blanket of grace around Him. Let Him sense that special grace and mercy to him. Why? Because You love him dearly. Amen."

"Amen," Joshua repeated, feeling a lift within him. "Thank you so much. Please continue to pray for me, would you?"

"Of course," Ms. Claremont said with a smile brushing away a black strand of her long hair. "You're a warrior for God. And I think you'll need extra doses of prayer. So, I will continue to lift you up."

"Thank you, Ms. Claremont," Joshua said opening the door. "You're pretty cool."

Ms. Claremont smiled and gave Joshua a friendly wave. "See you soon," she said as Joshua closed the door and headed, with a sense of dread, toward his front door. Yet he also felt a comfort knowing that he was returning to a safe place. Using his key to open the front door, he stepped into the living room not knowing what was about to happen or what was about to be said to him—if anything.

***

"Joshua," came his father's voice from upstairs. "Is that you?"

"Yes, Dad," Joshua replied and then he waited for what would be said next. Bailey came up to him and reared up on his hind legs. Joshua gave his childhood dog a rub behind the ears and a hearty hug. "So good to see you, boy!"

"You're running pretty late tonight, aren't you, son?" his Dad shouted.

Has Kris somehow covered for me? "Yes, Father," Joshua admitted. "I had to patch things up with Lydia."

"Oh, so that's the reason you lied to your brother?"

Joshua sighed briefly feeling the remnants of his strength seep out. "Yes," Joshua replied in an appeasing tone. "Sorry, Dad."

Dennis' head appeared at the bottom of the stairway. "How many weeks should I ground you? You were meant to return home just as your brother told you."

Joshua looked down at his hands as he sat down on the living room sofa, Bailey standing near him as if to give comfort. "A year? What does it matter, Dad?"

Dennis stepped down into the dimly-lit living room, his big frame blocking the light from the corner lamp so that Joshua couldn't identify his father's face. *Was he angry?*

318 | the Jesus boy

To Joshua's relief, his father stopped shy of the sofa where Joshua was seated and eased himself down onto the armchair nearest the kitchen. He sat back placing his hands behind his head before stretching out his legs in front of him before crossing them. "Are you okay, son? It's not like you to lie."

Joshua leaned forward lowering his head trying to keep himself composed. "No, Father," and then he couldn't stop himself. Joshua fell forward onto his knees as he felt all his internal conflict become unsealed. He began to sob. "I sinned against God." And as he remained on his knees, his father leaned forward immediately wrapping his arms around his son.

"It's going to be all right, my son," he said in a reassuring tone. "Don't worry, my boy. I'm here for you."

Joshua turned and wrapped his arms around his father—for the first time in a long time.

"I really don't need to know the details but was it something to do with Lydia?"

"Yes," Joshua buried his face into his father's chest. "I'm such a fool."

"Hey, hey!" his father said pulling his son even tighter to himself. "Don't say that about yourself. There isn't a single person alive who's perfect."

"But Father. He spoke to me. But I just pushed Him away. And I lied to Kris. And Lydia and I, we...if it wasn't for Lydia's Mom—"

"Okay, son. Just listen to me. You've been under a lot of strain of late. So, I just want you to bring your heart and mind back to the one thing that gives you strength."

"But I can't sense His closeness to me anymore," Joshua said pounding the carpet with his fist.

"Well," his father said reaching over to the bottom of a side table and pulling out his Bible. "Let's see what the Bible has to say about that."

Joshua looked up and watched his father turn the pages to the rear of the Book. Then he began to read. "'If anyone sins, we have an Advocate with the Father, Jesus the Righteous One.' What does that mean to you, Joshua?"

"He's not against me. Even though I've grieved and disobeyed Him," Joshua said. But as the words read to him from his father lingered in his mind, he saw for a moment a way out of the maze he'd created for himself.

"Aside from the fact that you are grounded for lying," his father said with a grin, "I don't think your heavenly Father will ground you when you have the Lord Jesus standing up for you and on your behalf."

Joshua chuckled as he nodded ever so slightly at his father's wisdom. "Is Kris upset that I lied to him?"

"No," his father said rising using Joshua's shoulder to stand up. "He actually thinks you're human like the rest of us, now."

Joshua laughed again. "Thanks for the encouragement, Dad. I'll just spend some time with the Lord down here before I go to sleep."

"Four weeks, if you're wondering."

"One?" Joshua opined.

"Three."

"Two?"

"Two and a half weeks," he said with a smirk as he neared the stairway to go up to his bedroom. "Your Mom will be home in the morning from the hospital before you head to school. Good night, son."

Joshua nodded with a smile. "Thanks, Dad."

After his father had gone up to bed, Joshua remained seated leaning forward in an attitude of prayer. The house seemed still, all-too quiet. Joshua squeezed his eyes shut as he focused on the One. "Lord, I seek Your forgiveness. I don't trust myself; I will trust You, however, to pick me up from this place I've fallen. I am sorry for hurting You and pushing away Your Voice. Please, make me a safe landing place for Your Spirit. I pray this in the Name of Jesus."

As he spoke the words "Amen," he sensed anew what had been so-familiar to him the past weeks and months—the abiding presence of the Holy Spirit. Comfort and hope seemed to wrap around him. Yet despite everything said to him, the truth of the Scriptures, and the comfort of the Spirit that surrounded him, there remained a lingering sense that he'd lost *something* when he'd chosen the voice of Lydia over and against the Voice of the One within him. "Please, Lord. Teach me to be rooted in You, to listen only to Your Voice. I pray for this, O God."

***

They clung to him, like wolves feasting on a downed deer. Every movement, every bite with razor sharp teeth taking from him what was so rare.

Then the ringing of that Word had sounded like bells in a church tower—the sound piercing and shaking all their surroundings. The truth settling into the heart, its life and light immediately brought forth the One—repelling them in one clean swoop. They tried to re-advance—and their onslaught was strong—but not strong enough.

Then, they saw in the distance—the little one's life about to be theirs. And they rejoiced.

***

 The call had come abruptly in the wee hours of the night. The landline phone's too-loud *twerp* invading the night's still silence with jarring effect. Joshua had heard the phone and sat up. Even Bailey at his bedside let out low barks as if sensing the circumstance. Then came the sound of footsteps in the hallway. He heard mumblings between his father and Kris, and he heard Bruce as well. Then Joshua's door opened.
 "Joshua?" his father said in a slightly panicked tone. "Quickly get dressed and come downstairs. We need to get to the hospital right away. Sammy's in trouble."

Part Four: Immovable Trees

"Storms make trees take deeper roots."
-Dolly Parton

Forty-Seven: The Funeral
Four Weeks Later

Trying to ward off the frigid cold, Cary stood on the trampled snow along with the mass of students, teachers, and even some from the Jaded Hearts who had grown disillusioned by the gang and its way of life. They'd come out and stood with Cary despite any repercussions. Heavy snow had fallen the previous night blanketing the grounds and piling high atop the tombstones, benches, trees and shrubs that covered the grounds as far as one could see. The sky seemed to reflect the ground—it's expanse as white and undefinable as the snow on the ground that seemed to merge the whole seen world into a collective white mass. The chill of a wind passed low-to-the-ground between the tombstones and trees causing everyone to clutch onto their coats in a futile effort to keep some semblance of warmth.

    Cary glanced over to the Phillips family who sat somberly in chairs alongside the casket—Dennis, Joan, and the three sons. Even their dog had been brought since, it was said, the dog had been such a part of the son's life. It sat still next to Mr. Phillips and moved not one inch—an occasional whine heard from the dog of many years. Upon the faces, there was a numbness and disbelief regarding the events that had unfolded the past weeks. Their eyes were fastened on the shiny brown casket which sat atop shiny gold railings, the deep hole with its pristine-edged dark brown walls open as if beckoning that which sat perched above it. Cary hated that the casket sat so separated from all the people—alone and isolated. It shouted finality. And it grieved Cary to no end that this had been the outcome, such as it was, for the Phillips son.

    Even as he heard without registering the preacher's words, Cary felt a tinge of anger and sadness the way things had turned out. If only he'd been around so that he could've done something—anything—to prevent the outcome as it had happened. Since his encounter with the One, Cary had come to see himself as a protector of sorts—the weaker, the smaller, and the vulnerable. And perhaps this was why so many in the gang had begun to regard Cary highly. On many occasions, they'd sought him out to get his advice, or get answers to the questions they had about spiritual matters. Sometimes, however, they just wanted to hear more about the Message and how it had removed the mess from his life. Some, too, requested his subtle help in getting them out of the gang. Even a few of the drug dealers had begun to reconsider their line of work and seek a way out. Some, however, likely sensed the tide turning on their activities and wanted to get as far away as possible from the sinking ship. Yet others seemed to genuinely feel an uncertain shame about their concealed actions.

    Enthusiastically, Cary had begun to show all that came to him not just in words, but also in his actions, about his God. Not only did he talk about the power, but he also demonstrated that power that resided within him. Cary had seen the healings begin to manifest because of his petitions. He'd also seen a few addicted to highly addictive drugs completely set free from their crazed need—and even their withdrawal symptoms were minimalized or non-existent when Cary would lead them in a prayer to receive Christ and then, subsequently, the power of the Holy Spirit. When they'd pray in the Spirit thereafter, the withdrawal symptoms seemed to be minimized and less tormenting. Then, usually after several hours, they'd finally break through the haze of their addiction. Everyone in the community saw with astonishment the change in Cary—and the evidence of something truly supernatural—that had come to be a regular part of his life.

    Despite any appearances of being strong or immovable, though, Cary knew himself all too well. When the news of the death of the Phillips son had reached his ears, it hadn't taken long before Cary had broken down; it had been the first time in his life he'd cried for another. If he were honest, that news had shook him to the core of his newfound faith. Yet after this time of testing and reflection, he'd been even more convinced and felt even more on task to do God's will—to show the world God's goodness and love.

    Looking around, Cary couldn't believe the numbers that had come. A gathering of hundreds had appeared—so many, in fact, that at least a third of the people were unable to enter the church sanctuary for the visitation and tribute. Yet they had all stood there in the foyer, and even outside the sanctuary in the wintry chill, silent, respectful—all come to commemorate and honor the poor lad who had met such a tragic end at such a young age.

    Pastor Hemmings from New Horizons Fellowship stood with his Bible as he finished his last words meant to give some sense of understanding and context—and how to somehow get past this maze of a loss. Several times during his homily the pastor's voice had broken though in the end, he'd maintained and completed his address—one that was as much inspirational as it was hopeful despite the circumstances. Chaplain Davis also stood to the side of the pastor with a long, drawn face. In the crowd, too, was the Snyder family, the man of whom Joshua along with Jennifer, Allistair, and Bradley, had prayed for at the hospital. Still in recovery, but alive and able to move about nonetheless. Earlier in the service, the chaplain had stood up and shared how impacted he'd been by the boy who had, on a few occasions, reminded and encouraged him to maintain a fire for those things which had brought him into ministry in the first place.

    Cary saw near the Phillips family Lydia along with Stacy and her Mom—all three wearing withdrawn and depleted faces. They stood huddled together, Lydia's head resting upon her mother's shoulder, Stacy held tightly from behind by Ms. Claremont. Behind Lydia stood the lady juvenile officer sent to chaperone the young lady from and to the Sioux City Juvenile Facility. Lydia wore a withdrawn look. She hadn't shed a tear, yet, but her face displayed a grave sadness. Cary shook his head slightly when he considered how Lydia, the teenager with the girl-next-door looks and the easy-going smile, had been discovered to be the mysterious "Mister Tony," the one who had orchestrated much of the drug trade for the county's schools for quite a good length of time.

    The last words spoken, the casket was slowly lowered into the earth wherein the family stood to their feet and approached the opening before dropping flowers. To the astonishment of those present, Bailey suddenly and for a moment again whimpering as well as looking agitated as the casket was let down into the depths. Mr. Phillips bent over and caressed the dog's head before trying to comfort the dog.

A few moments later, Cary stepped forward and approached Mr. Phillips. He leaned toward Mr. Phillips' ear. After speaking briefly in a low voice, Mr. Phillips nodded to Cary.

Turning and facing the crowd, Cary greeted everyone. "Hello, at one time, I promised Joshua I'd share my testimony. So, here we are. I'd like to share with all of us here what happened to me not too long ago. I'll keep this brief, but long-story-short, I was a person who had become hardened by life. I was brutal, rude, a bully, and didn't care what anyone thought about me. But the truth is, for all my years' experience as a gang member, I'd never known love. My father alien to me; my Mom, herself love-starved, unable to give love to me. Love was, I think, completely alien to me. I didn't even know it existed.

"But then," Cary said looking down at his hands, his voice shaking, "e-even when I was God's enemy, He blessed me through Joshua...literally blessed me. And when He did bless me, I found myself being...pursued—that's the only word I can think of—*pursued* by God's love. I found myself pegged down on the ground," he paused before allowing a chuckle. His dark eyes gleamed as he spoke. "And there I stayed—on the ground—till I finally surrendered. Me, a former thug and gang member, suddenly swallowed up by His love. I've never experienced what I experienced on that day. Turn to Jesus and you, too, will experience His love. And it was all due to Joshua."

After Cary finished, tears streaming down his face, the pastor gave his benediction.

Immediately after, little Samuel stepped over to Cary placing his small hand upon his arm and leaned into him for reassurance, the boy fighting the sobs that threatened to overtake his little body.

Forty-Eight: New Family

"Nice words," Samuel said, lowering his chin to his chest.

Cary looked the boy over and gave the boy a friendly grin and a slight nod. Samuel, smartly dressed, appeared so frail and barely holding up in the morning chill. Since what had been described by the locals as the "Incident," Sammy had become especially fond of him. The boy reached upward with his little hand toward Cary who gave a solemn smile before taking his hand and pulling the boy next to him and hugged him.

"Are you all right, Sammy?" Cary asked with a strengthening voice.

Samuel refused to look Cary in the face but instead, stared at the ground. His face—his eyes and mouth—showed great restraint in holding back the tears that threatened to come forth. "I-I don't know," Sam finally said before his mouth contorted into a barely heard moan. "I miss him so much."

Cary lowered himself and engulfed the boy in his massive arms. "I know you do. So do I, Sammy. So do I." He held him for a long while until he noticed Mr. Phillips standing next to them. He looked down upon them with a look of understanding. Cary stood up while pulling Samuel closer to himself.

Mr. Phillips began. "Cary, I just want you to know that you're always welcome in our home. In fact, my wife and I have talked about it. We'd like for you to come live with us. I've talked to a friend of mine who teaches at the vocational college. He says you can begin this Spring training in any area of study you're interested in—the first year entirely paid for."

"That's great, Mr. Phillips," Cary said. "Thank you for the offer. And maybe someday soon, I'll take you up on that. But for now," he said pausing, "I think I need to do the Lord's will. My vocation will be His vocation—reaching out for people that are empty and need His love and life—just like I once needed."

Mr. Phillips smiled and nodded. "I understand. Joshua really had an impact on you, didn't he?"

Cary could only nod and lower his face, his eyes again taking on a gleam.

Mr. Phillips reached his arm around Cary. "Would you join us at the house this afternoon? We'd be grateful if you'd come and hang out. We'll have lunch there."

"Sure, Mr. Phillips. I'd like that."

"You can ride with us if you'd like," Mr. Phillips said pointing to the stretched limousine.

At that, Sammy began to jump up and down, his face beaming for the first time this day. "Yes, Cary! Will you ride with us, please?"

Cary nodded and placed one of his hands on Sammy's head. "You bet."

The boy kept his eyes fixed upward on Cary's face as they moved toward the limousine.

Cary said his good byes to most of the gang members, some of whom no longer participated in gang activities. As per Cary's negotiations with the current gang leader who had come to regard Cary highly, those who wanted to leave would not be harassed or harmed in any way.

Cary caught a glimpse of Lydia several cars behind the limousine. Their eyes locked for an instant before she gave him a friendly nod. She looked well and there was something about her—something akin to peace on her face despite the unexpected tragedy of Joshua's loss. Close behind her stood an official-dressed prison female officer who had brought Lydia in a juvenile-prison van so she could attend the funeral of her boyfriend. Cary understood this had taken quite a bit of influence from the likes of Mr. Phillips, Pastor Hemmings, and even the hospital chaplain, Mr. Davis. Cary watched as Mr. and Mrs. Phillips approached Lydia with Ms. Claremont and Stacy standing nearby. Mrs. Phillips hugged Lydia and seemed to be thanking Lydia and her family for coming. There was behind each of their looks something that linked them: the sadness they shared for their loss.

The side door of the van open, Lydia volunteered her hands which the officer linked together with plastic zip ties before she stepped cautiously into the van.

Cary had read the paper headlines as they'd come out—Lydia having spilled the beans on the whole drug network including its leader, Frank, to the authorities to show cooperation and seek for a lighter sentence. Cary suspected there were other reasons, too. She knew Lydia to be a shrewd young lady—something he'd come to respect and even admire. Everything Lydia did involved calculation and purpose. Almost immediately, over a dozen teenagers from countywide middle and high schools had been brought into custody for drug distribution though there were said to be many more under investigation. And the numbers of adults, too, that had been involved, it was discovered, numbered in the dozens. Gang members from the Jaded Hearts, too, were placed under scrutiny by law enforcement for their involvement. Where there was evidence, gang members were taken into custody. National news networks had come to Sterling City to cover the story—how an attractive young teen girl, not even old enough to vote, had effectively run a network that spanned a whole county involving multiple schools and many dozens of adults. Thankfully, the law prevented her name or face being identified in the media.

Cary ducked his head as he climbed into the limousine taking up nearly half the rear seat—Sammy cozying up to his side as if seeking the assurance of protective safety. Three rear seats made up the limousine. Sammy patted the seat which drew Bailey to jump into the limousine and curl up in the remaining space. Kris and Bruce sat in the middle seat, while the front seat remained unoccupied, Mr. and Mrs. Phillips standing near the open limousine door still talking with several funeral visitors.

Looking down at Sammy, Cary was still astonished at the display of stamina he'd shown the past two weeks. Without hesitation, Cary reached down and hugged Samuel. The young boy looked up at his new big friend and allowed his shoulders to relax. Cary studied the little boy's face which now showed no hints of the onslaught that had previously ravaged his body. Although he displayed sadness, Cary also noticed something else—a childlike hope and optimism in his face—despite everything that had happened.

Cary still couldn't believe the events that had happened the past month—and truly they had been as much incredible as they were terrifying. He began to reminisce about the events of the past weeks even as the limousine began to move off—and the replay in his mind even at that moment unbelievable.

Forty-Nine: "The Incident"

As the limousine made its way back to the Phillips' residence, Cary thought back three weeks to the moment the inclination had dropped onto him—as if the weight of a small car had landed on his shoulders. The weight had settled upon him with such intensity that he felt there was no other recourse but to obey. So, to the hospital he went, a walk of twenty minutes at a brisk pace. When he entered his large mass into the hospital foyer, he had a feeling he knew this must be something to do with the Phillips boy, Joshua's youngest brother, Sam.

Cary locked eyes on the nurse's station. He thought he'd have a real problem getting past the station not being family and all, but then his eyes fell upon a nurse that looked familiar to him. Then he realized, the young lady had been his babysitter long ago. He'd not seen her in years yet her appearance was familiar plus the passage of time.

"Hi Lauren!" Cary said as he stood in front of the desk.

"Cary? Is that you?" she said with a surprised smile.

"Yes, it's me. How have you been?"

"I'm well. Hard to believe it's you."

"I know," Cary said with a grin. "I've changed a lot from when you looked after me." Cary laughed at the thought of his ancient small self and his larger-than-life self now.

Lauren nodded with a smile. "You've really grown up, Cary!"

"I like to eat!" Cary said with a grin. "It's the Italian in me!"

Lauren laughed at that.

Then his smile disappeared. "Lauren, are the Phillips family here?"

At his question, Lauren leaned forward. "I'm afraid it's been a sad night for them."

"Why?"

Her voice took on a whisper. "The little boy passed away just over two hours ago."

Cary heard the words and shook his head, a look of disgust appearing on his face. It took only a split second but already Cary was moving down the hall.

"But I'm not sure you're allow—"

Cary whirled around suddenly more versatile than his big frame suggested. "Be right back, Lauren."

Even before he reached the room, he could hear the soft crying inside the room. He stood in the doorway considering the darkened room. With their backs to him, Mr. and Mrs. Phillips rested on their knees with their elbows on the bed, their hands grasping Samuel's small hand and arm, the boy's hands and arms inactive and seemingly deflated. The brothers were in there too—each of the older brothers seated on the rooms' surrounding chairs behind their parents, their faces held behind closed hands or hidden in folded arms.

Joshua sat on the floor facing the far-right corner away from the rooms' occupants. He rocked back and forth silently while holding onto his knees, his face dropped downward against his chest, no noise coming from him at all. Seeing this mourning and brokenness, Cary stepped backwards. *What am I doing here at such a difficult time? What can I possibly offer these people?*

He turned and began to retrace his steps down the hallway until a voice called him. Cary stopped. It'd not come from anyone around him. His name had echoed *within* him. And then he heard the inner words, *Bless him.*

"Bless him?" Cary said quietly. "What do You—"
Speak My life into him.

The word began to echo within him and grow in intensity. Without arguing, Cary turned and went back to the room. He stepped inside and without hesitating, approached the bed. He knew he mustn't think too much about this directive. He just needed to do what he'd been told.

"The doctor said we could have time with him," Joan stopped crying long enough to say through brimming tears. "Please, don't take him yet—"

Cary realized she thought him to be hospital staff. He gave her a smile. "I've come not to take, but to give."

Immediately, Joshua whirled around and stood to his feet. "Cary?"

Cary smiled briefly to Joshua before turning back toward the boy. He seamlessly reached for Sammy's hand and held it with both of his big paws. The hand was heavy and cold. "I bless you, Sammy. It's time to wake up."

The sobbing and hidden faces now stopped and looked respectively on this strange big teen holding Samuel's hand. "Who are you?" Dennis Phillips asked him, a challenge in his voice.

Cary calmly turned and gave him a reassuring smile. "I am a friend." Then he turned his attention back to the lifeless boy. "I speak God's life into you, Sammy. Come on.

Get up," Cary said without a hint of wavering. "It's time for the Message to clean up the mess in the name of Jesus…"

"But he's not here with us anymore," Joan said weakly, a pleading in her voice. "He's gone."

***

The boy's life gone—all the prayers lifted on his behalf of no consequence—the darkness rejoiced. Their task complete, they now turned their faces toward the family—to take from them their faith, their trust in the One.

But then, there came a movement that shook all around them—as if a great giant were approaching. They saw, in the distance, a lightbearer. He appeared to be so distant from them, yet they sensed what was happening.

"What's going on?" they cursed and spat to each other. "Bring the strongest ones forward *now*!" they screamed. "We cannot lose this one."

When he came into the room, it was as if a hurricane's 150-mph winds struck them. They held on to the little boy with fevered determination.

***

Cary held the hand when it jolted as if struck by large amounts of *something* akin to electricity. The boy's hand squeezed and clutched onto Cary's hand and did not relent. Suddenly Samuel's chest started to rise and fall as the boy took in a deep breath as if life had just been emptied into him. Almost immediately his eyes popped open before fixing on Cary who hovered over him. The pale look on the boy's face began immediately to take on warm splashes of color.

Cary gave a smile. "It's about time!" he said with a grin.

Hesitantly and weakly, Samuel smiled upward at Cary, though the boy appeared extremely tired and disoriented. Then the boy turned his head ever so slightly to his parents.

"Mom? Dad?"

They immediately reached for him and held his hands. "Yes, honey?" Mrs. Phillips said, tears streaming down her cheeks—and her husband's cheeks.

"I'm so hungry!" he said weakly.

This caused the parents to laugh and smile in wonder as they glanced at each other—the joy now overflowing despite the dozens of questions at the back of their minds. However, those did not matter. Reality was happening in front of them. One moment he had not been there—gone and too far to reach. Now, he was back with them, simply and quietly.

The elder brothers stood behind astonished at all that was happening in front of them.

Cary stepped away. He'd completed what he'd been sent to do. He turned and made his way toward the room's exit. As he did so, Joshua ran after him grabbing his arm gently. "Cary?"

Cary nodded and gave Joshua a sidelong look while letting out a chuckle. "He told me to come," he said stepping outside the room.

"Thank you," was all Joshua could say through his tears standing in the doorway, throwing occasional glances over his shoulder at Samuel just in case this whole affair wasn't real. "Thank you so much."

Mr. Phillips also stepped out of the room, a slight tremor in his voice. "What did you do?" he asked shouting after Cary.

Cary just stood there and grinned. "I did what I was told, which is usually good for all around. Give glory and thanks to the Lord. He told me to come." Then the large, young man turned and began walking down the hallway toward the exit.

Mr. Phillips could only stare after Cary with a stunned look. But there was also incredible relief now easing across his face. And something else: *awe*.

Giving unceasing thanks and praise to the One, Joshua watched after Cary as he made his way toward the hospital exit, that young man who had, at one time, been his worst enemy.

***

As Cary walked toward the hospital exit, he considered the event that had just taken place. He had only known to come here. He had not known the reason. Yet somehow, he figured it must be something to do with Samuel. When he'd entered the hospital room and stepped to the bed, he'd known only one thing in his mind: He must be obedient and pray for the boy regardless of his state of body. He'd had no clue what would happen—if anything. Yet the boy's chest had begun to rise and fall under his touch. The reality of the moment had both frightened and astonished him. And it filled Cary with joy knowing that Joshua's brother would live despite evidence to the contrary.

Passing the nurse's station, Cary looked down at Lauren.

"I think they need you in there."

"What?" Lauren said. "What's happened?" she said rising to her feet, her face visibly disturbed.

"He's not dead. He's asking for food—hospital food which is a miracle in itself," he said with a laugh.

"What, Cary?" she asked again. "But the doctor—"

"Go see for yourself, Lauren," Cary said calmly, a smile spreading across his wide face.

Appearing troubled, almost distraught, the nurse quickly began heading with a quickened pace toward room 103. Another nurse walking toward the station intersected with Lauren. Cary heard her shout to the nurse. "You're with me. Let's go!"

Walking a bit further, he came to the waiting room. And there to his right were familiar faces seated in the foyer. Allistair, Sergio, Jennifer, and Bradley in his wheelchair. They looked to be praying. And then, all in one moment, Cary felt a nudge within. Stopping and turning, Cary approached the small group who'd remained to pray for the Phillips household. They all turned with puzzled looks on their face.

"Hi Cary," Allistair said.

Cary only returned a subtle nod to Allistair even as he continued walking toward the group. Then he stopped, kneeled, and placed his hands on the shoulders of a startled Bradley.

For a moment, Bradley tried to move backward in his wheelchair. But then he realized what Cary was doing and relaxed. Bradley closed his eyes even as Cary finished his prayer burst. Then the big boy rose before turning and heading toward the exit. As he got to the exit, however, he turned toward Allistair. "Samuel just awakened," he said with a smile, possibly the first the group had ever seen on Cary's face.

"But we were told Sammy's gone..." Allistair said.

Cary smiled. "Go and see for yourselves the goodness of God."

The group began to rejoice and give thanks to the One. They lifted their hands in praise and thanksgiving even as the burden for the Phillips family was lifted from their shoulders. Tears of joy began to fall. And then everyone stopped suddenly. They turned ever so slightly toward Bradley, their mouths agape.

Bradley turned toward them surprised at their attention suddenly set upon him. Then he realized something amiss. He looked downward to see himself now up and out of the chair, standing, his formerly twisted, confined form now upright and unfettered once again. He began to laugh even as the tears began to stream down his cheeks as he collapsed to his knees and threw up his hands in worship. The others almost leaped upon Bradley and embraced him even as they rejoiced even more for God's grace upon him.

***

The limousine pulled up in front of the Phillips' home. Looking down at Samuel seated beside him, Cary considered repeatedly in his mind the whole affair of Samuel's return to life. No matter what, he'd been astonished at the power of God in the boy's emaciated and lifeless body. Very quickly the event, what people in the community had come to call the "Incident," spread as incredible news to all the hospital's staff and, eventually, even to other patients, and then beyond the hospital's walls. The physician who had declared Samuel deceased had returned to the side of Samuel's bed, gob-smacked, to check the boy as did other doctors of the hospital—all with astonished looks on their faces. All the hospital staff remained dumbfounded at the mysterious reversal. It defied medical science. Tests were immediately started to find out what was happening within the boy's body. The next day, preliminary results showed the body free from any signs of leukemia. It had vanished leaving only a smiling, shrunken boy with an insatiable hunger for lots of food and drink. Even the local news media had run a piece on the event that had played the last five minutes of the news. "Something beyond comprehension had happened when it shouldn't have," the journalists had said regarding the mystery. But for Cary, the cause and effect had all boiled down to the power of One—the One Who lived within him.

Fifty: Salvation

A week later, Cary felt especially led to go to the Sioux City Juvenile State Facility. But before he could go, he sought the assistance of Chaplain Davis at the hospital. After a brief call, the chaplain said he'd be happy to contact the facility chaplain whom he personally knew and request from Lydia if Cary could be placed on her visit list.

Two days later, Cary received a call from the chaplain telling him that Lydia had added Cary to her list.

Travelling by bus some two hours north one way on Interstate 29, Cary watched as the world passed by. He quietly prayed, even as he sought to understand the Lord's directive for him to go to her. At last, he shrugged his shoulders. As long as he did what he was told, there would surely come direction when the moment demanded it. In some ways, he felt great joy and relief in simply walking along this uncertain, improvised edge—not knowing every detail for every step he made. He just needed to keep things simple—to trust and obey.

Arriving at the city center of Sioux City, Cary used his phone's map app to walk some thirty minutes to the state juvenile facility. This place housed hundreds of young people, the youngest aged thirteen. Some of these would remain on these grounds until they turned eighteen or, for especially heinous crimes, until aged twenty-one.

After almost an hour of waiting and being carefully searched, Cary was led into a long stretch of a room that held about a dozen metallic booths with inset large panes of glass. The facility was antiquated having been erected at the middle of the last century. Taking a seat near the end of the room, Cary sat down on a bolted down metal stool and kept his hands in front of him. He prayed quietly in the Spirit while awaiting Lydia's arrival. Finally, in she came dressed in an orange one-piece garment, her blond hair laying along her face and dropping to her shoulders. She sat down while at the same time giving Cary a Why-are-you-here? look.

Lydia sat there, uncommitted to picking up the phone. She tilted and laid her head on her hands. Cary remained peaceful enough. He didn't show any reaction whatsoever to the girl—just sat there with a neutral look fastened upon Lydia, the phone held to his ear. Finally, she reached for the black phone handset with its black cord and brought it to her ear pushing back her hair.

"What do you want, big boy?"

"I was told to come here."

"By who?"

"The Lord led me—"

Lydia rolled her eyes before looking Cary directly in the eyes. "Are you really sure you want to be following Someone who let Joshua get killed? What kind of God would allow that to happen to one of His own?"

Cary kept a neutral expression refusing to take the bait. "How are you doing?"

Finally, the defiance softened a tad. "I'm doing all right, I suppose," she said looking down at her hands.

"It was incredibly brave for you to give up Frank's name to the authorities."

"Brave?" Lydia said raising her voice. "What else was I to do? The network's existence had already been revealed to the authorities and linked to me to make my life unpleasant. I had to take control of the situation—even if it meant I'd lose everything. Besides, what he did to Joshua—" her words trailed off as she lowered her face.

Cary nodded with an understanding expression. "He must be a bit unhinged to literally dismantle the network in order to dismantle you, too."

Lydia nodded. "Because I was an uncertainty in his mind, I think he just felt he'd need to start it from scratch. Unfortunately for him, he didn't realize that I'm not afraid of consequences." Then she became impatient. "Why are you here? You didn't come here to discuss has-been news."

"As I said, He," he said pointing up at the ceiling, "put you on my heart."

"You don't know why you're here, either, do you?"

Cary smiled. "It's a bit like wandering around in pitch black with a small flashlight. It's a limited-perspective kind of thing. But I'll know when I need to know."

"That's handy." She turned around and glanced at the clock. "Well, you've got exactly fifteen minutes as the visits are limited to twenty minutes."

"I think He just wants you to know He's not far from you—that no matter what you've done or not done, He is near to you."

Lydia's expression really softened at that. "But—" Then she broke off her sentence. "Never mind."

"But what, Lydia?"

She hesitated before resuming her words. "If it hadn't been for me, Joshua would still be here right now."

"Lydia, if it wasn't for Joshua, I wouldn't be where I am now. Everything has a purpose—even the things we can't understand."

Lydia nodded slightly. "I can't believe he's gone." She looked down at her hands, a sadness coating her face.

Cary nodded and lowered his eyes to his hands. "Me either."

"I can't believe Frank would do such a thing."

Cary shook his head slowly. "I know," he said momentarily grinding his teeth.

Lydia shook her head, swearing under her breath. "If He's real, why would your God have allowed this to happen to him?"

"I don't know."

"You're okay with this?"

"No, I'm not okay with this. But blaming God isn't going to help anything."

"Let me guess," Lydia continued. "You've forgiven Frank already?"

Cary looked down for a moment and refused to reply. "No, I can't say I have, yet. It's a work in progress, Lydia. It's not going to be easy for me. But I know Joshua would want you to be at peace. And to know the God he followed. And that I follow."

Lydia locked her eyes on Cary as she leaned forward toward the glass. "Why would He want me?"

"Because *He* is good. We are not. But He still loves us."

"How did it happen for you? How could you be changed so much and so quickly?"

Cary grinned at her question before a smile began to surface. "I love to share this. I never knew love. It was alien to me—like a fairy tale. I used to hate people—especially families I'd see at the mall walking or eating together. They had something that was almost beyond my comprehension. My Mom never gave me much of anything except a hard time." Cary paused before pushing back a large strand of black hair that drooped slightly over his right eye. "When Joshua blessed me, it was as if I found myself in a dream. It was like being pursued by a swarm of bees. I thought I'd die if they caught up to me."

"You, running? Don't do that much in real life, do you?" Lydia said with a laugh as she looked over his large mass of a frame.

"Yeah, you're right about that one," Cary said chuckling. "But in the dream, I was running for dear life. When they caught up to me, I was caught in something not unpleasant but something entirely unexpected."

"What was it?"

"Love. I felt it for the first time. And the truth is, it hurt! Then, afterward, I began to read the Scriptures and study what He did *for* me, that He died for me, in *my* place. It was then that I knew it was more than just emotions or sentimental feelings. It was love-by-actions. I'd never been able to comprehend emotional love. But I could understand that kind of love—love by actions."

Lydia nodded slightly.

Cary resumed. "My gang. They'd die for each other. But they wouldn't do that for me if I was disloyal. Yet this Christ died for me despite me being His enemy."

***

Lydia stared at Cary through the glass barrier. Even as she listened to Cary, she felt all at once a hatred for him—

because of the words that were coming out of his mouth. She looked away looking instead at her hands in front of her. Yet even as he spoke, there was something of a comfort and of a hope in his words. Still, she couldn't help but think of her own life—the things she'd done, the words she'd spoken, the imaginations she had connived to enact in her life. She felt dirty from the lives that had surely been devastated by the drugs, by the thuggery of the gang who had been under her authority when needed. She felt a wave of shame wash over her and seemingly drag her downward into a darkened hole. For a second, she thought she'd scream at the big boy to shut the hell up, this boy who had appeared seemingly out of nowhere. But she let him drone on and on. After all, she surmised, there was nothing in this world that could truly comfort her or grant her genuine peace. She'd let him give his speech so he wouldn't feel he'd wasted all his time and energy to come see her. And after he'd finished, she'd leave this visitor's room the same way she'd entered it: living a mundane existence, on a heading with no destination. Thankfully, she'd been unable to see the night sky from her holding cell since coming here which meant her perspective was limited and earthbound thanks to the four drab walls surrounding her. There would be no comfort or peace for her—just the emptiness that gnawed at her from within.

    Since coming to the juvenile hall, she'd been harassed by many who had connections to Frank or the Hearts gang. She suspected they'd been told to attack her either physically or mentally every day—to make her life unbearable. The authorities had known this might happen and had taken steps to prevent her from being harmed. But there were still moments when she couldn't escape being with other prisoners. And then the attacks would ensue. In the time she'd been here, she'd gotten into several fights all because someone else had thought to take something from her—an apple, a carton of milk, whatever. But she could never allow that to happen, not without a response. She'd never let anyone walk over her before; she'd surely not allow it now—even in this place away from security and comfort, away from all that was good. At the rate she was going, she'd not be out of this place until she was at least twenty-one.

Even as Cary continued to talk as if he'd never stop, Lydia found herself remembering glimpses of Joshua—of the brief times she'd been with him. She pictured him with his infectious smile and the way he always seemed to embody life, of peace, and of joy. She felt suddenly ashamed that she'd set out to bring him down, to destroy what most mattered to him. The tears momentarily burned her eyes. She wiped at them quickly so not to allow Cary to think she was responding to his monotone. With earnest strength, she held back her emotions that were rising within her and threatening to burst forth. She missed Joshua unlike anyone else in her life. And, she had realized before, if it hadn't been for her connections to the drug network and Frank and the gang, Joshua would still be alive, still be helping people out, still be a light in such a dark world.

But would he forgive her if he were here? Would Joshua have approved of her course of action that Lydia had planned to take place as soon as it was possible—even later that evening? She couldn't do it—to live here day in and day out for another week, never mind for years. She had to let go of this life, to determine her own course of action—not be a twig on a river speeding toward an abyss. She'd do the controlling. She'd determine her own path and exit.

Yet despite her decision that had been made days before, despite how much it'd surely crush her mother's heart or her sister's heart, she began to hear in Cary's words something akin to what a fire-burned forest could receive—a new lease on life, a new beginning—borne of a fertile ground from which fresh seed gains traction and begins to flourish. Perhaps she had had to be brought to her lowest, to see no other outlet before His words could really lodge in her heart and bring life. She felt embarrassed, but her desperate state finally made her reach upward from her nadir.

***

Cary finally became quiet. He hesitated to say anymore in case he'd already said too much.

"What do I have to do?" Lydia said in a low voice, her eyes fixed on her hands in front of her.

Cary smiled faintly. He nodded quietly and mouthed thanks to the One. Then he began to lead her in a prayer of surrender—of losing control long enough to allow the One to take control—even as a guard knocked on the door giving a five-minute warning.

As Lydia finished repeating the prayer, the tears slipping down her cheeks, she looked up in amazement. "Wow," she said. "I really feel something different inside me. Something's really happened!"

Cary nodded. "This facility will have chaplains you can connect with. They can help you in your new-found faith."

Lydia smiled broadly. For the first time in Cary's interactions with her, the smile seemed genuine and unrestrained.

"I'll be praying for you, Lydia," Cary said.

"Would you come and visit again?" Lydia asked.

"Yeah, I think I can do that. Next week, same day and time?"

Lydia nodded and gave another smile.

Just then a guard opened the door and stepped into the visitor room. The female guard held the door open for Lydia. "Visit time is over," the guard said simply.

Lydia acknowledged the guard and then turned toward Cary. "Thank you for everything." She arose to her feet and began to walk out, the guard looking Lydia up and down and displaying a puzzled look at the sudden change in Lydia's demeanor from when she'd been brought in.

As Cary began to make his journey home, he was overwhelmed at the response from Lydia. She had opened to the Lord and finally received Him. He smiled for a moment glad he had the gift to talk to and open people's hearts to the Good News. His trip home went quickly even as he contemplated the change in Lydia. Truly nothing compared to sharing the Good News of Christ with people.

Fifty-One: The Temperature of Love

The following Monday, Cary made his way to visit his mother who lived in a small, one-bedroom apartment not far from Sterling City's city center. He'd made it a habit to visit her each Monday which had begun soon after he'd turned to the Lord. Up until that point, his relationship with his mother had been non-existent. As Cary rode the bus that would drop him just outside her apartment complex, he thought back to the very first time he'd gone to see her. It had not gone well. He'd felt like a total stranger in her home, and the great gulf between them seemed impossible to bridge. However, he'd not stopped visiting her—no matter how harsh and razor-sharp her words could sometimes be. He couldn't expect decades of old ways to die out just because he came to see her weekly. It'd take persistence and something even Cary understood was necessary: supernatural. Cary knew, however, that that could easily be an excuse to do nothing. But from what Cary had seen, the Lord would take his offerings and duplicate them. Cary had to do and give something before he could ever expect the Lord to do and give something supernatural.

    He walked up to the apartment complex entrance and then rung Apartment 3. A few seconds later, the intercom sounded a woman's raspy voice. "Oh, it's you!" she'd said. And then the buzzer sounded which temporarily unlocked the front door. Within less than five minutes, Cary stood in front of his mother's apartment door. He gave two quick, light knocks.

The door opened and a woman, thin and frail, immediately stepped away. Her red-nail polished fingers carried a cigarette. Her skin was tanned but the years had made her skin, openly revealed thanks to the tank top, and her face, age considerably. Yet there remained traces of an earlier beauty. She wore her dark hair in a bundle atop her head.

"What do you want?" she said with impatience as she plopped down on a recliner chair. Immediately she pulled a wooden lever which elevated her sandaled feet.

"Mom, why are you smoking again?" Cary asked.

"What, I can't smoke in my own home now?"

"No, it's not that. It's just not good for you."

Pushing the wooden lever on the chair, she sat up before flicking the ash into the ashtray. "Listen to me, young man. I'm not interested in your opinions." She eyed Cary directly. "And besides, it destresses me. Isn't that a good enough reason?"

"No, Mom. It's not."

In a burst of anger, she rammed the cigarette down into the ashtray which caused it to smolder and hiss in protest. "Happy now?" she said turning her face away. "Why do you come here, anyway? Is it just to make me miserable? If so, job *accomplished*!"

At that moment, Cary felt his anger begin to rise. But he'd not come here to get in an argument or to defend himself. He repressed his anger. "I guess I'll come back another day," he said and began to rise to leave.

"What, you're not hungry?" she asked looking at him, her voice softening. "You look like you're not eating properly? Who are you staying with these days, anyway?"

"A friend of mine. And yeah, I eat all right. Don't worry about me, Mom."

"Are you still running with those mongrels?"

"No, Mom. I've left them. Remember, I told you long ago."

"Smartest thing you ever did," she said with a hint of respect in her voice. "Well, do you want me to cook something for you or not?"

Cary nodded before allowing a brief smile. "About time you smiled," she said. "Was beginning to wonder if your religion allows a person to smile or not."

"Mom, if you could peek inside at my heart, you'd be astonished how good I am—to be at peace with God, with people, and with myself."

"Well, I can't, can I? So why don't you just tell me?" she said as she rose up and stepped into the small kitchen that adjoined the living room to the side.

"I guess before, my mind and heart, if you'd looked at it, would've been painted red with anger, and a lot of chaos there. But since I gave my life to God, since meeting Joshua Phillips, I've never been the same."

"All psychological, my dear," she said as the turned on the stove. "And I'd be careful who you associate with, if I were you. Haven't you heard of Jim Jones?"

"Why didn't you say something to me about the Hearts gang if associations were so important to you?" Cary asked, an edge in his voice. "Suddenly I'm hanging out with Christians and it's something to be cautious about?"

She stopped what she was doing and turned to look Cary directly in the eyes. "And would you have listened to me if I'd told you to stay clear of that gang? Would it have done any good to nag you?"

"No," he said accepting her words. "I suppose not."

"But now, you'll at least listen, right?"

"Yes, Mom."

"Then just be careful."

"But it's much more than psychological. I've seen what God can do and it goes beyond psychological. And besides, I know what He did in me."

"Good for you, honey," she said as she began to chop an onion. "Good for you."

Three-quarters of an hour later, spaghetti in a homemade tomato sauce was served along with long thin strips of heated and browned garlic bread.

"Thanks, Mom," Cary said as he began to twirl the pasta around his fork. Looking about the room, he couldn't believe he was here in his Mom's home having dinner. How far he'd come since God had penetrated his life with His Personhood and love.

Fifty-Two: The Mystery of Frank Gelb

The past three years had been productive for Cary. Not long after the funeral of Joshua, Cary had taken Mr. Phillips up on his offer to stay in a room in their home for a small monthly amount and to enter the community college to complete a business management degree. He'd learned he could always be an advocate for the Lord in regular life, too. He could build a future and do so in such a way that the Lord would continue to pour through him to those around him.

In line with his study, he was given the opportunity to work as an assistant-manager position in the local grocery store. Cary had even begun to shed some of the excess weight on his rotund frame. He made a point to play basketball twice a week with the Phillips' household and lift weights which took almost immediate effect in producing a change to Cary's look. Quite quickly, his rotund shape began to frame into an impressive stature. His jawline and cheeks became more pronounced and his black eyes more prominent.

Whereas before, he'd have been looked at for his prominent height or weight, now he was noticed because he was a good-looking man who displayed almost a natural charisma.

Not long after starting work, Cary had begun to send a weekly amount to his mother to help her out. He continued to visit her regularly. Though their relationship always bordered on raucous, there was, at the core, something slowly being rebuilt when it came to their relationship. Although arduous at times, it felt good. It made him feel grounded to have his Mom in his life. Cary would, too, regularly hug his Mom. At first, she'd been put off by his hugs and shunned them. Cary, however, had not given up. He made it his goal to hug her at least once, even twice, during each visit. And slowly over the weeks and months, she began to receive his love and, for the first time that Cary could remember, even give love back to him. Cary also prayed for her each visit—just simple prayers of blessing and what He thought about her.

This had the effect of dislodging blocked arteries in her heart until, finally, she began to change the way she used course language as well as the level of chain-smoking in front of him. Though she was indifferent to his or any other religion, Cary could tell she was softening to the Lord because he had never sought to present religion to her but instead give something vibrant and alive from the Lord Himself—His love, His peace, and His untamed desire to capture her heart.

Quite quickly, Cary had begun to see beyond the outer shell that had been built up over the decades. He could see just how vulnerable and frail she was despite the harsh outward displays. This made him love her even more.

Cary read the email on his phone that had come from the prison chaplain at the Sioux City Correctional Facility. Finally, at eighteen, Cary was old enough to join the pastor in coming with a small team from New Horizons Fellowship to the prison to share Christ to those who wanted to get out of their cell for an hour, or, who had a genuine hunger for spiritual matters.

There had been, too, another reason for Cary's desire to visit the prison on a regular basis. A singular name that had begun echoing in his mind every day for the past three years: Frank Gelb. It had trickled into his mind at first, and then began to drop into his thoughts almost unceasingly—sometimes even seeping into his dreams.

Cary knew that the man, once a leader of the Sterling City drug network and indirect leader of the Hearts gang, had finally been caught by the authorities in Florida and brought back to Iowa to be tried for the murder of Joshua Phillips and, separately, for his involvement in the drug network that had spread throughout Sterling City and the counties surrounding. Enough people had come forward, either on the inside or outside of correctional facilities, to incriminate the man for his leading involvement in statewide drug dealing network that had permeated local schools, colleges, and even fueled many adults' addictions. After a period of nearly six months, the man had finally been put behind bars for a period of no less than fifteen years at the Sioux City Correctional Facility with no possibility of parole due to the murder of Joshua Phillips, and, separately, the fact that the drug network had involved and been focused toward the delinquency and exploitation of many minors.

Coming to the prison the first time, Cary had prepared himself for this visit. With Pastor Hemmings, the two were checked into the prison and eventually led to the large chapel. It was, unlike the rest of the prison, cozy and warm—surely a temporary escape from the clanging doors and echoing voices that filled the inside of the prison all hours of the day and evening. Red-carpeted and with red-padded pews that sat in a semi-circular amphitheater setting, the pulpit stood at the center of a platform that sat at the bottom of the incline. Cary watched as prisoners, the first of three batches that would come to the service, were led into the chapel. Each chapel service, Pastor Hemmings led in worship playing his acoustic guitar followed by the giving of a short word of encouragement. Then during each of the three services, Cary would step forward and begin sharing his personal story of how God had intervened in his dead-end life.

As they climbed into the pastor's car to head home, Cary and the pastor both felt elated at the work that had been done. The men, in almost all instances, had been completely grateful and ecstatic for their visit. The worship had been full-on, and many at the end of each service came forward to commit or recommit their lives to the One.

"I keep hearing from the Lord the name Frank Gelb," Cary said.

"Why would you be hearing his name?"

Cary shrugged his shoulders. "I don't know, pastor."

"Could it be because you still haven't fully dealt with your anger toward him?"

"Of course. He killed the one person who was good, who wanted to be like Jesus. He took from me, from his family, from Lydia—from all of our community."

The pastor nodded. "What would be the purpose of your visit?" he asked as he started the car engine.

"I don't know. I'm just feeling like I need to see him face to face."

"When you were in the gang, did you have run-ins with him?"

"Not me personally. We only heard his first name and knew to stay on his good side."

"I see," the pastor said as he began to pull the car out of the parking slot toward the guard house where they'd be waved through the exit.

"Is there a way to be able to talk to him if he's not family and not coming to the chapel services?"

"I can talk to the chaplain there. Maybe he'll have some suggestions. How long has the Lord been placing him on your heart?"

"Since Joshua's death and his arrest."

"Hmm, a long time, then."

"It's been echoing in my mind and heart since that time."

"And what have you been doing about it?" the pastor asked matter-of-factly.

"Mainly just praying for the man. Lifting him up before the Lord. Is it possible that's all I'm supposed to do?"

"I wish I could say. You'll have to continue to ask the Lord about that. Meanwhile, I'll talk to the prison chaplain about getting you inside to meet Frank."

Cary nodded. "That'd be great."

***

One month later on a Sunday, the prison chaplain having made the arrangements, Cary was led into a visitor room where he waited several minutes until Frank Gelb stepped into the room. A glass and metal partition separated them. Frank wore a one-piece gray prison garb with a long number sewn on a strip of white fabric onto his breast pocket. Even in prison, he'd managed to maintain his sleek look—his jet-black hair combed back and tight upon his head, his goatee slickly trimmed. His skin had the glow of health, perhaps a tad light of a complexion since he was, for most of his time, kept indoors away from the sun. Cary thought he looked rested but with a tinge of boredom in his persona. He sat down before eyeing Cary.

"The prison chaplain said you have something to share with me? Is it a care package because that would be really nice?" he asked with a smug expression.

Cary looked at him calmly and with an easy-going appearance. He didn't want to come across the wrong way with Frank at the outset of their conversation. "Hi," he said simply. "I'll bring a package next time."

"Next time? Who said there'll be a next time?" Then Frank leaned forward slightly. "Have I seen you before?" Frank asked. "You kinda look familiar."

"I am here because God spoke your name to me over and over the past three years," Cary said simply.

At that, Frank gave an unbelieving nod and then quickly scanned the room for the guard who stood just beyond the visitor room door. He gave one condescending glance toward Cary indicating that the meeting was over and began to swivel and rise toward the rear door exit.

"Does that shock you? Or make me seem like a nut-case?" Cary asked forcefully.

Frank stopped his exit but refused to look Cary in the eyes, merely turning his head sidelong. He spoke but kept his eyes away from Cary. "Both."

"Why would God put your name on my heart all this time?"

"Wild imagination, perhaps?"

"No," Cary said plainly. "He's kept you on my mind, perhaps because you were convicted in the murder of Joshua Phillips."

"Oh, *that* boy," Frank said, now staring downward at his hands. "Such a thorn in my side."

Cary felt his face burning. He held his hands in front of him tightly, the knuckles becoming white under his clutching fingers. For a moment, he examined the glass between them wondering if he could get through it to reach this low-life.

Frank turned toward Cary and leaned forward. "Did I take away your boyfriend?" he jested with a mocking voice.

Cary hid his anger. If he'd been in the same room with the man, he'd surely have tested his own prowess against the murderer. "He was a good friend, and someone who genuinely cared for people. You took him from a lot of people."

Frank suddenly made three steps toward Cary before he bent over and slammed his hand on the metal table in front of him. "Good riddance!" he shouted followed by a full laugh. A guard appeared and looked through the exit door's window. "You coming here was a waste of my time *and* yours," he said simply.

"You're in here for the next twelve years. Surely you can give me twelve more minutes," Cary managed to say with forced control.

Frank sighed deeply. "This," he said forcefully, "is a waste of time." At that, the man began to walk toward the door at the rear of the room some five paces away.

"Did you know my Mother?" Cary asked toward Frank's broad back.

This caused the man to stop in his tracks. He turned slightly. "Her name?"

"Alba Adessi," Cary replied.

At that the man, his face remaining neutral, turned and made his way toward the rear door.

"I'll be back next week to see you," Cary said plainly. "I'll bring a care package."

There was no reply as the door opened before the man made his way out without saying a single word.

***

This one, theirs for decades, was surrounded by the strongest ones—some of them in the same league as those placed over nations. As the lightbearer, that troublesome one, came near, the strongest ones cupped his spiritual ears from start to finish—and whispered into his ears reminding him of his independence and his identity. He owed no one, feared no one, and didn't need anyone. A wall of pride, there for so long, kept the man aptly imprisoned. They clung to the man, their fangs digging into him, siphoning his very life—feeding his misery with porn and lust and violence.

***

Cary was troubled, to say the least. At the sight of Frank, within those first few seconds, Cary had noted within himself something altogether unfamiliar—at least since he'd given his life to the Living God. Yet it also reminded him of his old self. It was akin to hatred. And, he realized, he'd not been able to forgive the man for what he'd done to Joshua. This had been reinforced by the realization that if he'd been in the same room with the man, it wouldn't have ended peacefully. That look in Frank's face—of having absolutely no remorse about his actions even though he'd snatched a young man's life away from so many who loved him—it had reinforced Cary's desire to hurt the man if it were at all possible. Frank simply did not care what had happened to Joshua. The man's paramount concerns, it seemed, were only if his hair was in place and his skin pampered. Yet as if that wasn't enough, there was also something else— something nagging at the rear of Cary's mind. As a young boy, he'd been a witness to his mother's wayward living— and the large man who would often come to visit, and, as it was, also sometimes take out his violence on her. The details of the man's face he couldn't remember. He could only remember the man's black hair and his large frame. There was something about him—not to mention the way the One continued to highlight the man's name in his mind.

Coming out to the parking lot, Pastor Hemmings sat waiting patiently in his car. "You all right, Cary?"

Cary nodded but remained uncommitted to his response.

"What's wrong?"

"After seeing him, I'm more confused than ever."

"Did he react well to seeing you?"

"Not very good. And, sadly, I didn't react too well when I saw him, either," he said rubbing his temples with his thick fingers. "I wanted to kill him, pastor. He reminds me of myself several years ago."

The pastor nodded. "This man's effect on you has lodged within you with the effect that it's poisoning your spiritual condition."

"What do I have to do, pastor? I feel powerless."

"Start to pray about it, son. And let Him lead you. Maybe you just need to not do anything, but throw up your hands and acknowledge your powerlessness."

"That man. So stuck in his thinking and ways."

"We've all been stubborn at times, especially before He entered inside and did the changing needed."

Cary nodded in agreement. "So true. Can you please bring me back here next week too? I told him I'd be back and I intend to follow through. I'll send an email to the chaplain when I get home."

The pastor nodded again. "Let's pray together about this too. We need His help and direction on this issue that you're facing."

***

"I want to know about my father," Cary said as he sat down in his mother's living room.

She looked at Cary with disgust. "Why would you need to know that?" she asked caustically. "Why the sudden interest?" Her expression revealed nothing. She kept her eye on the television screen which showed *Jerry Springer* with its concoction of so-called entertainment. The screen showed one of three guests lifting and threatening to use his chair to attack a so-called best friend who'd apparently visited his girlfriend for illicit purposes.

Cary rose and reached for the TV before hitting the off button. "Why do you watch this trash, Mom?"

"What are you doing?" she asked appearing visibly hurt. "Are you going to do what you want in my own home?"

"I just need to know the answer to my question," Cary said in a calmer voice. "Please, Mom."

"What, are you looking for your Daddy so you can get a hug and feel better about your life?"

"No," Cary said flatly. "I'm already happy and content with my life."

"Is that right?" she asked with her gruff voice. "Well, I'm not! Especially with you here every week nagging me to death!" She stuck a cigarette in her mouth, lit it before dragging on it between her thin, cherry-colored lips.

Finally, trying to be patient, Cary interrupted her. "Mom, just tell me about my father."

She barely flinched. "Why do you want to know about that loser?"

"What was his name, Mom?" Cary asked plainly, his heartbeat increasing as he anticipated her answer.

She turned the television back on using the remote. Her eyes fastened on the television show which now showed both men holding plastic chairs in their hands threatening to swat each other while the girl sat sheepishly in the middle. "Gelb. Frank Gelb," she finally said as if giving the answer to a trivia question.

Cary lowered his face and closed his eyes as everything seemed to swirl around him causing him to feel momentarily dizzy.

***

Thursday, the day he'd see Frank again, came at a snail's pace. Cary sat at the glass staring at the metal stool that sat empty in front of him. I'm here, Lord, Cary said inwardly. And he sat there for another ten minutes. Finally, just when Cary was about to give up, the door swung open and in stepped Frank.

He sat down, having not once looked Cary in the eyes. Finally, he looked at the boy with a grin. "Why do you keep coming here, Big Boy? What you want with me?"

"I found out."

"You found out what?"

"You were the one I remember as a wee boy who used to beat my mother."

Frank nodded, indifferent. "Yeah, that was me. I thought I recognized your face from somewhere."

"And you made me," Cary said flatly.

Frank chuckled. "Yes, I did. I've made a lot of you if I'm to be honest. So, what do you want?"

"I want to forgive you. For what you did to my mother. What you didn't do for me as my father. And what you did to Joshua."

"Wow, that's a lot of forgiveness to give. Sure you're up to it?" Frank said, his eyes fueled by something that Cary could recognize as existing within him even now: rage.

Cary shook his head. "I can't do anything."

"Aww, thank you for wasting my time again," Frank said rolling his eyes. "Did you at least bring a care package?"

Cary leaned forward, anger burning in his eyes. "With God's help, I choose to forgive you!"

"Anything else?" Frank said. "I'm getting really bored with these family meet-ups."

"Yes," Cary said through semi-clenched teeth. "I'm praying for you."

"Does that mean anything to me?" Frank asked in a mocking voice. "Stop wasting everyone's time by coming here."

"I've brought you a care package. You'll get it at your next mail call."

"Really?" Frank asked. "And why did you bring a care package for me?"

"Because you've never known His love. And that's why you're here—so empty, and with no meaning to your life."

Frank heard his words before squeezing his eyes shut in frustration. "Listen, preacher. I've lived these last four decades-plus without needing anything. Thanks for the care package but keep the care. I don't need and don't want it!"

Cary rose and stepped away. Then he slowly turned around toward him. "I bless you. Because I love you. Because I was no different than you not too long ago. I was hurting good people. I was hurting my own mother. But it was all because I had nothing to fill my heart. I was so empty. Only His love could fill me and take away the pain. Only His love can fill you and take away your pain, *father*."

At that, Frank stood up and swung one of his hands toward Cary as if to swat away a bird. For the first time, nigh uncontrolled anger appeared on his reddening face. "Don't call me that!"

Cary turned toward the exit. "See you next week."

***

Cary had said he'd return the next week. But as he left the prison and stepped into the car where Pastor Hemmings waited for him, he sensed he'd not be back immediately. He'd send Frank a letter the next day to let him know he wouldn't be back for a while, if ever.

"You look different," the pastor said scanning Cary's face.

"I *feel* different," Cary responded with a smile. "I've been unknowingly shackled to Frank for the past three years—and honestly, for all my life."

"All your life?"

"I didn't tell you yet. But that man who caused so much pain for so many people in our city and Joshua—he's my father."

The pastor's jaw dropped. "Your father? My goodness..."

Cary gave a subtle nod. "I've been so angry toward him—never knew who he was, but still resented and hated him. Ever since I was a small boy."

"Have you been able to deal with your anger? I mean, Is it gone?"

"It'll be a daily battle for me. But at the least I've done what I was sent to do today. It's a start."

"What was you sent to do, Cary?"

"I'm not entirely sure. But I think it was important I be set free from the anger I felt toward him."

"How did he respond to what you said?"

"It wasn't all positive. But when you're stuck in a prison in mind and heart—and confined physically to a small space for hours upon hours per day, I suspect that God will eventually have his way."

"For him, that may take a long time."

Cary nodded. "He has a lot of years with almost inexhaustible time to think about his own life."

"Let's begin to pray for him daily until that happens," the pastor added.

"Thanks, pastor," Cary said, "for all your support these past years."

Fifty-Three: Change

The missive came. He opened the envelope and pulled out the pages within. He read the words from Lydia that had become something of a regular occurrence over the past few years. Lydia had completed her schooling receiving her high school diploma and, as a result of good behavior, been told she'd be released within the next six weeks prior to her nineteenth birthday. She asked Cary if he'd be at the gate to meet her along with her mom and sister. Without any hesitation, he acknowledged in his heart he would be there.

In the most recent letters over the past six months, there had arisen words of an intimate nature exchanged between Lydia and himself—of fondness, of waiting to be together after so much time apart and all the obstacles separating them, of regular talk that would've seemed uninteresting if coupled with any other person. But with her, it didn't matter what the topic; it held his interest. Then the word love had begun to be used. It had taken quite a long time to reach that moment. Yet their commonality of faith and their hunger to not have any barriers between them fueled the passion that existed between them.

On occasion, they reminisced about Joshua—the boy with the ready smile and the super-charged faith—the boy who had, by his very closeness with the One, sent out ripples of causality to all who crossed his life. He'd touched Lydia. He'd touched Cary. He'd even been the focal point for which now tens of hundreds of young people followed the One, choosing to be a bit different from the culture—alive in fasting, breathing prayer, their antennae raised for the slightest inclinations from the Throne to turn this way or that way. Most of these were in college now, or already working in vocations. Yet no matter what they did or who they met or where they went, their relationship with the One remained the most important relationship in their lives. The raising of Samuel, despite empirical evidence that he had died, had been a powerful impetus of these changed and charged lives. Cary might've been the one to pray for Samuel, but it had all begun with Joshua and his single touch. Even Joshua's brothers, all three, had been impacted and now took seriously their walks with the One. Samuel, now a teenager himself almost the same age as Joshua, was still looked upon in wonder by those who had seen or heard about his hospital visit and the subsequent events. At his side without fail, even old Bailey seemed resilient despite his old dog years.

    Arriving at the juvenile facility on the designated day, Lydia's Mom and sister stood just outside the facility doors while Cary leaned against the car. He'd remained at the car to allow Lydia's family the opportunity to have their first moments together. He couldn't believe that in just a few minutes, they would finally be together after so many years—no longer any barriers between them—only the goodness of godly love and the root of their faith connecting them.

    Finally, the door swung open and out stepped a smiling Lydia in civilian clothes, jeans and a light sweater, that her mother had brought for her on their last visit. Mother and sister immediately ran to her and warmly hugged her. After thirty seconds, Cary finally stepped toward Lydia looking trim and proper. Although Lydia was quite tall for a woman, Cary still had to lean downward to kiss and hug her. Almost immediately, they held hands as Cary took a minute to speak a prayer of thanksgiving to the One, the mother and sister happily joining together with them.

Over the next days and weeks, Cary and Lydia cemented their relationship. What had begun years before as simple correspondence now blossomed into a serious courtship. After six months, a glistening ring was given and accepted. And a date was set for the two to become one flesh. Cary also managed to find a modern apartment that would be a good place for them to start their new life together following their union under Pastor Hemmings.

***

A week before the marriage date, Cary helped to load the last bits of his stuff into the silver Audi A4 he'd bought a few weeks before. It was eight years old but with low mileage and nigh-pristine condition in terms of body and interior.

"Got everything?" Dennis asked patting him on his back.

"Thanks, I think so," he said with a happy grin.

"We're going to miss you, son," Dennis said.

Hearing him referred to as "son" surprised Cary and delighted him though he was too proud to let it show on his face. "Thanks," Cary said. "I'll miss you guys so much, too."

"I'm proud of the young man you've become," he said just as Sammy ran as fast as possible through the doorway followed by Mrs. Phillips. As they gathered around, Dennis handed Cary an envelope.

"What's this?" Cary asked.

"Open it and see," Joan said with an ear-to-ear smile.

Cary opened the envelope and saw a gift card contained within. "Huh?" Cary asked in wonder.

Dennis smiled and placed his hand on the young man's shoulder. Samuel, now a tall, slender teenager with a carefree disposition, stepped forward and reached up placing his hand on Cary's opposite shoulder. "We know," Dennis began, "you're moving into your own place. Here's a gift to help you choose some new furniture for your place. You can't be bringing a bride home to no sofa or bed, right?"

Cary smiled nodding slowly. "You're right about that." He fought back the tears. "I don't know what to say."

"Just invite us when you're settled," Mrs. Phillips said with a smile. "Oh, and this envelope came this morning for you."

Cary looked the envelope over. The return address showed the Iowa Correctional Unit in Sioux City. *Has the chaplain written me?* he wondered. He slipped the long envelope into his back pocket as he turned to hug the Phillips family and gave Bailey one last hug and rub. Then he climbed into his car.

"Come back when you want to get beat playing ball," Samuel said with a wide smile. There was in Samuel, Cary could see, a glimmer of the same light and love that had once been so evident in Joshua.

Cary grinned. "Oh, don't you worry. I'll be back to school you as soon as possible, Sammy." Samuel smiled before making a fist and jabbing Cary's shoulder gently. "I'll see you guys at the wedding," Cary reminded them. "And please remind Kris and Bruce I still need their ushering skills."

Mrs. Phillips smiled. "Of course they will. They're excited to do it. And we can't wait for your special day to celebrate with you!"

Cary smiled as he waved and backed the car out of the driveway before driving off heading to his new flat at the center of Sterling City. Most of his things were already in the apartment. And now, thanks to the Phillips' generosity, he'd be able to get some much-needed furniture prior to the wedding. Up until this point, he'd kept the apartment a secret from Lydia. He'd surprise her when he brought her home from the wedding. Then, the very next day, they'd fly to Toronto, Canada, for a seven-day honeymoon.

Reaching the apartment, he reached for the envelope before ripping it open. Pulling the letter out, he saw it wasn't from the chaplain at all but from his father, Frank Gelb.

Cary sat down on his carpeted living room as he stared at the words from his father. Then he silently prayed. "Thank You, Lord. Thank You!" even as he sensed the presence of the One surrounding him and filling him with a new joy.

Part Five: Fruit from the Branches

"Abide in Me, and I will abide in you. A branch cannot bear fruit if it is disconnected from the vine, and neither will you if you are not connected to Me."
-Jesus of Nazareth

Fifty-Four: The Outshining

Four Years Before

Following the complete reversal of Sammy's death and sickly body, Joshua, the next day, called all the Bible Group together. Of course, all knew by now that something extraordinary had occurred. Samuel had been raised from apparent death and no traces of the cancer remained. On top of that, Bradley had, too, also received a complete healing in his body. Bradley and his family had stopped at the local charity shop and dropped off the wheelchair; Brad and his family had concluded they would not be needing it again.

"The Lord is moving. So, let's move with Him," Joshua said grinning ear-to-ear. And just as he said that, Sammy ran up and leaped onto Joshua's back and held on while Joshua clutched onto his little brother's arms. Alistair, Jennifer, Bradley, and even Sergio stood in the group of thirteen.

"Hey, man!" said Sergio who stepped in front of Joshua. "I'm sorry about what's happened the past few months between us."

"It's all right," Joshua replied. "Paul and Barnabas also had an argument at the heights of their ministry."

Sergio nodded. "Yes. But I want to tell you I'm sorry. If it wasn't for you, I'd not even know the Lord today, or be able to serve Him as He leads me."

Joshua nodded and reached for him and hugged him, even with Sammy still clinging to his back. "It's good you're back, Sergio. Hope you'll always be around to check my blind spots."

"You bet!" Sergio said releasing him. "And you, mine."

Alistair also stepped forward extending a hand toward Joshua. "We're so overjoyed for what the Lord has done in Sammy," he said as he reached for Sammy's hand and grabbed his hand, too, followed by a smile.

"How's your parents? Have they begun to notice your witness?"

Alistair smiled, and his eyes shone brightly. "They've noticed changes in my demeanor—especially when they ask me to do something. And they're asking more questions about my faith. I think they're starting to believe it's something real in my life."

Joshua nodded. "That's great. Keep praying. Keep a servant's heart. He'll do the rest."

Samuel finally jumped down and stood next to Joshua.

"You called us here," Alistair said brushing away his long, slender black hair. "What's going on?"

As Joshua began to answer him, there came a sound from behind him. Someone running toward him, and then long, thick arms reaching, lifting, and squeezing him from behind. Joshua felt like he was in the ocean being tossed about by an all-too-large wave.

"Joshua!" came the voice joyously.

"Cary?" Joshua sounded.

"Yes, I felt the Lord lead me to come here today to this park," Cary said. "What's the plan?"

Joshua laughed. "You got my text, right?"

Cary chuckled and nodded at the same time. "Of course."

The sun shone above the trees, it's golden light and warmth blanketing all the grounds, trees, and distant hills. The deep blue sky was completely wide open as if anticipating this day. Although winter was encroaching, today at least, the chill was held back. There was expectation in the air. All things seemed joyous and overflowing. All over the park, people were picnicking or playing various sports—Frisbee, volleyball, badminton, and over at a set of courts, basketball. Over to the side of the park, remnants of a part of the city rested at the outside tables of cafes and restaurants—filled with people lounging while eating lunch or drinking coffee while sitting under the shade of colorful umbrellas. It might've been that most people sensed the seasons changing and that this day might be the last of the Fall season to enjoy.

"There is a simple plan," Joshua said. "We go out two by two. We ask people if they have pain in their bodies or any sickness or disease afflicting them. Then we act as His ambassadors and lay our hands on people commanding their healing in the name of Jesus."

"What if they're not healed?" asked one of the newer members of the Bible Club, a thin freckled boy with red hair. He seemed overly nervous and not comfortable in his own skin. This would be an exercise that remained outside most people's comfort zones.

Joshua smiled. "Then tell them you'll continue to pray for them. And simply bless them. Remind them that He loves them, that He's *for* them, *not against* them. The goal is to love people above all else."

The boy named Stuart nodded. "Who's going to be my partner?"

"Cary?" Josh queried, suggestion in his voice.

Cary immediately stepped over behind Stuart and placed his big paws on both boy's shoulders, the stark difference between their sizes quite apparent to all—Cary the height and width of a gentle giant, and Stuart short and about as thin as a telephone pole. "We'll be a great team," Cary said with a smile. Stuart looked up uncertain but managed a smile.

They began to move out over the park, all fourteen of them. Some headed straight to the café and restaurants while others headed toward the various people round about. The team began to ask people if they had any physical pains or needs. Without telling them they were Christians, they then asked permission to pray for them. Most people were open and said yes. Others were more unsure finding the whole set of questions to be abnormal. A few became hostile claiming they didn't believe in God. When this happened, the team members would offer a simple challenge. If God wasn't real, would it hurt for them to be prayed for then and there? Most accepted the challenge. And in most cases, the results were astounding.

Several hours after they began, the team regathered under the shade of a big oak tree that sat near the entrance of the park. All wore smiles, all were worn and tired and thirsty, yet this mattered little compared to the joy that was overflowing in and from them. Just then, someone approached their group.

"Hello?" said a frail woman with straight white hair. She smiled as she came. "We've been quite impressed by your group's actions today. We've been watching while picnicking over there," she said pointing to a large oak tree. She continued. "My husband's wondering if you'd pray for him? He's in constant pain."

Joshua stood up politely and invited the lady to come sit down on the single bench that rested near the tree. She obliged and drew near before sitting down.

"He's been experiencing back pain for the past three years," she said. "He struggles to sleep at night. I'm really feeling so helpless to help him," she said shaking her head.

"What's your name?" Joshua asked.

"I'm Michelle. My husband's name is Melvin. He's over across the field there," she said pointing.

Joshua asked Cary to accompany him. They came and in a friendly manner stood over the husband, Melvin, while Michelle remained standing nearby. "We hear you're in constant pain, is that right?"

The man nodded. He laid on his back on a picnic blanket. He said it was sometimes so difficult even to just stand or to get up from sitting. "I don't think anything can be done. But my wife insisted we ask," he said gruffly.

Joshua nodded. "I know that something can be done. Let's pray," he said before both he and Cary bent down and placed their hands on the man's side nearest the man's back. They prayed for less than five seconds and commanded all pain to go in the name of Jesus.

"Test it," Joshua said, as they backed off a bit.

The man began to shift slightly. "Sorry," he said kindly. "But thanks for trying," he added, the pain evident even on the man's face.

"Let's pray again, Melvin," Joshua said without a hint of seeking permission. He and Cary bent low again and released a prayer burst and commanded all pain to go. Then, again: "Test it out."

The man's face suddenly changed. "What?" The man began to twist his upper body, his face growing increasingly astounded. "I don't feel anything there now," he said visibly surprised.

Cary reached for the man to help him stand up.

"Oh, I think I don't need your help," he chuckled, visibly stunned. He stood up without any help or impediment.

"What's going on?" Melvin asked, his face suddenly somber. "The pains been constant for the past three years."

"We're just followers of Jesus doing what He did and what He continues to do through His people."

The man nodded. "But I don't believe in God," he said matter-of-factly.

"He," Cary said with a smile, "must believe in you."

Just then, the group gathered about. Joshua turned to the group. "Is everyone open to blanketing the city center?"

The group looked at each other and back to Joshua expectantly. Joshua continued. "Let's go bless people and let them know He loves them, that He's thinking of them," he said with a laugh. "And remember that if you pray for healing, to also share Christ with them. Give them the opportunity to know Him just like you know Him."

The couple stood in front of Joshua, pleased expressions on their faces. "We don't know what to say," the man said.

"Just know that He loves you. And that He is alive."

The woman turned to her husband. "Can't we join them? Just to see what happens? This is so fascinating." The man was hesitant but finally, he nodded with an uncertain smile.

***

The Lord moved through the fourteen young people over the rest of the day until the sun began to tilt toward the edge of the world dragging with it the light and warmth of the day. A chill of wind began to move across the city. Finding their way into a restaurant, the group ordered burgers and celebrated the day that had been simply amazing. After all had eaten their fill and talked till they had no more stories to tell, the group began to trickle out until only the elderly couple, who had not left the group's side since Melvin's healing, and Cary, remained.

"We want to follow Him, too," Melvin said.

And Joshua led them in a prayer of surrender to the Lord. Joy on their faces, they asked Joshua what their next step should be.

"Meet me or Cary at New Horizons Fellowship at 11 a.m. this Sunday. I'll introduce you to an awesome church that will help you in your new journey."

They nodded and gave Joshua and Cary hugs before heading out. The introduction of the Lord into their lives had been a dramatic moment for them. Joshua could tell they'd never be the same again.

***

Joshua stepped out and said goodbye to Cary who said he'd see him soon. Then Joshua texted his Mom to ask if she or Kris could come and pick him up. As he sent the message, Joshua noticed someone standing behind him leaning against a railing. Turning, he locked eyes with a face familiar—one that had become a face of dread over the past weeks.

"Joshua Phillips," the man said as he slowly stepped closer to Joshua.

"Yes, that's me," Joshua said trying to remain calm despite the fear that clung and weighed him down on his insides.

"I'm Frank," he said. "You've heard about me, right?"

Joshua gave a nod. "Lydia told me about you."

"What did she tell you about me?"

"Are you going to leave her alone?" Joshua asked as he felt a great irritation within him toward this man. He had turned toward Frank and squared his shoulders. He kept his chin up, and his eyes fixed on the man though he kept from entering a staring contest. His question was a genuine question. He didn't intend to disrespect the man, but simply ask the question because it needed to be asked. "If we're going to talk, let's talk about something worthwhile."

"Hmm," Frank stepped closer until he was standing in front of the boy. "You've been a thorn in my side for quite some time, junior," Frank said simply.

"It's not me who you need to worry about."

"Who, then? Tell me, please, so I can go and deal with him," Frank said with a calculated sneer.

"God," Joshua replied.

This made Frank chuckle. "I. Don't. Believe. In. God."

"That's interesting. He loves to go after the ones who think they are beyond His touch," Joshua said confidently. "And, to show you this is true, I dare you to let me pray for you."

"You're joking, right? What do I need prayer for?" Frank stepped away and looked away for a moment. "God is for the weak."

"Jesus said, 'Come to Me, and I'll give you rest.' Every one of us—no matter who—needs rest. Only He can fill our emptiness." Joshua dared to step closer to Frank. "Let me pray for you—just for a minute," he asked with a dare in his voice.

***

The ministering ones stood by waiting to intervene—the vacuum of darkness around the boy seemingly too great.
The light, though, was great upon this one.

***

Frank turned and offered his hand with the expensive gold watch and gold rings on his fingers. "Read my palm and tell me my future," he said laughing in a mocking tone.
Joshua looked up at the man with the sleeked back black hair, the goatee and darkly-complexioned face. He wore an expensive suit with a white dress shirt, opened at the top revealing several gold necklaces. From the intermittent light, Joshua could see he wore shiny crocodile-leather brown shoes that tapered smartly to a point. Every item on this man was deliberately chosen and meant to enlarge who this man was.
Joshua saw the hand extended toward him. "I'd give my life for Lydia, Frank."
"Would you?" Frank asked matter-of-factly allowing his hand to fall. "Are you sure she's worth it?"
"Yes, she is worth it."
"You don't really know her," he said taking out a cigarette and lighting it.
"I know she's worn masks since I met her. But slowly, she's become more transparent and removed them. And I still love her."

"She's played you like a fool," he said. "But maybe it's because you're just naïve. You do believe, after all, in spaghetti monsters in the sky, right?"

"I know all about Lydia. But I still love her."

Frank shook his head slowly. "What if I told you she's been in my hand like a puppet to cause problems for you?" He laughed. "*Love*. It can blind us to what's reality. And what needs to happen."

"I still love her, regardless. I'd give myself for her just like Christ gave Himself for the Church. What are you talking about?"

"Your love for her. It's a conflict with your faith, isn't it?" Frank asked as he finished puffing on his cigarette. He bent over a railing. The night air was still and quiet.

Just then, several people exited the restaurant, one of the persons stopping to lock the restaurant facilities. Joshua watched as these persons headed away from them toward the parking lot to get in their cars and head home. Then Joshua realized the particularly strange way Frank had made sure to keep his face unseen by the restaurant staff. It alarmed Joshua for a moment. Glancing at his phone, he saw that it was now just after 11 p.m. Quickly, he shuffled through several apps on his phone to find the one he needed that second.

"Joshua," Frank began. "You're not supposed to be in a relationship with Lydia since she doesn't believe in your God, in your way of life. Am I right?"

Joshua felt a growing irritation at the man's questions. He found the application even as he did what he needed to do. He considered Frank's question. The fact was, he couldn't deny the reality that there had been a conflict regarding his relationship with Lydia and with God. Perhaps, he'd thought many-a-time, he'd taken a big miss-step in being in relationship with her. It had always been a contention in his dealings with the Holy Spirit. Some part of him knew he'd gone against Scripture, yet the hope had been that he could and would win her to Christ.

Frank turned toward Joshua. "Am I right?" he asked with a stern voice.

"Yes," Joshua said. "You're right. It's been a conflict within me. And I've asked God to forgive me for any mistakes along the way."

"Would you like me to let her live?"

For whatever reason, Joshua considered his question not a question of exaggeration. This man had power, indeed. "Yes."

"Would you like me to stop harassing her?"

Joshua nodded slowly.

"Then promise me now, tonight, that you will end your relationship with her—that you'll never speak to her again."

"So you can use her? So you can go on to ruin her life by using her to commit your business crimes?"

"So she'll live," Frank said. He stood upright and pulled downward on his shirt before stepping in front of Joshua and looking down at him. "You want her to live, right?"

Looking upward at Frank, Joshua gave no answer, but inwardly, he was praying. Finally, he conceded an answer. "But yes, I'd give up anything for Lydia. I'd do anything to make her happy and have peace—for her to live."

Frank nodded giving an impressed look. Then, with an upbeat voice, he asked, "So are you going to pray for me or what?" he asked extending one hand toward Joshua.

"I will pray for you," he said in an even voice. "Would you close your eyes and relax?"

"No thanks," he replied. "I've kept my eyes open all my life till now. Not going to change that just for a prayer."

"Very well," said Joshua. "Father, I want to take this time to lift up Frank Gelb to you. I pray You'd allow Your presence and Your love to come upon Mr. Gelb—let Him sense Your reality. I pray You'd begin to reveal Yourself to Him, and fill his emptiness with Your love—that He'd know You love him dearly. I pray You'd give him rest. I pray You'd—"

Joshua felt the blow into his gut; it knocked him backward and then he felt it—the slicing, nauseating sharpness radiating throughout his mid-section. Joshua instinctively reached for his gut and felt the warm sticky outflow that began to cover the front of him. It had come before Joshua had known what had happened. He immediately felt unwell even as Frank stepped toward him and eased the boy down to the pavement.

"How very noble. I know you'd give your life for her," Frank said as he stood over Joshua. "And you'll stop being a thorn in my side from this moment on, won't you?"

Joshua sensed his own demise. In fleeting moments, he thought of Jesus. He thought of his Mom and Dad. He thought of Lydia. He managed several words even as he strained to breathe. "Frank," he said through belabored breaths, the blood now sputtering out of his mouth. "I *forgive* you." He strained to breathe even as a second breath was not found as the boy's life ebbed away. Joshua's vision became blurred as he fixed his eyes on an overhead lamp, the light of which seemed to grow and intensify all around him. Then he closed his eyes.

***

On His Throne, the One looked down from His place. He stood.

Over a long distance, he came. He received His lightbearer, embracing him with gladness and gratitude.

Evil *had* struck—but from the death of the seed would come the flourishing of life that can only come from ultimate sacrifice.

***

Despite the life that had been dispatched from Joshua's body, the police would later discover his hastily-buried remains in nearby woods. Then, too, they'd discovered his phone which had been found under some shrubbery right outside the restaurant. Under a voice app, an entire conversation had been uncovered that had revealed enough to pinpoint the murderer as Frank Gelb. Within two days of his murder, a warrant was sent statewide and then countrywide by police officials on the lookout for the man.

Although he'd not be caught for almost one month following the murder, there had also arisen, weeks later and due to Lydia who had learned about the murder of Joshua by Frank, direct eyewitness testimony and evidence regarding Frank's involvement in the drug network. This had been the result of Lydia opening and revealing the whole of the operation and the names of all those involved to the police authorities. Although Lydia was uncertain what the ramifications would be for herself, she felt it entirely worthwhile so to bring the whole ship and its crew down with her. They had thought they would make her suffer dearly for her lack of loyalty. Yet they did not fully know her.

Live or die, she'd do as she wished to whomever she wished. They had thought they'd jettison her and, in time, launch a new project with all new leaders. But their actions had only served to anger and cause Lydia to become more defiant and, arguably, dangerous to their dark affairs. Soon and very soon, they'd learn they'd seriously underestimated Lydia Claremont.

Fifty-Five: Legacies
Present Day

Cary had been surprised, even shocked, that the letter had arrived. He'd read the missive repeatedly and kept it in his pocket this entire time.

It had read:

> *"Son, I'm a broken man. Sorry.*
> *-F. Gelb."*

He'd stared at the six words over and over. He'd looked at the size of the handwriting, not too big, not too small. He'd looked at the slanting of the letters hoping to see if their direction was uniform—perhaps any particular word not uniform would indicate dishonesty or lack of integrity? He'd stared at the placement of the words—at the dead center of the page—written in black ink. No part of the letter displayed Cary's name save for the front of the envelope.

Arriving and entering the prison, he now sat silently with his thoughts as he awaited the arrival of his father. Finally, after just a few minutes, Frank Gelb was allowed to enter the visitor room. Almost immediately he looked at Cary with a softened, laid back look.

"Cary," he said, almost immediately. "Thanks for the care packages since I last saw you."

"Not a problem," Cary replied, his mind racing at the already open discussion they were having.

"How long's it been, now?" Frank asked, looking upward at the ceiling as he tried to recollect the time that had passed.

"Close to a year?" Cary suggested. "How've you been?"

"Not bad for where I am," Frank said matter-of-factly but with a hint of something akin to hope in his voice. "What's new in your life?"

"I'll share after you," Cary replied with a defiant look. There was a wait-and-see expression on Cary's face.

Frank nodded. "Sure," he said. "I respect that. Well, first, I want to say that I'm sorry for the misery I caused you, your Mom, and—"

Cary remained quiet as he studied this man who appeared to have aged considerably since he'd last saw him. His hair wasn't so in-place, and his goatee had spread to form a dark beard with touches of silver. And the most significant change came looking at his father's eyes—they no longer darted this way and that. They were settled and now had a soft focus to them.

"—the Phillips family."

Cary slowly nodded even as he looked at the face of his friend's killer. There was something happening in the man— something he thought impossible: Tears being shed.

"Why the change in you?"

"It's not me. It's all Him," he said pointing up with a grin. "I finally received him not long after you last visited me— about nine, ten months ago."

"Why didn't you write me sooner?"

"I wanted to. But I also wanted to make sure this was real in me, first. I didn't want to contact you until I knew this was genuine and not just some sort of phase."

"I see," Cary replied. "How did it happen?"

"One of the first weekly care packages you sent, I found the New Testament you included. Well, one day I found myself opening it. I began to read about Jesus—His teachings, His life, His sacrifice. How He died for His enemies. And how He forgave them which blew my mind. I was definitely His enemy and deserving to be destroyed and never remembered again."

Cary continued to listen.

Again, tears filled Frank's eyes. "Joshua, your good friend—the one I took from you and his family," he said trying to keep his voice strong. "I hated him. Not personally, but what he represented. Here he was not even fifteen years old and he had more peace, more guts than I'd ever had. He stood up to me and tried to stand up for the love of his life—even though I stood there in front of him. Surely, he knew about me, had heard stories from Lydia about me. Yet he didn't hold back."

Cary nodded. And then, finally, he spoke up again. "How did this change happen?"

"I've had a lot of time in my prison room, you know. I read all the newspaper articles that followed. I even read a newspaper when I first arrived at the prison that was months old that had a small article about Joshua's brother—declared dead but suddenly alive again... What was his name?"

"Samuel," Cary said simply.

"And then the outpouring of support—the hundreds that had come to that Joshua's funeral. I read everything printed

I could about it. And I couldn't get him out of my mind. How could such a small person such as Joshua have carried such a big influence on so many? His last words..."

"What were they?" Cary asked in a low voice, almost not wanting to know.

Frank lowered his head. He fought to maintain his composure. "H-His last words were that he had forgiven me! Can you believe that?" Frank said with an astonished, incredulous look.

Cary heard the words coming from Frank but he couldn't believe them. As bad as he felt for being suspicious, he wondered if at any moment this would all prove to be some sort of sick joke. Yet, there was something happening within Cary—within his deepest parts—that seemed to attest to what Frank was saying. Something had happened in Frank that had completely awakened and changed the man from his old ways.

"After I received Christ, everything changed. My life became what you might call fine-tuned."

"What do you mean?" Cary asked.

"I'd awaken every morning at 7 a.m. and for the next twelve hours-plus, I'd have my three meals throughout the day, and, so much time to read from the New Testament, and pray, and grow inwardly as a follower of Christ and outwardly as a Christian toward the other prisoners."

"I see," Cary replied. "Joshua had said something long ago to me when we first met."

"What's that?"

"He'd told me that the Lord had whispered something within him about his life." Cary fought to keep his emotions in check. "The Lord had spoken something to Joshua saying, 'The one who will change the world.'"

"Was that true in his life, Cary?"

Cary nodded in deep thought. "Yes, it has been true. But not the way we might've expected it. The one who would change the world isn't Joshua per se, but the One within Joshua, within me, within you, and within all of His people the world-over."

Frank nodded getting it. "I see the evidence of His changing-force in this prison. He's changed me and He's changing so many I know that I meet here. They've had to increase the chaplain services to four services per Sunday!"

Cary smiled for the first time even as the tears threatened to spill over onto his cheeks. "He changed me the same way," Cary said.

"I know He has," Frank whispered.

"Dad?"

"Wow, you've just called me 'Dad'!" he said beaming a smile. "I think I like that!"

"I like it, too," Cary said with a kind grin.

"Son," he said, his voice gathering strength. "Please, please, please if you can—if not today, tomorrow or the next year—can you forgive me for the way I treated your Mom, the way I treated Lydia, and," his voice lowering with shame, "what I did to your friend… I'm so sorry," he said, and he swallowed a gulp even as he struggled not to break down completely.

Cary nodded slowly. "I forgave you last time I was here, remember? But it hasn't been without challenges. But just in case I haven't done it fully, I forgive you now, too, Dad."

"Thank you," Frank said. He lifted his hand to his face and for a few seconds, sobbed quietly. Then, regathering himself, he locked eyes with Cary and smiled briefly.

"Dad?" Cary begun.

"Yes?"

"I'm getting married tomorrow."

"You are?" Frank asked with a soft, approving voice.

"Lydia and I—we both believe in Jesus. We both want our lives to be intertwined and remain together for the rest of our lives."

"I'm so happy for you. And I'm happy Lydia is going to be with someone like you—and you with her!"

Cary nodded. "Thanks Dad. I just want to say that I need and want you in my life."

Those words struck Frank almost like a hammer. He began to shudder and shake under the declaration. And he spoke slowly and deliberately, "I need and want you too, son." He paused. "But what about Lydia? Will she forgive me too?"

Epilogue: The Coming and Going of Seasons

Eleven Years Later

One could not fathom the changes that begun so strong in the Phillips family and Cary Adessi and Frank Gelb—all because of the Master's touch that had been birthed in surrender joined with invitation beginning with Joshua Phillips.

On the eleventh year, so much had changed in Sterling City. The city had grown higher and wider within those years. Yet almost all within the city could remember the events of their city—the moments of clarity in a select few who had known their identity rooted in the One and who had gone out touching so many. Healings. Interventions. And sometimes, simply the loving touch of someone that genuinely cared. There wasn't enough love in the world. And yet those who surrendered to Him were given the power to love and to share the truth that was, actually, not a thing or institution or denomination, but a Living Person.

Joshua Phillips had been no greater than anyone else. He had found surrender to be the entry door into a wide-open expanse. He'd awakened to the extra dimension that exists in co-habitation with this world—the results of which had come as God led him daily. Yes, he struggled with temptations—and sometimes lost battles. But he never stopped relying on the grace of His God. He never stopped seeking to walk in concert with His Holy Spirit. He was always quick to go to his knees to be lifted up again and be renewed for Spirit-led service again.

Out walked Frank Gelb to meet Cary and his wife, Lydia, along with two wonderful boys, aged three and six, not to mention Dottie and Stacy, the latter now married and expecting—all beaming with smiles on that day. Included in that moment was an older lady by the name of Miss Alba Adessi.

The change in her, too, had been great, though she could still be seen on rare occasions smoking a cigarette—never around the grandkids, of course. In time, she'd responded to the prophetic words spoken over her by her son, Cary. In time, she and the Lord Jesus were in a relationship. Off went the television with its *Jerry Springer* and soup operas—and in their places came times with the Lord—reading her Bible or spending time in prayer. She had learned to redeem her days—to make them count. There had even been letters exchanged between Frank and Alba, and of a rekindling of that old relationship between them—but this time, their relationship built on entirely different, and eternal, foundation.

Finally, Dennis Phillips and his wife, Joan, plus a young man by the name of Samuel Phillips, had also accompanied Cary to the prison that day. Cary had given a fair warning to his father that the parents of Joshua wanted to meet him after all the things he'd been able to share with them about Frank over the years.

When he'd stepped out of the prison establishment, he'd met Cary and his family with outstretched arms and faces full of joy. Yet when, moments later, he'd come to stand before the Phillips family standing there together, quiet and reserved, he'd gone to them and collapsed to his knees before them. He'd sobbed with little restraint as he sought their forgiveness for his long-before crime against Joshua. And, amazingly, somehow, with God's grace and strength, forgiveness had been given despite all the possible reasons why it shouldn't have been given.

There were many tears shed that day. Several families, linked by the One, changed and rearranged, and forever living in the light of His countenance. It wasn't without testing, temptation, or the troubles of life. But they had learned that with the Lord, one can go further and longer and deeper—whatever's required in life. They had learned they are not ever alone—for they had allowed His love to penetrate and fill them until their actions and thought-life produced the practicality of actions.

***

It was in a small and seemingly insignificant people that the sweeping change began to become a tidal wave of change the world over. It had not begun in great and powerful ministries or churches. It had begun in everyday people—the simple people of the earth and the happiest people on earth—those who had said with all-consuming desire to the Master, "I will follow You with all my heart, mind, and strength." And to those ones, after sacrifice and dedication, had come the Holy Spirit landing upon them with such intensity of love and purpose that all the works of Jesus began to appear through their hands and through their lives, too. It happened in remote places and in the huge metropolitan cities of the world. It began on farms and in the waiting rooms of doctors' offices. It was the stranger walking across the park or the man ordering a well-done steak who looked up, and, with a natural-supernatural look in his or her eye—and one of genuine love—would begin to speak life to their waitress or waiter or cook. It began to happen in governor's mansions or at the top floors of immaculate, glamourous penthouses—the cleaners, the chefs, the nannies and the mothers—all who'd open themselves up to being used by Him to bring a changing of trajectories to those put in their paths. Destinies could be rearranged and redirected—all because the One Who had loved them and given Himself for them had stepped into their lives through regular, every day, grass-roots people. The One in them would bring change to the world—no matter how old, no matter what the background, no matter what the challenges or the struggles. All it took was the surrender not unlike that of one Joshua Phillips. Then the doors would open and the blessings would flow without restraint and to unlimited reaches just as the Master had always intended for His people.

|The End|

Books Now Published from Sean Elliot Russell, author of *the Jesus boy*

(Fiction)

Shiloh's Rising: The Day after the Second Coming
Many stories have been told that lead up to the Second Coming. This is the adventure that begins at His Return and takes us on a journey to the edge of Eternity itself. Fifteen years in the making, this novel will thrust the reader into a world unseen by most—a world in which the Great King, Jesus, finally returns and establishes His rule and reign from His Holy City, Jerusalem. This is the epic adventure of those who enter that new world:

-Amai Azuma, who thinks his life at an end, planning his own demise, when the King arrives. His wife and daughter ravaged by evil, Azuma sets himself on a path to get revenge for their murders when he learns the killer, Mitchio Ito, is alive and well;

-Allister Talbot, a young teen left to fend for himself after the simultaneous deaths of his parents in the western Canadian wilderness;

-Ammar, the young prince of the Suranan tribe in the southeastern region of Africa;

-Avidan Ish-Shalom and his family, including his daughter Rebecca and son-in-law Jude, native to a war-ravaged Israel.

Each must deal in their own ways with the new world with each on a heading that will bring them face to face with the Jerusalem King Himself. Will the people's inner conflicts be resolved in time for salvation to be realized within each one before the danger fast approaching comes—one that will test all allegiances leaving only the resolute left standing.

A recent reviewer has given the book 5-stars saying it's "a great read" and brought them closer to the Lord. The same reviewer wrote: "It was a book about me meeting God as much as the characters meeting God." Yet another reviewer called the novel anointed and a work that "captures the true heart of God." Two reviewers said, respectively, that the book was "riveting" and said, "prepare to be swept away." Get your copy today!

***

Should the Oaks Fall: Short Stories to Enliven the Heart
A compilation of eleven stories which will enliven the heart needing rejuvenation—especially to the one who's missed feeling something good on the inside of late. Most of the stories are of everyday people who are on a search for one thing or another. They may be, indeed, reflections of you & me. These stories will uplift your heart as well as amuse and entertain you.

One reviewer who gave 5 out of 5 stars has written regarding this short story collection that the stories were "very uplifting and made my heart smile."

***

Non-fiction/Devotional)

The Journey Home: Papa-God is Waiting for You
This book is directed toward those who are aloof or have no relationship with Papa-God for whatever reason. Written in a style that may not quite feel like a traditional devotional, I seek to draw the reader to begin a journey with me to explore the character and heart and Person of God as revealed through the Old Testament Tabernacle and its various furnishings. Through this exploration, we participate in a journey of sorts as we make our way to toward the One Who alone can fill our emptiness and give us the identity and value we've always sought after. This book will encourage you—and challenge you!—to face the things that trouble and keep you aloof from God. By the end of the book, we'll find our way Home to Papa-God who actively waits, arms extended, for each of us to draw near to Him.

Coming Soon from Inspirational Writer, Sean Elliot Russell

(Fiction)

Darkness Rising
The prequel to the SHILOH'S RISING novel, this story showcases the world as it falls into a season of darkness and evil unparalleled in world history. A young man finds himself in the presence of an unexpected visitor—someone only he is able to see and interact with. And with this bizarre appearance comes a new glimpse to a world around him he *thought* he knew. But visitors from Heaven hardly make an appearance without something happening thereafter—something usually not very good. **Coming soon!**

***

The Day Jesus Moved Next Door
When the King of Heaven moves next door, the impact is immediately felt even as those on the street try to come to terms with the Son of God living amongst them. What will be the result as people seemingly forgotten by God suddenly find themselves in His crosshairs?

***

(Fiction Short Story Collection)
Path of the Honeybee: Short Stories to Enliven the Heart
Various short stories to uplift the heart and soul.
***

(Non-Fiction/Devotional)
40 Days with the Fairest of Ten Thousand
This is part of the Face2Face Devotional Series. These are writings written to help the believer grow to a new depth of intimacy with the Lord Jesus, indeed the Fairest of Ten Thousand! Included in this work are challenging questions (for journaling) as well as "prayer starters" in order to assist the reader go deeper in his/her relationship with the Lord. My aim in writing this series of devotionals is that as one goes through the forty days, they'd indeed encounter the One and begin to know and walk with Him in the intimacy available to all believers in Christ. Indeed, all of these devos are written with the goal that as we come to know Him more fully, that we'd allow His love and power to pass through us to a hurting and dying world.

***

30 Selah-Moments with the Holy Spirit: Reflections on the Book of Acts
(Volume 1 of 2: Ch1-13)
A DCI (Devotional Commentary Interactive work) written to build up the worldwide Body of Christ in their pursuit after the heart and plan of God for their lives through reflections on the Book of Acts. Included in this study are relevant background information as well as thoughtful questions for persons/groups to journal and/or reflect upon as they seek to be a man, woman, or child who walks daily and in every circumstance as an Acts believer led and empowered by the Holy Spirit.

Printed in Great Britain
by Amazon